D.E. STE
FIVE WII

Born in Edinburgh in 1892, Dorothy Emily Stevenson came from a distinguished Scottish family, her father being David Alan Stevenson, the lighthouse engineer, first cousin to Robert Louis Stevenson.

In 1916 she married Major James Reid Peploe (nephew to the artist Samuel Peploe). After the First World War they lived near Glasgow and brought up two sons and a daughter. Dorothy wrote her first novel in the 1920's, and by the 1930's was a prolific bestseller, ultimately selling more than seven million books in her career. Among her many bestselling novels was the series featuring the popular "Mrs. Tim", the wife of a British Army officer. The author often returned to Scotland and Scottish themes in her romantic, witty and well-observed novels.

During the Second World War Dorothy Stevenson moved with her husband to Moffat in Scotland. It was here that most of her subsequent works were written. D.E. Stevenson died in Moffat in 1973.

NOVELS BY D.E. STEVENSON
Available from Dean Street Press

Mrs. Tim Carries on (1941)

Mrs. Tim Gets a Job (1947)

Mrs. Tim Flies Home (1952)

Smouldering Fire (1935)

Spring Magic (1942)

Vittoria Cottage (1949)

Music in the Hills (1950)

Winter and Rough Weather (1951)

The Fair Miss Fortune (written c. 1938, first published 2011)

Green Money (1939, aka *The Green Money*)

The English Air (1940)

Kate Hardy (1947)

Young Mrs. Savage (1948)

Five Windows (1953)

Charlotte Fairlie (1954, aka *The Enchanted Isle*, aka *Blow the Wind Southerly*)

The Tall Stranger (1957)

Anna and Her Daughters (1958)

The Musgraves (1960)

The Blue Sapphire (1963)

(A complete D.E. Stevenson bibliography is included at the end of this book.)

D.E. STEVENSON

FIVE WINDOWS

DEAN STREET PRESS

A Furrowed Middlebrow Book
FM78

Published by Dean Street Press 2022

Copyright © 1953 D.E. Stevenson

All Rights Reserved

The right of D.E. Stevenson to be identified as the Author of the Work
has been asserted by her estate in accordance with the Copyright,
Designs and Patents Act 1988.

First published in 1953 by Collins

Cover by DSP

ISBN 978 1 915014 44 3

www.deanstreetpress.co.uk

FOREWORD

THE story about David Kirke, his mother and father and his friends, was in my mind for a long time before I put pen to paper. In a way it was an experiment for I wanted to put myself into the skin of a little boy and see the world through his eyes. A story told in the first person limits one's scope considerably, for nothing must go into the story except what the writer sees. Nothing must go into the story except what the writer feels. With David Kirke I ran about the hills and moors, and went to school. It all had to be told in very simple language. Then as he grew older and developed the outlook became more adult, the reactions more mature . . . but David was still a simple creature, the product of his sheltered upbringing. People have criticised David and have told me he was a sap—too good to be true. But he is not intended to be a "hero". And surely, even in this sophisticated world, there must still be Davids. Perhaps they feel a little bewildered when they adventure forth and meet with dragons. David did not know much about Life, he did not even know much about himself. All this was difficult at first but soon it became easier and my pen ran on happily to the end. I think it would be true to say that *Five Windows* gave me more pleasure to write than any of my other books.

THE FIRST WINDOW

"My window looked out over the garden to the bridge and the hills. In summer this view was hidden by a glorious old chestnut-tree which had grown as high as the house. I loved this tree at all seasons of the year: in spring there were the candles to watch and I saw the pink flowers unfolding: the leaves were fresh and green, they waved with the wind or hung quietly drinking in the golden sunshine. The tree was full of birds chirping and building their nests—they would fly to my window for crumbs to feed their nestlings. In winter when the leaves had fallen my view of the world was enlarged and through the delicate tracery of twig and branch I could see the countryside: the bridge, the woods and the hills."

CHAPTER ONE

"The farmer's in his den,
The farmer's in his den,
Heigh ho ma Daddy O!
The farmer's in his den.
The farmer takes a wife,
The farmer takes a wife,
Heigh ho ma Daddy O!
The farmer takes a wife."

THE other children had begun to play when I came out of the school-house; they were forming circles and dancing round, chanting the well-known rhymes in their shrill voices. I stood on the steps of the school-house for a few moments blinking my eyes in the bright sunshine which was so dazzling after the dim coolness of the classroom. From the four corners of the playground children were running to break the circles and join in the game; some of them saw me and shouted to me. "David!" they cried. "Come and play!" But to-day I had something better to do than to join in childish games, to-day was my birthday, I was nine years old, and Father had given me a fishing rod. I had brought it with me to school and had left it hidden in the wood amongst a tangle of brambles. It was there, waiting for me: the rod, the reel and a tin full of worms. I set off to find it.

The other children called after me. "Come back! Where are you going, David?" and Freda Lorimer, who was my special friend and often came with me on expeditions, began running towards me across the playground; but I waved to her and took to my heels for I wanted no companion. Fishing is a solitary sport. I wanted to wander up the stream, rod in hand, with nothing to distract my thoughts. I wanted to catch a basket of trout for breakfast. Four would do, four shiny brown trout, one each for Father, Mother, old Meg and myself.

The village of Haines lies in a bend of the Ling. The main street of the village winds steeply down to the bank of the stream and a solid stone bridge carries the road across the water. Just beside the bridge is the church, standing upon a green hillock, and beside it is the manse with its walled garden and tiny orchard. The manse is a solid stone-built house (a very comfortable dwelling, as I had reason to know; for Father was the minister of Haines and we had come there when I was two years old and had lived there ever since). The front windows of the manse look out across the bridge to the rounded hills of Nethercleugh and westward down the green and beautiful valley of the Ling with its woods and fields and prosperous farms. These windows have red blinds and as one comes across the bridge on a winter's evening it is a pleasant sight to see the red glow of the fights behind the blinds and to imagine the comfort and warmth of the rooms inside. To me, at least, there is no more pleasant sight in all the world.

My bedroom was at the front of the house; my window looked out over the garden to the bridge and the hills. In summer this view was hidden by a glorious old chestnut-tree which had grown as high as the house. I loved this tree at all seasons of the year : in spring there were the candles to watch and I saw the pink flowers unfolding; the leaves were fresh and green, they waved with the wind or hung quietly drinking in the golden sunshine; the tree was full of birds chirping and building their nests—they would fly to my window for crumbs to feed their nestlings.

In winter when the leaves had fallen my view of the world was enlarged and through the delicate tracery of twig and branch I could see the countryside: the bridge, the woods and the hills. This opening view was one of the compensations for cold wintry days and dark evenings.

Above Haines village the scene is different. There are no snug farm-houses nor tilled fields. The country is wild and becomes wilder and more deserted with every step one takes. The hills are steeper and higher; there are tumbled rocks and bogs; every few hundred yards a burn swirls amongst brown peat or trickles over grey stones or leaps from bare rock to bubbling pool. It was this wild country—the upper reaches of the Ling—to which I hastened with my new rod and my tin of worms on that fine May evening of my ninth birthday.

The woods were green with new bright leaves, the marsh-marigolds were gold in the sunshine and the banks of the stream were starred with tiny wild-flowers. Larks rose from the tufted grasses at my feet and soared into the blue sky. Spring was here and summer was on its way and the knowledge lifted my heart and made me happy, but it was the Ling itself that drew my eyes and filled my conscious thoughts. The stream was in perfect condition; there had been rain in the night—warm, soft rain—and the water was discoloured by peaty sediment. It was not in spate, but it was the colour of beer, and, like beer, it foamed in the pools where it was trapped for a moment between the boulders.

About a mile above the village there was a heap of stones and a cluster of nettles. Once, long ago, this had been a little house with people living in it but now it was utterly deserted. Owls nested in the ruined chimney, grass and ferns sprouted on the walls. Freda and I had discovered this place on one of our expeditions and often used it in our games. Sometimes we pretended it was a shop and collected stones and leaves and laid them out on a slab to represent eggs and biscuits. We brought paper bags and filled them with fine white river sand; this was sugar, of course. It was usually a grocer's shop but sometimes it was a confectioner's with brown gingerbread cakes, made of mud, and tiny round pebbles which did very nicely for toffee or peppermint balls. Sometimes our games were wilder and more active; the place was a smugglers' cave or a bandits' lair or the haunt of a Covenanter pursued by the soldiers of Claverhouse. "Our Cottage" we called it . . . and indeed we had never seen any other human being near it to dispute our claim.

Close by the ruined cottage there was a pool in the stream and it was here I intended to catch my basket of trout. I assembled my rod and, baiting my hook with a worm, began to fish.

I had often fished before, but never with a real rod and the spring in the rod bothered me, but after a little I got the hang of it and began to enjoy myself. I dropped my hook into the current and let it drift down into the pool.

At first there was nothing doing . . . and then suddenly it happened. There was a sharp tug, the rod bent and the reel ran out. The fish was a big one, there was no doubt of that, I could feel it struggling to escape. I kept the fine taut, winding it in and letting it out, my hands were trembling with excitement.

What a monster it was! How strong and full of fight! It rushed across the pool from side to side, it leapt half out of the water in a shower of spray—a gleaming shiny trout—it sulked under a stone and then dashed out again. Presently it began to tire and very carefully I coaxed it towards me. But when it was almost within reach it saw my shadow and away it went across the pool with the reel screaming. I realised that I should have had a net; I should have borrowed Father's net and brought it with me. The small fish I had caught before had been easy to land, I had flicked them out of the water. This fish was different, this fish was a monster, I should never be able to land this fish without a net.

"Stick to it, David!" said a voice behind me. "Keep a hold on him. Wind in the slack." The speaker was Malcolm. I would have known his voice anywhere.

"I've no net!" I cried. "Malcolm, I've no net!"

"I'll land him, David," said Malcolm. He waded into the pool and, taking off his cap, scooped the fish neatly out of the water.

"Oh, Malcolm, how lucky you were there!" I exclaimed rapturously.

"He's a good one," declared Malcolm as he disengaged the hook and knocked its head on a stone. "He's a fine wee fish—every bit of a pound."

"I thought he was big! I thought he was enormous!"

"He would have been if he'd got away," said Malcolm, smiling. "Maybe it's a pity he didn't get away—he would have been two pounds at least—but on the other hand he'll make a nice breakfast for the minister. Now you'll need to catch another nice one for Mistress Kirke."

"Oh, Malcolm, it *was* lucky! If you hadn't come—"

"You'd have managed, David. The fish was well hooked. You'd have landed him yourself." While we were talking he was baiting the hook and we were ready for the next one.

I caught my other three fish quite quickly, they were small compared with the first, and then I took down my rod and went over to Malcolm who was sitting on a tree-stump, smoking his big briar pipe.

"Are you finished, David?" he asked in surprise.

"I've got four," I explained. "One each for breakfast. That's what I wanted, you see."

"I see," he said, nodding.

We sat there together in the pale spring sunshine. The little river prattled by and the birds were singing and chirping in the trees. Malcolm was in a silent mood but I did not mind, it was enough just to be near him, he made me feel rested and happy and safe. The restful thing about Malcolm was the fact that time meant very little to him; he ordered his days by the sun and not by the clock. He could do this quite easily because he was a shepherd and lived alone except for his dog Bess, so he could get up when he liked—which was usually very early—and have his meals when it suited him. He was a giant of a man with broad strong shoulders and big rugged features. His face was brown and weather-beaten from going out in all weathers to care for his sheep. I had known Malcolm all my life and often, when school was over, I used to go up the hill to his little cottage above Nethercleugh Farm; he was always pleased to see me.

There was an odd sort of excitement in visiting Malcolm, because I never knew whether or not he would be there. I would hurry up the hill with my heart beating fast and climb on to a rock from which I could see the cottage from afar. If the windows were shut I knew that Malcolm was out and I would turn and go home (somehow it was less disappointing to turn back then; it was unbearable to. arrive at the door and find it locked). If the windows were open I knew Malcolm was in and I would shout to him and run on. Then Malcolm would come out, bending his head because the lintel of the doorway was low, and stand there shading his eyes with his hand and watching me approach. Bess would be at his heels, she would look up at her master for permission and when he nodded she would bound down the steep path to meet me with her feathery tail waving in the breeze.

"Well, Davie lad!" Malcolm would cry, his eyes creasing at the corners as he smiled. "Come away in and tell me the news. I've been wearying to see you."

I was thinking of all this, sitting on the bank of the river, and presently Malcolm turned and said, "What are you thinking about, lad?"

"Well," I said slowly, "I was thinking it's nice to go and see people who want to see you. It's the nicest thing I know."

"You're growing up, David," said Malcolm, looking at me thoughtfully.

"Yes, I'm nine," I said.

CHAPTER TWO

ALL the children in the district went to the village school; there were children from the big farms—like the Lorimers of Nethercleugh—and children from the village. Most of them spoke two languages: the local dialect and a reasonable imitation of English. Unlike the others my home-language was English of course but when I was playing with the other children I spoke as they did; it was more friendly somehow. I was rather proud of my accomplishment and sometimes I amused Mother with it. She would hold up her hands in mock dismay and cry, "Davie, what are you saying!"

As a matter of fact the dialect was so broad as to be practically unintelligible to anybody who had not been born and bred in that part of the country.

"It's Haines language," I would tell her.

Then Mother would smile a little doubtfully and say, "Well, I suppose it's all right as long as you keep it separate but don't get it mixed, will you?"

I saw what she meant of course and I never got it mixed. As a matter of fact the two languages were so different that there was little fear of it.

Mr. Semple, the schoolmaster, had a good deal of trouble with the dialect and children who came to school from the outlying cottages spent most of their first year learning to speak. Mr. Semple sometimes came to supper at the manse and I remember listening to a conversation between him and Father on the subject. Perhaps conversation is hardly the word, for Mr. Semple was a great talker and Father was a silent man.

"They must learn to speak English," declared Mr. Semple earnestly. "We can do nothing with them until they've learnt that. They can speak as they please at home. You see, Mr. Kirke, apart from anything else these children will get out into the world some day (it's unlikely that they'll remain *here* all their lives) so it's essential that they should be able to make themselves understood."

"Quite," agreed Father.

"I've been accused of trying to stamp out the local dialect," continued Mr. Semple fretfully. "It is untrue. I couldn't stamp it out if I tried—and I've no wish to stamp it out. The dialect is picturesque and, what is more important, it's useful. These children have little difficulty with the pronunciation of foreign languages—especially German. The vowel sounds are similar; that's the explanation, Mr. Kirke."

"Yes," said Father.

"Of course they all have the radio now and listen to it in their homes so they understand English—or what they are pleased to call Oxford English," said Mr. Semple with scorn. "Oxford English—that's what they call it, Mr. Kirke. Did you ever hear the like of that?"

"A misnomer, certainly," agreed Father.

"Before the advent of the radio the children from up the glen had never heard their own tongue properly spoken; they would come to school and sit with blank faces unable to understand a word that was said."

"Deplorable," said Father mildly.

"Deplorable!" echoed Mr. Semple fiercely. "Simply deplorable. There was one family in particular . . ." and Mr. Semple embarked upon a long story about the family of a shepherd, the members of which had caused him more trouble than all the rest of his scholars put together.

Mr. Semple continued to talk and Father continued to make suitable comments and rejoinders . . . but I could see that Father had ceased to listen and was thinking of something else. Father could do this quite easily, he withdrew inside himself and meditated, leaving a sentry to guard the door of his inner room. People who did not know him well would go on talking quite unaware of the fact that he was not attending to a word they said.

I was very proud of Father. My proudest moment was on Sundays when he went up into the pulpit and stood there for a moment without speaking, looking down. He had wavy grey hair and dark flashing eyes and his voice was deep and musical. When I was a child I did not understand his sermons, of course, but I liked to sit beside Mother and listen to his voice. Then gradually as I grew older I began to follow his arguments and appreciate what he said. His sermons were well thought out and interesting and they were always Bible sermons; he never preached about secular matters nor topical affairs.

Father was a good deal older than Mother and, because his nature was grave, he seemed older than his years. Mother was proud of him—as I was—she understood him through and through and managed him beautifully. Although we never spoke of it we both tried to shield Father and this made a queer sort of secret bond between us. Mother was only eighteen years older than myself; she played games with me when I was little and enjoyed the games as much as I did. We played singing games together and sometimes we played hide-and-seek all over the house. When I was older we started keeping a diary about the weather and the birds and things that happened in Haines, and we collected wild flowers and pressed them between sheets of blotting-paper and we made drawings and painted them. Mother was good at drawing and she taught me all she knew. She tried to teach me to play the piano, too, but we never got very far with that. I preferred to listen to Mother playing.

Sometimes when the organist was ill or away for a holiday Mother played the organ in church, but she was not good at it and it made her very nervous. I hated it when Mother had to play the organ; it was sheer agony to see her sitting there on the high bench struggling with the pedals and occasionally playing wrong notes. My hands got wet inside and cold shivers ran up and down my spine.

One Saturday father came in to lunch and said, "Thomson has just heard that his mother is ill, he wants to go at once. I said it would be all right and that you would play the organ to-morrow, Mary."

"No!" I cried. "No, no, no!"

Father gazed at me in astonishment.

"She's not to!" I cried. "You're not to make her! You don't understand."

"Mary!" exclaimed Father, looking at her.

"It's all right," she said quietly. "I'll—I'll do it, of course."

"No!" I cried. "You're not to make her! I won't let you!" and I burst into tears.

I never knew what happened after that, because I was sent up to my room, but Mother did not play the organ. She never played it again.

Other children had brothers and sisters and sometimes they said to me it must be dull being an only child. "What do you do?" they asked. "Fancy having nobody to play with!"

I was never dull; there was plenty to do and I had Mother to play with. I never thought of Mother as being "old" or "young." In fact I never really thought of her at all. She was just Mother. One day I was talking to an old woman in the village; she had been ill and I had been sent to take her some books. She said to me, "Will Mistress Kirke be coming again soon?"

"She'll be coming to-morrow," I said. "She's rather busy to-day."

"To-morrow," said the old woman, nodding. "That's fine. Mistress Kirke is a gay, pretty creature. It makes your heart glad to look at her."

I went home and looked at her—and it was true. She was gay and pretty and nobody could look at her without feeling happy. I saw she had grey-blue eyes and light brown hair curling naturally at the back of her neck and round her ears, and I saw she had rather a large mouth which curled naturally into a smile and I saw that she was not very tall but looked taller because she held herself so bravely.

"What are you looking at me like that for!" she cried. "Have you never seen me before, Davie boy?"

"No," I said seriously. "I've never seen you before."

Our home was very happy. I took it for granted of course, it was only when I got older that I realised all homes were not as happy as ours. Father was good and patient and kind and he never spared himself. I understood Father very well but I knew he did not understand me. He did not understand children. Sometimes he expected too much of them, and sometimes too little. He believed sincerely that "of such are the Kingdom of Heaven."

I have often wondered about that saying of Our Lord, because my experience of children is that they have a great deal of "the old Adam" in their make-up. Quite often they are ruthless and unkind to one another and deceitful to their elders. There are exceptions of course but on the whole they are more like savages than saints and therefore further from the Kingdom of Heaven than most grown-up people. That was my opinion (and it still is) but Father thought otherwise. He tried hard to understand the children of his parish and to make friends with them. Perhaps he tried too hard, for children are suspicious of a man who seeks them out and talks to them and are apt to be more friendly with somebody who disregards them.

When Father spoke to children he put on a special manner, and many is the time when I have stood by, in agonised embarrassment, while he endeavoured to make contact with a group of my playmates. I remember one occasion in particular; we were playing tip-and-run on the village-green, and Father, who happened to be passing on his way to visit a sick parishioner, stopped to talk.

"Cricket is a fine game," said Father. "I'm glad to see you playing cricket. How many runs have you made, Sandy?"

Sandy was older than I was and a great deal bigger, he was growing so fast that all his clothes were tight—he seemed to be bursting out at every seam. He had a shock of carroty hair which looked as if it had never been brushed or combed and his face was fat and pink all over with no eyebrows and queer little eyes like boot-buttons. To my mind Sandy was the ugliest boy in Haines and his personality matched his appearance for he was a bully and a sneak.

Father did not know these facts about Sandy but even if he had it would have made no difference. He would have spoken to Sandy just as kindly. I knew that.

"How many runs, Sandy?" asked Father again.

Sandy stood first on one leg and then on the other. "Three," he said.

"Three?" said Father. "That's a good start. You'll have to go on and make a lot more before they get you out. The great thing is to be cautious at first. Play yourself in before you start hitting sixes."

Sandy remained dumb.

"It's tip-and-run," I murmured. "You've got to—"

But Father took no notice. Perhaps he had never played tip-and-run when he was a boy. As a matter of fact I could not imagine Father as a boy. I could not believe he had ever been young and small with dirty hands and untidy hair—it was incredible.

"Cricket was my favourite game when I was a lad," continued Father. "I was fond of reading too. On a wet afternoon when you can't play cricket you can be happy with a book. I expect you all like reading stories."

There was silence for a moment and then one or two of them said gruffly that they liked it fine.

"I wonder if I can guess your favourites," said Father, smiling. "Perhaps *Robinson Crusoe*. That's a grand story."

They gazed at him in silence. I could have told him that when they read anything—which was seldom—they read the Adventures of Three-Gun Dick which appeared in a weekly "Comic," but it was not for me to interfere.

"You've all read the story about Robinson Crusoe and Friday, I'm sure," said Father encouragingly.

None of them had, but it was obvious that the minister wanted a reply in the affirmative so there was a murmur of assent from all.

"And where did Robinson Crusoe live? Robert will tell us."

"On an island," muttered Robert. Everybody knew that.

"Quite right," nodded Father. "He was wrecked on an island, poor man, and he lived there for years. It's a good story. We can all learn something from Robinson Crusoe."

Father passed on and the game was resumed without comment but the incident had its sequel.

That evening when we were all in the school changing-room getting ready to go home a voice suddenly remarked, "And where did Robinson Crusoe live? Robert will tell us."

It was Sandy, of course. Sandy was a mimic and he had got Father's voice and intonation pretty well. His effort was greeted with a gale of laughter.

As I said before Sandy was older than I, and a good deal bigger, but I was too angry to count the cost; I turned and hit him as hard as I could on his grinning mouth. It was only when my knuckles crashed against his teeth that I came to my senses. *He'll kill me*, I thought.

After that I had no time to think of anything; I was too busy shielding myself from blows, dodging them when I could and trying to get in an occasional blow in return. At last I was sent reeling into the corner and lay there, dazed and breathless, amongst a welter of dirty boots.

"That'll learn you!" cried Sandy, standing over me, his face red as fire and the blood dripping from his mouth. "Say you're sorry, you little—!"

I could not speak and perhaps it was just as well, for I might have recanted.

"Och, leave him," said Robert, taking his friend by the arm. "You've skelved him properly. There'll be trouble if you kill the wee runt."

Twenty minutes later I was on my way home with a swelled nose and a rapidly closing eye. My knuckles were skinned and bleeding; I was stiff and sore all over and my collar had been torn off my shirt. It had been a most inglorious battle as far as I was concerned and my only consolation was that my opponent had lost a tooth. When I reached the manse I hid in the shrubbery for a few minutes to see if the coast was clear and then made a dash for the back-door. Father was a man of peace but old Meg would help me. I could wash in the scullery and make myself look more respectable. Unfortunately, however, old Meg was out and Father caught me on the stairs.

"You've been fighting again!" he exclaimed. "Oh David, will you never learn! Why do you like fighting?"

"I don't like fighting," I said; nor did I, for I was no hero and I hated getting hurt.

"Why do you do it then? The Book tells us to turn the other cheek. You know that."

"Yes, I know, but—but—"

He looked at me. "Did the other boy strike you first?"

"No," I said.

"You struck him first, David!"

"Yes," I said.

The punishment was not severe. It was bed and no supper—and I was feeling so sick and giddy that bed and no supper was exactly what I wanted.

Presently Mother came up to my room and looked at me.

"Oh Davie!" she said sorrowfully. "Oh Davie, your poor face! Did you have to fight!"

"Yes, I had to," I said.

She asked no more but busied herself preparing a wet dressing and binding it over my eye with a big silk handkerchief.

The psychologists will tell you that when children are punished unjustly it creates a complex but as a matter of fact it did not seem unjust that Father should punish me. I understood Father and respected him. He practised what he preached.

I can see now that the affair had its comic side but at the time I saw no humour in it. The affair seemed quite ordinary and all in the day's work.

CHAPTER THREE

MR. LORIMER was an important man in the district; he owned the big sheep-farm of which Malcolm was the shepherd. His house was about half a mile from the village, across the bridge and up the hill. I remember how surprised I was when I discovered that "Malcolm's sheep" really belonged to Mr. Lorimer. There were three girls in the Lorimer family: Freda, who was a few months older than myself and Janet and Elsie who were twins and several years younger. Freda was clever and pretty, she had two long plaits and rosy cheeks and dark eyes. We usually walked home from school together for our ways lay in the same direction and in the holidays we sometimes took a picnic lunch and went for long expeditions. Freda was as good as a boy at making dams and climbing trees and walking over the hills. She would have liked to be a boy.

"You see, David," said Freda, one day when we were going home together. "You see, if I had been a boy I could have been a farmer. Nethercleugh will be mine some day. Of course I *shall* be a farmer, but it would have been easier if I had been a boy."

"You're just as good as a boy, Freda."

"Boys have a much better time than girls."

"I don't see how."

"You would if you were a girl! I wish I could cut my hair," declared Freda, shaking her pigtails impatiently. "I wish I could wear shorts. I wish Mother wouldn't keep on telling me it isn't ladylike to climb trees and whistle. I don't want to be ladylike." Then suddenly she laughed and shouted, "I'll race you to the bridge, David!" and off she went like an arrow.

It was not a fair race because she had taken me by surprise and was away before I started, so of course she won. I did not mind (if it pleased Freda to think she could beat me, she could go on thinking it) but I would have minded if she had been a boy . . . and this was rather funny if you thought about it.

Mrs. Lorimer was a friend of Mother's; she often came to tea at the manse and brought the twins with her. They were very alike, with straight silky brown hair and solemn dark-blue eyes. I did not like them much, they were too young to be interesting, but mother seemed to like them. She always baked special cakes for them, little iced cakes with pink sugar on the top.

One afternoon when they came, Mother had two little dolls for them, she had made the clothes herself and after tea she sat on the floor and showed the twins how to take off the clothes and put them on. The twins leant over her and breathed down her neck and she pretended they were tickling her and had fun with them. Mrs. Lorimer sat and said nothing and I went out into the garden and ate gooseberries.

When it was time for them to go we saw them off at the gate. One of the twins ran back and hugged Mother again and said "Thank you!" I did not know which of them it was, and did not care, but Mother knew it was Janet. We watched them walk over the bridge.

"Do you wish I had been a girl?" I asked.

"Davie!" she cried, turning and looking at me. "What a thing to say! What a ridiculous thing!"

"You seem to like playing with them," I said uncomfortably.

"Oh Davie, you mustn't be jealous! There's more misery caused by jealousy than anything else in the world. Jealousy is wicked and foolish too. It's like a disease," said Mother earnestly. "It's like an awful creeping disease. It's like ivy strangling a tree."

"I'm not jealous," I told her. "I just thought you liked them. I just thought perhaps you were sorry you hadn't got a girl."

The three figures were still in sight walking up the hill: Mrs. Lorimer in the middle and a twin on either side.

"I would have liked a wee girl," admitted Mother with a sigh. "It would have been good for you to have a sister. I had no brothers or sisters, and I know I missed something valuable in life."

"I'm happy as I am."

"I know," she agreed. "But it would have been good for you all the same. Only children are too old in some ways and too young in others. They're too sensitive; they never learn to tease and be teased and there's nobody to be rude to them and break their toys, so it's much harder for them when they have to go out into the big wide world and have their corners rubbed off. That's why I should have liked a sister for you, Davie; but we can't choose. Some people get what they want and some don't."

"Mrs. Lorimer—" I began.

"Poor thing!" exclaimed Mother. "She was *set* on having a son, and she got twin daughters! Mr. Lorimer wanted a son, too. Perhaps Mr. Lorimer wouldn't be so difficult if he had got what he wanted. They say it's bad for you to have everything you want but some people can't bear to be thwarted. Nethercleugh would be a happier house if there were a laddie in it."

"Yes," I said thoughtfully. "It isn't very happy."

Mother could never be serious for long. She took my hand and added, "But I'll not swap with them, Davie. I wouldn't exchange my son for a dozen daughters. Oh Davie! Think of a dozen daughters! Think of them sitting round the breakfast-table eating porridge!"

"You'd need a leaf in the table—"

"Two leaves!" cried Mother.

We looked at one another and laughed.

Perhaps I had been a little jealous of the Lorimer twins, because after that I liked them better, and the next time they came to tea I played horses with them and gave them rides on my back. Elsie was good and obedient, but Janet was naughty. She ran away and hid when it was time to go home and I had to go and look for her. When I found her she did not want to come and I was obliged to pick her up and carry her to the gate. She did not scream or kick, she just looked up at me and said, "I want to stay here with you and Mrs. Kirke."

"You can't," I told her.

The twins were so alike that when they arrived with Mrs. Lorimer it was impossible to tell them apart—they looked identical—but after they had been playing in the garden for half an hour there was no difficulty about it. Janet would rush about wildly and tear her frock and get hot and dirty and Elsie still looked as if she had been washed and dressed that very minute. I found this difference very convenient, it was a nuisance not knowing which was which.

Mother had said that the Lorimer's house was not happy and this was true. Sometimes Freda asked me to tea but I never went if I could avoid it. There was a queer sort of atmosphere about Nethercleugh and it made me feel uncomfortable. Mr. Lorimer was a boisterous sort of man; he was pleasant to me but not so pleasant to his family.

"Well, David, here we are again!" he would say, seating himself at the tea-table. "You're a brave man to come to Nethercleugh. It's a houseful of women. What was it John Knox called the female sex? A monstrous regiment! Hand the scones, Janet. Don't sit there gaping like a fish. Women should be ornamental—or useful. Hand the scones to David."

Sometimes Mrs. Lorimer would talk to me about Mother or ask whether old Meg's rheumatism was better and Mr. Lorimer would chip in.

"Women's talk!" he would say scornfully. "David doesn't want to be bothered with women's nonsense. You don't know how to talk to boys, Edith."

For a long time I did not know what was the matter. I knew Mr. Lorimer was being unkind and I hated him for it, but I did not understand. It was not until Mother told me that the Lorimers had wanted a son that I understood. The next time I went to Nethercleugh I held the key to the mystery and it was a mystery no longer—or rather it was a different mystery. Mr. Lorimer wanted a son, but whose fault was it that he had not got what he wanted? It was not Mrs. Lorimer's fault, it was not Freda's fault, nor Janet's nor Elsie's. If Mr. Lorimer had thought for a moment he must have seen how illogical it was to make their lives miserable for something they could not help. He made his own life miserable too for nobody can be happy if he has a grudge.

When I was out of temper Meg would say, "Och, away, David! You've a black monkey on your shoulders!" and, like so many of Meg's sayings, it hit the mark. I could feel that black monkey sitting on my shoulders; I could feel the heavy weight of it. One day I looked in the mirror and I almost imagined I could see it sitting there, grinning malevolently. The thing to do was to shake it off and be free of it, and usually I could. Mr. Lorimer's black monkey was his constant companion, at least I never saw him without it.

CHAPTER FOUR

WHEN spring came and the lambing started Malcolm used to spend his nights on the hill. There was a sheep-fold up there, a round of closely-cropped turf enclosed by a solid stone wall (Malcolm called it the stell), and there was a wooden shed with iron wheels which was dragged up the hill by the farm tractor and placed in the shelter of a rock. I had been to the stell with Malcolm often enough in the daytime but I wanted to go at night. I wanted to spend the night up there on the hill with the stars shining overhead and the cool night wind rustling in the grasses. Malcolm said he would take me sometime *if I were allowed to come.* We both realised that this might not be easy.

One evening when we were having supper Malcolm came in. Father asked him to sit down with us, but he said in his polite manner that he was going up to the hill.

"I just called to ask if David could come with me," Malcolm explained.

"It's rather late for David," said Mother.

"Oh Mother, I'd like to go with Malcolm!" I cried.

Father shook his head. "I think not, David will be better in his bed."

"I would take care of him," said Malcolm in his deep voice. "It's a mild night and there's a good stove in the wee shed. He would be warm and comfortable, Mr. Kirke, I'll promise you."

"Do you mean you're spending the night on the hill?" asked Mother incredulously.

"It's lambing-time," explained Malcolm. "I thought it would be interesting for David. The stars are beautiful tonight. Presently the moon will come up from behind the hills. I think David would like it."

"Oh no!" cried Mother in dismay. "Davie's too young!"

I wanted to go with Malcolm more than I had ever wanted anything before. It would be the most marvellous adventure. I said nothing, of course (it was no use saying anything) but I shut my eyes and prayed silently that they would let me go. "Please God make them let me!" Over and over again I said the words under my breath.

Ten minutes later Malcolm and I were walking up the hill together.

"It *was* a miracle, Malcolm," I told him. "It really was a miracle. God made them let me come."

"Prayers are not always answered," Malcolm replied. "Sometimes it's better for us that they're not answered; sometimes they're answered differently from what we expect."

"My prayer was answered."

"That's so," he said, but he said it casually. He did not believe in the miracle.

"It was a miracle," I declared. "They said no, and I thought it was hopeless, and then quite suddenly they changed their minds."

"That was the way of it," he agreed, looking down and smiling.

"Listen, Malcolm, if I had not prayed, they wouldn't have let me come, would they?"

"No, David, they would not."

"It was because I prayed so hard. I was praying very hard, Malcolm."

"I could see that," he said. "Your father saw it too. We all saw how hard you were praying." Malcolm began to chuckle to himself—I could hear him as I followed him up the stony path—but when I asked him what the joke was he would not tell me. (It was not until long afterwards when I was writing my story about Malcolm that I saw why he had laughed.)

The stell looked quite different at night; it looked mysterious, and the cries of the wild creatures were weird in the stillness. I could hear the bark of a fox and an owl swept past on silent wings. The sheep were calling too. Some of them had lambs already and others were moving about restlessly waiting for their time. Malcolm had collected some of them into the stell so that he could keep an eye on them. In the darkness their fleeces were a pearly grey, almost the same colour as the boulders. There was no moon as yet but the sky was dazzling with stars, I could see Orion with his shining belt and the seven bright stars of the Plough.

Malcolm opened the door of the little shed and busied himself lighting the stove. He used the stove to warm the shed so that he could bring the lambs in and warm them. Most hill lambs are hardy and need little care, but some of them, when they arrive in a cold wet world, decide it is not worth the struggle. It was Malcolm's job to coax them to live and usually he succeeded.

The shed was neat and tidy. In one corner was a pile of clean hay and a tartan plaid.

"That's your bed," said Malcolm. "You'll be warm and comfortable. Hay makes a fine warm bed."

"But I'm not going to bed!" I cried. "I'm going to help you. I'm not a bit sleepy."

"Well, we'll see," he said, smiling. "You'll do as you feel inclined, that's the best way. Are you ready for your supper?"

I had had one supper of course but that did not prevent me from enjoying another with Malcolm. He cooked it on the stove and we ate it together: sizzling hot sausages and bacon and strong tea with plenty of sugar in it. It was a grand supper and I said so.

"You're a good doer," he declared. "I like to see folk enjoying their food. It's a wonder to me you're not bigger."

"I'm strong," I said quickly.

"Och, I know that fine . . . and you'll grow," said Malcolm. "I wouldn't wonder if you grew into a great big chap one of those days."

While we were having supper we talked about the weather, for weather was important to Malcolm. I said it was fine and warm for the lambing.

"There's the borrowing days to come," Malcolm replied. "You know the old rhyme, David? It goes like this:

> *"March said to Aprile,*
> *'I see three lambs on yonder hill,*
> *Three days auld style gie tae me*
> *I'll find a way tae gar them dee.'*

"The first day was wind and weet,
The second o' them was snaw and sleet,
The third o' them was sic a freeze
As froze the birds' nebs tae the trees.

"But when the days were past and gane
The wee lammies came hirplin' hame."

"So they didn't die?" I said in relief.

"Not that time," agreed Malcolm.

"But Malcolm," I said. "It says in the rhyme that March borrowed days from April, but really and truly it's April that borrows from March."

Malcolm smiled. "You're a great one for getting to the bottom of things, David. Maybe they borrow from each other. . . . Aye, that's the explanation. We get April days in March and then they've got to be paid back; so we get March days in April. Does that satisfy you?"

"Yes," I said doubtfully. "It sounds all right—but it ought to say it in the rhyme."

We had finished our meal by this time and after we had washed up the dishes and put them away we went out into the stell. It was colder now, though not really cold; the moon had risen from behind the hill and hung in the dark blue sky like a great lantern. All the world was black and silver—it was beautiful.

The sheep looked alike to me but Malcolm knew then apart quite easily, and they knew him and were not frightened when he approached. He was like the Good Shepherd in the parable, I thought. The parable came alive for me that night. Malcolm moved slowly and deliberately amongst the sheep and his shadow followed him—a great black shadow. Some lambs had been born already, and had begun to totter about on unsteady legs, a few were born that night and I helped Malcolm with them.

Sheep are curious beasts. The young ewes which had not lambed before were uninterested in their lambs. They would look at the lamb with a surprised sort of expression ("What's this strange object?" they seemed to be saying) and they would leave it lying on the ground and stroll away and begin to nibble grass. Once you had managed to coax them to lick the lamb it was all right, there was no more bother, but sometimes it was not easy.

"They'll know next year," said Malcolm.

"They're stupid," I said.

"Och no, they're not stupid!" objected Malcolm. He did not like to hear his beloved sheep miscalled.

"They are, Malcolm. What other creature in the whole world doesn't know how to take care of its own baby?"

"That's true," said Malcolm thoughtfully.

"Of course it's true! Look at cats and rabbits—look at wolves!"

"They're wild. Maybe it's because we've tamed sheep."

I said no more, but I thought a lot about it. Sheep are not tame, they roam about the hills as wild and free as any creature on God's earth. They are much wilder than cats, and who ever heard of a cat that would leave its kittens to die and walk away! Even birds know how to care for their nestlings . . . and I once read in a book that earwigs are very good mothers. Earwigs! Malcolm would not have liked it if I had told him that.

Once or twice Malcolm asked if I were sleepy but I did not feel sleepy at all. I have no recollection of feeling sleepy, but I suppose I must have been. It seemed to me that one moment it was silver moonlight and I was helping Malcolm with the lambs and the next moment I was lying on the pile of hay wrapped in Malcolm's plaid and the shed was full of golden sunshine.

I sat up and looked round. I could not believe it.

Suddenly the shed was darkened and there was Malcolm standing in the doorway. "My, you're a grand sleeper, Davie lad," he said.

"You should have wakened me!" I cried. "I never meant to go to sleep. I can sleep *any* night."

"Nothing would have wakened you," declared Malcolm, smiling. "I doubt if the Last Trump would have wakened you. I picked you up and carried you into the shed and you never stirred."

"It's such a waste," I said.

"Och, I don't know. Maybe it's just as well. If you were tired you'd not be allowed to come another time," said Malcolm sensibly.

Malcolm was always sensible. He was so patient that it was never too much trouble to explain a thing thoroughly and to keep on explaining until he was sure I understood. I learnt a great deal from Malcolm. I learnt about sheep and birds and stars. Malcolm taught me to use my eyes as I went about Haines.

Malcolm's rhyme about the borrowing days had stuck in my mind (perhaps because I was still doubtful about its meaning) so I wrote it in the diary which Mother and I were keeping and which, by this time, contained all sorts of interesting things about Haines. When Mother saw it she was surprised.

"That's different from the rhyme I know," she said. "When I was a child I used to hear about the borrowing days. Let me see if I can remember how it went."

She took the pen and wrote her version underneath mine. I thought it was much better.

> *Said blustering March to fair Aprile:*
> *'Ye see three lambs on yonder hill?*
> *Gin ye will loan three days tae me*
> *I'll blaw on them an'gar them dee.'*
>
> *The borrowing days were cauld as sin*
> *The clouds were dark: fierce blew the win',*
> *But when the borrowing days were gane*
> *The three wee lammies hirpled hame.*

CHAPTER FIVE

BEHIND Malcolm's cottage there was a shed made from old railway sleepers; he had made it himself and fitted it up with a bench and a vice, with saws and planes and all things necessary to a carpenter. Usually a workroom is a bit of a muddle but this one was so tidy that Malcolm could have laid his hand on any tool in the dark. There was a shelf with a row of tins upon it and each tin was for different sizes of nails and screws. Malcolm was very particular about the wood he used and even more particular about the way he used it. He chose pieces of wood carefully and he made plain, sensible furniture. This was his hobby.

One day when I went to see him I took a little frame which I had made at school and showed it to him. It was an oblong wooden frame ornamented with fretwork and I was rather proud of it.

Malcolm looked at it. "David!" he exclaimed in dismay.

"Did they learn you to make that at school? It's dreadful! And the wood is good, too. A good piece of wood doesn't need to be cut about and ornamented with whirly-gigs and scrolls. A piece of wood has its own beauty which just needs to be brought out."

"I was going to give it to Mother for Christmas."

Malcolm's face changed. "Och, I'm a fool! Never heed what I said. Your mother will like the wee frame; she'll be as pleased as Punch."

"But I don't like it!" I cried. A moment ago I had been as pleased as Punch with my handiwork but now I saw it for what it was: a tawdry thing, an unworthy gift.

"It's clever," said Malcolm earnestly. "It's neatly done. It must have taken a long time. Mistress Kirke will like it fine."

The little frame lay on Malcolm's table between us. The table was of plain polished wood with a sheen on it like satin and it made the frame look gimcrack and cheap.

"No," I said, looking at it. "No, I don't want to give it to Mother."

"She'll like it, David."

"Oh, I know. She'll like it because I made it, but that's no use."

There was silence for a moment or two.

"Och well," said Malcolm with a sigh. "It just shows . . . what's said can never be unsaid. It should be a lesson to me. Well, lad, I tell you what we'll do. We'll choose a piece of wood and you'll make a box for your mother. You'll do it all yourself—every bit of it—and I'll show you how."

The box took a long time to make. Malcolm was a slow, careful worker and he made me go slow; every bit of the box had to be perfect to satisfy him. No nails nor screws were used, the joints were dovetailed, the only metal in the box was its brass hinges. I spent most of the Christmas holidays in Malcolm's workshop, sometimes Malcolm was there and sometimes I was there alone. When the holidays were over there was less time, but I went up to the cottage after school and on Saturday mornings to complete the task.

One day in March the box was finished. It was a solid chest, made of beautifully grained wood, about three feet long and two and a half feet broad, perfectly plain, with no nonsense about it. The lid fitted as snugly as the lid of an air-tight container. It stood upon the bench shining like a chestnut and I saw it was beautiful.

Malcolm ran his hand over it and said, "You've made something worth-while, Davie. That box will still be a good, useful box long after you're gone."

"After I've gone?"

"When you're dead," explained Malcolm, smiling. "It'll last a hundred years and more. When you're dead and gone—and perhaps forgotten—that box will be as good as ever. The work of your hands, Davie!"

It was a new idea to me—rather a frightening idea, but interesting too. Somebody would own that box, he would open it and shut it and use it to keep things in, and he would never know who had made it.

"I'll put my initials on it!" I exclaimed. So I carved my initials on the bottom of the box where it would not show, unless you looked for it, and they are still there: "D.J.K. 1939."

I was glad it was finished and yet in a way I was sorry and I said so to Malcolm.

"It's just as well it's finished," Malcolm said. "I'll carry it down to the manse to-morrow and you'll give it to your mother. I'd like to see her face when she gets it. It's just as well it's finished," he repeated. "I'll not be here much longer. I've promised Mr. Lorimer to stay for the lambing and then I'm going away to be a soldier."

"To be a soldier," I cried in astonishment.

"Och, Davie," he said, looking at me and smiling. "Why are you so surprised?"

I was surprised. Anybody less like a soldier it would have been impossible to imagine. I tried to imagine Malcolm dressed in uniform—and failed.

"Why are you so surprised?" he repeated. "There's going to be a war. You know that, surely?"

"But I thought they'd settled it. I thought there was going to be peace."

"There'll be a war, sooner or later. They're making guns as fast as they can and they're wanting soldiers to fire them."

"But Malcolm, why not wait?"

"That would be foolish," he said thoughtfully. "You see, Davie, if I was wanting a man to help me with the lambing I'd never wait until the lambing had started. I'd get him into the way of things before. He'd be some help to me then. It's the same with war. I'll need to learn to be a soldier before the fighting starts. That's the sensible way of doing."

"You can shoot already," I said.

"There's more than shooting in it. Shooting is important for a soldier but there's other things as well. I'll be no good until I've learnt. That's the truth."

"Supposing there isn't a war after all?"

"Then there's no harm done. Mr. Lorimer will take me back, either way. If there's no war he'll take me back and if there's a war he'll take me back when it's over. He was very good about it."

"Oh Malcolm, I don't want you to go."

He smiled. "I'm not sure I want to go myself, but it's the right thing. I know that. I was too young for the last war and I'm almost too old for the next . . . almost but not quite." It was absolutely staggering. It was the first big thing that had ever happened. Life had run smoothly for me and I had never thought there would be any change.

Malcolm was standing at the window looking out. "Maybe I've been here too long," he said slowly. "I'll miss my window with its view of the hills and the sheep. There'll be a different window with a different view. That's life, Davie."

"What do you mean?" I asked.

"Life is like looking out of a lot of different windows," explained Malcolm. "At least that's the way I think of it. My father was a fisherman, our cottage was close on the shore, and when I was a laddie I slept with my brother in a room with a wee window that looked out over the sea. Since then there's been a good many different windows in my life. This one has been the best. I've been well-contented here . . . but it's the right thing to do. There's no sense in letting Hitler have everything his own way. We've got to put a stop to it." He sighed and added, "I've a cousin in the Black Watch; maybe I'll get in beside him."

"You'll write to me?" I asked.

"Why, surely. I'll tell you how I'm getting on and whether they're managing to make me into a soldier. It'll not be an easy job for them. Maybe I'll get leave and come to Haines and see you later on. You'll not forget me, David?"

"No, never," I said. "Of course not, Malcolm."

"Look," said Malcolm. "You keep this for me, David. It'll be safer with you. I might lose it." He dropped something into my hand. It was a little gold locket and chain.

There were five pink pearls set in the locket and Malcolm told me about them; he explained that he had found them himself in the river near his home. He showed me how to open the locket by pressing a little spring. Inside there was a tiny coloured photograph of a young woman with dark hair and grave eyes—eyes which were curiously like Malcolm's.

"It's my mother," he said. "The wee locket was hers. I gave it to her. There's a story about yon wee locket. I'll tell it you someday—someday when I come back from the war. Meanwhile just you keep it safe for me, there's a good lad." When Malcolm had gone I felt at a loose end. The box had taken up all my leisure for so long that now it was finished I had difficulty in finding things to do. It was the Easter holidays by this time, which made it worse. I think I would have been glad to go to school, I was so bored with my leisure.

"You're like a knotless thread," said Mother. "You never used to have difficulty in finding things to do. Why don't you go up to the garage? You used to like going there and helping Dochie. You've not been up to the garage for months, have you?"

The garage was in the village street. It was owned by Mr. Grigg, a small perky little man with a flourishing moustache. Mr. Grigg was an elder of the church and took himself very seriously. He did not work in the garage himself, he was too neat and tidy. You could not imagine Mr. Grigg in dirty overalls crawling under a car. Most of the time Mr. Grigg sat in his office adding up accounts and writing letters while all the real work of the garage was done by Dochie.

Dochie was rather a mystery. Years and years ago he had suddenly appeared in Haines and Mr. Grigg had taken him on as his assistant. Nobody seemed to know where he had come from or anything about him. He was tall and very thin with very large hands and feet and a round head which looked too big and heavy for his thin neck. He had light grey eyes and scrubby sort of hair and he was always very dirty. People said Dochie was silly, and of course he was in some ways, but he was not silly where cars were concerned. He loved engines. He would take bits of engines to pieces with his enormous oily hands and put them together again and all the time he would talk to them in a crooning sort of way, like the way women talk to their babies. I liked watching Dochie and I used to spend a lot of time at the garage in holidays. Dochie would show me what he was doing and let me hand him the tools.

"There," he would say. "It was a wee bit o' grit choking her carburettor. See that, Davie! She'll be better noo. She'll run sweet. See that . . . and that . . ." and the tiny pieces of metal would all go back and fit into their right places as if by magic. It reminded me of the conjuror who had come to show us his tricks at the school party.

Dochie was shy of strangers. He talked to me a bit but he did not like questions. One day I asked him how old he was and he said he did not know. Another day I asked him whether Dochie was his real name or just a nickname, but he did not seem to know that either. He lodged with a woman in the village and Mr. Grigg paid for his board and lodging and bought him what he needed in the way of clothes. It was no use giving Dochie wages because he spent it on drink, but if he had no money he never bothered about it. He was quite happy as long as he could work with engines.

"Why don't you go up to the garage and see Dochie?" repeated Mother. She was busy and I expect she was tired of having me hanging about the house.

It seemed a good idea so I went along and Dochie was quite pleased to see me. After that I went along every morning, there was always something doing at the garage, people came from far and wide and brought their cars to Dochie to be overhauled.

One day an American gentleman drove up to the garage, he was on his way north and had been delayed by engine-trouble. Usually when strangers called at the garage Mr. Grigg came out of his office and talked to them, but Mr. Grigg had gone to Dumfries for the day. The gentleman explained to Dochie that the engine was knocking and there was no power.

Dochie said nothing. He stood and gazed at the car in admiration; she was a beautiful car with a long shining bonnet.

"Can you find out the trouble?" asked the gentleman impatiently.

Dochie was dumb.

"Is he hard of hearing?" asked the gentleman, looking at me.

"No," I said. "He's just shy. But he's a very good mechanic. He'll put it right for you, won't you, Dochie?"

Dochie still said nothing.

The gentleman looked at me and then he looked at Dochie. I could see he was not very happy about it.

"It's all right—honestly," I told him. "Dochie looks silly but he knows all about engines."

"O.K., cully," said the gentleman smiling. "If you say so—" While Dochie was busy with the engine the gentleman talked to me and asked me all sorts of questions about myself: who I was, and what I did and things about Haines as well. I had never seen an American before in real life, though I had seen plenty on the films. It was funny to hear him talk. Presently he asked if I would like to go back to America with him (he did not mean it, of course) and I said, "What would you do with me in America?"

He laughed and said he would put me on show and charge a dollar for people to talk to me . . . and I realised my way of talking seemed just as funny to him as his way seemed to me.

"You should hear Dochie talk," I said. "You wouldn't understand a word."

"I guess that wouldn't be so interesting," he replied with a twinkle in his eye.

By this time Dochie had discovered the trouble. He started the engine and it began buzzing merrily like a bumble bee. "That sounds swell!" exclaimed its owner in surprise. "Yes," I said. "I told you Dochie could do it."

"You did," agreed the gentleman. "Doggie is a wizard. He seems dumb but he's a wizard all right."

Before the gentleman drove away I tried to make Dochie talk but he would not open his mouth, he just stood there looking silly. I think he knew I wanted to show him off and was determined not to be shown, he could be very stubborn when he liked. Presently the gentleman said he must go. He took a pound note out of his note-case and gave it to Dochie and then he got into his car and drove away.

Dochie took the money and looked at it in a dazed sort of way, then he put down his tools and walked off For a few moments I did not realise where he was going . . . and then I remembered. I called to him to come back but he took no notice so I ran after him and seized him by the arm.

"Come back!" I cried. "Mr. Grigg is away. You must come back to the garage." But he shook me off and walked on like a man in a dream. He went up the street and disappeared into the Black Bull—and that was that.

The next day we heard that he had spent every penny of the money on whisky and they had to carry him home and put him to bed. Poor Dochie was ill for days and when at last he was able to go back to work he was thinner than ever; he looked pale and wretched, and his clothes hung on him as if he were a pole.

Some people blamed Mr. Fletcher at the Black Bull for giving Dochie the whisky, but Mr. Fletcher said he was there to sell whisky and if people came and asked for it he could not refuse them. Besides, he did not know Dochie had had too much until he suddenly passed out. What fun did Dochie have? asked Mr. Fletcher. Toiling and moiling all day and never speaking to anybody? That was no sort of life. Why shouldn't he have a bit of a blind now and then?

There was quite a row about it. Everybody in Haines took sides; some took sides with Mr. Grigg and said Mr. Fletcher should have known better than to let Dochie have the whisky, and others took sides with Mr. Fletcher and said Dochie had a right to drink if he liked. The only person who seemed unaffected was Dochie himself. He went back to his engines and said nothing at all. Of course in time the battle died down and everything was the same as before, except that Mr. Grigg and Mr. Fletcher were not on speaking terms.

Sometimes when I was at the garage a car would drive up and the people would ask for petrol, and if Dochie were busy he would let me work the pump. I got quite good at it and could add up what it cost and give the right change—in fact I was a great deal better at it than Dochie.

One day when I was working the pump Mr. Grigg came out of the office and saw me. He waited until the car drove away and then he came towards me, walking in his funny jerky way with his feet turned out.

"This'll not do!" he exclaimed. "This'll not do at all."

"It's all right, Mr. Grigg," I said. "Dochie was busy. I often do it when he's busy. I can do it quite well and I know how much to charge and everything."

"No, no! It's not the right thing. The minister's son serving petrol!"

"But Dochie was busy!" I cried.

"No, no! Away home, David! I'll not have it. The minister would be affronted if he knew."

"Father wouldn't mind—"

"He would be black affronted," declared Mr. Grigg. "It's not the right thing for you to be here at all, and Dochie is not a fit person for you to consort with. Away home, David, there's better things for you to do than hang about a garage all day."

Mother used to say I took notions to things (perhaps most children do); sometimes I took a notion to fish and nothing could keep me away from the river, and sometimes I took a notion to help Malcolm with his sheep—but of course Malcolm had gone. At the moment my chief pleasure in life was to hang about the garage, so the decree that I was not to do so any more was a crushing blow.

I ran home as fast as I could and burst into Father's study like a whirlwind.

Father was writing his sermon; he looked at me over the top of his spectacles. "Well, David?" he asked.

It was some time before I could get my breath, but he waited patiently and when I was able to speak he listened patiently to my tale of woe. "You don't mind, do you?" I panted. "I'm useful, Dochie says so. He said Dochie wasn't a fit person for me to consort with—of course he swears sometimes—and he gets drunk when he has enough money—but I like him."

Father rarely laughed; he did not laugh now, but I caught a glint of humour in his dark eyes. "Well, David," he said. "I see no harm in it, but then I'm the servant of a man who got into trouble for consorting with wine-bibbers and such-like riff-raff."

"Then I can!" I cried, preparing to fly.

"Wait, David. Wait, now! There's been enough trouble in Haines over Dochie."

"Yes," I admitted, hovering in the doorway. "Yes, but if you say I can—"

"It's not my garage, David, and Grigg is one of my elders. Just let's hear what you're proposing to say to Mr. Grigg."

"Oh—" I said doubtfully.

"You see," said Father nodding. "The matter needs consideration. I believe the best way would be to ask your mother. She'll know what to do."

Mother knew. "Yes, James," she said. "It's quite easy. You must have a wee chat with Mr. Grigg. Tell him you want Davie to learn about cars and ask him to let Davie come to the garage—as a favour."

CHAPTER SIX

AS THE summer wore on it became obvious that Malcolm had been right and that there was going to be a war. I had several letters from Malcolm, he seemed cheerful and contented (learning to be a soldier was less difficult than he had thought) and I wrote to him in return and told him all the news and sent him a pair of socks which Mother had knitted for him. The war started in September, as everybody knows, and as Malcolm's regiment was in the Highland Division it was one of the first to be sent to France. He was pleased at this. He had given up his work to be a soldier and he wanted to fight. His letters from the B.E.F. were short but even more cheerful. The war would be over by the New Year and he would be back at Haines for the lambing.

The war was unreal to me. Everything at Haines was the same as usual. It was difficult to believe that we were at war. I was disappointed when it was not over by the New Year and even more disappointed when people began to say it might last until the autumn but there was so much to do that I had little time to think about it. Now that I was eleven I had moved into a higher form and I had to work harder. In some ways I liked being in the higher form, the lessons were more interesting, but in other ways it was not so good for I had caught up Sandy and Robert and some of their friends who were older and bigger than myself. This little gang of boys stood together and made my life as unpleasant as they could.

One day in March, a cold dry breezy morning, I was running off to school when Father opened the window of his study and called to me.

"I'm late, Father!" I cried, hesitating at the gate.

"Never mind that. I want you, David."

I came back and stood on the path outside his window, looking up at him and wondering what I had done. "There's bad news, Davie," said Father gravely.

"Bad news? You mean—about the war?"

"In a way," he replied. "I've just heard. They sent me a message from the post office. There's been fighting over in France. You know that, don't you?"

"Yes," I said. I kept on wondering why Father was delaying me like this. Mr. Semple would be angry if I were late.

"Davie," said Father. "You'll need to be brave. There's bad news about a friend of ours . . . about Malcolm."

I could say nothing. I felt as if something had happened inside me. I felt sick and queer.

"He's—he's been killed, Davie," Father said.

"Malcolm," I whispered. Somehow I had never thought of that.

"You'd better come in," said Father. "Come and talk to your mother. You needn't go to school."

But I could not talk to anybody. I had to get away. I turned and ran out of the gate and up the path beside the river. Tears were blinding me so that I could hardly see and I stumbled over the stones and the tufted grass. I wanted to get away, that was all. I hardly knew where I was going, it was not until I reached the little ruined cottage that I knew I had meant to come here. I flung myself down and buried my face in the grass.

For a long time I lay there sobbing helplessly and thinking of nothing except that Malcolm was dead and I should never see him again. I should never again go up to his little cottage and call for him; I should never again go up to the stell and help him with the sheep; I should never again see his kindly smile, with his eyes crinkling up at the corners, nor hear his slow deep voice saying, "Well, Davie lad, and what have you been doing with yourself? How's the fishing these days?" Malcolm was so clearly in my mind that I could almost see him; I could almost hear him.

After a bit I began to hear the prattle of the river over the stones and the singing of the birds, and I began to feel ashamed. Father had said I must be brave. I was eleven years old and I was behaving like a baby. I sat up and dried my eyes and tried to be sensible about it. I wondered why I had never expected this to happen—it was war and soldiers got killed and Malcolm was a soldier—but I had never thought about it for a moment. Perhaps it was because Malcolm was so big and strong and full of life . . . even now it was difficult to believe that the Germans had killed him. I wondered if it had hurt, being killed, and I wondered what he was doing at this moment. I wondered if Malcolm still cared about what happened in this world and whether he could see me. Then I remembered his locket which was wrapped up in cotton wool in a little box in the drawer of my dressing-table and I said aloud, "Malcolm, are you listening? I'll keep your locket safely for you, like you said, and I'll never never forget you." I felt a little better after that, because it was something I could do for Malcolm.

Presently I heard a little rustle in the bushes and Mother came out. She did not speak to me but sat down on the bank a little way off and looked at the river. I knew she must have followed me and I wondered how she knew I would be here. At first I felt I could not speak to her but after a bit I felt I could, so I went over and sat down beside her.

"Malcolm is in Heaven," I said.

"Yes," said Mother.

"I wonder what it's like," I said. "I wonder if he's happy. I mean he wouldn't be happy unless there were useful things to do—things like making beautiful boxes or looking after sheep, but there are no sheep in Heaven, are there?"

"I don't know, Davie, but I'm sure there are useful things to do. Nobody could be happy doing nothing."

"Those are the two things Malcolm liked doing," I told her.

"Davie," said Mother thoughtfully. "You remember the disciples. They were fishermen, weren't they? I expect they liked fishing and could do it well . . . but Jesus called them away from their fishing and gave them more important things to do. They followed Him gladly and did what He told them and listened to all He said. They were happy just to be with Him. It was better than fishing; it was better than being at home with their families; it was much, much better than anything they had known before."

"Yes," I said. "Yes, of course. It was silly of me."

We sat there for a long time saying nothing but just looking at the river as it flowed past.

It had seemed an easy thing to promise that I would never forget Malcolm. How could I possibly forget him? But after a bit I realised I was not thinking about Malcolm quite so much and I realised that people who die are apt to be forgotten even by their best friends; or at least not remembered very often. I knew this was true because several people in Haines had died and amongst them Willy Mackie. I had liked Willie a lot, but how often did I think of him now? The words of that fine hymn, by Isaac Watts, came into my head (as a "son of the Manse" I had many hymns and psalms by heart): "They fly forgotten, as a dream dies at the opening day." I saw what it meant, now. Dreams fade very quickly. You awaken with a dream clear and bright in your head, and in a few minutes it has gone. How dreadful if that happened with Malcolm!

The idea worried me; I thought about it and wondered what to do; and at last I decided to write down everything I could remember about him. That was the best way. Then there would be no danger of forgetting him.

It was early morning when I thought of this plan, and it was Saturday, which meant that I had the whole day to do it. I got up at once and found my history exercise-book, which fortunately was almost new, and I turned it upside down and began at the other end. I began by describing what Malcolm looked like: a giant of a man with high cheek-bones and blue eyes, his face brown and hard from going out in all weathers to care for his sheep. His hands were large, but very neat and clever, and his feet were so enormous that he had to have his boots specially made by the cobbler in the village. I described his cottage and the big black pot which hung on a hook over the fire, and I described his workshop and his tools and the beautiful solid furniture he had made. I described his garden, fenced with wire-netting to keep out the rabbits, and the geraniums which he grew in barrels, cut in half and painted with creosote. When I had written all I could about Malcolm and his cottage I began to put down things he said and did and my own memories of him.

It was impossible to do this all in one day—or in two days—or three. I had known Malcolm all my life—I could not remember a time when I had not known him—so the story went far back into the mists of the past and the more I thought about him the more I remembered. At first I found it difficult to put my thoughts into words, for I had never tried to write anything like this before, but after a bit I found it came quite easily and in a way I enjoyed it. The story went on and on, it overflowed into several exercise-books; I began to think it would never be finished.

The story was written in pencil and it was very untidy, I had written it just as it came into my head, so after a bit I stopped and read it over to see if I could put it in better order. Some parts were better than I expected and other parts were worse, but the thing that bothered me most was the discovery that there was a lot about myself in the story. I could not understand how it had happened. The story was supposed to be about Malcolm Fraser, not about David Kirke. I tore up several pages and tried again but it was no good. I could not keep David Kirke out of the story however hard I tried. (It was like poor Mr. Dick in *David Copperfield* who kept on writing about King Charles's head.) At last I gave up struggling; I had to let David come into the story and make the best of it.

When I had remembered all I could I copied it out neatly in another book and made some little drawings of the cottage and of Malcolm walking up the hill with Bess at his heels. I drew the stell and the sheep and the little shed on wheels where I had spent the night with Malcolm. At the beginning of the story I copied out the verse from the hymn, because that had been the beginning of the whole thing, it had given me the idea of writing Malcolm's story:

> "Time, like an ever rolling stream,
> Bears all its sons away;
> They fly forgotten, as a dream
> Dies at the opening day."

The story had been a secret, I had said nothing about it to anybody, but now that it was finished I took it to Mother. She was in the sitting-room, darning socks, and she looked up and said, "What's this, Davie?" but I did not answer. I put it down beside her on the sofa and went away. I went up the hill a bit and sat down beside a rock and looked out across the valley. I thought of Mother reading it and wondered what she was thinking. Perhaps she would think it was silly. Perhaps she would not understand why I had done it. Perhaps I should have explained.

When it was supper-time and I had to go home I felt quite sick. I was afraid she would say something about it . . . but she said nothing at all. We sat down and had supper as usual. Father talked about the affairs of the parish and about Mrs. Mackie who was ill.

It was not until I was in bed and Mother came up to say good night to me that the subject was mentioned. She brought the book with her and she sat down on the end of the bed.

"Oh, Davie, I don't know what to say!" she exclaimed.

I did not know what to say either, and I could not look at her. "The spelling is all wrong," I muttered.

"The spelling!" she cried, lifting her arms as if to throw it away. "The spelling! What does that matter? It's the love that matters . . . and all the remembering. Malcolm is not dead as long as you're alive!"

I knew what she meant because it was like the box that I had made. It was the same sort of thing. Malcolm had had a hand in making me.

"And it's beautiful," Mother was saying. "The idea is beautiful and you've done it beautifully. It made me laugh and it made me cry! Oh, David!"

We hugged each other and it was all right. After that I could talk about the story without feeling shy. I wanted Mother to make suggestions and to correct the spelling but she said it was better just as it was and the spelling did not matter. We talked about it for a long time and I told her how it had been difficult just at first and then easier . . . and about David Kirke cropping up where he was not wanted like King Charles's head. There was no need to explain why I had written the story, she understood that.

Just as Mother was going away she stopped at the door and looked back. "You'll write other stories," she said.

"Other stories!" I exclaimed—but she had gone.

I was sure Mother was wrong. There was nothing more in me. I felt quite empty. Everything had gone into my story about Malcolm and there was nothing left.

CHAPTER SEVEN

ALL this time I had been at the village school but I could not go on there much longer. Father began to talk about the future and to say he wished he could send me to Fettes—he had been there himself—but that was impossible. There was not enough money to send me to a public school; I knew that so I did not worry. I did not worry about the future at all for I could stay at Haines for another year, and a year seemed a long time. Freda was going to school in Edinburgh in the autumn, she was excited about it and about all the new clothes she was going to get.

The weather was beautiful that summer. The war went on and all sorts of dreadful things happened but it did not affect our lives. The war was like a cloud far-off in the sky. In Haines the sun shone and the birds sang and the Ling ran on as usual. Freda and I went for long walks over the hills or played in "our cottage"; sometimes I went up to the garage and helped Dochie.

It was that summer I first met Cliffe. He was the nephew of the blacksmith at Haines. His home was in Edinburgh and his father kept an ironmonger's shop in Leith Street. Cliffe had had measles very badly so he came to stay with his uncle for a change of air. He was just about my age but a good deal bigger and although he was pale after his illness he looked pretty sturdy. Cliffe had never lived in the country before and knew very little about it. He did not know the difference between bulls and cows; he knew nothing about birds. One day he stood and gazed at a field of oats and said, "It's super! I've never seen such a fine big field of wheat." The other boys laughed at him and said he was barmy, but there was nothing barmy about Cliffe. We would have made stupid mistakes if we had gone to live in town.

I took Cliffe fishing. I asked him to come because I thought it would be fun showing him things, but after that I took him because I liked him and found him good company. He was merry and he had plenty to say; sometimes when he got excited he stammered. I had to keep an eye on him of course; he would pound along beside me talking, and not looking where he was going, and would catch his foot in a heather clump and fall flat on his face. One day he walked straight into a bog and nearly lost his shoes in the sticky slime. It was quite a job pulling him out and when at last I managed it he sat on a rock and laughed until the tears ran down his cheeks.

"You silly donkey!" I exclaimed. "Why don't you look where you're going?" It had given me a fright and I was rather cross with him.

"But I did!" he cried. "How was I to know that smooth green patch was nothing but mud with scum on the top of it? Gosh, how it stinks! I'll need to wash my shoes in the river." It was that day Cliffe caught his first fish. I lent him my rod and showed him how to let the baited hook drift down the current. The hook fell in with a splash and away it went and the next moment a fish had taken it. Cliffe was so excited when he felt the tug that he forgot everything I had told him. He danced up and down on the bank waving the rod and shouting like a lunatic.

"David, I've caught it! What am I to d-do? I've caught a f-fish! It's a b-big one! It's pulling like m-mad! It's p-pulling the rod out of my hands! Gosh, it's a m-monster! David, quick, what am I to d-d-do?"

I shouted instructions, but it was useless. The only thing was to wade into the water and net it. More by good luck than good guidance the fish was well-hooked so I gathered the slack line in one hand and netted the fish and brought it to him.

It was a miserable wee trout, not much more than four ounces (if I had caught it I would have put it back) but Cliffe was delighted with it. He took it in his hands and examined it carefully, he opened its mouth and looked inside, he admired its pretty markings.

"Could I send it home?" he asked. "The girls would like fine to see it. I could send it by post, couldn't I?" Fortunately I managed to persuade him not to.

After that we were both so exhausted that we sat on the bank and talked. Cliffe told me about his home and about his father's shop and about his sisters. He had five sisters, all younger than himself He told me under a frightful oath of secrecy that his name was really Cuthbert.

"Cuthbert!" I exclaimed in dismay.

He looked all round and lowered his voice. "Cuthbert Clifford Dodge," he said. "It's awful . . . but not many people know. I made them call me Cliffe."

This confidence touched me profoundly and I assured him that nothing would make me reveal his secret.

We fished all the afternoon but caught nothing; Cliffe did not mind. He was completely satisfied with his catch and went off saying he was going to ask his aunt to cook it for breakfast. I hoped Mrs. Dodge would not be too damping about the wee trout.

That night I dreamt that Sandy and Robert were trying to make me tell them Cliffe's name; they were twisting my arm and screwing my thumbs and employing various other forms of torture. I woke in a sweat of terror and found myself shouting, "No, no, I won't! I *won't* tell you!"

It was dull when Cliffe went back to Edinburgh and I looked about for something else to do. One Sunday afternoon when I was lying on the bank of the river I saw an otter swimming about in the pool; he was diving and swimming under water, you could see where he was by the bubbles of air which rose to the surface. Presently he came out quite near me and sunned himself on the bank. I watched him for a long time and I began to think about a story. It was a made-up story of course (not a true story like the one about Malcolm). The otter had his hole in the root of an old tree and he lived there with his mate and three cubs. I drew a picture of the dog-otter and it came out rather well. The otter's face looked quite human and, by some fluke, it had a slightly malicious grin which amused me a good deal. The only thing was I had to change the story for I had intended my otter to be of a benevolent disposition. Mother liked the story; she said the otter resembled Mr. Lorimer—in more ways than one—and we laughed about it. She had put Malcolm's story into the wooden box and she put this one beside it.

"There's plenty of room for more," she said as she closed the lid.

I wrote some more stories. One or two of them seemed quite good and I was pleased with them but the others seemed very bad. I wrote some plays, too, and Freda and I took our tea to the ruined cottage and acted them together for our own amusement. It was difficult when there were only two actors but we managed it by doubling and trebling the parts.

Freda always wanted a man's part; the play she liked best was one about a King's Messenger who was riding north with valuable papers. Freda was the hero of course. The hero rode tip to the cottage (which had become a small inn) and called for wine and food and stabling. I was the innkeeper and received the King's Messenger humbly and hospitably . . . then I drugged his wine and stole the papers. I handed them to an accomplice—who was myself—and he took to his heels with them. When the King's Messenger awoke and discovered what had happened he went after the thief and the play ended with a wild hunt on the hillside amongst the bracken. It was a good game—though I should not say so—and we both enjoyed it.

One afternoon when Freda called for me she had the twins with her; they were dressed alike in kilted skirts and pullovers and I would have defied anybody to say which was Elsie and which was Janet.

"Look!" exclaimed Freda, pointing to them. "Isn't it absolutely sickening? Mother's going out so I've got to look after them. We shan't be able to play the game."

"They can be part of the gang," I suggested.

"You mean take them to the cottage?" asked Freda, looking at them doubtfully.

"Yes, why not?"

"They're so silly," replied Freda.

The twins looked dejected and I did not wonder. It is not much fun being foisted upon people who obviously do not want you.

"They'll be all right," I said. "It will be fun having more people to play."

Freda did not agree. "You don't know them. They'll fall into the river or get lost or something—however it can't be helped."

By this time the twins were eight years old; they were country-children, used to playing on the hills, and I did not see what could happen to them. We set off together, carrying the basket with our tea in it, the twins tagging along behind.

There was a cloud over that expedition from the very start. Freda was out of temper and the twins were silent and depressed.

"Let's make the best of it," I said to Freda. "They're not bad kids. Let's all enjoy ourselves."

"I am enjoying myself," declared Freda and she began to whistle. Whistling was one of Freda's accomplishments, she was proud of her whistling and practised it in and out of season . . . whistling was a boy's thing.

By the time we reached the cottage one of the twins had lost her hair-ribbon, and her socks had nearly disappeared into her shoes; the other was still as neat as a new pin, so there was no difficulty in knowing which was which.

"Come on," I said. "We'll have tea first and then we'll teach you the game."

We sat down on the soft green turf and opened the tea-basket.

"It's nice here," said Janet. "I like it. We'll come here often."

"You won't," replied Freda. "This cottage belongs to David and me. We brought you here to-day because we had to. Where's your hair-ribbon?"

"She took it off," said Elsie. "I told her not to but she wouldn't listen."

Janet had collected a little posy of wild-flowers and had tied them together with the ribbon. The posy was lying beside her in the shade of the wall.

"What a nuisance you are!" exclaimed Freda, seizing it and scattering the flowers. "Come here and let me tie on your ribbon, Janet."

No comb was available; a strand of hair was dragged back from Janet's forehead and tied so tightly that it stood out from her head in a loop.

"Ow! You're hurting me!" cried Janet.

"I'm not," said Freda. "And even if I am, it serves you right. You had no business to use your ribbon for tying up flowers. I don't know what Mother would say. There, that won't come off in a hurry," added Freda with satisfaction.

"Doesn't she look funny?" exclaimed Elsie, giggling. "You *do* look funny, Janet. You look like a tea-pot with a handle."

Janet's face was very red and a tear rolled down each cheek, but she made no sound. She was collecting the flowers and putting them together carefully. Her hands were very small and somehow that made me feel even more sorry for her. I found a little piece of string in my pocket and dropped it into her lap.

"Say thank you to David," said Freda.

"She can't," said Elsie. "She's crying because you tied up her hair. I didn't take my ribbon off. I'm not a nuisance, am I?"

"There's no need to be smug about it," Freda told her.

The picnic was not a success. It had started off badly and it went from bad to worse. The strange thing was that Freda was really fond of the twins (I knew that because when Elsie was ill Freda had been miserable). It was just that she had not wanted them to come with us, she had wanted to play our game. I looked at her face and suddenly I saw she was very like Mr. Lorimer. She had the same grim, miserable look.

"Shake it off!" I exclaimed impulsively.

"What?" asked Freda in surprise.

"The black monkey, of course. Oh, Freda, do shake it off and be happy!"

"I don't know what you mean," said Freda crossly . . . but she did know; we had laughed together often over old Meg's black monkey.

"Come on," I said. "Let's play ordinary hide-and-seek. I'll take Janet and hide and you and Elsie can look for us."

"That's no fun," declared Freda. "There's no time, either. The twins go to bed at six."

"It's only just five," I said. "There's time for one game. This place will be the den. Hide your eyes and count two hundred slowly. Come on, Janet."

I started off there and then; Janet ran after me and slipped her hand into mine. It was warm and soft and very small. "Where shall we hide, David?" she asked.

"I know a place . . . but we'll have to hurry." I told her. There was a little bluff higher up the river with a few stunted trees growing on it. One day when I was fishing I had taken shelter from a shower beneath the overhanging bank and I had found a tiny cave between two rocks with gorse bushes masking the entrance. Freda did not know about the cave and I was pretty certain she would not find it. We ran along the path by the edge of the stream and climbed the slope and crawled into the cave. Janet's face was crimson and she was panting like a steam engine.

"Goodness!" I exclaimed. "You *are* hot! You should have told me I was going too fast. Why didn't you tell me?"

"It's—all—right," she gasped. "I'll be—better—in a minute." She was even more dishevelled than before, her skirt was torn and her hair-ribbon had come off again. It had caught in one of the gorse bushes. She handed me the ribbon without speaking and turned her head so that I could tie it on. By this time the little piece of blue ribbon was so crumpled and dirty that it was like a piece of boot-lace but I realised that if Freda saw her without it there would be trouble. I smoothed it out and divided her hair carefully. It was soft silky hair which accounted for the fact that the ribbon slipped off so easily. I was not an experienced tier of ribbons so the job took time, but when I had finished it and arranged the bows I was pleased with the effect. I had made a better job of it than Freda, anyway.

By this time Janet had recovered her breath and had begun to chatter excitedly. "This is a lovely hidey-hole, David. Does Freda know about it?"

"Nobody knows about it," I told her.

"That's good. They'll never find us here. It *was* nice of you to show it to me—I won't tell anybody, I promise. It's a secret, isn't it, David? A secret between you and me."

"Yes, it's a secret."

She clasped her hands ecstatically. "I do love secrets," she said. "D'you think this dear little cave belongs to a fox—or an otter—or perhaps a badger? D'you think it belongs to a badger, David?"

"I think it's too small for a badger."

"It *is* small," she agreed. "There's only just room for you and me. I *do* think it's a dear little cave. It would be fun to sleep here all night. We could make a bed of heather like the Covenanters, couldn't we? Oh, David, it *would* be fun! Couldn't we? Couldn't we just stay here—?"

" What would Mrs. Lorimer say?"

Janet sighed. "That's it," she said. "You never can do anything really thrilling when you're eight. I wish I was eighteen. When I'm eighteen I shall do exactly as I like."

"What will you do?"

"See things," said Janet vaguely. "Go about alone."

"Go about alone?"

She nodded. "I want to be me," she said. "It's awfully sickening being half another person and nobody ever knowing whether you're you or somebody else."

"I thought twins liked being twins," I said.

"I want to be me," she repeated. "I want to go right away. I want to go to places where there are lots and lots of flowers—great big beautiful coloured flowers and butterflies . . ."

"Wheesht, they're coming!" I whispered.

They were walking along the path by the river, Freda in front and Elsie trailing along behind. They passed so close to our hiding place that I could have tossed a lump of earth on to their heads quite easily. It was amusing to see them and not be seen. Janet evidently thought it was funny too for she gave a little smothered giggle.

"Come on, Elsie!" exclaimed Freda. "You aren't looking for them. You don't seem to take any interest in the game."

"I don't like this game," complained Elsie.

"You're just a mutt, that's all."

"I'm not a mutt."

"Yes, you are."

"I'll tell Mother you said I was a mutt."

"I don't care what you tell her," Freda declared. "Tell her anything you like, you horrid little clype."

"I'm not a clype."

"Yes, you are."

They walked on up the river and disappeared.

When they had gone Janet and I crawled out of the cave and went back to the ruined cottage. Janet was quite happy now, she ran about and collected some more flowers.

"Look, David!" she cried. "Look at this darling little orchis! And here's a clump of speedwell! Don't you love its tiny blue flowers? It's almost a pity to pick them—but nobody would see them here, would they? I think flowers like to be seen. Look at these great big golden buttercups!"

Fortunately I had another piece of string in my pocket so she made another posy. She sat down and put the flowers together carefully with her tiny hands; there were buttercups and scabious and thrift and big heads of mauve clover.

"It's very pretty," I said.

"Yes," she agreed. "Yes, it's a lovely posy. D'you think Mrs. Kirke would like it?"

"I'm sure she would."

"Are you really sure, David? They're only wild flowers, you know. Some people think wild flowers are just rubbish."

"Mother doesn't. I'm really truly sure Mother would like it."

Janet smiled and gave it to me. I found some sphagnum moss and packed it round the posy to keep it fresh.

"They like that," said Janet nodding approvingly.

We sat down and waited. It was some time before the others returned.

"Oh, there you are!" said Freda crossly. "Where were you? We looked *everywhere*."

"You didn't," laughed Janet. "You didn't look everywhere. If you'd looked in the right place you'd have found us. We saw you."

"Where were you?"

"That's a secret. It's a secret between David and me. You passed quite close, didn't they, David? It was awfully funny to see you, wasn't it, David?"

"All right, I don't care," declared Freda. "You were hiding in the bracken, I suppose."

Janet did not answer.

"Come on," said Freda. "We must go home. I don't know what Mother will say when she sees you. You're a perfect sight"

"I'm not!" cried Janet.

"You are! Look at that great jagged tear in your skirt! and your face is filthy! You're not fit to be seen. Come on, Janet . . . and don't hang on to David's hand. David doesn't want to be bothered with you!"

"But, Freda—" began Janet.

"Oh, come on and don't argue. You can walk in front with Elsie and then I'll see what you're doing."

The twins walked on and we followed.

"They're such a nuisance," complained Freda. "You're lucky not to have any sisters, David."

"Well, I don't know," I said doubtfully. "Janet is rather sweet—"

"She's very naughty—*much* more bother than Elsie. Oh, it's all very well for you, just seeing them now and then! If you had them under your feet all the time it would be a different story."

"I suppose it would."

"You'd soon get sick of them," declared Freda with conviction.

It had been a wretched afternoon. The only nice thing about that picnic was the little posy. I gave it to Mother with Janet's love and she put it in a bowl on her desk.

"Janet's mad about flowers," I said.

"So am I," said Mother smiling.

CHAPTER EIGHT

SOON after that unsuccessful picnic Uncle Matthew came to stay with us. It was early September so I had not gone back to school and I was involved in the tremendous preparations which were made for his comfort. The whole house was scrubbed and polished and all the curtains and cretonne covers were washed. In fact it was like spring cleaning all over again, only more so.

"I don't know why you bother," Father said. "Matthew will never notice."

"Never notice!" cried Mother. "Your brother Matthew notices every-thing. He's very particular: His own house is twice the size of this and as spick and span as can be."

"It's like every other Edinburgh house; tall and grey and hemmed in by its neighbours, with a wee cat-walk at the back. I wouldn't exchange houses with Matthew for a king's ransom."

"I never said I would exchange," replied Mother smiling.

"Why has he never been to see us before?" I wanted to know.

"He's coming for a change of air," replied Mother. "He's had 'flu and the doctor said he must get away for a holiday." This explained the reason for his visit, but it did not answer my question, so when I got

Mother to myself I asked her again. We were hanging up the curtains in the spare-room.

"Why?" I asked. "Why has Uncle Matthew never been here before?"

"Oh well, sometimes brothers and sisters don't see eye to eye about things. I never had any brothers or sisters and neither have you, so we can't judge, can we?"

I thought of the Lorimers. "No, I suppose we can't," I said slowly.

"They have different ideas, that's all."

"Isn't Uncle Matthew nice?"

"Oh Davie! What a boy for questions!"

"Well, isn't he?"

"He's always been very nice to me—in his own way."

I saw I should get no further information on that point. "Mother," I said. "I've got an aunt too, haven't I? Does she live with Uncle Matthew?"

"She lives near him in Edinburgh."

"You'd think she'd live with him, wouldn't you?"

"No, I wouldn't, Davie."

"Why?" I asked. "I mean neither of them is married. Why doesn't Aunt Etta live with Uncle Matthew and keep house for him?"

"Oh Davie, how should I know!" exclaimed Mother as she stood back and arranged the folds of the curtains. "I've told you brothers and sisters have different ideas about things. When you see Uncle Matthew you'll understand."

It was a damp rainy evening when Uncle Matthew arrived. Father hired Mr. Grigg's car and drove over to Drumburly to meet him at the station. It was a five-mile drive. I peeped out of my bedroom window as they came up the path together and my first impression was that they were very alike. They were the same height and had the same wavy grey hair. Later I changed my mind and decided that no two men could be more unlike.

"Well, David," said Uncle Matthew when I went downstairs. "So this is you, is it? We've met before but I dare say you've forgotten me."

"Yes," I said doubtfully. "I'm afraid I have."

He shook his head sadly and said, " Some people have short memories. It's ten years—that's all—since you and I foregathered. I remember the occasion as if it were yesterday, but you've forgotten! Well, well!"

"I must have been two—" I began.

"You know how to do subtractions!" he exclaimed raising his eyebrows in surprise.

I saw now that it was a joke. Perhaps it was dense of me not to have seen it before but I was shy and nervous; besides he looked like Father and Father never made jokes.

"David is quite well on with his lessons," said Father encouragingly.

"And what are you going to do with him?"

"David hasn't decided what he wants to be," said Mother. We sat down to supper. It was a good supper—Mother had seen to that—and Uncle Matthew did full justice to it. He ate and talked and told us funny stories and laughed uproariously at his own jokes.

"How is Etta?" Father asked.

"Etta enjoys bad health," replied Uncle Matthew. "I can't tell you whether there's much wrong with her or not. She likes nothing better than to tell you about her pains and aches but she looks uncommonly well."

"It's terribly sad!" exclaimed Mother.

"Sad!" echoed Uncle Matthew. "There's a lot of people worse off than Etta. She's got comfortable rooms and a pleasant, kindly woman to look after her. It's my belief that if Etta would take a little exercise it would do her all the good in the world. I've no sympathy for people who sit about and do nothing all day long. They're bound to be unhealthy."

"Etta should have married," said Father.

"Who'd marry Etta?" cried Uncle Matthew.

"She must have been very pretty when she was young," said Mother gently.

Mother hated unkindness; she always found something good to say about everybody. (She even found something good to say about the tramp who came to the back door begging bread and, while Mother was cutting him a piece and spreading it with butter, made off with her purse which was lying on the kitchen table. "I expect he needed the money," Mother said. "He had such kind eyes; I'm sure he would never have taken it if he hadn't needed it very badly.")

Uncle Matthew had come to Haines to throw off the after-effects of his illness; but he did not look ill and he was very cheerful; in fact he was boisterous. He talked a great deal and even when he was silent it was impossible to forget he was there; the house seemed full of him. Fortunately the weather was fine and he was able to spend most of his time sitting in a deck-chair in the garden. Every morning immediately after breakfast he walked off to the village and returned with a sheaf of newspapers which he read and strewed about. The *Scotsman* was delivered daily of course and he read that too.

"What a waste!" said Father one day. He was looking out of his study window at the figure in the deck-chair.

"They'll be useful for the fires," said Mother smiling.

"I wasn't thinking of the money so much; it's the time," explained Father. "He could be reading something worth while."

This was the only criticism I heard, and yet I knew that Uncle Matthew did and said a good many things of which Father disapproved. I knew Father thought he was the World, the Flesh and the Devil all rolled into one man. In spite of this I liked Uncle Matthew—I could not help liking him—and I had a feeling that Mother liked him too. He was always kind and cheerful and he was certainly very amusing. Some of his stories were very funny indeed. Uncle Matthew was a solicitor, he was a partner in an old-established Edinburgh firm, so many of his jokes had a legal flavour and he told them in a dry pawky way, which made them seem even funnier than they really were. The only thing was they amused him so much that he usually began to laugh before he came to the end. It would have been better if he could have kept a straight face over them.

Towards the end of Uncle Matthew's visit I became aware that there was "something in the wind." Several times when I went into the room there was a sudden uncomfortable silence and then they would all start talking about the news.

I was wondering about this, and sawing up some wood, when Meg came to tell me I was wanted in the study.

"What have ye done, David?" asked Meg anxiously. "Ye must have done something bad. They're all sitting there mim as mice waiting on ye. Maybe ye'd better wash before ye go in."

I had not finished cutting up the wood and it seemed a waste to wash, so I put down the saw and went in just as I was.

"David," began Father in a serious tone, "there's something—"

But Uncle Matthew interrupted him. "Hold your tongue, James," said Uncle Matthew. "Let me speak first. You can have your turn later."

It was very funny to see Father's face of astonishment at being told to hold his tongue and if I had not been so anxious about what was coming I might have laughed. But I *was* anxious so I did not feel like laughing; I just looked at them and waited.

"Now, David," said Uncle Matthew kindly. "You're a sensible boy and it seems to me you've the right to have a say in your own future. You've done well at your lessons but you can't continue at the village school much longer. You're aware of that, of course. The question is what's to be done. Well, I've offered to defray the cost of your education. I've offered to have you to live with me in Edinburgh and send you to a good day-school. What do you say to that?"

I looked at Mother. There were tears in her eyes but she made no sign; Father was tapping on the desk with his pencil and gazing out of the window. I did not know what to say.

"I don't know!" I said uncomfortably. "It's awfully kind of you, Uncle Matthew, but—but—"

"But what?" asked Uncle Matthew.

There was a little silence.

"You're all crazy," said Uncle Matthew at last. "You all say, but—but—but—and you've no alternative plan. What do you propose doing with the lad? Is he to leave school at fourteen and become a ploughboy?"

"We thought of Dumfries," began Father in a low voice. "It wouldn't cost much. We could manage—"

"What do you say, David?" asked Uncle Matthew. "Would you rather your parents pinched and scraped and sent you to school at Dumfries, or would you rather accept my offer and come to Edinburgh?"

"Now, Matthew," said Father. "It's not fair on the boy to put it like that. Mary says we'll manage."

"The Lord will provide!" exclaimed Uncle Matthew scornfully. "That's your attitude, James. The Lord will send ravens to feed you and provide Mary with a winter coat!"

"Matthew, that's no way to talk!"

"It's blasphemy, I suppose. Well, James, I've no wish to offend you so I'll take it back. The fact is I'm a man who says what he thinks. I've worked hard and I've made money. I've always found that God helps those who help themselves. If you'd taken my advice ten years ago you'd not be in this pickle now; but that's all over and done with. It's the future we've got to think of—David's future."

"We're very grateful to you," said Mother. "It's just—we feel we ought to be responsible for our own boy."

"And so you are!" cried Uncle Matthew, hitting the table with his fist. "That's what I've been trying to make you see for days. You're responsible for David. Well, here's a good offer. Have you a right to refuse?"

I was still standing by the table. I was dazed and bewildered but even so I realised how difficult a problem it was. Father had often said he wished he could send me to school in Edinburgh and here was his chance to do it . . . but on the other hand Father disapproved of Uncle Matthew and was loath to accept a favour from him.

They went on talking about it and at last Uncle Matthew said, "Well, James, you're very high and mighty, but I'd like to ask you one question; how do you know this is not the Lord's way of providing for your son's education?"

"It's a thing I've thought of, Matthew."

"You've thought of that?"

"Yes, indeed. How could I not think of it? Our prayers are often answered in an unexpected way. But I can't see light," added Father miserably.

"You'd see light if you opened your eyes. It's your pride that's blinding you."

There was a short silence and then Uncle Matthew rose. "Well," he said. "I've made my offer and I'll leave you to discuss the matter yourselves. If David comes to me I'll treat him as if he were my own son. He's a good lad and I'm fond of him. David and I fadge very well together." He went out and shut the door.

Mother was crying now, and Father was still tapping with his pencil.

"Well, David—" began Father.

"No," said Mother, drying her eyes. "No, James, you're not to put it on David. This is a thing we've got to decide ourselves."

She signed to me to leave them and I went towards the door.

"It's not pride, Mary," said Father earnestly. "If he were a different sort of man I wouldn't hesitate. I don't trust Matthew—"

"I think you're wrong," said Mother. "He's very fond of David, and you can trust David, can't you?"

I knew then that the thing was settled and as I shut the door and went back to the wood-shed I tried to make up my mind whether or not I was pleased. What would it be like to live with Uncle Matthew and go to a big Edinburgh day-school? I hated the idea of leaving home but that was not the point for in any case I should have to leave home . . . and it would not be for another year so it was far away. It seemed to me that it would be much more pleasant to stay with Uncle Matthew than to go to Dumfries and board with people I did not know. I knew Uncle Matthew and liked him, it was true that we fadged well.

Another advantage of being in Edinburgh was that Cliffe lived in Edinburgh. It would be fun to see Cliffe. Perhaps Uncle Matthew would let me ask him to tea occasionally. Cliffe had said that if ever I came to Edinburgh I must let him know. It would be good to start my new life with a friend.

That evening Uncle Matthew was in great spirits, for he was a man who liked to have his own way; he was as kind as possible and told me what a fine time we would have when I came to stay with him.

"Two bachelors, David!" he cried. "Two bachelors setting up house together? My word, we'll make things hum!"

"David must work—" began Father, frowning.

"Oh, of course, of course," agreed Uncle Matthew hastily.

"We'll both need to work, David and I. We'll be off to our work every morning, regular as clockwork. Don't you worry about that. And every Sunday morning we'll go to St. Giles. Rain or fine," said Uncle Matthew nodding to Father reassuringly. "Rain or fine David and I will go to St. Giles' every Sunday morning. On my honour we will."

I could see that Uncle Matthew thought he was making a tremendous sacrifice when he made this promise, but Father did not see it. To Father it seemed quite natural that every Sunday morning should see us at St. Giles'. It was a typical instance of how they misunderstood one another.

Uncle Matthew's approach to Mother was on different lines and was much more successful. He was never done telling her how pleased he was that I was coming and how much he was looking forward to having me. He told her about the room he was going to give me; it was on the second floor, facing south; he would have it papered and painted and newly furnished. He described his domestic arrangements in detail: his cook-housekeeper would look after my comfort. She and her daughter ran the house between them; they would mend my socks and sew on my buttons.

"What about air-raids?" asked Mother.

"There's the cellar," he replied. "I've had the cellar shored up with beams . . . but who knows! The war may be over before next year. Don't you worry, Mary. I promise you I'll take good care of David."

THE SECOND WINDOW

"My window looked out on to a chequer-board of gardens, each separated from its neighbour by a solid stone wall covered with ivy. The gardens were rectangular and very small indeed: some of them were unkempt and tawdry: some had stanchions fixed to the walls and the family washing fluttered upon ropes: a few were carefully tended patches with chrysanthemums or dahlias or little rockeries planted with variegated heaths. . . . Beyond the gardens was a somewhat grim row of tall grey houses—the backs of the houses of which the next crescent was composed."

CHAPTER NINE

UNCLE Matthew's house was in a crescent of tall grey houses not far from Haymarket Station. It was a quiet, sedate crescent and in the middle there was an oval-shaped garden with lawns and paths and trees. Number nineteen looked prosperous and well-kept, the front door was painted green and there were white lace curtains at the shining windows. My room was at the back on the second floor; my window looked out on to a chequer-board of gardens, each separated from its neighbours by a solid stone wall covered with ivy. The gardens were rectangular and very small indeed; some of them were unkempt and tawdry; some had stanchions fixed to the walls and the family washing fluttered upon ropes; a few were carefully tended patches, with chrysanthemums or dahlias or little rockeries planted with variegated heaths. Uncle Matthew's garden was neat and tidy, it boasted a crazy path and a couple of beds of roses. Beyond the gardens was a somewhat grim row of tall grey houses—the backs of the houses of which the next crescent was composed.

There were iron bars across the window of my room which showed that at one time it had been a nursery, but now it was furnished as a bed-sitting-room, with an electric fire, two comfortable basket chairs and a solid desk with a reading lamp. The bed was low and covered with a brown bedspread to match the curtains.

"It's a boy's room," said Uncle Matthew proudly. "It's yours, David, you can do what you like in it—there's nothing to spoil. I thought you might want to ask a friend in, now and then. It doesn't look too much like a bedroom."

"It's a splendid room," I said.

"Well, I hope you'll be comfortable here. If there's anything you want you've only got to tell me."

"You've thought of everything," I declared. "You *are* kind, Uncle Matthew."

"Yes," he said nodding and puffing out his cheeks. "Yes, I think you'll find practically everything you need. I've taken a good deal of trouble over it . . . but I can see you're pleased, David. You might call me Uncle Matt," he added. "It sounds more friendly."

For a day or two I felt homesick and miserable but after a bit I settled down into the new ways. Uncle Matt and I had breakfast together every morning at eight o'clock in the big heavily-furnished dining-room, then he went off to his office and I to school. Sometimes we had tea together and sometimes not but we always met again for dinner at half-past seven. It was real dinner, not supper, in Uncle Matt's establishment. Mrs. Drummond was an excellent housekeeper and cook; Uncle Matt sometimes grumbled about "war-time fare" but I thought the food was delicious.

There was no lack of conversation at the dinner-table. Uncle Matt was really interested in how I got on at school and what had done and seen during the day. He loved jokes and I found I could make him laugh quite easily. Sometimes what I told him reminded him of things that had happened when he was a boy (and if all he said was true he must have been an exceedingly troublesome boy). He talked about present-day experiences, too, and talked as if I were his contemporary. He told me what clients he had seen and what advice he had given them. At the moment he was particularly interested in the case of a lady who was suing her husband for "alimony." I heard a great deal about this alimony and at last I asked Uncle Matt what it meant.

"Goodness, David!" he exclaimed. "Why did you not ask me before? Here have I been talking for hours and you no whit the wiser! Always ask if you don't know the meaning of a word or you'll never learn anything. Always ask."

"Yes," I said nodding.

"Alimony," continued Uncle Matt. "Alimony is the money which is due to a woman who is separated from her husband by law. He's got to make an allowance for her support. . . ." He went on explaining quite patiently until I understood. "Will your client win her case?" I asked.

"Win her case! I can tell you this: if she doesn't win her case it will be a serious miscarriage of justice. Do you understand what that means, David?"

"Yes," I said, grinning at him. "It means that the court doesn't agree with you."

Uncle Matt roared with laughter. He rather liked me to be cheeky.

On Saturday afternoon we went for a drive in Uncle Matt's car. It was an old car and it trundled along sedately. Uncle Matt was a very poor driver and he was nervous into the bargain; he did not give the car a chance.

"There's something the matter with the damn' thing," said Uncle Matt impatiently. "It doesn't go any faster when I press the accelerator."

"Have you had it long?" I asked.

"Long!" he exclaimed. "About ten years, that's all. I had a chap to drive it but he joined up at the beginning of the war." The car went slower and slower; eventually when we were half-way up a hill the engine stalled and we began to run backwards. Uncle Matt put on the hand-brake and sat there looking at the dashboard and cursing violently. When he had called the car every name he could think of he got out and raised the bonnet. I followed him.

"It's no good," he said. "The blasted thing has died on us. We'll just need to walk to the nearest garage and get a man."

"I think it's the plugs," I said, giggling feebly.

"The plugs? Where are the plugs?"

"There," I said. "They're oiled up, that's all."

"Don't touch it," said Uncle Matt nervously. "For pity's sake leave the thing alone. You might get a shock, David. We'll wait a bit and see if somebody comes along—somebody who knows what to do."

I saw no sense in waiting so I found the tools and took out the plugs. "Look at that!" I said. "They're in a frightful condition."

"What's wrong with them?"

"Well—look! They're oiled up. Goodness knows what Dochie would say if he saw these plugs."

"Be careful, David—"

"It's all right. I know what to do. I've seen Dochie do it hundreds of times."

Uncle Matt did not believe me. He fluttered round like an old hen beseeching me to be careful but I just went on with the job and took no notice. I could not clean the plugs properly of course because there was no wire brush amongst the tools but I scraped them with a knife and put them back, hoping for the best.

"Are you sure it's all right?" asked Uncle Matt anxiously. "Have you done it properly, David? Maybe we'd better not start the engine in case the whole thing blows up."

"Go on," I said. "It's all right. Start the engine."

Fortunately for me the engine started without the slightest trouble and off we went.

Uncle Matt was amazed—he was absolutely flabbergasted—and all the way home he kept on saying how clever I was. But there was nothing clever about it; I had learnt quite a lot about engines from Dochie so it was easy enough to clean the plugs. If it had been something else—something wrong with the carburettor for instance—I could not have coped with it.

This incident made me think and I decided that if we were going for more drives together I had better learn a bit more about the car, so I took the handbook up to my room and studied it assiduously whenever I had time.

On Sunday morning we went to St. Giles'. I discovered from Mrs. Drummond that Uncle Matt usually stayed in bed on Sunday mornings and read the papers and I was not really surprised. I had had a feeling that his promise to Father was a great concession and was costing him something he valued. Uncle Matt said nothing about it to me, so I did not mention it. We went off together as if it were the most natural thing in the world.

That first week-end with Uncle Matt set the pattern. Nearly every fine Saturday afternoon we took out the car and had a spin out into the country. We went up to the Pentland Hills and got out and walked; we went to Gullane and had tea on the sands; one very fine day we took lunch with us and went over Soutra Hill and picnicked near a burn. When it became too wet and cold for out-door expeditions we went to a picture-house together, and sometimes on a Saturday evening we went to the theatre and saw a play. I realised that all these expeditions were planned for my benefit but there was no doubt Uncle Matt enjoyed them as much as I did. He had a natural capacity for enjoyment, he was full of energy and there was a boyishness about him which made him an excellent companion.

One Sunday afternoon hen I had been in Edinburgh for about three weeks Uncle Matt called me into his study and handed me a letter.

"It's for your aunt," he said. "You might take it along and wait for an answer. She'll probably ask you to stay to tea."

"But I don't know her!"

"She knows you. She wants to see you." He hesitated for a moment and then added, "Etta's a bit daft so you needn't pay too much attention to what she says."

I gazed at him in dismay. "But Uncle Matt—"

"Och, away with you!" he said laughing. "She'll not eat you, David. You'll have to go sometime so you may as well get it over."

These words were anything but reassuring and as I put the letter in my pocket and let myself out at the front door my heart was in my boots. I was shy of strangers at the best of times and an unknown aunt who was "a bit daft" sounded most alarming. I would have given a good deal to escape my fate. I walked along the quiet Sunday streets as slowly as I could but even so I arrived at my destination far too quickly.

The door was opened by a very nice-looking middle-aged woman in a black dress.

"For Miss Kirke," I said and I handed her the letter.

"Oh," she said, looking at me. "You'll be Miss Kirke's nephew. She was hoping you'd come and see her."

"Are you sure she wants to see me?" I asked.

"Of course," said the woman briskly. "You'd want people to come and see you if you could never get out, wouldn't you?"

There was no reply to that. I followed the woman upstairs without another word.

Aunt Etta was sitting in an easy-chair by the fire. She was a large woman with silvery hair parted in the middle and looped back over her ears; her face was round and fat and she had very pale blue eyes with a slightly bewildered expression.

When I was shown into her presence I was suddenly afflicted with dumbness but fortunately that did not matter; Aunt Etta had plenty to say.

"There now!" she exclaimed laying down her book and taking off her spectacles. "I knew you'd come to-day. It was the first thing I said when Jean brought my morning tea. I said 'David will come to-day,' didn't I, Jean?"

"Yes, Miss Kirke," agreed Jean. "But you've said the same thing every morning for a fortnight."

Aunt Etta looked a little crestfallen for a moment and then she smiled and said, "Never mind, I was right to-day."

I was sorry I had not come before but it was no good saying so.

"Well now, David," continued Aunt Etta. "You'll stay and have tea with me, won't you? We'll have a nice chat. There are all sorts of things for us to talk about. How are James and Mary? Sit down and tell me about them. Are they happy?"

For a moment I could not think whom she meant and then I pulled myself together. "Yes, thank you," I said.

"You're sure they're happy? Mary was so much younger than James. I was at the wedding and I thought how pretty she was—so young and pretty."

"She still is," I said, thinking of her.

"I was pretty once. It's difficult to believe, isn't it?" said Aunt Etta looking at me anxiously.

"No," I said. "I mean I'm sure you were . . . besides Mother said so."

"Did she really, David?"

"Yes, really."

Aunt Etta smiled happily. "Someday I'll show you a photograph which was taken when I was eighteen; then you'll see for yourself. I'll look it out and have it ready to show you next time you come." She paused and then added, "You're more like Mary than James."

"Yes," I said. It was rather embarrassing to be stared at by those very pale blue eyes.

"But there's Kirke in you, too. There's a distinct look of my father in you, David. It's your brow, I think. You ought to be proud of being like my father; he was a very fine man. I sometimes wonder what he would think of the world if he were alive to-day . . . but of course he would be over ninety. Do you remember him, David?"

"No, he died before I was born."

"That's a pity," said Aunt Etta, shaking her head sadly. "I wish you had seen him. But I remember now. He died before you were born. Then Matthew and James had a quarrel. That was a pity too."

"What did they quarrel about?" I asked with interest.

"Let me see," she said. "It was so long ago. You were a baby at the time so of course you couldn't know about it, could you?" She looked vague for a few moments and then her face cleared. "Matthew wanted James to go to London. Yes, that was it."

"To London?"

She nodded. "James had the offer of a Presbyterian Church in London but he went to Haines instead and Matthew thought it was very stupid of him. Yes, that was it," repeated Aunt Etta. "There was a great deal of unpleasantness about it. You see James would have got quite a lot more money if he had gone to London, but James never minded about money. Matthew likes money, you know."

"Yes, I know."

"He's clever about it, too. He manages all my business affairs for me. To tell you the truth, David, I don't know what I would do if I had to manage my own affairs. I'm not very good at business."

This was easy to believe.

So far she had not opened the letter, she had been turning it over and over in her fat white hands, but now she held it up and looked at it. "This is from Matthew?" she exclaimed in surprise.

"Yes, he gave it to me to bring you."

"Oh dear, it will be business! Is it about the house, David?"

"I don't know what it's about," I said.

"I'm sure it's about the house," declared Aunt Etta, looking at the envelope with distaste. "I *know* that's what it's about—so I don't think I'll open it."

"But Uncle Matt wants an answer!"

"Listen, David," said Aunt Etta, leaning forward and dropping her voice confidentially. "Matthew wants me to sell the house. You don't think I should, do you?"

"I don't know anything about it, I'm afraid."

"I'll tell you," she said. "I'll tell you all about it and then you can advise me what to do. It's a little house near London and it's called Green Beech Cottage; isn't that a pretty name? It used to belong to a great friend of mine and long ago I went to stay with her. It was a dear little house with a veranda at the back and it had a lovely view. We had tea on the veranda sometimes. Vera was very badly off, poor thing, so I gave her some money. Then when she died she left me Green Beech Cottage in her will. It was nice of her, wasn't it? So you see, David, Green Beech Cottage belongs to me. You understand don't you?"

"Yes," I said.

"You're a very clever boy!" declared Aunt Etta admiringly.

"It's quite easy to understand," I told her.

"You don't think I should sell it, do you?"

"Well, it's yours," I said. "You can do what you like with it, can't you?"

"It's my very own," she agreed. "Matthew thinks I ought to sell it, but some day, when the war's over, I might want to go and live near London and then I would have no house."

"But would you want to?" I asked. It seemed to me that if Aunt Etta never went out it would be all the same where she lived, whether here or in London.

"I won't sell it," she declared, pursing her lips stubbornly. "No, I won't. Matthew can't make me sell it." She looked at the letter and added, "I won't open the letter, either."

"I think you'd better open it. I mean it might be about something else. Uncle Matt said it was important."

"No, David, it will just upset me."

I looked at her and wondered what to do. "I shall get into trouble if you don't open it," I told her.

"Will you?" she asked. "Well, you open it. That's the best way. Then, if it's just telling me to sell the house I needn't read it." She gave me the letter and sat back with her hands folded. Uncle Matt had said she was daft—and she was—but there was a sort of sense in her. I had been a bit scared of her at first but now I just felt sorry.

"Open it, David," she said. "Read it and see what it says." There was nothing for me to do but open it.

19 Ruthven Crescent
Edinburgh

Dear Etta,

Since seeing you I have instituted inquiries regarding the small property bequeathed to you by Mrs. Marsden and have received a report on same by a competent valuator. The house stands in its own garden of about half an acre surrounded by a beech hedge. The building is of red brick and is in reasonably good repair. The accommodation consists of two public rooms— one large and one small—and two bedrooms, one bathroom, kitchen, etc. As you do not require the house yourself you have no option but to sell. It will deteriorate if it is allowed to stand empty. This being so I propose putting the property into the hands of a House Agent in London and shall be obliged if you will write me a short note giving me permission to act for you in the matter. This will save you further trouble. When I spoke to you about this before you seemed unwilling to sell but I hope you have considered the matter carefully and will take a sensible view. The property should have a ready sale and the money therefrom will be useful to you.

Believe me,
Your affectionate brother,

MATTHEW KIRKS

"Well," demanded Aunt Etta. "It's about the house, isn't it? Matthew wants me to sell it."

"Yes," I said. "He thinks you should sell it. The property will deteriorate if it is left standing empty. That's what he says."

"I know. That's what he said before; but it's mine and I can do what I like with it." She chuckled and added, "Matthew will be very cross. He likes people to do exactly as he tells them."

"But perhaps he's right. I mean—"

"He's usually right," agreed Aunt Etta. "That's what's so annoying—and usually I do what he tells me because it's easier and more pleasant, but sometimes I don't. Sometimes I dig in my toes and refuse to budge; I just have a feeling that I want to. Do you never have that feeling, David?"

I could not help smiling because she looked so like a naughty child with her round fat cheeks and the mischievous glint in her eyes. "Yes," I admitted. "Yes, I sometimes feel like that—but what am I to say to Uncle Matt?"

"Tell him the truth," she replied and she leant forward and seized the letter and threw it into the fire. "There," she said, dusting her hands together. "That's finished with. Now we can talk about other things, can't we? You haven't told me about James. Tell me all about him."

"He's—quite well," I said feebly.

"That's not telling me about him! I want to know lots more. He's my brother, you know. I remember when James was born. He was small and red and quite, quite bald. I cried when I saw him. You see, David, I was very disappointed because Mother had told me I was going to have a little sister. I had two brothers already."

"Two brothers?" I asked.

"Henry died," she explained. "He died when he was eight years old. It was dreadfully sad. You won't remember Henry, I'm afraid."

"No, he must have died long before I was born."

"Such a lot of things happened before you were born," said Aunt Etta, and she looked so sad I was afraid she was going to cry.

Fortunately at that moment tea was brought in and Aunt Etta cheered up a lot. She enjoyed her tea; she ate scones and jam and cakes and chocolate biscuits. I had a very good tea myself but Aunt Etta ate twice as much as I did; no wonder she was fat! While she ate she talked all the time and she was really very amusing; she told me about Father when he was a little boy. According to Aunt Etta, Father was very naughty indeed and was never out of mischief. Somehow it gave me a new idea of Father to hear that he was not always good and grave.

"You'll come again, won't you, David?" said Aunt Etta when I rose to go. "Come again soon."

"Yes, of course. I'd like to come again," I told her—and it was true.

CHAPTER TEN

WHEN I returned from having tea with Aunt Etta it was nearly six o'clock. Uncle Matt came out of his study and met me in the hall.

"Goodness, David, I thought you were lost!" he exclaimed. "You haven't been all this time with Etta, have you? Where's the letter?"

I had forgotten all about the wretched letter.

"Don't stand there gaping like a fish," said Uncle Matt testily. "You've got that note for me, I suppose."

"She didn't—write a note."

He glared at me. "Why didn't you wait for an answer? I told you to wait for an answer, didn't I?"

"Yes, but she wouldn't—" I began.

"What did she say?"

"She said she didn't want to sell the house," I replied. I could see Uncle Matt was getting very angry and I was not going to tell him that his letter had been thrown into the fire. Aunt Etta could tell him that herself if she wanted to.

"What on earth do you mean!" exclaimed Uncle Matt. "You know perfectly well I wanted a proper answer to the letter. You should have waited until she had written it. I can't do anything until I get that note. What's she going to do with the damned house!"

"She just said she doesn't want to sell the house. That's all."

"That's all!" he cried. "I write her a business letter and she sends a verbal message that she doesn't want to sell the house! That's all, is it! That's gratitude! I toil and moil and do her business for her and all I get in return is this infernal nonsense. What does she think she's going to do with the place? She can't go and live there! She can't leave it to rot!"

"I couldn't help it, Uncle Matt!"

"You couldn't help it!" he exclaimed scornfully. "Of course you could have helped it. You should have made her write an answer. You're a perfect fool!"

Uncle Matt's face was as red as fire; he called his sister every name under the sun. "The stubborn old mule!" he shouted. "She's crazy! I could have her locked up to-morrow! That would teach her a lesson and save a deal of trouble—" I had never seen anybody in such a fury before and to tell the truth I was terrified. I had heard that people sometimes had fits when they flew into rages and I expected that any minute Uncle Matt might fall down dead. I dodged past him and ran up the stairs, pursued by the sound of his voice, hoarse with anger.

For a long time I sat on the end of my bed thinking about Uncle Matt, and the funny mixture he was, wondering what it was going to be like living with him for years. People had been angry with me before (sometimes old Meg was furious with me) but never unless I deserved it. Uncle Matt had raged at me for something I could not help; that was what upset me. I thought of Haines and the manse and the gentle voices of Mother and Father. I began to realise that the world was different from what I had thought. Perhaps my home had been too sheltered. Perhaps I had been coddled—not coddled physically but mentally. Perhaps Mother had been right in saying that only children were too sensitive and it was much harder for them when they went out into the world and had their corners rubbed off. Uncle Matt had rubbed off one of my corners effectually; he had destroyed the illusion that you could depend upon grown-up people to be sensible and just.

When the gong rang for dinner I crept softly down the stairs and listened. Voices were coming from the study, cheerful voices, and I heard Uncle Matt's hearty laugh. I opened the door and saw him standing with his back to the fire in his favourite position looking as pleased as Punch; a tall thin man with long legs and a long sad face was sitting on the sofa.

"Here's David!" cried Uncle Matt. "I told you about him, didn't I? David, this is Mr. Blackworth."

It was obvious that Uncle Matt and Mr. Blackworth were great friends (indeed afterwards I discovered they had been at school together); they called one another Tom and Matt and talked hard all the time. Mr. Blackworth's long sad face was deceptive; he was extremely funny and made the most comical remarks without the ghost of a smile. I never heard him laugh once all the time I knew him; but he was very good at making other people laugh, especially Uncle Matt.

We went in to dinner. Uncle Matt had opened a bottle of especially good claret for the benefit of his friend and they insisted that I should have some too. The first sip surprised me, for I had never tasted wine before, but when I had drunk half a glass I decided that I liked it. Uncle Matt was pleased, he said claret was a gentleman's drink and every gentleman should have a cultivated palate. Mr. Blackworth said sadly that if Uncle Matt thought it a necessary constituent in my education it would come pretty expensive. They talked about claret at length and I found it interesting. Long ago claret had become a favourite drink in Edinburgh because the town had such a close connection with France. The finest French wines and spirits were brought over by smugglers and found their way free of duty to the tables of the good Edinburgh burghers. In those days it was thought no crime to have dealings with the Free Traders (as they were called more politely by those who enjoyed their wares). The smugglers and the Jacobites worked together and it was natural that they should for they both worked under cover of darkness and both worked against the law of the land. The Free Traders smuggled in their wines and smuggled out the followers of Prince Charles. It was convenient and a matter of principle as well.

"There's a wee poem about claret," said Uncle Matt. "My father was fond of quoting it—your grandfather, David—I'm not very sure that I've got it right but it went something like this:

> *"Guid claret best keeps oot the cauld*
> *And rives awa the winter sune.*
> *It mak's a manny wise and bauld*
> *And heaves his saul beyond the mune."*

"I've heard it somewhere," Mr. Blackworth said. "Maybe I heard it from your father, Matt."

Like Uncle Matt, Mr. Blackworth was a solicitor and when they had finished discussing claret they began to talk about a law suit which had been tried quite recently in the Edinburgh courts. I did not understand all they were saying but I listened and went on with my dinner. Uncle Matt and Mr. Blackworth were dissatisfied with the verdict and they were especially annoyed with a man called McFluster who had asked one of the witnesses a leading question and got away with it. "What's a leading question, Uncle Matt?" I said.

"Bless me, I'd forgotten the boy!" he exclaimed. "What do you make of all this rigmarole, eh?"

They both looked at me and waited for an answer. "Not very much," I said. "I didn't understand all of it but it sounds to me as if there had been a miscarriage of justice."

"A Daniel come to judgment," said Mr. Blackworth.

Uncle Matt was laughing uproariously. I think he had forgotten that he had taught me the term himself. "A miscarriage of justice!" he cried. "Did you hear that, Tom! That's rich! McFluster would like that."

"You haven't explained the term 'leading question,'" said Mr. Blackworth. "Our young friend, Daniel, asked you what it meant."

"You tell him," said Uncle Matt feebly. "You tell him what it means. I'm nearly killed."

"Well, Daniel," said Mr. Blackworth. "I would have you know that when a witness is being examined in court he may be asked a great many questions about what he saw and heard, but these questions must be straightforward and must on no account give him a lead or presuppose an answer. For instance—"

But Uncle Matt had recovered now and interrupted him. "You're not making it clear, Tom. The boy doesn't know what you're talking about." And with that he began to explain the matter himself.

Soon they had forgotten me again and were hard at it, arguing with one another about questions which they had heard being put to witnesses and debating hotly whether or not they were leading questions. To tell the truth I was not much wiser at the end of the discussion than I was at the beginning and it seemed to me that it must be very difficult for a judge to decide what was a leading question and what was not.

When I went up to bed at nine o'clock, which was my usual time on Sundays, the two of them were still talking. They were sitting beside the fire in the study and as I paused at the door and looked back at them I thought they made a good picture; they were so different from one another and yet there was something about them the same.

As time passed I got to know Mr. Blackworth quite well for he often came to dinner with Uncle Matt; they both loved talking but they were quite fair about it and willing to listen to what each other had to say. Mr. Blackworth always called me Daniel; it had started as a joke but after a bit I believe he forgot about the joke and was under the impression that Daniel was my name. I used to look at him and wonder—his face was so inscrutable that it was impossible to tell whether he was making a joke or not.

Mr. Blackworth had a nephew called Miles, a big upstanding fellow with dark curly hair. Miles Blackworth went to the same school as I did; he was in my form and we became fast friends. I had always been small for my age and I had mousy fair hair, so I admired Miles tremendously; he was exactly the sort of fellow I should have liked to be. He was a back at rugger, he was dashing and gay, he never suffered from shyness. Sometimes I used to wonder why Miles bothered about me; he could have had anybody he liked as a friend. One afternoon—it was a half holiday—we went to the Zoo together and he came back and had tea. Another day we went to a film and enjoyed it tremendously. Miles never asked me to go to his house, he explained that his family were "a nuisance."

"It's no good asking you to my place," said Miles. "We couldn't talk or anything. I've got three sisters and a brother all older than myself. It's frightful, really. They're so interfering."

This surprised me, for Miles seemed to be able to do exactly as he wanted.

"It's sickening," Miles continued. "I suppose it's because I'm the youngest of the family. They seem to think I'm still a child. The parents are just as bad; I can't go out without them asking where I'm going and when I'm coming back and all the rest of it. I suppose you're perfectly free, David?"

I found this question difficult to answer. As a matter of fact I felt perfectly free, but it had never occurred to me to go out without consulting Uncle Matt and telling him my plans. But how could I say this to Miles? He would think me a ninny. Of course Miles was different—naturally Miles did not want his family interfering with his liberty to come and go as he pleased.

"Does your uncle interfere with you?" asked Miles, putting his question differently.

"No," I said. "He's all right. We get on splendidly."

"You're lucky," said Miles with a sigh. "I wish to goodness they'd let me go to Loretto. Then I'd get away from the family. My brother's at Loretto—but of course I'm the youngest so I've got to stay at home and go to a blinking day-school. It's rotten, isn't it?"

"It doesn't seem fair," I agreed.

"Just because he got a scholarship! I mean," said Miles confidentially. "I mean of course it was all right Robert getting a scholarship. Robert is clever, he doesn't have to swot. But Father could easily afford to send me to Loretto without me bothering to get a scholarship. That's what's so unfair."

"But if you got a scholarship—"

"Gosh!" exclaimed Miles. "You won't see me swotting. There are lots of other much more exciting things to do."

"People are different," I said. "You're so keen on rugger. You'll be in the first fifteen before very long."

"Oh—well—perhaps," he said, but I could see he was pleased.

CHAPTER ELEVEN

ONE morning when Uncle Matt and I were having breakfast together he suggested that I might ask one of my friends to lunch on Sunday.

"We could go for an expedition," said Uncle Matt. "We could go to Peebles or somewhere. Perhaps you'd like to ask Miles."

"Can I ask Freda?" I said.

"Freda!" exclaimed Uncle Matt in horrified tones. "A girl! Great Scott, where did you meet a girl, David?"

"I didn't meet her," I said laughing. "I've always known Freda. Her father is a farmer at Nethercleugh, and she's at school in Edinburgh."

"When I was your age I had no use for girls."

"But Freda isn't an ordinary girl, she's different."

"They're all different, David," said Uncle Matt with a sigh. "They're all different—and they're all the same. Most of the trouble in this world is made by the sex that wears the petticoats. But there's no need for us to argue about it because they'd never let her come."

"Why wouldn't they?"

"Because—Och, David, what a question! They're terribly particular at these posh schools; they'd never let the girl go out with two fascinating bachelors."

"But I *know* her!" I cried. "I know her father and mother—I've known them all my life!"

At first Uncle Matt was adamant, but when he heard that Freda was at Dinwell Hall he changed his mind, for Miss Humble, the headmistress, was one of his clients and he knew her well. He grumbled about it, of course, and he teased me quite a lot but he consented to write to Miss Humble and ask if Freda could come. Miss Humble replied that Freda would be delighted to accept the invitation and we could fetch her at twelve-thirty on Sunday morning.

"We can't go to St. Giles'," said Uncle Matt, looking at me sideways. "There wouldn't be time. We'll need to give it a miss—but maybe it will not matter for once."

Dinwell Hall was a large square house in a big park with fine trees. We drove up to the door in the funny old car and were shown into Miss Humble's presence. Miss Humble was large and fat with grey hair, cut short like a man's, and large flashing spectacles set firmly on her fleshy nose. She shook hands with us in a masterful fashion and invited us to sit down.

"I have sent for Freda," said Miss Humble. "She will be here in a few minutes."

"There's no hurry at all," said Uncle Matt politely.

We sat and talked. Uncle Matt was on his best behaviour and I could not help smiling to myself when I looked at him. Here was quite a different Uncle Matt—a polished, pleasant man-of-the-world making polite conversation with a lady. Nearly everybody is made up of a whole lot of different people but Uncle Matt was more of a mixture than anybody I have ever seen . . . and as a matter of fact I saw yet another side of him when Freda appeared and we managed to escape from Miss Humble. Uncle Matt treated Freda as if she were grownup; he was gallant, he even flirted with her a little in an elephantine way.

We had a very happy time together. Freda was at her best, she was friendly and amusing and enjoyed every moment of the outing. We lunched at the Hawes Inn at Queensferry and then we went for a drive in the car and home to Ruthven Crescent for tea. After tea Freda and I went out into the gardens in front of the house and sat on a seat and talked.

"Your Uncle Matt is a dear," said Freda. "I wish I had an uncle like that."

"You have," I told her, smiling. "He's yours, Freda. You've got him eating out of your hand."

Freda laughed. "Yes, I think he likes me quite a lot. You'll ask me again, won't you, David? It's lovely to get away from school."

"Don't you like school?" I asked her.

"Of course I like it," she replied. "But all the same it's nice to get away. Nearly all the other girls go out on Sundays; their parents come and take them or they have friends in Edinburgh; but I've got nobody to take me." She hesitated and then added, "It's awfully mean of Father and Mother, they could easily come from Haines and take me out for the day."

Freda's face, which had been so happy, clouded over and she set her lips in a thin straight line.

"But Freda, how could they?" I exclaimed. "They wouldn't have enough petrol to come up from Haines."

"They could do it if they wanted," declared Freda. "It isn't that I *want* them to come, it's just that it seems so funny . . . all the other girls go out on Sundays."

"Well, don't let's talk about it," I said. "We've had a lovely time to-day and we'll have lots of other outings."

Freda looked at me and smiled. "You're just the same, David. You don't like talking about anything unpleasant."

"Who does!" I exclaimed.

"But it's like an ostrich, burying its head in the sand!"

"Not really," I said thoughtfully. "It's better to be happy and think of nice things instead of being miserable and worrying over nasty things."

"That's what an ostrich does," said Freda emphatically. It was no good arguing with her of course, so I left it and talked about something else, and presently it was time to take Freda back to Dinwell Hall.

Soon after this I wrote to Cliffe and told him I was in Edinburgh and Cliffe rang up in great excitement and invited me to supper the following Sunday. Uncle Matt was amused when he heard about the invitation but he knew Mr. Dodge's shop and told me how to get there.

"You've an odd selection of friends," said Uncle Matt as he saw me off at the door.

"Cliffe isn't odd," I said. "Cliffe is a frightfully good sport. You'd like Cliffe. He'd make you laugh."

"All right, all right," said Uncle Matt cheerfully. "Ask him to tea if you want to."

The Dodges' shop was a big ironmonger's establishment in Leith Street. It was shut, of course, but there was a side-door with DODGE written on the bell. Cliffe opened the door himself and fell upon me with cries of joy.

"D-David! This is grand!" he exclaimed. "I thought it must be you when I heard the b-bell! Gosh, it's grand to see you!"

"You're bigger than ever, Cliffe!"

"Well, what did you expect!" laughed Cliffe, seizing my arm. "Of course I'm b-bigger. You're b-b-bigger too, you old silly. Come on, David, they're all p-panting to see you. I've told them all about you."

The Dodges' flat was over the shop. It was a biggish flat and very comfortably furnished. Mr. Dodge was small and fat, he was very bald and wore some strands of dark hair brushed across the top of his head. I could see his resemblance to his brother—the blacksmith at Haines—but his manner and way of talking were ludicrously different. Mrs. Dodge was large and statuesque, she was wearing a black silk dress and a gold brooch with a cameo in the middle of it. The five little girls had round faces and fair hair and blue eyes, they looked exactly alike, except for their sizes, and when I saw them sitting round the big dining-table I suddenly thought of Mother and her "dozen daughters." The room seemed full of little girls.

"We've been looking forward to seeing you, Mr. Kirke," said Mrs. Dodge grandly. "You were so good to Cliffe."

"Cliffe has told us all about you," added Mr. Dodge.

We were all shy and on our best behaviour so at first the conversation was somewhat stilted. I was even more embarrassed when I discovered that the Dodges were under the impression that I had saved their son's life. Cliffe had given them a garbled account of his adventures in the bog and it was impossible to disabuse them of their absurd idea without saying outright that Cliffe was a liar.

"It beats me how you got him out," declared Mr. Dodge. "You must be a deal stronger than you look."

"He's terribly strong," put in Cliffe.

"It was brave," said Mrs. Dodge. "It was very brave. You might have been sucked under yourself."

"David never thought of *that*," declared Cliffe. "David's not that sort. He came right in after me and p-pulled me out."

"It was nothing," I mumbled. "There was no danger at all."

"There I was," continued Cliffe dramatically. "There I was in the b-bog—*sinking*. I could feel myself sinking. The slimy m-mud was b-b-bubbling round me—and the smell was awful. I've never been so frightened in my life. You've no idea what it's like to feel the ground all quaky and sinky under your f-feet and your f-f-feet sticking like glue so that you can't move them. I tell you I wouldn't be here now if it wasn't for D-David."

"Oh rot!" I exclaimed. "You weren't a bit frightened. You laughed like anything when I got you out."

"I was a bit hysterical," said Cliffe solemnly. "It was enough to m-make anyone hysterical."

"Nonsense, Cliffe!" I said.

Mrs. Dodge had become quite pale. "The country is awful dangerous," she declared. "We'd never have let Cliffe go to Haines if we'd realised how dangerous it was."

"Dangerous!" I exclaimed in surprise. "It's not nearly as dangerous as town. Every time I cross the street I'm nearly run over by a bus or a lorry."

"Och, there's no need to worry," said Mr. Dodge comfortably. "They have no wish to run over you, Mr. Kirke."

This seemed such a comic idea that I could not help laughing, and of course Cliffe laughed too—it took very little to make Cliffe laugh—soon we were all laughing together and the ice was broken.

"I've no idea what the joke is," declared Mr. Dodge, taking a large green silk handkerchief out of his pocket and blowing his nose.

"Nor me," agreed Mrs. Dodge. "Mr. Kirke will be thinking we're all mad."

"Please call me David," I said.

"Well, it would be more friendly-like," nodded Mr. Dodge. "And Cliffe having talked about you so much it would be easy, too. David is a nice name. He was a sweet singer, so we're told. If we'd had another son we would have called him David."

"It's a pity I hadn't an elder brother," said Cliffe a trifle bitterly.

By this time we had finished supper and the two eldest little girls had begun to help their mother to clear the dishes. I wondered if we ought to help but apparently this was not expected of us.

"What are you two lads going to do?" asked Mr. Dodge. "Are you going out, or what?"

They all looked at me.

"I wonder if I could see the shop?" I said doubtfully. "It's Sunday, of course, so perhaps—but that's what I'd like."

"Well, of course you can!" cried Mr. Dodge smiling delightedly. "You're welcome to see the shop. Look now, Cliffe, you take David downstairs and show him round. Maybe he would like a knife to put in his pocket—one of those new knives that's just come in. You see to that, Cliffe."

We went downstairs together and Cliffe opened the door of the shop. It was all shut up of course and rather dark and shadowy but we switched on some of the lights and looked about. The place was large and spacious and full of all sorts of interesting things, and it was fun looking at them with Cliffe, who knew all about them.

"What a splendid shop!" I exclaimed.

"Yes, it's a good business," he agreed. "Dad built it up from a wee poky ironmonger's store. That takes a lot of hard work, you know. I help as much as I can when I'm not at school; some day when I've left school I'll be here for good. I like the work, it's very interesting."

"Yes, it must be," I said. I envied Cliffe. Here was his future all ready for him.

"What about you?" asked Cliffe. "Are you going to be a minister like your father?"

"No—not that," I told him. "I couldn't be a minister. I don't know what I'll do. I'd like to be a farmer but you've got to have money to buy a farm. I suppose I'll have to go into an office or something."

We spent a long time looking round and at last Cliffe produced a big tray of pocket-knives and put it down on the glass counter.

"You're to choose one," he told me. "Choose any one you like."

"No, Cliffe," I said.

"But Dad said so! What d'you mean, David?"

"I mean I don't want one."

"But David, they're fine!"

"I know, but I couldn't take it, Cliffe. He said I was to have it because of that stupid story about the bog and you know perfectly well it was all lies."

"Not lies," declared Cliffe cheerfully. "It was maybe a wee bit exaggerated, but I had to make a good story of it."

"Well, I wish you hadn't. I felt a perfect fool—and anyway I'm not taking the knife, that's flat."

"David, you must! Look, here's one with three b-blades and a corkscrew and a thing for taking stones out of a horse's shoe."

"I can't," I told him. "Honestly, Cliffe, I'd be taking it on false pretences. Don't you understand?"

Cliffe stood and looked at me with the knife in his hand.

He was serious for once. "I see what you mean," he said slowly. "I'm sorry, David . . . but I didn't do it on purpose. I was just telling them about the bog and they sort of jumped to the conclusion that it was a wee bit worse than it really was. Mum has never seen a bog but she's read about people sinking in them—and I was sinking. If you'd not been there I might have sunk up to my neck, so you see—"

"That's nonsense!"

"It's not! And anyway that's what they think and you can't explain things when p-people get an idea into their heads. Look, David," said Cliffe earnestly. "You m-must try to understand. I d-didn't set out to exaggerate the b-bog. It just happened . . . and it seemed a p-pity to spoil the story when they liked it so much."

He looked at me to see if I understood and of course I did understand, but all the same I was not going to accept the knife.

"Listen, David," said Cliffe. "You *did* pull me out, didn't you? And if it had been d-dangerous you'd have p-pulled me out just the same, wouldn't you?"

"I don't know."

"What? Would you have g-gone away and left me to sink?"

" I don't know what I'd have done."

"Well, I know," said Cliffe. "I know what you'd have d-done. You'd have p-pulled me out of that b-bog and never thought about whether it was dangerous . . . so you can take the knife with a clear conscience."

I could not help smiling at Cliffe's reasoning, but I still shook my head.

"Oh, all right," said Cliffe sadly. "Dad will be hurt, of course. He'll think you're too p-proud to t-take a p-present from him—that's what he'll think."

This was true. I had not thought of it before but now I saw that Mr. Dodge would think just that. He would think I was too proud to accept the knife.

"Wait," I said quickly. "Don't put them away, Cliffe. I'll choose a knife. It's very kind of Mr. Dodge."

Cliffe was delighted. He helped me to choose a knife and I went home with it in my pocket.

After that first visit to the Dodges I went to see them quite often and Cliffe came and had tea with me . . . but unfortunately Uncle Matt and Cliffe did not like one another. Uncle Matt was at his worst with Cliffe, he was stiff and patronising, and Cliffe was so nervous that he stammered and stuttered and made inane remarks, and was quite unlike his usual cheerful self. There was nothing I could do about it except to decide that I would never ask Cliffe again unless I was sure Uncle Matt would be out when he came. It seemed very odd when I liked them both so much that they should not like each other—it seemed illogical. I puzzled over it a lot.

CHAPTER TWELVE

THE first term I spent in Edinburgh seemed endless, and I was nearly mad with excitement when the Christmas holidays approached, but after that the years flew by very quickly. There was so much to do that I had no time to think. My days were full of lessons and games and expeditions with Uncle Matt. I went to see Aunt Etta as often as I could; Freda came to lunch; I made friends with several boys at school and visited their homes; I took the tram to Leith Street and called at the Dodges'.

Uncle Matt and I got on well very together. I learnt to understand him and to manage him so that I could usually get my own way. When he flew into one of his rages I left him alone and made myself scarce until he recovered. I decided that his rages were a sort of disease. Uncle Matt could not help flying into a rage when things annoyed him; it was a pity, but it was not his fault. I realised that although Uncle Matt was old in years he was young in character, he had never grown up. There was a naïveté about him which was rather pathetic. He was both proud and humble. For instance he would boast about his cleverness and tell me what wise advice he had given his clients and what fools they were when they did not follow it; and then, a few minutes later, he would say with absolute sincerity, "It's dull for you, David, cooped up with a silly old buffer of an uncle. You'd better get Miles to go to a show or something. There's a good play on at the Lyceum this week."

"Why don't you come?" I would say. "I'd rather go with you."

Then he would smile all over his face and exclaim, "Would you really, David?"

Rages or no, you could not help liking Uncle Matt. When I had been in Edinburgh for about a year I suddenly began to grow at a tremendous rate. Uncle Matt said it was the East Coast air. I was delighted, of course, for I had always wanted to be a giant and I had almost given up hope of being anything more than a pigmy. The only trouble was that I outgrew all my clothes; every garment I possessed became too small for me. Mrs. Drummond did what she could to make my clothes wearable but even she could not work miracles and at last I had to write to Mother and tell her about it. Fortunately mother was quite pleased at the news, she came up from Haines for the day and we had a great shopping expedition. We bought clothes that were too large for me and for a bit I felt completely lost in them, but I was growing so fast that I soon filled them out.

Looking back upon the years in Edinburgh they seem to telescope and it is difficult to remember when this incident or that incident occurred. Here and there a day stands out like a little bright picture, but for the most part those years are hazy in the extreme. There is a little bright picture of a sunshiny afternoon when Uncle Matt and Freda and I went over to Peebles and had lunch at the Hydropathic Hotel; there is the day when Cliffe and I took a tram to Fairmilehead and walked over the Pentland Hills . . .

Another incident which I remember clearly—but for quite a different reason—is the Saturday afternoon when Miles came to tea and we talked about the future. Miles was to have played rugger but the rain had been coming down in sheets all day and the match had been postponed.

"Do they think we're made of butter?" grumbled Miles as we went upstairs to my room together. "We could easily have played. Fothers is just an old woman to put off the match."

"You may not be made of butter but the pitch is like treacle," I replied. "It would have ruined the pitch for the whole season if you'd played."

Miles laughed and settled himself comfortably in one of the basket-chairs. "Oh well, we can talk," he said.

We talked. The rain was lashing against the window, but my room, with its electric stove, was cosy and comfortable.

"What are you going to do when you leave school?" asked Miles.

"National Service, of course."

"I know—but after that? I'm going to London."

"London!" I exclaimed in surprise.

"That's the place to make money, David. London is the hub of the world," declared Miles.

"Yes, but—"

Miles leaned forward eagerly. "Look here," he said. "Why don't you come too, David?"

"I couldn't possibly!"

"Why not? We could join forces. We could both get jobs and live in digs together. Gosh, it would be fun!"

"Do you mean it?" I asked incredulously.

"Of course I mean it. We could have a marvellous time—you and I in digs together. It's a grand idea."

"But Miles, how could I?"

"Don't be an old stick-in-the-mud!" cried Miles. "Think of it, David! Think of what fun we could have!"

I thought about it. "Could we?" I asked doubtfully. "I mean, could we get jobs in London?"

"We could," declared Miles. "I've gone into that. As a matter of fact I spoke to Uncle Tom and he promised to help me. He knows a firm of lawyers in London who would take me on as a clerk. Of course that would only be a beginning; I don't intend to stay a clerk all my life. Once I was actually in London I could look about and find something better. That's my idea."

"You could do that here, couldn't you?"

"Here!" he cried scornfully. "Good Lord, I don't want to settle down in Edinburgh. I don't want to be on a leading-rein all my life. I want to strike out on my own."

The idea of going to London and living in digs with Miles appealed to me tremendously. The only thing was I had promised Uncle Matt that when I had done my National Service I would come back and start work as a clerk in his office. His idea was that later on I should read Law at the Edinburgh University and take my degree and become a junior partner in the firm. The prospect did not fill me with enthusiasm but there had seemed no alternative. Uncle Matt liked me—I knew that—and it was a good opening. I explained all this to Miles.

"Gracious!" exclaimed Miles. "What a dreary prospect! Cut it out and come to London with me."

"Miles, listen—"

"No, you listen to me. You want to get on, don't you? There's no scope *here* for a young fellow who wants to get on in the world and make good. Are you going to moulder here all your life and turn into an old fossil like your uncle—and mine?"

"No, of course not!" I cried.

"You will," said Miles, looking at me and smiling. "I can see it coming. I can see you forty years from now and, believe it or not, you look just like Uncle Tom."

I had a horrible feeling he was right.

"Come on, David," continued Miles. "Be a sport. Come to London with me and make your fortune."

"But how could I get a job?"

"That's easy. You could get one to-morrow if you wanted. Your uncle could fix a job for you. Why don't you speak to him about it and see what he says?"

After that Miles and I talked about it often and at last he persuaded me to broach the subject to Uncle Matt. I sounded Uncle Matt as tactfully as I could for I did not want to hurt his feelings.

"London?" exclaimed Uncle Matt in surprise. "Why on earth do you want to go to London?"

"Miles is going," I said. "He suggested we might live in digs together, but of course I wouldn't dream of going if you want me here."

"Miles is going?" asked Uncle Matt.

"Yes, it was his idea, really."

"Well, I don't know," said Uncle Matt thoughtfully. "We'll need to think about it."

"Yes, of course. We needn't decide straight off."

Uncle Matt was silent for a few moments and then he said, "It might be quite a good plan. Supposing you tried it for a couple of years and then came back here to me?"

I gazed at him in amazement. I had been so sure that he would be averse to the plan and turn it down off-hand that I was completely taken aback; it was like pushing against a door that you think is shut and finding it open.

"Fred Heatley would take you," continued Uncle Matt. "Heatley and Frensham—it's a good solid firm. We often do business with them. I'll write Fred Heatley and see what he says."

"You don't mind?" I asked. "I mean you've been so awfully good to me."

"I don't mind at all," declared Uncle Matt cheerfully. "Why should I mind? Everybody's got a right to decide his own future. And it will be a great advantage if you have a little experience before you come to me. If you go to Heatley for a couple of years you'll learn the way an office is run." He paused and then added, "You know, David, the more I think about it the more I like your plan. It will do you good to get away and be on your own for a bit. Try your wings, my boy! Have a look at London! You'll settle down better when you've seen a bit of life."

Uncle Matt was so pleased with the idea that he wrote to Mr. Heatley at once and Mr. Heatley replied that he would be delighted to keep a vacancy for me. I was to let him know when I had done my National Service.

The whole thing was settled in a few days and I ought to have been delighted . . . but I was not. Instead of being delighted at having my future settled I felt as if I had been caught in a trap, and the fact that I had walked into the trap with my eyes open did not make it less dismaying. Miles was full of enthusiasm of course, and when I was with him and he was painting our future in glowing terms I felt a bit better about it. Certainly it would be fun to share digs with Miles and although I had doubts as to whether we would make our fortunes as rapidly as he expected his enthusiasm was infectious.

CHAPTER THIRTEEN

THE wind was cool and fresh upon my cheek when I stepped out of the train at Drumburly Station. The sunshine had the shallow brightness of autumn—there was little warmth in it—and the hills looked more gently rolling, less high and bold. Perhaps this was merely a trick of light (the mellow sunshine cast only the softest of shadows upon the slopes) or perhaps they looked less high to me because I had not seen them for so long and my fond imagination had magnified them. I stood for some minutes on the station platform enjoying them, loving their roundness and their baldness and the clean sweep of them against the sky. My National Service had taken me first to Salisbury Plain, where there were no hills worth speaking of, and then to Germany where the mountains were clothed with trees. It was fine scenery no doubt but it was not my kind of scenery; it did not lift up the heart or soothe the spirit like my hills of home.

"Are ye wanting a lift tae Haines?" inquired a voice behind me. "Ye're David Kirke, are ye no'?"

I looked round and was amazed to discover the speaker was Sandy, my enemy of long ago; there was no mistaking him for he looked the same as ever—big and beefy with small eyes stuck like currants in his pink face. His carroty hair was still shaggy and still had the odd appearance of growing from one place on the crown of his head and spreading in all directions over his skull.

"Sandy!" I exclaimed.

"Aye, it's me," he agreed. "I'm driving the milk-lorry. If ye're wanting a lift tae Haines I'll take ye."

The offer was too good to refuse and soon I was sitting beside Sandy on the front seat of the lorry and we were rattling out of the station yard.

"You've not changed a bit," I told him.

"I'll no say the same," he replied. "Ye were a wee skinny speldron and noo ye're no' sae bad at all. Mebbe it's the army that's set ye up and made a man of ye. That's what folks say it does."

"Yes," I said doubtfully.

"What were ye doing in the army?" inquired Sandy. "Ye were an officer, I suppose."

"No, I was driving the colonel's car most of the time."

"Hmff! Yon's a cushy job!"

In some ways it had been a cushy job, but all the same I was slightly nettled. There are colonels and colonels—mine had been pernickety and had liked the car kept in a highly polished condition. He had been chary of praise when all went well and lavish with blame when it did not. He had kept me waiting long hours in the cold while he fed and feasted.

"Yon's a cushy job," repeated Sandy scornfully. "Ye'd get oot of drills and fatigues and all the rest of it. Some folk are danged lucky. It's inflooence, that's what it is."

"It wasn't," I replied. "I know a bit about cars—that's why I was chosen for the job."

Sandy snorted.

"Have you done your National Service?" I asked.

"What d'ye think?" he replied. "I'd have got oot of it if I could. I knew fine I'd hate it—and it was wurrse than I expected." He was silent for a few moments and then added, "Och, weel, it's past. I'm hame noo, and hame I'll bide. There's no place like Haines tae my mind."

This was interesting, not because I disagreed but because I shared his feelings wholeheartedly. It seemed odd that two people so completely different as Sandy and myself should be in agreement.

"Why do you like Haines?" I inquired.

"Why?" he echoed as he changed his gear with a heart-rending crunch. "Why dae I like Haines? Dae ye no like it?"

"Yes, of course."

"Weel then," said Sandy as if that settled the matter.

"But you may like it for a different reason."

He made no reply. It was obvious that the subject did not interest him.

"What's the news?" I asked after a short silence. This was the usual gambit to a conversation in Haines, as it is in most rural districts.

Sandy understood this better and was only too ready to oblige. He launched out into a history of the Haines Football Club during the last two seasons with particular emphasis on his own prowess in the field.

"We've lost Robert," he said sadly. "Robert was coming on fine—but we've lost him."

"Not—not dead?" I asked in suitably muted tones.

"Just marrit," replied Sandy. "An awful niminy piminy lassie oot o' Dumfries. It's a wonder what he could see in her, so it is. She's made him give up football—did ye ever hear the like?"

I asked for information about other people in the district and received the usual tale of births, marriages and deaths; finally I asked about Nethercleugh.

"It's the same as ever," Sandy replied. "Mr. Lorimer got a good price for his lambs . . . but maybe it's his lassies ye're wanting tae hear of?" He leered sideways at me as he spoke.

"I just wondered if they were all at home," I said coldly.

"None of them is," chuckled Sandy. "Ye'll need tae find a lassie some other road. Yon Freda is away in foreign pairts and the twins are in Edinbro' at a school for cooking . . . a school for cooking!" repeated Sandy scornfully. "Did ye ever hear the like? Could they not be learnt cooking at hame like other lassies? Och, they're just snobs, the whole jing bang of them."

By this time I regretted having accepted a lift from Sandy. I had detested him in the old days—with good cause—and he was still detestable. I wondered whether I should take a strong line and tell him to speak respectfully of my friends or whether it was more dignified to ignore his rudeness. Glancing sideways at his fat pink face I remembered the occasion when I had hit it with all my might—and the subsequent horrible results of my action—Sandy was still much bigger than I, but I was not the least afraid of him and I was pretty certain that if it came to blows between us I should have the best of it. The idea amused me a good deal; I imagined Father's horror if I were to arrive home with a black eye or a bloody nose.

"What are ye grinning for?" asked my companion.

"I was remembering our fight," I told him. "The time when you nearly killed me in the changing-room at school. We'd be better matched now."

He grunted crossly but said nothing. Perhaps he had caught the hint of a threat in my suggestion and decided that discretion was the better part of valour. I had not intended it as a threat but I realised it might be taken as such by a creature of Sandy's mentality.

We were nearing Haines by this time; we rattled over the bridge and drew up with a screech of brakes at the manse gate. The dear old house looked exactly the same as ever; there were asters and chrysanthemums in the garden and the Virginia creeper was rioting like flames upon the west wall.

Mother must have been watching from the window for as I said good-bye to Sandy and pushed the gate open she came flying down the path to welcome me home.

It had been arranged that I should have a month at Haines before going to London and starting work in Mr. Heatley's office. I had been looking forward to this and intended to make the most of it for in future I should get no more than a fortnight's holiday in the year.

Quite often when one looks forward to something with keen anticipation one is disappointed in the reality, but in this case it was not so. The reality was even better than my expectations. Now that I had been so far away and had seen a bit of the world I appreciated my parents more than ever; I was able to measure them by a new standard and they stood the test. Although they lived in a backwater there was nothing stagnant about them; they were wiser and more alert in mind than I had remembered. I found endless pleasure in talking to them, telling them what I had done and seen and listening to their views. To me they seemed younger than before; perhaps this was because I was older. I appreciated my home; my own dear room with the chestnut tree whispering outside the window; I revelled in the peace and leisure, the comfortable chairs, the bright log fire in the evenings and the delicious food. Last but by no means least I enjoyed the long walks over the hills in the crisp September air.

Sometimes I had to stand still and look . . . the colours were so startling that they almost took my breath away. The withered bracken was golden brown; the withered heather dark brown and amongst the dark green conifers were deciduous trees burning like flames.

One of my first walks was up the path by the side of the Ling to the ruined cottage and as I sat down upon the smooth turf and leaned against the wall I had the strange feeling of moving back in time . . . all that had happened since my last visit to this place was nothing but a dream. Rip van Winkle must have had the same feeling when he returned to his home after his sojourn with the fairies. I was a bit hazy about the details of Rip van Winkle's story but how clearly I understood his feelings!

But Rip and I were quite different from each other in some ways, for this glimpse of home, this return to the past, was just a "breather" in my race; time to look back upon what had gone and to look forward to the future. Until now I had not thought a great deal about the future (I had looked forward to this holiday and only vaguely beyond) but now I tried to envisage what it would be like to live in London and work in an office every day. During my period of National Service I had taken a course of shorthand, typing and book-keeping, but it had all seemed very difficult and there had been little time to practise. I had written and warned Mr. Heatley that I was slow and he had replied that it did not matter—but would it? Supposing they found me too slow! Supposing the work was beyond me! The idea of plunging into an office amongst a lot of other clerks who knew their jobs was alarming to say the least of it.

Would Mr. Heatley's office be like Uncle Matt's—a quiet sleepy place with huge desks and thick carpets, where a stray sunbeam, finding its way through the window, was laden with millions of specks of floating dust and the only sound was the subdued chatter of typewriters and the tinkle of a discreet bell—there was nothing very alarming about Uncle Matt's office, but probably a London office would move more quickly.

It was pleasant sitting there in the still air with the sun shining softly and the river rippling past. It was soothing. My pipe was in my pocket and I took it out and looked at it. A smoke would have completed the soothing process but I had no tobacco. I was giving up smoking because it was too expensive a luxury for a junior clerk in a lawyer's office. It would be difficult enough to make ends meet without that. I wondered if Miles smoked. He and I were sharing digs in London and if by any chance he had acquired the habit in a big way it would be . . . rather a pity. But Miles was booked for the same sort of job as myself and presumably would receive much the same weekly salary, which meant he would not be able to afford it either.

What fun it would be to see Miles again! I had not seen him for nearly two years and his letters had been few and short so I had only the vaguest idea of what he had been doing. He had not answered my last letter at all (not even by sending a picture postcard, which was one of his ways of answering) but probably he was too busy enjoying his spell of freedom in his own way with girls and social gaieties. My idea of enjoyment was different. For a moment a doubt crossed my mind as to how Miles and I would fit in with one another in London. Then I realised that Miles and I would be on our own with no outside interests; we would make our own life and share one another's pleasures. . . . it was a cheering thought.

The days passed quickly (it was glorious weather) and every day I felt more settled at home and more disinclined to go away and start my new life in London.

One morning when I was cutting the grass Mother came out to speak to me and I saw from her worried expression that there was something on her mind.

"What is it?" I asked, pausing in my labours.

"Nothing, really," she replied. "It was just—I wondered—you're not finding it dull, are you?"

"Dull! How could I find it dull?"

"There's nobody for you to talk to—nobody young. I'd hoped the Lorimer girls would be here. Freda will be back next month but you'll be gone by then." She hesitated and then added, "I wish you were to be here longer; you've been here nearly a fortnight and it's gone like the wind."

I had been wishing exactly the same thing, but it was too late now to change my plans.

"We ought to be thinking about your clothes," Mother continued. "You'll need a town suit for London; you've nothing fit to wear."

She was sitting on the garden-seat and she looked so small and dejected that I went over and sat down beside her. "Don't worry," I said. "We'll go to Dumfries to-morrow and see about clothes. I had better start with a decent outfit and then I shan't have to bother about clothes when I get to London."

"What about your room?"

"Miles has arranged that. We're going to a boarding-house in Blooms-bury. Miles heard about it from a friend. He was to write and get rooms for us both. The only thing that hasn't been fixed is the actual date we're travelling south. Miles thought it would be a good plan to go a bit sooner so as to settle down and have a look round before we start work."

"Sooner than you need?" asked Mother rather sadly. "Just a few days," I said. "I wrote to Miles and asked him about the date but he hasn't answered my letter."

"Perhaps you should ring him up."

"Don't fuss," I said, smiling and patting her hand. "Your little boy is grown-up now and he's been in all sorts of funny places."

"I'm not fussing," declared Mother. "I just like to have things arranged in good time. It's old-fashioned of me I know, but that's how I'm made. Nowadays people leave everything to the last minute and somehow or other they muddle through. It's an uncomfortable way of doing things to say the least of it."

"I've written to Miles."

"If you take my advice you'll ring him up."

"All right, I'll ring him up to-night," I promised. "But that's not to say I'll be able to speak to him. Miles doesn't spend many evenings in the bosom of his family, he's a gay lad is Miles."

Contrary to my expectations I got through quite easily and Miles answered the telephone himself.

"Hallo!" he said eagerly. "Is that you, Iris?"

"No, you old donkey, it's David," I replied, chuckling. "Disappointing for you, isn't it?"

"David?"

"Yes, David Kirke of course."

"Gosh, what luck!" he exclaimed. "Look here, you old stiff, we're having a tremendous beano to-morrow night and we need another man. What about it?"

"I'm at Haines—"

"Well, what of it? You can get a train, can't you? We'll give you a bed for the night. You must come, David. It's going to be a whale of a party."

"Look here, Miles," I said, interrupting him. "You never answered my letter. Have you decided what day we're travelling south?"

There was a moment's silence.

"Are you there?" I cried. "This line is frightful. I want to know what day you've decided to travel. Can you hear me?"

"Yes, of course I can hear you. As a matter of fact I meant to answer your letter ages ago, but you know what I am—the world's worst letter-writer! Look here, David, it's a bit too complicated to explain over the phone. You come up to-morrow and I'll tell you about it."

"Complicated?" I said. "What's complicated? All I want to know is what day we're going to London so that I can make my plans."

"Look here, David—"

"Have you fixed the day?"

"Well—er—no. You see things have changed a bit since we talked about going to London. I'm afraid it's all off as far as I'm concerned."

"All off!" I exclaimed incredulously.

"I shan't be coming to London, old boy—at least not at present. You see—"

"Not coming! But Miles—"

"Change of plan," said Miles's voice cheerfully. "It's a pity in some ways. It would have been rather fun (you and I in digs together, wouldn't it?) but it can't be done. The fact is I'm starting to read Law in the jolly old University, so London is washed out."

"Miles! It was all fixed!"

"Not fixed, old boy. It was just an idea—"

"It *was* fixed!" I cried. "You know it was. You said you would write to the boarding-house and engage our rooms."

"Did I? Oh, well, I must have forgotten about it. I'll send you the address and you can write yourself. How about that?"

"But Miles," I said desperately. "I can't understand it. The whole thing was your idea. You said nothing would induce you to stay at home. You said there was no scope—"

He laughed. "Oh, I know I talked a lot of hot air. As a matter of fact it will be a lot better to read Law and graduate than to go to London and swot in a mouldy office. There's more future in it. You must see that, David."

He paused but I did not reply.

"I meant to write to you," continued Miles. "But you know how it is. Look here, old boy, why not come up to-morrow? I haven't seen you for centuries."

"No, thank you," I said.

"You're not fed-up, are you?"

I did not answer.

"I say!" exclaimed Miles. "Don't be an ass, David. Come up to-morrow and I'll explain the whole thing. Come and stay the night. It will be fun. I want to tell you about my experiences in the army. Some of them were pretty colourful."

"No, thank you," I repeated and I put down the receiver.

It was a bitter blow. Miles had persuaded me to go to London; he had pushed me into it and now he had backed out and left me in the lurch. If he had written and told me of his change of plan I would not have been so angry but he had treated the whole affair casually: "Not fixed, old boy. It was just an idea—" He had not even apologised for letting me down.

The fact that Miles had let me down was harder to bear than the disappointment caused by his change of plan—and that was hard enough in all conscience. I had looked forward to sharing digs with Miles, to going about with him and seeing London together. It would be a very different matter to go alone. My feelings were bitter and resentful. Looking back I remembered other occasions when Miles had let me down; this was not the first time—nor the second time. I had made excuses for him because I had admired him so tremendously. I had told myself that it was his nature; Miles was so gay and dashing and brilliant that you could not blame him for being a bit casual. I had told myself that you could not be angry with Miles. But now I was angry with him and angry with myself as well. What a fool I had been to trust Miles!

Mother was distressed when she heard that Miles was not going with me, but to her I made light of the matter and explained that Mr. Blackworth had arranged for Miles to go to Edinburgh University instead.

"He should have let you know at once," said Mother, putting her finger on the spot in her usual sensible fashion. "You'd never have known if you hadn't rung him up. I think it was bad of him, Davie."

I thought it was bad of him too. I could not sleep for thinking about Miles and the rotten way he had treated me.

The next morning, after breakfast, I took a heavy spade and started digging the garden and presently Father came out and sat on the seat.

"Digging is a good thing," said Father when I stopped to rest. "It's the oldest cure for a sore heart. Adam dug when he was turned out of Eden and I've no doubt it helped him to get over his trouble. 'In the sweat of thy face shalt thou eat bread.'"

"Yes," I agreed, mopping my heated brow.

"What a deal of resentment and bitterness can be purged from the human system by honest sweat!" said Father thoughtfully.

I leant on my spade and looked at him. I knew what he meant all right. "Yes, I *do* feel a bit resentful. Miles has treated me very badly," I said.

"So it appears, David. I'm sorry for *him*."

"Sorry for him! You don't need to be sorry for him!"

"I wonder," said Father. "It's a bad thing to be let down by a man you've trusted, but it's worse to let down a man who trusts you."

"Miles doesn't care. He was quite casual about it—he was quite cheerful. I daresay he couldn't help his plans being changed but he should have written at once and told me. It was rotten of him not to let me know."

"That's true; but I daresay he's not fond of writing unpleasant letters; few of us are. If you think about it you can see how it happened: he would say to himself I must write to David, but what shall I say to him? I'll wait and do it to-morrow.' Then he would forget about it for a day or two, and then he would remember and say the same thing again." This was exactly what Miles would have done. "But Father, you don't know Miles!" I exclaimed.

"I know a wee bit about human nature."

"You're making excuses for him."

"Not excuses. He's behaved badly, I admit. I'm just pointing out how the thing might have occurred. As a matter of fact—whatever you say—I'm sorry for that young fellow. I don't envy his state of mind."

"You needn't worry about him," I said bitterly.

"Och, David, you're not asking me to believe he's happy about it? Nobody with a spark of decent feeling could feel happy."

"He hasn't," I declared. "He's an absolute rotter."

Father was filling his pipe. He smoked very little—I think he had one pipe a day—but he made the most of it. I saw it was part of the pleasure to fill his pipe very slowly and carefully.

"That's even more difficult to believe," said Father thoughtfully. "Surely there must be quite a lot of good in him or you would never have made plans to go with him to London."

I could not help smiling. "Father," I said. "I believe you'd have made as good a lawyer as Uncle Matt."

I dug another row while Father sat quietly on the seat and smoked.

Then I stopped and looked at him. "It's Saturday morning!" I exclaimed.

"That's so," he agreed.

"But you always write your sermons on Saturday mornings!"

Father smiled gravely. "Sermons are important, but they're not my principal duty, David. Sometimes it's more important to sit in the garden and smoke."

That answer gave me a lot to think about.

Whether it was the digging or whether it was my talk with Father I began to feel better about Miles. My hard feelings about him softened. Two days later I received a letter from him saying he was sorry he had been a swine and enclosing the address of the boarding-house. It was quite a short letter but all the same I knew it must have cost him something. Miles hated to acknowledge himself in the wrong; he was one of those people who like to think that whatever they do is right.

Unfortunately the boarding-house had no room available (it was too short notice) but the proprietor enclosed a list of places in the same district which might or might not have vacancies. One of these was run by a certain Mrs. Hall and we decided to try her. By this time Mother was really worried—I think she envisaged her son sleeping on the Embankment—so she took the address and said she would write to Mrs. Hall herself. I have no idea what Mother said in her letter but Mrs. Hall's reply, though somewhat illiterate, was cordial and reassuring. Fortunately she had a vacancy (the gentleman had left that very morning) and she would be delighted to let the room to me. It was a nice quiet room with a fixed basin and she was sure it would suit me. Her other guests were friendly and pleasant so I would not be lonely and she would do all she could to make me feel at home. Mrs. Hall's terms were reasonable but if I wanted the fixed basin that would be extra of course.

"What happens if David doesn't want the fixed basin?" asked Father as he folded the letter and handed it back. "Does Mrs. Hall tear it out of the wall?"

"But he does want it!" exclaimed Mother.

Poor Mother, her sense of humour was not working as well as usual; she was too worried and upset. As a matter of fact I have no idea to this day whether or not Father intended it as a joke—he seldom made jokes—but I thought his remark very funny indeed.

The day before I left Haines was cold and damp, with a thick white mist shrouding the hills. Mother lighted the fire in the sitting-room and got out her mending-basket; we settled down for a quiet chat.

"London is a big place," said Mother rather sadly.

"So it is," I agreed, trying to smile cheerfully. "London is a very big place—and I've got a job there."

"You're happy about it, Davie?"

"I'm happy here," I told her. "I don't want to leave home—not one little bit—but I shall make the best of it."

"If only you could be a farmer! The life would have suited you much better. Do you remember how you loved going on the hill with Malcolm and helping him with the sheep?"

"Yes, of course, but—"

"He said you were wonderful with the sheep, Davie."

"But you can't be a farmer unless you have the capital to buy a farm. Where could I get the money?"

Mother sighed. "I can't help worrying," she said.

"You didn't worry when I was in the army."

"Not so much," she agreed. "You weren't on your own. You had friends and companions and, although it was rough, I knew you were being looked after. In London you'll have nobody. Oh Davie, if you're unhappy or if anything goes wrong you must promise to tell us."

"What could go wrong?"

"I don't know—but you're all we've got—and you're so young."

"I'm twenty," I reminded her.

"That's a great age I admit, but you're very young all the same. Perhaps you'll always be young."

"Like you," I suggested, smiling. "Who would think, to look at you, that you had a grown-up son. The thing's ridiculous."

Mother smiled and shook her head but she was not to be turned from the subject. "You're young," she repeated. "You've never had to—to manage for yourself, to stand on your own feet—"

"Goodness!" I cried. "Do you think the army was a kindergarten?"

"It was different, Davie. I'm afraid you may be lonely without any friends and you won't have much money. When you've paid for your board and lodging you'll have very little left."

I knew that, of course, but I had decided to have a try at writing short articles for the papers. Ever since I had left home and gone to school in Edinburgh I had been too busy to think of writing but now it would be different. I could not afford to spend money on entertainments so in the evenings I would settle down and write. Somehow I felt I could; there was an urge in me to express my ideas on paper.

Mother agreed that this was an excellent plan. "You can write," she declared. "I know you can."

"On the strength of a few childish stories," I said teasingly.

"But they were good," she declared. "They were not just childish drivel. There was laughter and tears in your stories . . . and your letters were so interesting."

"Well, we'll see."

"I hope you'll be comfortable," continued Mother with a sigh. "We don't know anything about that boarding-house."

"Mrs. Hall seems pleasant, judging from her letter."

"Yes, it was a welcoming sort of letter. She said she would look after you and do all she could to make you feel at home. She couldn't say more, I suppose."

"I'll be all right," I said confidently. "If I can't manage to make ends meet I can fall back on the money in my Post Office Savings—and Uncle Matt gave me twenty-five pounds."

"Don't spend that," said Mother earnestly. "Don't fritter it away. Keep it until you need it for something important. If you can't make ends meet we could help you a bit."

"I'll manage," I said. I was determined to manage. I knew very well that my parents could not afford to help me.

THE THIRD WINDOW

"My window looked out on to a blank wall. The wall towered up some thirty feet from my window: it was of dingy brick and there was no break in it except for an iron ventilator. Once upon a time the wall had been painted white—presumably to lighten my room—but the paint had nearly all flaked off and what was left was streaky and discoloured with London soot. Even on the sunniest day my room was dim: even on the breeziest day my room was airless."

CHAPTER FOURTEEN

MRS. Hall's boarding-house was tucked away in a back street. It was tall and dingy—and Mrs. Hall was tall and dingy too. Her skin had the curious grey look of a person who does not go out very much and is not fond of soap and water; her eyes were narrow and her lips thin and blood-less. But, although her appearance was unprepossessing and somewhat grim, she welcomed me effusively, asking if I had had a good journey and inquiring after my parents' health.

"Such a nice lady your mother is," declared Mrs. Hall. "I could tell that by her letter—and so fond of you, too! It's a wonderful thing to have a good mother, Mr. Kirke. I expect you're hungry after your long jour-ney so we'll just leave your things in the 'all until you've 'ad your supper. We're just having supper now and it'll be a good opportunity for you to meet the other guests. They're all looking forward to meeting you."

Mrs. Hall spoke quickly in a monotonous voice, and she was very careful to sound her aitches except when she forgot about them.

I would rather have washed before having supper, for I felt dirty and untidy, but she gave me no chance. She opened the door of the dining-room.

"Here's Mr. Kirke!" she exclaimed.

There were six people sitting round the table and they all looked up when I came in. Afterwards I got to know them quite well, but in that first moment they were six strange faces beneath a hard bright light. There was Mr. Owen, a thin dark Welshman with a shock of wiry black hair; Miss Bulwer who was thin and pale with fair hair, turning grey; Mr. Kensey who was fat and pale and bald; Ned Mottram, pale and heavy-eyed, with smooth brown hair and a small moustache; and Madame Futrelle, a short stout Frenchwoman, whose bright red hair and heavily made-up face contrasted strangely with the pallid countenances of her fellows. Last but not least there was Beryl Collingham . . . and to be honest Miss Collingham's was the only face I saw distinctly in that first uncomfortable moment. It was a heart-shaped face, framed in fair curls, and her brown eyes met mine across the room in a welcoming smile.

My place was laid between Mrs. Hall and Miss Collingham; I slipped into it as quickly as I could and did my best to answer all the questions which were put to me. Quite obviously my fellow guests were anxious to be friendly and although it seemed to me that their friendliness was a little overdone I could hardly blame them for that.

"You're Scotch, of course," said Mr. Kensey. "I have a cousin who lives in Glasgow, perhaps you've met her. Mrs. Fraser is her name."

"No," I said. "No, I'm afraid I don't know anybody in Glasgow."

"Where do you live?" asked Miss Bulwer.

"At a little village called Haines. My father is the minister—"

"That's a Scotch clergyman, isn't it?" Mr. Kensey said.

"A non-conformist," nodded Miss Bulwer. "I know all about it because my aunt was Chapel, you see."

I could not help wondering what Father would have said to this and how he would have explained. I was about to try to explain the matter myself but a plate of soup had been placed before me and as everyone else had passed on to the next course I decided I had better leave explanations to a more convenient moment. The soup did not help matters, it was a hell's broth of liquid mustard.

"Mulligatawny," said Mrs. Hall, nodding at me encouragingly. "I hope you like mulligatawny, Mr. Kirke. I always say a nice plate of 'ot soup is the best thing after a long journey."

"Yes," I said. I could say no more for my eyes were full of tears after the first hasty mouthful.

"You are verree young," said Madame Futrelle, gazing at me intently. "Is it permitted to ask what you will do in London? 'Ave you got a job?"

"Yes," I said. "Yes, I'm starting to-morrow in a lawyer's office, Messrs. Heatley and Frensham."

"You are a lawyer, then?"

"No, just a clerk."

"I am modiste. I 'ave a leetle place in Knightsbridge—verree chic. It is a verree good business; I sell gowns and 'ats to the verree best people. Some day when I 'ave made enough money I go back to Paree. I do not like London—no. Do you like London, Mistaire Kirke?"

"I don't know. I've only just come."

"It's the only place to live," declared Ned Mottram. "There's so much going on in London. I was in Cardiff for a bit, but I jumped at it when I got the chance of coming here. I sell cars on commission. I should hate to sit in an office all day. Beryl is on the stage," he added, smiling across the table at Miss Collingham.

I said I had never met an actress before.

"You 'ave not met one now," declared Madame Futrelle. "You 'ave only met a girl who would like to be an actress if someone would give her the chance. But nobody is likely to do that."

"Beryl is resting!" exclaimed Ned Mottram.

"She needs so much rest," said Madame Futrelle, laughing maliciously. "Per'aps if she did a leetle real work she would not feel so tired."

Miss Collingham said nothing.

"I expect it's difficult to get started," I said, turning to her.

"Very difficult," she replied in a low voice. "People don't understand. The stage isn't like other jobs that go on all the time, and it isn't any use having talent unless you have influence. You've no idea what a lot of wire-pulling goes on. For instance I know a girl who has got a part in a new musical comedy—she's a friend of the producer, that's why. It's terribly unfair."

"Some people can't afford to sit back and wait for work," declared Miss Bulwer. "Some people have to work for their bread and butter."

"Bread and marge, you mean," put in Mr. Owen.

Miss Bulwer paid no attention to the interruption. "I learnt shorthand and typewriting," she continued. "I work all day in a typewriting office. I can't afford to rest. Sometimes I would give a great deal to be able to take a day off. I have a very delicate stomach."

"We all know about that," declared Mr. Kensey.

"Mr. Kirke doesn't know—" began Miss Bulwer.

"He knows now," said Mr. Kensey. "He'll hear enough about your stomach in the next few days to last him a lifetime."

"You will all tell poor Mistaire Kirke about your troubles," said Madame Futrelle. "So many troubles you 'ave! It is verree sad."

"We aren't all as lucky as you," said Mrs. Hall.

"Lucky!" cried Madame Futrelle. "I work 'ard and I use the brain the good God 'as given to me. That is not lucky."

"I'd change places with you any day," declared Mrs. Hall. "The worry I have running this 'ouse! The price of food! Only yesterday I was asked sixpence for an ounce of carraway seeds done up in a fancy packet! Sixpence! Well of course I said, 'No thanks, you can keep it.'"

"That's good news," declared Mr. Kensey. "If it means we don't have any more seed-cake it's the best news I've heard for a long time."

"I never eat seed-cake—" began Miss Bulwer.

"Why don't we have fruit-cake?" asked Mr. Owen in his sing-song voice. "In my home there was always a big juicy fruit-cake. My mother used to make one every week."

"Fruit-cake!" exclaimed Mrs. Hall with withering scorn. "I could make a 'big juicy fruit-cake' if I 'ad the fruit to do it with. Where's the fruit, Mr. Owen? There isn't none in the shops nor 'asn't been for months."

"I always say there's nothing nicer than a plain sponge," declared Miss Bulwer.

"Plain sponges are useful for the bath," said Madame Futrelle. "To eat, they are not so good . . . when they are made by Mrs. 'All. One must beat the eggs and beat and beat, that is the secret. I 'ave not tasted a good cake in this countree. In Paree it is so different; the cakes light as a feather and prettee to look at with coloured sugar on the top and cream inside."

"Eggs, sugar, cream!" cried Mrs. Hall. "What about the rations—that's all I ask! What about the rations? If you 'ad to stand in a queue to get a bit of meat for dinner perhaps you wouldn't be so particular."

"They always talk about food," said Miss Collingham with a little sigh. "Even if they begin to talk about other things they always come round to food. It's so greedy, Mr. Kirke. Don't you think so? I never notice what I eat—I'm funny like that—I just like simple things. Sometimes Ned and I go to a little restaurant and have supper together and then go to a picture. Perhaps you'd like to come with us one evening."

"Yes, I should like to," I said.

After supper I went up to my room and began to unpack. I felt home-sick and miserable—I felt like a lost dog. My room did little to cheer me; it was a dreary apartment with shabby furniture, and the carpet on the floor was so dirty and threadbare that all vestige of pattern had disappeared. The wallpaper was striped yellow and brown; the curtains had once been yellow but were now a dingy fawn; the mirror over the dressing-table was spotted with damp. The bed itself looked uninviting and when I examined it I discovered that not only was it hard and lumpy with a deep hollow in the middle but it had a curious musty smell. The only pleasant thing in the room was a fixed basin with hot and cold water laid on; it looked quite new and I remembered that Mrs. Hall had mentioned it in her letter and was charging me extra for it—and I remembered Father's joke. Somehow the joke did not seem so funny to-night; I was in no mood for jokes.

My experiences in the army had accustomed me to rough living but not to dirt, and as I looked round my new quarters I decided that I would willingly change them for a barrack-room with a scrubbed wooden floor—and my fellow-boarders seemed a good deal less agreeable than my comrades-in-arms.

Presently there was a knock on the door and Ned Mottram looked in.

"How are you getting on?" he asked. "This is a ghastly hole, isn't it?"

"Yes," I said. "It seems—rather grim."

He sat down on the bed and looked round. "Pretty ghastly," he said. "This room has been empty for months—Old Hall was lucky to let it—I don't suppose you'd have taken it if you'd seen it."

"I thought somebody had just left."

"Oh, she'd tell you that of course. Old Hall is a prize liar . . but you've got a fixed basin which is something. I wish I had. There's only one bathroom and everyone wants it at the same moment. Old Kensey usually gets in first and takes half an hour to shave, or if he doesn't make it in time the Bulwer bags it—and then you're properly sunk. Futrelle doesn't wash, of course." He sighed and added, "The food is the worst."

"I thought the supper was quite good, except for the soup."

He laughed. "That's because you're new. There's always a decent supper laid on when a new victim arrives. To-morrow we'll go back to greasy sausages and sludgy cabbage."

Ned lighted a cigarette. He stuck it in the corner of his mouth and it dangled from his lip as he talked. Somehow this appendage completed the picture of misery and wretchedness presented by my new acquaintance.

"Why do you stay if it's so uncomfortable?" I asked.

"Oh well—it's difficult to find a decent room—and this place is cheap—and there's Beryl, of course. Beryl can't leave because she owes about four week's board to Old Hall, and I can't leave because of Beryl. She's a peach, isn't she?"

"Yes, she's very pretty."

"She's a peach. It's a shame she can't get a break, isn't it? If only she could! It's jealousy, that's ah. You've no idea what a lot of jealousy there is on the stage. They do all they can to keep girls like Beryl from getting a chance because they're afraid of them."

"You mean other actresses?"

"Yes, of course. You see Beryl's got talent; she'd make a tremendous hit if she got the chance, so they take damn' good care to keep her out. Sickening, isn't it?"

"Yes."

"What do you think of the inmates?"

"The inmates?"

"Bulwer and Kensey and co. They're frightful, aren't they? Beryl and I call them the inmates. Futrelle is the worst, she's poisonous, but the others aren't much better. Take old Kensey, for instance, he makes me sick. He's got plenty of money but he never spends a penny except on himself; he wouldn't lend his best friend half a crown—that's Kensey for you! Bulwer is a dried up old maid, always grousing and grumbling about something . . . just wait till you you've been here a week!"

"Yes," I said.

"Of course I'm out all day. I'm only here for breakfast and supper, otherwise I couldn't stick it. I have a snack at a place in the city near the showrooms. I suppose you'll do that too."

"Yes."

"I told you I sold cars, didn't I?"

"Yes, it sounds interesting."

"It's all right if you can sell them," said Ned lugubriously. "Business has been bad lately—flat as a pancake—and as a matter of fact I've had the most rotten luck. People are so extraordinary; they say they want a Rolls and you show them the car and take them for runs and waste hours dancing attendance on them and then they sheer off and you never see them again. There was one old dame—you'll never believe this—who kept me on the hop for days swithering between a Jaguar and a Bentley and then went to another showroom and bought a second-hand Morris . . ."

Ned had a monotonous voice and he went on talking. He talked and talked and he made everything sound hopeless and depressing. I had felt miserable enough before, but when at last I managed to get rid of him I felt absolutely wretched. I finished my unpacking and then pulled back the heavy curtains. I expected to see the lights of London, pinpoints of light from lamp-posts which lined the streets and chinks of lights from the windows of neighbouring houses, but there was nothing to see at all. I might have been looking into a cupboard. The mystery puzzled me but was resolved in the morning. My window looked out on to a blank wall.

The wall towered up some thirty feet from my window; it was of dingy brick and there was no break in it except for an iron ventilator. Once upon a time the wall had been painted white, presumably to lighten my room, but the paint had nearly all flaked off and what remained was streaky and discoloured with London soot. Even on the sunniest day my room was dim; even on the breeziest day my room was airless.

CHAPTER FIFTEEN

THE work at Mr. Heatley's office was easier than I had expected and I soon discovered that the qualms I had felt were needless.

Mr. Heatley was small and dark with bright shrewd eyes and a brusque manner. He was not a patient man but he made allowances for my inexperience. "Mr. Penman will show you the ropes," he said, looking at me as if he could see right through to my back-bone. "If you please Mr. Penman you'll please me. You'll make mistakes at first of course, but I hope you'll make as few as possible. That's all, Kirke."

"Yes, sir," I said meekly.

Mr. Penman was the head clerk, he had been in the office for thirty years and knew his business inside out. He knew my business too, and showed me exactly what was wanted. I found him helpful and kind. The other two clerks were not much older than myself: Wrigson belonged to a motor-cycling club and Ullenwood was a football enthusiast. I had hoped to make friends with them but it was obvious from the very beginning that they had no use for me and resented my intrusion. A third desk had been put into the room where they worked and they found this inconvenient. My advent was inconvenient to them in other ways as well. When Mr. Penman was there they applied themselves industriously but when he was absent they relaxed and chatted about girls and racing and football pools and other things that interested them. It was impossible for me to join in the conversation—even if I had wanted to—because it took me all my time to cope with the work; but what they did or left undone was no business of mine so I shut my eyes and ears and carried on to the best of my ability. Naturally they were annoyed with me. It had been much more pleasant before I came. Before I came they had had the room to themselves.

One of my duties was to keep Mr. Penman's desk tidy. I filled his fountain pens every morning—one with black ink and the other with red—and I put out clean blotting-paper. The job had been Ullenwood's before I came but apparently he had not bothered much about it. I had no idea of this of course and nothing was said openly but I happened to overhear a snatch of conversation between the two friends which showed how the land lay.

"All that fuss about the old man's desk!" exclaimed Ullenwood scornfully. "It makes me sick to see him trying to worm his way into Penman's good graces."

"Trying!" echoed Wrigson. "He's succeeding. Penman thinks he's the cat's whiskers . . . so keen!"

They both laughed.

That was all I heard but it was quite enough and it upset me a good deal. In a way it was true, for I was trying very hard to please Mr. Penman and to earn his good opinion . . . but surely this was no more than my duty. It was what I was paid for. I thought it over as I walked back to Mrs. Hall's and wondered if there were any way of justifying myself— but of course there was not. If I tried to explain my view to Wrigson and Ullenwood they would think me more of a prig than ever and in any case I could not attempt to explain without telling them that I had overheard their conversation.

As I was the junior clerk it fell to my lot to do the messages; to deliver a letter and wait for a reply or to collect a parcel for Mr. Heatley. This was another grievance to Ullenwood who had enjoyed an occasional break in office work. He suggested to Mr. Penman that he should continue to be the office errand-boy.

"Kirke doesn't know his way about, sir," explained Ullenwood. "It will take him ages to find the place."

"If it takes him longer than you I shall be surprised," replied Mr. Penman dryly. "Kirke can ask his way, I suppose."

It certainly was not easy to find my way about London but the policemen were helpful. There they stood like rocks in a sea of traffic, directing it with efficiency, and at the same time they were able to give me clear and detailed instructions as to how best to reach my destination by tube or bus.

Ned Mottram had said, "Wait till you've been here a week." Long before I had been a week in London I had begun to think I could not bear it . . . and yet I knew I must. This was the life I had chosen for myself so I must make the best of it. Somehow or other I managed to write home cheerfully in answer to Mother's anxious inquiries as to how I was getting on.

The worst of my troubles was loneliness. I had not a single friend nor any prospect of making one. The jostling crowds surged past me on the pavements (hordes of people chattering to one another) but I knew nobody and nobody knew me or cared whether I lived or died. If Miles had been here it would have been entirely different. We could have talked about our experiences and had jokes together. If Miles had been here I would not have minded what Wrigson and Ullenwood thought. If Miles had been here . . . but Miles had let me down and I had never been so lonely in my life.

There was Ned Mottram of course—and I must admit that he seemed willing to be friendly—but although he talked to me a great deal he was interested only in himself and his own affairs. He did not want to hear what I had been doing; all he wanted was to tell me what he had done. I found this unsatisfactory; it was one-sided to say the least of it.

The other boarders at Mrs. Hall's had much the same mentality; one after another they managed to get me alone and proceeded to pour out their troubles. Mr. Owen was discontented with the World. The World had treated him badly. Why should he have to work hard, day in and day out, while other people lived at ease on money they had not earned? Mr. Owen could talk for hours on end about the Unfairness of the World and it was difficult to escape from him. Mr. Kensey was miserable because nobody wanted him. His son was married and lived at St. Albans with his wife and family; they were only a few miles away but Mr. Kensey scarcely ever saw them. They had a nice big house and Mr. Kensey had offered to go and live with them and share expenses, but they did not want him. Nobody wanted you when you were old, said Mr. Kensey. It was dreadful to be old; you were just a nuisance and better dead.

Miss Bulwer was unhappy too. The secretary at the type-writing office where she worked had a down on her and took every opportunity of being rude and disagreeable. If anything went wrong it was Miss Bulwer who was blamed. She suffered acutely from indigestion and no doctor was able to help her. Sometimes she felt she could not carry on— but what was she to do? Miss Bulwer told me about her childhood; her parents had been well-off and had brought her up in luxury. She had never expected to have to work for her living.

"It was the Slump," explained Miss Bulwer. "Father was a stock-broker, you see. He lost everything in that dreadful Slump. He was so shattered by his misfortunes that he died, and Mother died soon after-wards. When the house was sold most of the money went to pay off the debts; there was just enough left for me to take a course in shorthand and type-writing."

I said I was sorry. It seemed inadequate, but there was nothing else to say.

Mrs. Hall was always complaining. She complained about "the girl" who helped her in the house; she complained about her "guests"; she complained that food was expensive. "You've no idea what I have to put up with," Mrs. Hall declared. "If only I could give up this place and retire! I wouldn't mind living in one room. I do my best to make my guests comfortable and what thanks do I get? There's nothing but grumbles. There's no gratitude for all I do. You needn't expect gratitude in this world, Mr. Kirke. You needn't expect kindness or consideration. It's a 'ard world for people that 'as to make their own living—a 'ard cruel world."

Madame Futrelle complained about the weather. She compared London with "Paree" and declared that she could hardly bear her exile. The people in London were "'orrible." So shabby, they were, so wanting in "chic," so mean and stingy. As for her assistants there was not one she could trust. Directly her back was turned they became slack and disinterested.

I listened to them all and sympathised as best I could. I was very sorry for them. In fact I was so sorry for them that their troubles upset me. They were all unhappy but I could do nothing to help them. Nobody could help them. Perhaps the worst part of it was their unkindness to one another—yes, that was the worst. I had never before met people like this: people who were bitter and unkind and hopeless, people who had no happiness in life nor any expectation of happiness. Sometimes as I walked home from the office through the streets I looked up at the rows and rows of dingy houses and wondered if they were all full of miserable people. It became a sort of nightmare to me.

The boarding-house was dirty and uncomfortable; the food was wretched and badly cooked. There was no privacy. If I wanted to read I had to go up to my room—and my room was cold and dreary. Mrs. Hall was inquisitive, she pried into everything. One day I found her looking through the drawers of my dressing-table (she pretended she was "tidying up") and another day when I came in she was examining a letter which was waiting for me on the hall table, holding it up to the light and trying to see through the envelope.

"Oh! This is for you, Mr. Kirke!" she exclaimed, handing it to me. "It's from your mother, isn't it?"

I hated to see her pawing Mother's letter with her dirty hands. After that I wrote and told Mother that I wanted all my letters sent to the office; it was more convenient, I said.

One evening I got back earlier than usual and found Beryl Collingham sitting in the lounge. So far I had not had much opportunity of speaking to her except when we met on the stairs and said "Good morning."

"Hallo!" she said, looking up from the paper she was reading. "You're early to-night, aren't you? How are you getting on?"

"All right, thank you," I told her.

"I was wondering if you were feeling lonely."

"A bit," I replied. "I haven't any friends in London. I expect I shall get to know people in time."

"You won't. London is different from a small place where you bump into people and get to know all about them. I was very lonely when I came here first."

"Were you?"

She nodded. "I tell you what. Shall we go out and have supper together instead of having it here? It would be a change, wouldn't it?"

"Yes," I said. "Yes, why shouldn't we?"

"Every reason why we should!" she cried, springing up from the chair. "I'll go and get my coat."

As I waited for her in the hall I began to be a little dubious about the expedition. Would Ned mind? But what could I have done? I could hardly have refused to take her out to supper . . . and I did not want to refuse. It would be a pleasant change from the dreary atmosphere of the boarding-house.

"This is fun!" cried Beryl as she came running down the stairs. "I know a nice little restaurant in Soho. We'll go there, shall we? I think you'd like it. The food is quite good and it isn't expensive."

The restaurant was called The Three Lamplighters; it was quite a small place in a back street but it was comfortable and, as Beryl had said, the food was good. We ate and talked. My companion was pretty and gay, she was enjoying herself and so was I.

"You must call me Beryl," she said. "Everyone calls me Beryl. It sounds so funny when you say Miss Collingham—it sounds old and dowdy. I'm not old and dowdy, am I?"

"No, Beryl," I said. "You're young and pretty."

We laughed.

"You're funny, David," she said. "You're different. Why are you different, I wonder?"

"Different from what?"

"From the others, of course. Different from Ned and Harry and all the others. I mean of course you are. For instance if I'd said to Harry that he was different he'd have come back at me with some silly nonsense, but you just said 'Different from what?' When you say a thing you mean it."

"That's true."

"Why do you?"

"Because I've never learned to talk. It's a thing you have to learn."

"Don't learn. You're nice as you are," said Beryl, smiling.

"I feel an awful ass sometimes."

"We all do!" she cried. "It doesn't matter as long as you don't look an ass."

"Well, perhaps," I said. "But sometimes when I'm with a lot of people and they're all talking and making jokes I feel like an uncle."

"Oh David, you are a scream!"

"I do, honestly," I told her. "Perhaps it's because I haven't any brothers or sisters. I've always been with people a lot older than myself."

"Have you got a girl friend?" inquired Beryl.

"There's Freda of course."

"Tell me about Freda."

"We're just friends," I explained. "There's no silly nonsense about Freda."

"What on earth do you mean!"

"I mean we're not in love with each other or anything like that. Freda and I have always been friends just as if she were a boy."

"Is she pretty?"

"Yes—yes, she is," I replied, thinking of Freda. "She has dark curly hair and brown eyes. Yes, she's very pretty, but she doesn't bother about her looks."

"She must be a queer girl!"

"Not really," I replied, smiling. "Of course she's quite different from you. I couldn't imagine anybody falling in love with Freda."

Beryl laughed. "Oh, David! That means you *could* imagine somebody fading in love with me, doesn't it?"

"Well, there's Ned. I don't need to imagine it, do I?"

"Oh—Ned!" said Beryl. "Yes, of course. Poor Ned, he's rather a nuisance sometimes. Of course he's better than nothing; but you know, between you and me, he's so selfish. He thinks of nobody but himself."

"He thinks of you."

"Not properly," said Beryl, frowning. "I mean he only thinks of me because I mean something to him. He doesn't think of me as a real person. It's difficult to explain but I know what I mean."

I knew what she meant, too.

"He never wants to know things about me," continued Beryl. "He always wants to tell me about himself."

"Yes, he is rather like that, but he's very fond of you." She nodded. "I know—but what's the good?"

"What's the good?" I echoed in surprise.

"He'll never be anything. He'll never make any money. A man like that isn't any good to a girl."

I was dumb with amazement.

"Oh, David!" she cried. "Oh, David, I wish you could see your face! You're shocked. What a funny boy you are! I suppose you've been brought up on romantic novels."

"No," I said. "It's just a new idea to me, that's all. I've never been in love, but I've always thought if you were really in love you wouldn't mind about anything except the other person."

Beryl sighed. She said, "Perhaps you're right. Perhaps I've never been in love either."

We talked about all sorts of things. I am afraid I did most of the talking for it was a delightful change to find somebody who was interested in what I had to say. It was a delightful change from the role of listener which I had played ever since I came to London. When I looked at Beryl she smiled and nodded. "Yes," she said. "Yes, David, I feel like that too. Tell me more, David. Tell me about your home."

It was late when we rose from the table. The waiter brought the bill and to tell the truth it startled me considerably. Beryl had said The Three Lamplighters was not expensive, so I had not bothered. We had had a very good dinner and a bottle of Italian wine, Beryl had had a peach and some cigarettes. I did not grudge the money for I had enjoyed it and fortunately I had just received my week's salary so I had enough on me to pay the bill. I comforted myself by the reflection that I could easily draw some money out of the Savings Bank to pay Mrs. Hall. It did not matter for once in a way.

"It's been lovely," said Beryl as we came out into the narrow dark street. "You're a pet and I've enjoyed it terribly. Let's do this again often."

"Yes," I said doubtfully. "The only thing is—"

"Oh, David, haven't you enjoyed it?"

"Yes, of course, but you see—"

"It's good for people to enjoy themselves," said Beryl earnestly. "Life is a bit drab, isn't it? Look at Miss Bulwer and Mr. Kensey and all of them!

They go on day after day getting older and drearier. They give me a pain in the neck. What's the good of being alive if you never have any fun?"

I had been wondering the same thing myself.

CHAPTER SIXTEEN

CHRISTMAS came and went. Mrs. Hall provided turkey and plum-pudding and Mr. Owen a box of crackers but in spite of these seasonable luxuries there was no jollity in the boarding-house and a singular absence of good will. To me it was a travesty of Christmas and I was thankful when it was over and normal conditions were resumed.

Ned and I left the boarding-house at the same time every morning and as our ways lay in the same direction we had made a habit of walking together. It was his choice rather than mine for I found Ned a depressing companion and although I needed a friend badly I knew that I could never be really friendly with Ned. To be friends with a person you must be able to share his interests and he must be able to share yours. Ned's interests were different from mine and he did not care a brass pin what my interests were. In addition, Ned was an inveterate borrower. He was always "on the rocks." He was constantly borrowing half a crown and rarely found it convenient to pay me back. Money was pretty tight with me and I had very little to come and go on, so half a crown meant a good deal, but somehow I could not refuse Ned. The odd thing was I could have refused quite easily if I had liked him better. I felt I ought to like Ned. He seemed to like me and because I could not return his liking I was unable to refuse him the half-crowns.

One morning we set out together as usual. It was a bright sunshiny morning, the sort of morning when Haines would be looking perfectly beautiful; I could not help thinking about it and wishing I were there. As a matter of fact I preferred dull rainy weather, it made me feel less homesick.

"I say, David," said Ned. "It's Beryl's birthday on Saturday and we're having a beano. Would you like to come?"

"It's very kind of you, but—"

"But what?"

"I'm not very good at parties. Besides I wouldn't know anybody, would I?"

"It isn't a big party. There'll be six of us, that's all."

"I don't think I'll come, Ned."

"Nonsense, of course you must come. We're going to a hotel near Richmond; it's a frightfully good place. A fellow I know told me about it, he said it was absolutely tip-top."

"Well, if you're sure you really want me—"

"Of course we want you!" he cried. "You must come, old boy."

"All right. It's very kind of you," I said. After all, it would be a change. If they really wanted me it seemed stupid and ungrateful to refuse.

"Good!" exclaimed Ned. "That's fixed then. Beryl will be pleased; she wants you to come."

"How do you get there?" I asked.

"Oh, that's all right. I can easily get the loan of a car. I'll get one that will take us all—you don't need to worry about that. The only thing is, I wondered if you'd mind paying something towards the dinner, would you? It's a bit odd to ask you to come to a party and help to pay for it, but—well—" said Ned, looking at me anxiously. "The fact is I'm a bit short of cash. I told you I'd had a run of bad luck lately, didn't I?"

"Yes," I said. "Yes, you told me."

"It's like this, you see: I promised Beryl ages ago that I'd give a party for her birthday and—well—there you are! I can't let her down, can I? She'd be so disappointed. I'm in the devil of a fix, that's the truth."

"Yes," I said. "Yes—of course."

"I say, you are a good pal!" he exclaimed. "You're one of the best. I'll never forget this—never! I've been worrying myself silly over it."

"How much would it be?" I asked.

"Oh—say three quid. I'll manage the rest."

"Three pounds!"

"We want to put up a good show, don't we? I mean it's Beryl's birthday. I hate doing things on the cheap, don't you? It's horrible to do things on the cheap. I mean it would be better to call the whole thing off than to be mingy about it. I tell you what, David, we'll call it a loan, shall we? My luck's sure to turn and then I'll pay you back. I must have it—honestly, old chap. I simply must have it."

"All right," I said. "But we won't call it a loan. It will be my share of the party."

Fortunately we had reached the parting of our ways so I was able to escape from his gratitude. It was all the more fortunate because I was annoyed and I could not be gracious about it. Three pounds for a party I did not want to go to! I was annoyed with Ned, but even more annoyed with myself for being such a fool. As for calling it a loan I knew Ned well enough by this time to be pretty certain that whatever we called it the money was gone for good.

That afternoon I drew some money from my Post Office Savings account and after supper I went up to his room and gave him the three pounds.

"Hallo, what's this!" he exclaimed. "Oh, of course . . . but why not keep it and share the bill?"

"No, you take it," I said. "It's your party."

This was not as generous as it sounds. I had a feeling that it was safer. I had a feeling that when the bill appeared Ned might say, "Oh, look here we're going shares in this, aren't we, David?" and my share might come to more than I had bargained for.

Ned took the notes and put them in his pocket-book. "You're a good sport," he said. "But I don't mind taking it because I know you'll enjoy the party. It's going to be no end of a beano. We've got two girls—friends of Beryl's—and a chap called Harry Elder. He's an absolutely tip-top fellow. As a matter of fact we were lucky to get him because he goes about all over the place—parties every night, that's Harry's form. Everyone knows Harry."

"Splendid!" I said. Somehow or other I felt quite certain I should not like Harry.

"It'll do you good," continued Ned. "It'll do us all good to have a real slap-up dinner. So long. David. See you tomorrow at seven-fifteen on the dot. I'll pick up the others and then call here for you and Beryl."

I was ready at seven-fifteen but there was no sign of the party. At seven-thirty Beryl came down the stairs; she was wearing a bright scarlet dress which matched her lips and nails and she was carrying a scarlet hand-bag. Her fair hair was in wavy curls upon her shoulders. I could not help wondering what people in Haines would have thought if they could have seen Beryl in her war-paint . . . but Haines was far away. Here things were different. Beryl looked fine.

"Hallo, David!" she exclaimed. "Where are the others? Oh well, never mind. We've got the whole night before us, haven't we?"

"Ned said seven-fifteen."

"Ned's always late. It's no good fussing, is it?"

We sat down on the little sofa in the parlour and waited. Beryl smoked and talked. Her eyes were shining with excitement and her cheeks were flushed.

"I love parties," she declared. "I wish we could have a party every night. That's one reason why I'm so keen to be an actress; they're always having parties, aren't they? I'm going to an audition to-morrow. Perhaps this is going to be my chance—perhaps some day I shall be a great actress—a star! Will you come and see me, David?"

"Yes, of course. I shall say 'That's Beryl Collingham, I knew her before she was famous.'"

Beryl laughed. "You *are* sweet," she said. "Oh, David, I am so excited. It's going to be a lovely party. Harry's coming, you know."

"Yes, Ned told me."

"Harry's an absolute scream. You'll like Zilla too. Zilla is awfully good value at a party. She makes things hum."

"There's another girl, isn't there?"

"Joan," said Beryl, nodding. "Joan is all right. She isn't quite so amusing of course but I had to ask her because I've known her for ages. It's rotten to forget old friends—at least I think so. Besides Joan has lots of money. It's useful, isn't it? I mean it's useful to have lots of money."

"Yes, very useful," I said.

"She gave me this hand-bag for my birthday. Wasn't it sweet of her?"

"Yes," I said. I realised I should have got something to give Beryl, but I had not thought of it. I wondered whether Beryl knew I was helping to pay for the party. I could not say anything, of course.

Beryl was showing me her bag when a car drove up and stopped at the door, announcing its arrival by prolonged blasts upon a Klaxon horn.

"That's them!" cried Beryl, leaping to her feet and rushing out of the room.

I followed more slowly.

In the car there were two girls, Ned and another man. Ned was driving. "Come on!" he cried. "Don't keep us waiting."

"I like that!" exclaimed Beryl. "You've kept us waiting for hours."

"It was Zilla's fault!"

"It was Harry's fault. He was chatting to his girl-friend on the phone."

"Which one—that's what I'd like to know!"

"The last but one—at least that's what it sounded like to me!"

"Ha, ha, that's a good one!"

They were all talking at once, greeting one another, laughing gaily.

"This is David," said Beryl. "That's Zilla and that's Joan. Oh, and Harry, of course. I nearly forgot Harry."

"Happy birthday to you!" cried Harry. "Lots of happy birthdays! I went to Tiffany's this morning but they hadn't anything *worthy* of you, Beryl dear, so I was obliged to fall back on Woolworth's."

Zilla screamed with laughter. "Isn't Harry marvellous?" We all got in. (The three girls in the back, Harry in front with Ned, myself perched somewhat precariously upon a tip-up seat.) Beryl was busy opening the parcels they had brought her and exclaiming rapturously over her presents. "How sweet! Just what I wanted! You are dears!"

"Not us," said Ned. "We're stags, Harry and I. You should have heard Harry's conversation on the phone."

"It wasn't Anne, was it?" asked Beryl mischievously.

"How did you guess?" inquired Harry. "It was Anne all right—wanted me to take her to a picture."

"You should have *heard* him!" said Ned chuckling. "'Not to-night I'm afraid . . . terribly sorry, darling . . . no, it's absolutely hopeless, my pet. No, dearest, I'm working. I've got a *lot* of work on hand and I must get it done to-night'!"

"Working!" exclaimed Joan. "Oh, Harry, what made you say that? Anne wouldn't fall for that one. She knows you too well."

"Rather too well," admitted Harry. "It was the only thing I could think of at the moment."

"You'll catch it!" cried Zilla with a shrill scream of laughter. "You'll catch it, Harry. She'll ring you up later and find you've gone out. That's what I'd do."

"Anne isn't like you," declared Harry. "Anne has a beautiful soul."

They all laughed uproariously and went on laughing and talking and referring to mutual friends. I had a feeling that they were showing off, leaving me out of the conversation deliberately, but perhaps they were not. Perhaps it was my fault for being out of harmony with them. I could do nothing about it for their jokes about Anne and their allusions to Jim and Thora meant nothing to me.

Harry was the life and soul of the party; they were all trying to impress Harry, teasing him and drawing him out. Ned was playing stooge, currying favour with the hero. It reminded me of school and of the way fellows used to "suck up" to people in the rugger fifteen. The only difference was that at school people had hated it and Harry was in his element.

"Look out, Ned!" cried Harry. "You nearly ran over that old hag—not that it would have mattered. She's a U.M. if ever there was one."

"What's a U.M.?" asked Beryl.

"Useless mouth, of course," said Ned.

"Unmarried mother," suggested Joan.

"Now, now, girls!" said Harry with mock solemnity. "Keep it clean."

"Ow!" screeched Zilla. "I bet Harry was thinking of something awful! I bet you were thinking of something awful, Harry."

I sat and listened. I tried to laugh when they laughed.

Presently we arrived at a road-house, a huge building, garishly painted, with blazing lights in the windows.

"Here we are, chums!" said Ned. "This is the place where we eat. I'll just park the car and then we'll go in."

"Drinks first," said Harry, leading the way into the American Bar. "Never eat before drinking, that's my motto. Come on, you blighters, the drinks are on me. Who's going to have what?"

"They shake a very pretty cocktail here," declared Ned. "You'd like it, Harry."

"I'll try anything once," said Harry, laughing.

"Is that another of your mottoes?" asked Beryl.

"You bet it is," he replied. "I'll try anything once. If it's good I'll keep on trying it."

The bar was hot and crowded. It was so noisy with chatter that its patrons had to shout to make themselves heard. Harry forced his way through the scrum and presently returned with a tray of small glasses containing a curious cloudy liquid.

"Here we are!" he said. "Six of them! Happy birthday to Beryl!"

We drank Beryl's health. The cocktail had a pleasant velvety taste. I had expected something more fiery—there was no bite in this potation—but before I had finished the stuff I had changed my mind about it. Quite suddenly I began to feel slightly muzzy, the voices became louder and the floor seemed to be swaying a little beneath my feet. I remembered that I had had nothing to eat since lunch; so perhaps that was the reason.

"Have another," Harry was saying. "Another all round."

The others accepted with alacrity but I refused.

"What!" cried. Harry. "Oh, come on. You need some ginger. It'll cheer you up and make a man of you. It'll loosen your tongue, old boy."

"He hasn't got a tongue!" cried Zilla with one of her shrill screams.

"No thank you," I said, trying to smile. "I won't have another—honestly, Harry."

"Mother wouldn't like it," said Joan.

This was considered a tremendous joke.

"It isn't Mother at all," said Beryl, giggling. "It's Father. Father's a Covenanter, isn't he, David? Father holds religious meetings and sings psalms. Mother plays the piano. Then suddenly in the middle of it the soldiers clatter up to the door and they all jump out of the window and hide in a cave."

"Oh Beryl, you *are* a scream!" cried Harry, laughing.

"It's true," she declared, opening her eyes very wide. "David told me all about it."

I smiled and said, "Beryl's got it a bit wrong," but I was angry all the same. She had persuaded me to talk about my home; I had told her about the old days when the Men of the Covenant were persecuted and hunted like hares amongst the Border hills. She had led me on to talk about the things I cared for and now she was using my confidence to amuse her friends.

"I haven't got it wrong," declared Beryl. "You told me about the Covenanters. You know you did! You said they sang psalms and hid in caves. You said your father was one of them."

"No, I didn't. I said—"

"They must have been batty!" exclaimed Harry. "Nobody who wasn't batty would live in a cave. No baths, I suppose? Or did they have hot and cold laid on? And what about the piano? Did they take that to the cave?"

"Father carried it on his back," suggested Ned.

It was amazingly silly but there was something nasty about it too. There are different ways of making jokes.

"Were you born in a cave, David?" asked Joan, giggling.

"Of course he was!" cried Harry. "He's a cave-man. That's why he's so strong and fierce."

"Yes," I agreed. "You've guessed it. I'm a cave-man."

"Ow!" screamed Zilla. "Everything's going round. I'm tiddly! You'd better give me something to eat."

CHAPTER SEVENTEEN

WE MOVED into the dining-room and found the table which Ned had reserved. It was in a corner near the service-door where the waiters kept coming in and out with trays. I was thankful we were going to have dinner, not only because I was starving with hunger but also because I was beginning to be anxious about my companions. Zilla was not the only one who was suffering from the effects of too many cocktails.

The dining-room was cool and pleasant after the crowded cocktail-bar; it was large and well-lighted and full of little tables. There was a quiet hum of voices in the air.

"This seems a good place," said Harry, looking round.

"Not bad," agreed Ned. "I often come here when I want a decent meal. By the by I've ordered the dinner—hope everybody likes what I like—it saves a lot of bother if you order in advance."

"You *said* there was a band!" exclaimed Beryl in disappointed tones.

"No," said Ned. "No band—"

"But you said there was!" Beryl declared. "You said there was a tip-top band. You know you did."

"They used to have a band," began Ned.

"No sir," said the waiter, who had begun to serve the *hors d'oeuvres*. "We never had a band. Our patrons don't like a lot of noise."

Poor Ned looked rather uncomfortable. He had pretended he had been here before and he had never been here before in his life.

"Never mind the band," I said. "Food is the main thing."

"Food and drink," agreed Harry. "What are we going to drink?"

"I've ordered white wine," replied Ned.

"Not fizz!" cried Zilla. "Not fizz—to drink Beryl's health!"

"It's hock," explained Ned. "Hock's much nicer."

It was obvious nobody agreed with him.

The wine was slightly fizzy and very sour. If it was hock, which I doubt, it was a very inferior brand of that noble wine. Fortunately—or perhaps unfortunately—the others seemed quite pleased with it; their glasses were filled and emptied and more bottles were ordered. Joan was the only one who seemed to share my aversion to the wine. "I'd rather have water," she said.

We both had water. It amused the others a good deal.

By contrast the dinner was excellent and I should have enjoyed it thoroughly if I could have eaten it in peace, but as time went on the behaviour of my companions was more and more uncontrolled. Zilla's shrieks became louder and shriller and they all laughed inordinately at every silly joke. They rolled little balls of bread and flicked them across the table, a wine-glass was upset and its contents flooded the cloth and dripped on to the floor.

The people at the other tables began to look round and stare in a disapproving manner. I did not blame them, but it was most embarrassing.

"Look here," I said. "We've finished now. Let's go, shall we?"

"Go!" cried Beryl. "The party's only just started."

"It's David's bed-time," suggested Harry. "Father likes him to be in bed by ten."

Beryl gave a wild hoot of laughter and the others joined in.

"Let's have coffee," said Joan.

"Not for me," declared Ned. "I hate the stuff. We'll have another bottle of hock instead."

Another bottle of "hock" was ordered and cigarettes were handed round. By this time they were all flushed and dishevelled and I wondered what would happen next. How on earth was I going to get them away? What could I do?

"I'll tell you something funny," said Zilla in blurred accents. "I'll tell you—something—damn' funny. It'll make you laugh." She began to laugh herself, swaying backwards and forwards in her chair. "I've forgotten it," she screamed. "I've forgotten—what it was—that's damn' funny, isn't it?"

"I don't think thass funny," said Ned. "Beryl doesn't think thass funny, do you, Beryl? I could tell mush funnier—story."

Beryl's face was pale and her eyes were glassy. She said slowly and carefully, "You're tight, that's what. This is my birthday and it's a lousy party. I've been looking forward—to my birthday—for years and years—and it's lousy. There's no band." Tears began to roll down her cheeks.

"I think so, too!" shouted Zilla. "I think shame as Beryl—no band!"

"Harry," I said. "Let's go. People are looking at us."

"A cat may look at a king," said Harry.

It was at this moment that the waiter approached and tendered the bill.

"But we haven't finished," said Ned, waving it away.

"This table is required, sir. There's another party waiting."

"Put them somewhere else," said Harry. "There's lots of empty tables."

"I'm sorry, sir, but you must go," said the waiter. "If you don't go I shall fetch the manager. People are complaining about you."

"Complaining!" exclaimed Harry. "What d'you mean, complaining? We've got as much right to be here as them."

"Come on," I said, rising and pushing back my chair. "We've finished dinner. Come on, Ned, pay the bill and we'll go."

"I don't want to go home!" cried Beryl. "It's my birthday! It's my birthday party!"

"My burshday too!" shrieked Zilla. "My burshday shame as Beryl. All our burshdays!"

The waiter turned to me. "Please make them go, sir," he implored. "The manager doesn't like this sort of thing. It gives the place a bad name."

My face was burning and my hands were clammy with perspiration. I had never felt so ashamed in my life. "Come on," I said, taking Ned by the arm. "Pay the bill and come. We don't want to stay where we're not wanted."

"Not wanted!" cried Harry. "That's a funny thing! Not wanted!"

Ned took out his pocket-book and began to count out the money.

"I'll go shares," said Harry. "It's been a good party. I don't mind paying for my fun."

"And David—" said Beryl looking at me. "David'll go shares too."

I looked at Ned but he was busy paying the bill and objecting to some of the items. "Whass this?" he was saying. "We didn't have coffee; nobody had coffee."

"Here you are!" said Harry, throwing down a wad of notes. "Pay the blinking bill. Nobody can say I'm stingy."

"David's stingy," said Joan with her irritating giggle. "David doesn't want to go shares. I don't think much of your new boy-friend, Beryl. He's too Scotch; that's what's the matter with him."

"Stingy," agreed Beryl, looking at me with glassy eyes. "David's stingy. Don't like stingy people."

I said nothing. My one idea was to get them on the move and presently after a good deal of argument the bill was settled and we trailed out to the car. Zilla could hardly walk and Beryl was not much better but somehow or other we managed. Ned opened the door of the car and climbed into the driving seat.

"Here!" exclaimed Harry. "You better let me drive. You're tight."

"I'm not. Just a bit lit up—thass all. We'll go to Chertsey—I know a pub at Chertsey—nice little pub—do us good to have a drink."

"I want to go home," said Joan. "Let Harry drive! Ned, let Harry drive! I want to go home."

"I don't want to go home!" cried Beryl.

"Harry's tight too!" screamed Zilla. "We're all tight excep' David. David thinks we're awful. Beryl, look at David! He thinks we're awful!"

I lifted her into the car and the others crawled in after her. Ned and Harry were still arguing about which of them was to drive. Obviously neither of them was fit to drive and I decided that I must take a firm line and drive the car myself. My licence had expired months ago but that could not be helped.

"Where's your bag, Beryl?" exclaimed Joan.

"My bag!"

"Yes, your handbag; the little red bag I gave you for your birthday. You've lost it!"

"I've lost it!" wailed Beryl. "I've lost my bag!"

"It's all right," I told her. "I'll go back and look for your bag. I expect it slipped under the table."

The last thing I wanted to do was to go back to that dining-room for Beryl's bag. I walked back slowly (they can wait for me, I thought. It will do them no harm to wait). I walked back through the car-park and up the steps. When I got into the hall I hesitated. Could I do it? Could I go back to the dining-room and grope under the table for that horrible little bag? Everybody in the room would look at me. "That's one of those awful people!" they would say.

I was still hesitating when the waiter came out of the dining-room with the little red bag in his hand. He handed it to me and said, "I'm sorry; but we have to consider our other patrons, you see. This is a quiet sort of place. People come here and bring their families."

"I know," I said. "I'm sorry about it, too—and ashamed."

He smiled at me. He had a nice open face and he was quite young, not much older than I was. "I could see that," he said. "But I shouldn't worry if I were you. There's no harm done. These things happen sometimes."

"It's never happened to me before and it never will again!"

"I shouldn't worry too much," he repeated. "The only thing is—you came in a car, didn't you, sir?"

"Yes."

"You'll drive, won't you? There might be serious trouble—if you see what I mean."

"Yes, I'll drive," I said, nodding. I gave him a tip, for I knew he had not got much from Ned and he thanked me and said good night.

Somehow talking to him had made me feel better. He was sane and sensible—the first sane, sensible person I had spoken to for hours. As I walked back to the car I had an absurd feeling that I could be friends with that waiter. I wondered what his name was and where he lived . . . it was foolish, of course; I knew nothing about him, nothing except that he was sensible and kind.

When I got back to the car-park there was no green car to be seen. For a moment I could not believe my eyes. I stood there gazing at the empty space in blank amazement. The big green car had vanished. They had gone without me.

Suddenly I began to laugh. It was a cracking joke. They had gone without me! Perhaps they had got tired of waiting; quite possibly they had forgotten me. I did not care. I was so delighted to be rid of my companions that I did not care a hoot. If I had to walk all the way back to Bloomsbury I did not care!

In my pocket there was a sixpence and three pennies (I had given the waiter ten shillings and that was all I had left) so it looked as if I should have to walk most of the way, but it was a fine starry night and the air was sweet and clean. I started off down the road. Perhaps I should have been worrying about the fate of the green car and its occupants but the plain truth is that I was not worrying at all. The plain truth is I did not care a pin what happened to them. I was utterly fed up and disgusted with the whole crowd.

It was my own fault of course. I should never have accepted the invitation to the party. I had known from the very beginning that Ned was not my sort. It was nothing to do with class, it was his character; Ned was a third-rate person and his friends were of the same pattern. Oddly enough I was much more angry and disgusted with Beryl—perhaps because I had liked her—I was so furious with Beryl that I could not think of her without a curious sort of constriction in my chest.

There were streets and streets, all quiet and deserted with scarcely a creature to be seen. I threw back my shoulders and stretched my legs and strode along at a round pace. The fresh night air was exhilarating and presently I began to feel better. I remembered what Father had said about digging—digging was the best cure for a sore heart—and I decided that walking at night was almost as good, especially if the stars were bright in a clear dark-blue sky. Why didn't more people walk at night in London? Why didn't I, for that matter? The pavements, which in the daytime were thick with crowds of pedestrians, were wide and empty and free.

I had walked for about an hour when I came to a coffee-stall drawn up at the corner of a street. The smell of coffee was tempting and after a moment's hesitation I joined the little group of people who had gathered round the stall. They were an odd collection: a tall man in evening dress, two navvies, a stout individual with a check cap (who might have been a bookie) and several others. The proprietor had grey hair and a red face; he was pouring coffee into big thick cups and serving sausage rolls and sandwiches. "Wot'll you 'ave?" he asked.

"What can you give me for ninepence?"

"Ninepence!"

"That's all I've got," I told him.

He looked at me. "'Ave you 'ad your pocket picked?"

"No," I said. "I was with some friends and they went off without me, that's all."

The other people had stopped chatting and were gazing at me with interest.

"Funny sort of thing to do," said the man in the check cap. "Not my ideer of a joke. I'd see them far enough before I gave them another chance."

"They won't get another chance," I said with feeling.

The coffee-stall proprietor gave me a cup of steaming coffee and a sausage roll. "There you are, young feller," he said.

"Where are you going?" asked the man in evening dress.

"Bloomsbury," I replied. I fished out the sixpence and the three pennies to pay for the food and handed it over.

"You better keep it," said the coffee-stall proprietor, smiling at me, "you've a long way to go. You might get a bus or something—"

"Not now, 'e won't," declared one of the navvies.

"It's all right," I said. "I like walking and it's a lovely night. I've been wondering why more people don't walk at night in London."

"They've enough to do in the day," suggested the man in the check cap.

The man in evening dress looked at me thoughtfully. "You aren't a Londoner," he said.

I laughed. "No, I'm a country cousin."

A big tall fellow at the other end of the stall leant forward and stared at me. He had red hair and a ruddy complexion and his eyes crinkled at the corners. "I'm thinking ye come frae the norrth," he declared.

"You're right, I've done most of my walking on the hills."

"See here, I'll tak' ye tae Bloomsbury—it's a wee bit oot o' my way but niver heed."

The sound of his slow Scots voice with its lilting cadences was music in my ears. I exclaimed impulsively, "You're a Hawick man!"

Back came the answer. "Na, na, ye're oot o' yer reckoning, laddie. I'm frae Tushielaw." He grinned at me and added, "I'm awa' back hame the morn's morn. Wull ye come?"

"What's he saying?" asked the man in evening dress and I was not surprised for my brother Scot had tendered his invitation in the broad dialect of the district where he was born and which I had recognised at once. (Tushielaw is less than twenty miles from Hawick.)

"It's double Dutch," declared the man in the check cap. "That's what it is."

"Sounds like Danish to me," said the man in evening dress. "He looks like a Dane, too."

"He's a Scot," I said, laughing. "So am I. He's offering me a lift home to Scotland, and I'd give my ears to take him at his word."

"I thought you wanted to go to Bloomsbury."

"I don't want to go to Bloomsbury, but I've got to," I explained.

"Come awa' then, laddie," said the Scot. "If I'm taking ye tae Bloomsbury we'll need tae get stairted. D'ye ken the road?"

I had only the vaguest idea of the way to Bloomsbury but they were all interested by this time and all joined in a discussion of the best and shortest route, but the advice we received was so varied as to be almost useless and after listening to it for a few moments my friendly Scot lost patience.

"Och away!" he exclaimed. "There's too mony roads hereabouts. We'll trust oor sense o' direction."

I said good-bye and followed him to his van. It was a big furniture van painted green, a solid-looking vehicle. We climbed into the front seat and set off.

"They're kind, mind you, but they're awful silly whiles," said the Tushielaw man reflectively.

Fortunately we had little difficulty in finding our way—the river was our guide—and as we went we chatted comfortably about Haines and Tushielaw and other matters of interest. It was nearly three o'clock when the green van drew up before the door of Mrs. Hall's boarding-house and I thanked my new friend for his kindness.

"Ye're welcome," he said simply, and we shook hands. The key of the front door was in my pocket; I let myself in quietly and crept up the stairs. So much had happened that it was not until I was safely in bed that I remembered Ned and Beryl and the other members of the party and wondered whether or not they too were safely in bed.

CHAPTER EIGHTEEN

NEITHER Ned nor Beryl appeared at breakfast and I was not surprised. It was Sunday, of course, so there was nothing to prevent them from sleeping off the effects of the party.

Mr. Kensey asked if I had had a good time but before I could think of a suitable reply Miss Bulwer chipped in:

"I heard you come in," declared Miss Bulwer. "It was after three o'clock. Disgraceful, I call it! Do you realise it was Sunday morning, Mr. Kirke?"

"They were home before twelve," said Owen in his sing-song voice. "Yes, indeed they were. I heard Ned and Beryl talking on the landing. They were having a row. Very noisy, they were. It shows little consideration for others to be talking so loudly on the landing at that time of night. So you see, Miss Bulwer, you were wrong. It was twelve o'clock that they came in and not three."

"It was three o'clock," interrupted Miss Bulwer. "I heard Mr. Kirke come in. His room is next door to mine. I looked at my watch."

They argued about it. Oddly enough it did not seem to occur to them to refer the matter to me, and this being so I went on eating my breakfast and did not interfere.

It was my habit to go out for the whole day on Sundays and I saw no reason to break it. I went to St. Paul's for the morning service; I lunched in a small restaurant not far from the Cathedral and then I walked in the Park. When I got back Ned was alone in the lounge sitting beside a smoky fire and reading a Sunday paper. He was even paler than usual and his eyes were swollen and puffy; in fact I had scarcely ever seen a more miserable-looking object.

"David!" he exclaimed. "Good heavens, where have you been? I've been waiting for you all day. I want to talk to you."

"Talk away," I said.

"You're not angry, are you? I mean it was all a mistake. Look here, old boy, I'll explain the whole thing. It was like this you see; Harry wanted to drive, but I was blowed if I was going to let him. He kept on trying to drag me out of the seat—he was as tight as a drum—I couldn't let him drive, could I? It wouldn't have been safe. So I just stepped on the gas and drove off. I thought you were in the car—really I did, David. The girls kept on yelling at me to go back but I didn't understand—I mean I didn't want to go back to that foul place. I just drove on and took no notice. As a matter of fact I had a devil of a job getting out of that beastly car-park; the gate was so narrow that I scraped off half the wing. They were all screaming their heads off in the back and Harry was bawling in my ear and clutching at the wheel."

I laughed. I could not help it.

"What are you laughing at?" he said. "There was nothing to laugh at, I can tell you. I was absolutely boiling with rage. I just drove on and took no notice of them and it wasn't until we'd gone some distance that they stopped behaving like a pack of lunatics and explained that you'd been left behind. We went back at once—honestly David—we went straight back but you weren't there. That's how it happened."

"It doesn't matter," I said.

"I couldn't help it. The whole thing was a mistake."

"It doesn't matter," I repeated.

"But it does. You're as sick as mud—I can see that. You're fed up because we drove off without you—but we were only gone a few minutes and when we got back you weren't there. What could we do? It was no good hanging about waiting for you. We didn't know where you'd gone."

"I walked home."

"You walked home!"

"Most of the way. Then I got a lift in a van."

"Why didn't you wait for us?"

"I never thought of it. I didn't know you were coming back. But you needn't worry. As a matter of fact I was very glad when I realised you'd gone without me. I had had enough."

"That's a funny thing to say!" cried Ned. "You'd had enough. My hat, we'd had enough of you! We asked you to the party and you were no more use than a sick headache. Harry said you were a stuffed shirt and so you were!"

Quite suddenly I was angry. I had made up my mind to say nothing but this sensible resolution was swept away. Harry thought I was a stuffed shirt, did he?

"I didn't like your party—or your friends," I said. "I've never seen such a crew! You all got drunk and behaved so badly that we were kicked out of the hotel."

"We weren't kicked out!"

"We were—and I didn't blame them. I've never been so ashamed before in all my life."

"Oh lord," groaned Ned. "My head's splitting!"

"Small wonder!" I said unsympathetically, and I sat down and opened the paper.

"It was that hock. I don't believe it was good stuff."

"It was foul," I replied shortly.

He was silent for a few moments and then he continued in a dreary tone. "It was a stinking place for a party—absolutely lousy—we should have gone somewhere and danced. I wish I'd never suggested having a party. It was an absolute wash-out. I did it for Beryl and instead of being pleased she's fed-up to the back teeth. She keeps on saying there was no band. How could I know there wouldn't be a band? Of course I thought there'd be a band at a place like that. That party cost the earth and it was no good at all. I suppose you couldn't lend me a few quid to go on with, David?"

I could hardly believe my ears.

"David, could you?" he asked. "It would only be till the end of the week. I'm absolutely cleaned out."

"Cleaned out?" I said, putting down the paper and looking at him. "How can you be cleaned out? I gave you three pounds and Harry shared the bill with you. How much did you have to pay? Precious little!"

"It was the car. I mean I'll have to pay for the wing to be repaired."

"Wasn't it insured?"

"Well—no—" he muttered. "Not really. I mean it's insured when the boss is driving. I mean it's a bit difficult to explain to anyone who doesn't understand." He paused and looked at me. "I had to have a big car," he said miserably. "There were six of us. How could six of us fit into a mouldy little bus? Harry's used to doing things in style. Oh hell, don't know what the boss will say to-morrow when he sees that wing!"

"You seem to have got yourself into a serious mess."

"Mess isn't the word! It's ghastly—and it's such rotten luck, isn't it?"

"I wouldn't describe it as rotten luck."

"It was! I've driven that blinking car dozens of times. I can drive that car with my eyes shut. How did I know Harry would grab the wheel just as we were going out of the gate! Look here, David, you might lend me a few quid. If I could raise a fiver I could square up the whole thing. I'll pay you back—sure as death I'll pay you every penny."

The idiotic thing was that I could not say no. I was annoyed with Ned and disgusted with his underhand dealings—but I was sorry for him.

"How much do you want?" I asked.

"Oh, David, you *are* a brick! How much have you got?"

I turned out my pockets. I had a pound and a ten shilling note and some small change. I gave him the notes and returned the change to my pocket.

"Is that all?" he said in disappointed tones. "Oh, well, it's better than nothing. I'll have to get down to the show-rooms early to-morrow morning and see if I can fix things up."

I could not help smiling as I went upstairs to my room. Ned was incorrigible. He had treated me abominably but he seemed unaware of the fact. Nothing was his fault; it was all bad luck. Everything that happened to Ned was bad luck. But in spite of my amusement I was uneasy for I realised that unless I could harden my heart he would continue to look upon me as a milch-cow. The fact was I could not afford Ned.

Presently there was a knock on the door and Beryl appeared.

"It's all right," she said in a low voice, and she came in and shut the door. "It's all right, David. I won't stay a minute. I just had to talk to you and there's no chance of talking downstairs."

She stood and looked at me. Her face was drawn and pale and there were dark smudges under her eyes.

"David," she continued in the same low voice. "Why don't you say something?"

"I've got nothing to say," I told her.

"You're cross! Oh, David, I was afraid you would be cross. It was a frightful party; I know you hated it but it wasn't my fault."

"It was my fault. I shouldn't have come. I told you I was no good at parties."

"Listen, David. I didn't know you'd helped to pay for the party. I didn't know until last night when we got home and Ned told me. He should have told me before and then I'd have known. Ned and I had an absolutely blazing row. I never want to see him again."

"You'll see him at supper—in about ten minutes," I said. "Don't be horrid!" she exclaimed, looking at me piteously. "It wasn't my fault that we drove off and left you behind. It wasn't my fault—really it wasn't. I tried to make Ned stop, but he wouldn't. Then at last we made him stop and we went back, but you weren't there. That's the truth, David. You see how it happened, don't you?"

"Yes," I said. "It's all right."

"So now you understand, don't you?"

I did not answer that. I took her bag out of the drawer and gave it to her. "There's your bag," I said.

"Oh, David!" she cried. "Why are you so horrid? I've explained everything, haven't I?"

"No," I said. "You haven't explained why you encouraged me to tell you about my home and then made fun of it."

"I didn't!" she exclaimed. "I don't know what you mean."

"Oh well, never mind, it doesn't matter . . . but you'd better go away."

"I'll go in a minute. I just came because—because I want to be friends. Please, David! I didn't mean to be horrid. Say you'll forgive me."

"All right," I said uncomfortably. "But you'd better go away. Miss Bulwer's room is next door . . . so you'd better go away."

"Listen, David," said Beryl, coming nearer and reducing her voice to a whisper. "Please listen. I like you so much—really and truly. That's why I wanted to talk to you and explain. I can't bear us not to be friends.

I mean you're different; I've never met anyone like you before. Don't be cross with me."

"I've told you it's all right."

"You keep on saying it's all right, but it isn't," said Beryl miserably. "You don't like me any more."

This was so true that I could not deny it. I had liked Beryl quite a lot; she was gay and friendly, and I had enjoyed our evening together at The Three Lamplighters. Now, as I looked at her, I could not believe that I had ever liked her. I had thought her pretty, but now I saw that her eyes were too close together and her skin pasty and unhealthy beneath the layer of powder. It was as if I had been wearing a pair of rose-coloured spectacles and had taken them off.

"David, don't look at me like that!" she exclaimed.

"I'm sorry," I said, turning away. I was sorry. It seemed unkind, but I could not help it. I was through with Beryl.

Fortunately at this moment the gong rang and, after I had reconnoitred to see that Miss Bulwer was not prowling about on the landing, Beryl slipped out of my room and ran downstairs. I waited for a few moments and then went down myself.

CHAPTER NINETEEN

THE following evening, walking home after work, I took a different route and, getting lost amongst the maze of streets, found myself in the Covent Garden district. The market was over of course, but there were a few men tidying the place. It was getting dark and the lights were going on. I strolled along looking about with interest and deciding that I must come some morning when the market was in full swing.

Just round the corner I came upon a little bookseller's shop; it was in an area below the level of the street. I leant upon the railings and looked down at the lighted window which was full of all sorts and conditions of books. There were old books with shabby covers, and new books with gay jackets, and a whole shelf of cheap editions. The fact is I can never pass a book-shop and although I had no money to spend on books it gave me pleasure to look at them.

In one corner of the window there was a small card which said FLAT TO LET. TOP FLOOR. I gazed at it for a few moments and then, quite suddenly, I made up my mind to inquire. It would be no good, of course, but still . . .

As I went down the steps a man came out of the door; he was a tubby little man with light blue eyes and shaggy brownish-grey eyebrows. His hair was of the same indeterminate colour and his forehead was unusually broad.

"I'm just shutting up shop," he said, looking at me doubtfully. His voice seemed to come from deep down in his chest.

"Oh," I said, hesitating. "It was just . . . I see you have a flat to let."

"That's right. It's an attic flat—right up on the top floor. If you're looking for a flat in Mayfair with a lift and a man in uniform there's no use bothering."

"I wasn't, really," I said, smiling. The little man was gruff and obviously a little out of temper, but somehow I could not help liking him.

He went back into the shop and I followed him.

"There have been people here all day," he continued in a grumbling tone. "Women with babies, who wanted to know how they could get the pram upstairs; people with rheumatism in their knees, people with pianos and dogs—"

"I've got none of those things. Not even rheumatism in my knees."

He glanced at me from beneath his shaggy brows and there was the ghost of a twinkle in his eye. "Well, I have," he said. "And I'm not going up those stairs again—not for nobody."

"Perhaps I could go and have a look at it, myself?"

"You can if you like. I'll wait here till you come down and say why it won't suit you."

I took the key and hesitated. "Is it expensive?" I asked.

"No, it's cheap. The fact is—and I may as well tell you—there's no bathroom. I could have let it over and over again if it had a bathroom with chromium-plated fittings. I've often thought of putting in a bath but I've never got round to it. That's the truth."

"There's hot and cold water?" I asked.

"Lord, yes! There's a good big sink, too. You better go and have a look—that is if you can do without a bath."

I thought I could. The fact was that at Mrs. Hall's one could scarcely ever get into the bathroom and I was used to washing piece-meal.

"I'll tell you what," he said. "If the flat suits you I don't mind letting you have a bath in my own place. I've got a little flat behind the shop. This whole house belongs to me; it's divided into five flats, they're all let except the top one."

"You're Mr. Coe?" I asked. John Coe was the name over the window.

"That's right," he said. "You take the key and have a look. We shan't quarrel about the rent."

I went through the shop and up the stairs. It was a very old house, but the woodwork was in good repair. In the old days it must have belonged to a family (perhaps some important family) but now, as Mr. Coe had said, it was divided up and on every floor there were different people with a front-door of their own. I went up and up until I came to the top-landing with a skylight overhead. Here I found a brown-painted door. I put the key in the lock, turned it and went in.

The door opened directly into a good-sized room with two windows facing west, so that the last rays of the setting sun streamed into it, lighting it with a soft yellow radiance. The room was empty, completely empty.

I suppose it was foolish of me to have expected the flat to be furnished, but I *had* expected it so the bare room gave me a shock. I very nearly turned round and went out again. However I had come up all those stairs to see it so I decided to have a look round.

The flat consisted of two rooms, one opening out of the other, and a small kitchen with an electric stove and a sink and shelves all round. The ceilings were low, but the rooms were well-proportioned. The floor was of plain solid wood, stained with brown varnish, and the walls were distempered in egg-shell blue. When I had had a good look round I went back to the living-room and sat down on the window seat. If only it had been furnished! But it was not furnished and I did not possess a stick of furniture . . . so it was no good. . . . or was it? How much would it cost to buy what I should need? I should not want much: just a bed and a table and a couple of chairs and a few other odds and ends.

I had some money in the bank. Mother had said, "Don't fritter it away. Keep it until you need it." Well, I needed it now, didn't I? Living here, buying my own food and cooking it myself, would cost much less than the boarding-house—and how much more pleasant it would be!

There was a friendly atmosphere about the little flat and the longer I stayed in it the better I like it. There was peace and privacy; it was like a haven in the turmoil of London.

Presently I heard somebody coming up the stairs and Mr. Coe appeared in the doorway.

"What's happened to you?" he inquired crossly. "I've been waiting for you. I thought you must have thrown yourself out of the window or else that you were taking the knobs off the doors. How long does it take to look at two empty rooms and decide that you don't want them?" He switched on the light as he spoke and the bare room was illuminated.

"I've been thinking," I said.

"The thoughts of youth are long, long thoughts," declared Mr. Coe.

"Mine are a bit complicated. I like this place no end—but I haven't any furniture."

Mr. Coe said nothing.

"Do you think I could buy some furniture second-hand?" I asked.

"Well, of course. That's what second-hand furniture shops are for."

"I want peace," I told him.

"Peace! Well, I daresay this is just about as peaceful as you could get. Nobody's going to climb up all those stairs to badger you."

"No, that's what I thought."

He sat down beside me on the window-seat and we discussed the matter. I explained how I was situated and he listened and nodded. He told me that he had a friend in the second-hand furniture trade and would give me an introduction to him if I liked.

"Look here," he said at last. "I don't want to rush you into it. Suppose you think it over and let me know. Suppose you sleep on it."

But by this time my mind was made up. I was determined to have the flat. I wanted it here and now. I told him so.

"All right, it's yours," he said, looking at me and smiling.

It was mine. I looked round my domain with satisfaction. I felt as if a burden had fallen from my back.

We went downstairs together. The shop was shut; there were big shutters on the windows, it was dim and shadowy, in the book-lined room. Mr. Coe took me into his parlour and set out two glasses and a bottle of rum.

"We must seal the bargain," he said. "I'm a seafaring man—or was in my young days—so rum's my drink. I don't hold with gin, it's rot-gut stuff. I can give you beer if you'd rather."

"I'll try your rum, please," I told him.

The room was small and full of large old-fashioned furniture and heavy curtains, it was stuffy but very clean. Mr. Coe explained that he had a woman who came in every morning and cleaned the place and cooked his dinner. He suggested that I might have her for an hour three times a week. I said I would if I could afford it. I should have to see how things worked out.

"That's right," he said. "You wait and see." He sat down in an easy-chair and looked round the little room with pride. "Cosy, isn't it?" he said. "I like being cosy. As a matter of fact I picked up most of this stuff second-hand. If you know what you're doing you can pick up good furniture for half nothing—even now, you can—but you've got to be pretty fly. Good solid stuff is what I like—none of your modern stuff that falls to pieces if you look at it too hard."

"I don't know much about furniture."

"No?" he said, looking at me doubtfully. "Well, it takes experience, of course. Look here, how would you like me to come with you to Mackenzie's and give you a hand at choosing the stuff? You have to keep your eyes skinned; I mean those second-hand furniture blokes are pretty smart."

"That's very good of you, Mr. Coe."

"Not a bit! I'd like to. We'll go round to-morrow when I've shut the shop. That suit you?"

"Down to the ground," I declared. The idea of having Mr. Coe to help me to choose the furniture relieved my mind considerably.

CHAPTER TWENTY

IT WAS late when I got back to the boarding-house (supper was nearly over) and as I opened the door of the dining-room I saw them all sitting round the table. Seven faces turned and looked at me—it reminded me of the night I had arrived—but now the faces were no longer strange to me. It flashed across my mind that in a few days I should have left here and, more than likely, I should never see any of those faces again.

Mrs. Hall was annoyed with me for being late. "We've nearly finished," she said. "If you'd said you'd be late—but of course you never thought of *that*! Some people 'ave no consideration. There's sausages if you want them—over on the sideboard—you can 'elp yourself."

"They'll be cold," said Beryl.

"I daresay," agreed Mrs. Hall. "People that come in late 'as to put up with cold food. I suppose you think the food ought to 'ave kept 'ot! Well, it 'asn't been—and it won't be. Not in *this* 'ouse."

Somehow I did not feel hungry, and the greasy sausages in the cracked dish revolted me. I cut a piece of bread and helped myself to raspberry jam. This was an added insult, of course. Mrs. Hall glared at me.

"Mr. Kirke is 'appy to-night," said Madame Futrelle slyly. They all looked at me and I could feel myself blushing.

"You see!" she exclaimed. "You see 'ow 'e looks 'appy! I wonder what it is that 'as pleased 'im so much."

I smiled at her across the table but did not reply.

"Mr. Kirke is not going to tell us," she continued. "It is a secret . . . but I think I can guess."

"It's spring," said Mr. Kensey. "We all know what happens to a young man in spring—ha, ha, ha!"

"Can't you leave him alone!" exclaimed Beryl angrily.

"They can't," declared Miss Bulwer. "There's no privacy here. Even one's thoughts are public property, it seems."

"That's why I'm leaving," I said.

"Leaving!" exclaimed Mrs. Hall in amazement.

"Yes, I shall be giving up my room at the end of the week."

"Well, I never!" she cried. "That's a surprise, that is! I'm sure I've done everything I could to make you comfortable."

"Comfortable!" exclaimed Mr. Kensey. "D'you call this comfortable? I don't blame Kirke for moving. I'm not sure I shan't move myself."

"What d'you want?" asked Mrs. Hall angrily. "You get your meals regular. Why don't you take a room at the Savoy?"

"Regular meals!" cried Mr. Owen. "Is that what you call a meal—one sausage for supper!"

"You could 'ave 'ad two if you'd wanted."

"Well I didn't," he told her. "Half-cooked it was—nasty—all red inside."

Mrs. Hall left him and returned to me. I was the villain of the piece. "You never complained," she said. "You never said a thing about not being settled. Sly, that's what I call it! You might 'ave said you was looking for something else."

"I wasn't looking for something else. I just happened to find the flat by accident. That's why I was late."

"A flat!" exclaimed Mrs. Hall. "You've taken a flat!"

"Yes, it's a flat in a friend's house." This was true—or so I felt. Compared with Mrs. Hall my new landlord was a very good friend.

"My, we *are* going up in the world!" said Mrs. Hall sarcastically. "A flat in Kensington, I shouldn't wonder, with a page in buttons to open the door and a 'all full of palm trees!"

I could not help laughing.

"Where is it, David?" asked Beryl.

"In an attic," I replied.

"But where? Is it near here?"

"David is not going to say," declared Madame Futrelle with a malicious little twinkle in her eyes. "Me, I do not blame 'im that he wants to shake the dust off 'is feet. No, I do not blame 'im."

"Of course 'e'll leave 'is address," said Mrs. Hall, looking at me.

I took no notice, but just went on eating my bread and jam. I had intended to leave my address but now I realised that there was no need. All my letters came to the office. As Madame Futrelle had suggested I could shake the dust off my feet. There are certain advantages to be gained from living in London; one of them is the ease with which one can disappear. Although only a few miles of streets would separate me from Mrs. Hall and her guests I could "disappear" as easily as if I had been going to Australia.

All this time Ned had said nothing. He was preoccupied with his own thoughts. He looked a bit chastened and I wondered what had happened when "the boss" saw his car with its crumpled wing. I wondered whether Ned had got the sack or merely a dressing-down, but there was no need to wonder. I knew Ned would tell me the whole story in detail as soon as he could get me alone.

After supper Ned followed me to my room and began his tale.

"I've had an awful day," he declared. "I don't know when I've had such a ghastly day. I've had nothing to eat except aspirin tablets; couldn't face any food. I went down to the show-room early to look at that wretched car and see what I could do about it . . ."

The story went on. Ned was so taken up with his affairs that he never mentioned mine; perhaps the fact that I was leaving had not penetrated his mind or perhaps he thought it was an empty threat on my part. Mr. Owen and Mr. Kensey often threatened to leave the place and it never came to anything. At any rate, whatever the reason, Ned seemed oblivious of my future plans. He talked and talked, describing how he had bribed the foreman to camouflage the damaged wing and how the boss had arrived in the middle of it with a brow like thunder, and what the boss had said, and what he had said to the boss, and how at first it had looked as if he were going to be thrown out, but eventually the boss had come round and said that if he paid for the damage he could stay on in the meantime.

"So that's that," declared Ned. "I shall have to mind my step for a bit until he's forgotten about it, of course."

"You'd better," I told him.

"Oh, I shall. It wouldn't suit me to get the boot. Fortunately I managed to sell a car this afternoon—at least I think I've sold it—but of course you can never be certain till the deal is absolutely through. You've no idea how people behave, backing out at the last minute."

I had a very good idea of the way Ned's customers behaved. He had described their vagaries over and over again until I was sick of the subject.

I let him talk on and did not listen and presently I told him I was going to bed and managed to get rid of him.

There was a lot to think about. I got into bed and tried to read but I was too full of what had happened and was going to happen in the next few days. Soon—as soon as I could manage it—I would say good-bye to this dismal room and this lumpy bed and start fresh in new surroundings. I would say good-bye to Mrs. Hall and Mr. Kensey and all the rest of them. I would have peace to live my own life. I would be able to write. I had intended to write when I came to London but I had been so badgered and so miserable that I had not been able to write a word; I had even not wanted to write a word. Now the mere idea of having quietude to think my own thoughts without interference stirred my imagination. Yes, I would write. One thing I must have in my new abode was a large steady table. I would put it near the window. I knew exactly where it would stand.

Just as I was getting sleepy and was about to turn out the light I heard a slight noise at the door. The handle turned slowly and the door opened. It was Beryl.

"Beryl!" I whispered. "Beryl, you can't come in."

She came in and shut the door softly. She was wearing a pale pink dressing-gown and her fair hair was fluffed out round her face. "I had to see you," she said. "I couldn't go to sleep—I was so miserable. David, why are you going away?"

"We can't talk now," I told her. "Miss Bulwer will hear. I'll talk to you in the morning."

"But we can't!" she whispered. "We can't talk with all those frightful people listening to every word. David, listen—"

"No," I said. "I don't want to listen."

She came nearer. Her dressing-gown was trimmed with lace, it was greasy round her neck (dirty and greasy and stuck together, so that the lace looked like string) and as she approached there was a smell of strong sweet scent. It made me feel quite sick.

"Go back to bed," I said as sternly as I could. It is difficult to speak sternly in a whisper.

"I'm so lonely," she murmured. "I'm so miserable. I don't want you to go away. I can't bear it—"

I leapt out of bed and took her firmly by the shoulders and pushed her out of the door. I shut it and turned the key. For a moment or two I waited, listening, but I could hear nothing. Then I went back to bed.

At first I was furiously angry with the silly little fool but after a bit my anger faded away and I saw the funny side of it. I was not at all sure what Beryl's intentions had been, but I had shown her mine.

CHAPTER TWENTY-ONE

THE next day when I had finished work at the office I went straight to the book-shop. Mr. Coe was waiting for me and we set off together.

"I've been thinking," said Mr. Coe. "You'd better leave the bargaining to me. I know the tricks of the trade, and I know Mackenzie."

"It's very good of you."

"I like it," he replied frankly. "Now look here, Kirke, have you ever played a game called 'Sergeant Murphy'? It's a silly sort of game. We used to play it when we were kids."

"We used to play it too," I said in some surprise. "It's squad drill, but you don't obey orders unless they're prefaced by the words, 'Sergeant Murphy says . . .'"

Mr. Coe chuckled. "That's it. You and I are going to play that game with Mackenzie, see? For instance if Mackenzie says 'Two pounds' and I say to you, 'What about it?' or 'Could you run to that?' Then you say, 'No, it's too much.' But if Mackenzie says 'Two pounds' and I say, 'Well, Mr. Kirke, what about it?' Then you say, 'Yes.' You don't say it eagerly of course, you say it a bit reluctantly, but if I say 'Mr Kirke' you know it's O.K."

"Kirke is the password."

"That's right—and your password to me is Coe."

I had expected, not unnaturally, to meet a fellow-Scot but there was nothing Scots about Mr. Mackenzie except his name. Mr. Mackenzie was well-dressed; he spoke well and had a dignified and benevolent air.

The conversation opened politely with introductions and remarks about the weather and the deplorable conditions of the trade. Mr. Mackenzie told an amusing story and told it well and we all laughed heartily. It was not until we had been chatting for about ten minutes that Mr. Coe mentioned business.

"My friend Mr. Kirke wants a few odds and ends of furniture," he said.

"Certainly, we'll have a look round," said Mr. Mackenzie, nodding, and he led us to his store.

The battle began. It was a most amusing performance and was conducted with the greatest dignity upon high diplomatic levels. For a time I listened in silence and in some bewilderment, but before long I began to understand the rules of the game. We looked at rugs first. Mr. Coe extolled the beauties of those we did not want and deprecated the merits of the one we wanted. The password was extremely useful to us both. If I did not like a rug I said, "Yes, it seems a nice rug. I believe that would suit me." If I liked it, I said, "That's not a bad rug, Mr. Coe."

"Three pounds," said Mr. Mackenzie.

"Three pounds!" echoed Mr. Coe in horrified accents.

"Two-seventeen-six to you," said Mr. Mackenzie. "I wouldn't sell that rug to anyone else for less than three-ten."

Mr. Coe turned to me. "What about it?" he inquired.

"Too much," I replied firmly.

"I want you to have this rug," declared Mr. Mackenzie. "It's a good rug. It came out of a good house. I'm losing money on it—but I'll let you have it for two-ten."

"Look at that burn!" said Mr. Coe. "Somebody must have dropped a cigarette on it . . . no, I wouldn't advise my friend to pay a penny more than two-five."

"Two-seven-six," suggested Mr. Mackenzie. "That's giving the rug away."

"Well, I don't know," said Mr. Coe reluctantly. "What do you say, Mr. Kirke? It's for you to say."

"I might run to that, Mr. Coe," I replied in reluctant tones.

In addition to the rug I bought a solid table, a divan with a broken leg, an easy-chair and two upright chairs with wooden arms and leather seats. I bought two pairs of blue rep curtains which matched the rug, a cupboard with shelves for books and a shaving-mirror. Mr. Mackenzie endeavoured to persuade me to buy a bed, but I refused for I had decided to have a new one. The bed in Mrs. Hall's boarding-house with its queer musty smell had given me a horror of second-hand beds and bedding. My refusal pained Mr. Mackenzie and to soothe his injured feelings I consented to buy a large old-fashioned chest of drawers and a standard lamp with a parchment shade.

It was nearly nine o'clock when we came out of the furniture-store and I was weak with hunger so I invited Mr. Coe to dine with me, and he took me to a small restaurant not far from his book-shop and we had a comfortable meal.

In some ways the place reminded me of The Three Lamplighters, where I had gone with Beryl, but it was smaller and a good deal cheaper.

It was called The Wooden Spoon and Mr. Coe knew the proprietor who was an Austrian and cooked the food himself.

"You'll find this place useful," said Mr. Coe. "If you get tired of cooking your own food you can nip round here and have a decent meal. I only hope it isn't discovered."

"Discovered?"

"That's what happens. These little places where you can get a good meal are all right until they're 'discovered' by nobs. Once they're discovered the nobs come in droves and up go the prices."

Mr. Coe was in great form. He discussed our purchases and declared that on the whole we had done well.

"You tumbled to it," he said, laughing. "I could hardly keep my face straight over that wooden table. I couldn't believe you really wanted that table—a great clumsy thing! I couldn't believe my ears when you said, 'That's not a bad table, Mr. Coe.' Why didn't you take the other table? It was a good bit of furniture."

"I wanted a solid table," I said.

"You've got that," he declared. "It's solid. It would take an elephant to knock that table over. It's all scratched too."

"It needs to be sand-papered, that's all."

"We paid too much for the mirror but the chest of drawers was a bargain; so was the divan. If you're handy with tools I'll lend you some and you can mend that leg yourself."

Next day I got off early from the office and went to a good shop in the Strand. I bought a plain iron bed and a mattress, a pillow, blankets and sheets. I also bought a kettle and a couple of saucepans. Woolworth's provided me with knives, forks and spoons and the necessary china. These things cost nearly as much as all the other stuff put together but I had to have them. I nearly forgot towels and dish cloths and cleaning materials—it is amazing all the odds and ends one needs to set up house.

I spent Friday evening cleaning the flat and on Saturday afternoon the furniture arrived from Mr. Mackenzie's store. Two men brought the stuff and they were not pleased when they discovered they had to carry it up to the attic. The bed and the other things came too, and a very neat little electric radiator which I had not ordered. Mr. Coe said it was a present from him and told me to air the mattress and blankets.

"I don't want you to get rheumatism," said Mr. Coe when I thanked him. "If you get rheumatism in your knees that flat will be empty again. I'm sick of having that flat empty." It was late when I got everything settled; the rug on the floor, the curtains hung, the furniture just as I wanted it. When I had drawn the curtains and lighted the standard lamp I was delighted with the results of my efforts. The room looked snug and cosy, there was a friendly feeling about it. I had made a home.

If I had planned things better I could have moved straight in but I had no food and the shops were all shut so I had to go back to the boarding-house for the week-end. On Monday evening I packed my suitcase and told Mrs. Hall I was going.

"Not now—this minute!" exclaimed Mrs. Hall, looking at my suitcase.

"Yes, now," I replied. "I'll pay you up to Wednesday of course."

"And two pounds over and above," said Mrs. Hall firmly. "People what leaves their rooms sudden pays two pounds over and above. That's only fair. It takes time to find a nice respectable guest and I'll be out of pocket."

"But I gave you a week's notice."

"Two pounds over and above," she repeated. "That's what's done under the circumstances. It's the right thing, Mr. Kirke."

I was pretty sure it was not the right thing but I was anxious to escape before the other boarders came down to supper. I took out the two pounds and gave it to her without a word.

"What's the address?" she asked, pursuing me on to the doorstep.

"It doesn't matter," I told her and I ran down the steps for the last time.

Mr. Coe was shutting up the shop when I arrived. I helped him to put up the shutters and he asked me to come and have supper with him. It was all ready in his little parlour; rabbit stew and onions, a pot of tea and a tin of condensed milk. It was an odd sort of supper but the stew was well cooked and I enjoyed it. I enjoyed Mr. Coe's company as well. He was cheerful and amusing and full of odd bits of knowledge which he had picked up in a varied and interesting life. When he was young he had joined the Merchant Navy and had been all over the world; then he had fallen heir to his uncle's book-shop and had settled down to read and improve his mind.

"That's the right way to do it," Mr. Coe explained. "See the world when you're young and nippy, and then sit down and read. I've never been married—never wanted to marry—but that doesn't mean I've never had a sweetheart, you know."

"A girl in every port?"

"Well, that's a bit exaggerated," declared Mr. Coe, chuckling. "A girl here and there but nothing serious. I'll tell you about some of my adventures one of these days. I could make a good story if I could write."

"Have you tried?" I asked.

"H'm," he said. "I've had a try but it isn't my line. Comes out dull as ditch-water. But we were talking about marriage, weren't we? Marriage is a mug's game. Don't you get married, Kirke."

"No, I don't intend to."

He smiled at me and continued, "You'll have your work cut out to escape. They're after you all the time. You've got to run pretty fast to escape the females."

"Or live in an attic," I suggested.

"H'm," he said. "You think you're safe in an attic, do you?" We talked about books after that. He adored Dickens. "Dickens was a Londoner," said Mr. Coe. "He walked the London streets and he knew the people. He knew them inside out. You may say his characters are overdrawn— the bad ones too bad and the good ones too good—but that's a healthy way to see people, Kirke. In modern novels the good and the bad are mixed up so you never know where you are. More often than not the hero behaves like a cad and you're expected to like him just the same. Give me Dickens," said Mr. Coe earnestly. "I know where I am with Dickens. The hero is good and the villain is bad—that's what I like."

I had read most of Dickens but not *Our Mutual Friend* which was Mr. Coe's favourite. When Mr. Coe discovered this lamentable fact he rose at once and we went into the little shop and found a copy of it, an ancient dog-eared volume with Cruickshank illustrations.

"Read it," said Mr. Coe, handing it to me. "It's well worth reading. I envy you, Kirke. I wish I was going to read it for the first time . . . and take anything else you like so long as you put it back in the same place. Not new books, of course, but any of the old ones."

I thanked him warmly and said good night.

THE FOURTH WINDOW

"My window looked out on to roofs of all shapes and sizes sloping in all directions: upon jutting gables and hundreds of chimney-pots. The whole aspect was topsy-turvy, it was a choppy sea of roofs. The gables cut sharply across the night sky: in the bright moonlight their slates shone like silver and their shadows were black as pitch. It was a curious outlook, quite different from any of my other windows, and strictly speaking it was ugly . . . but it was ugly in an interesting way. There was history here: not the sort of history which finds its way into books but the history of ordinary people."

CHAPTER TWENTY-TWO

THE stairs were steep and my suitcase was heavy so I was somewhat breathless when I arrived at the top landing. I opened the door of my flat and went in, bolting it behind me. Here I was at last in my own place; it belonged to me, everything in the room was mine. I could do as I liked; I could live my own life.

The room was full of moonlight; I could see the moon, far and peaceful, floating like a huge silvery balloon in the dark sky. I did not put on the light but went across to the window and opened it. Then I kneeled down with my elbows on the sill and looked out.

I had been too busy putting things in order to take much notice of the view from the window of my new abode; I had glanced at it hastily and had gained a vague impression of roofs and chimneys but now that I had leisure to look at it properly I saw what a very curious view it was. My window looked out on to roofs of all shapes and sizes sloping in all directions; upon jutting gables and hundreds of chimney-pots. The whole aspect was topsy-turvy; it was a choppy sea of roofs. The gables cut sharply across the night sky; in the bright moonlight their slates shone like silver and their shadows were black as pitch. It was a curious outlook, quite different from any of my other windows, and strictly speaking it was ugly . . . but it was ugly in an interesting way. There was history here; not the sort of history which fords its way into books, but the history of ordinary people. Thousands of people had lived in these houses and had reshaped them to suit their needs. This one had thrown out a gable; that one had built on a room; somebody else had wanted more light and enlarged his window or wanted more space and heightened his roof. There was something very human and cosy and friendly about the view from the window of my room.

Thousands of people had lived here and died—or gone away—but there were hundreds of people living here still, behind those curtained windows—mysterious people, living their own lives, sleeping quietly in their own beds—and although they lived within a stone's throw of my flat I should never know them.

By leaning out of my window and looking down to the left I could see a section of the street and a lamp-post which made a pool of amber light upon the cobblestones. A man and a girl were dallying there, and the night was so still that I could hear the murmur of their voices and their laughter. I leaned out a little further and looked to the right; some distance away there was a taller house with a high straight side in which were eight windows. Most of these were dark, some showed chinks of light at the corners, but one was brightly lighted and uncurtained so that the whole room was visible and I could see a man in grey trousers and a white shirt with the sleeves rolled up above his elbows. The man was alone in the room but he was behaving in a very curious way. He was walking to and fro, talking and gesticulating wildly. Every now and then he paused and threw up his hands in a gesture of despair or shook his fist threateningly in the face of a non-existent antagonist. For several minutes I watched him in bewilderment (what on earth was he doing?) and at last I came to the conclusion that he was an actor rehearsing a theatrical rôle.

Presently my new neighbour grew tired. He came to the window and stood there quite peacefully, looking up at the sky. Then he stretched his arms and drew the curtains; I could hear the rattle of the old-fashioned rings upon the rod. The play was over.

It was bed-time now so I pulled my own curtains and began to undress, emptying my pockets as usual and laying their contents upon the table. It was only then that I realised the condition of my finances: I had four and elevenpence, no more and no less, to last me until Friday.

What a fool! I thought, looking at the coins in dismay.

As a matter of fact it was not quite so foolish as it sounds. I had budgeted very carefully and left myself enough to carry on quite comfortably, but Mrs. Hall had forced me to pay her two pounds "over and above." It was a ramp, of course (she had no right to the extra money and I had known it at the time), but it had been easier to pay than to argue, so I had paid.

Four and elevenpence to last me until Friday! It would be all right after that, for on Friday I should get my week's salary from Mr. Heatley, but how was I going to exist until then?

I thought it over seriously. Should I borrow from Mr. Coe? I was sure he would lend it to me if I asked him . . . but Ned's little games had put me off borrowing and I did not want to begin my acquaintanceship with Mr. Coe by asking him to lend me money. The mere idea was distasteful. Besides it was my own fault entirely. Only a mug would have paid Mrs. Hall that money and paid it without a murmur. It was my own fault and I must make the best of it.

There was no food in the flat—literally nothing—when I went into the little kitchen to get a drink of water the clean dishes on the shelves and the gleaming aluminium pans seemed to be laughing at me.

"All right, you can laugh," I said aloud. "I'll manage somehow. I shan't starve."

It did not take long to complete my preparations for the night. I got into my new bed, stretched out my legs and relaxed utterly. How comfortable it was. How firm and straight and clean! Nobody had ever slept in it before, nobody had ever laid their head upon my nice new pillow . . .

When I awoke it was eight o'clock and the sun was shining brightly. I woke slowly and luxuriously; I came up to the surface from the depths of sleep like a diver emerging from a deep dark pool of placid water. The bedroom was bare. There was nothing in it except the bed and the chest of drawers (I had put all the other stuff in the sitting-room). The window was wide open and the noise of the market came to my ears, the noise of cars and carts and shouting, but it seemed to me a friendly noise and it did not worry me. After a bit I got up and drank a glass of water and set off to the office.

There was a coffee bar at the corner and I was so hungry that I stopped and had a cup of coffee and a roll. I knew it was foolish but I had it all the same.

The day seemed long. I had no lunch and when I came out of the office I was ravenous. But I had made up my mind what I was going to do. On the way home I bought four large loaves of brown bread and I went into a fish shop and asked for a cod's head.

The fishmonger looked at me in surprise.

"It's for the cat," I mumbled. "Any odds and ends will do."

He gave me a bag of unsavoury looking scraps and when I had paid him for it I had fivepence left. Then I went home and boiled the scraps and ate what I could with the brown bread and washed it down with water. I spent the evening reading *Our Mutual Friend* and went to bed.

Hunger woke me early, but not too early for the market which already was in full swing. I had wanted to see the market and here was my chance. I went downstairs and let myself out of the shop and in a moment I was in the middle of it. The narrow streets were full of huge lorries; the open bazaars were full of men and packing-cases and crates. The noise was deafening, everybody seemed in a hurry, shouldering along, calling, shouting, bargaining. There were stalls piled high with vegetables, flowers and fruit. The whole place was in such confusion that it was impossible to stand still and look on—which was what I wanted to do. Everybody else was moving; men with trollies came rattling past calling out "Mind your back!"

"Look out there!" Men with crates balanced on their heads or with hampers upon their shoulders pushed through the crowd. There were a few policemen about; they were endeavouring to keep the traffic moving but without much success. I spoke to one of them and asked if it were always like this.

"It's worse at week-ends," he replied. "But they're not so bad—not really. It looks 'opeless but it sorts itself out. If you want to stand still and 'ave a look you could park yourself be'ind that pillar . . ."

He raised his voice and shouted, "Look out, there! This is a one-way street and you know it as well as I do. You'll 'ave to back."

There was a girl sheltering behind the pillar, she was dressed in slacks and a loose coat and I put her down as an artist.

"It's fun, isn't it?" she said. "It gives me something. It's so old and so new . . . and it's mostly good-natured."

"It's very English," I suggested.

She smiled and nodded. "Have you been here before?" she asked.

I told her that it was new to me and explained that I had just moved in to a flat near-by—an attic flat in a very old house.

"What fun!" she exclaimed. "Of course this part of London used to be very fashionable at one time. All sorts of interesting people lived here."

We chatted for a few minutes. She knew the history of the district and told me (what I had always wanted to know) that the name Covent Garden, was a corruption of Convent Garden. Long ago it was the garden of the Abbey of Westminster and people came here to buy fruit and vegetables from the monks. Gradually it became a market and at the beginning of the nineteenth century the Duke of Bedford built the big hall of Arcades which is now known as Charter Market.

"I like the architecture, don't you?" said the girl. "Many of the buildings were designed by Inigo Jones—and of course he designed the Church of St. Paul's at the same time. The buildings are Italian in style; you can't see them properly in all this hurly burly."

"It seems a mixture of architecture."

"Oh yes," she agreed. "That's what happened last century. They built all sorts of rubbish and hid the beautiful bits . . . all these crowded narrow streets!" she laughed and added: "I met an American here the other day and he said the whole place ought to be pulled down and a market built upon the site on modern lines. I was a bit horrified at first, but of course he was right from his point of view; Covent Garden is the most inconvenient market in the world. We happen to like it—that's all. We don't mind the inconveniences and cramped quarters; we shouldn't be nearly so happy in a well-designed, modern market run on properly disciplined lines. My American couldn't understand this, of course. Why should he?"

"No," I said slowly. "It's rather interesting when you think of it."

"The inconvenience of Covent Garden is beyond words," continued the girl. "It isn't only the market itself, it's the approaches. Every street for miles around is blocked every morning by hundreds of lorries converging upon the place from all directions: the Strand, Kingsway, Bedford Street all blocked! You couldn't do anything about that unless you pulled down half London."

"You explained that to your American of course."

"Oh yes! He was all for pulling down half London," laughed the girl.

"Tell me more," I said. "Tell me how it's run."

"There isn't much plan," she replied. "The whole affair is a bit haphazard in true English style. The lorries time themselves to be on their pitch between four and five o'clock and are off again about nine. By that time most of the business of the day is over. Most of the big growers have their own pitches so that anyone who wants to do business with them knows where to find them. They have their own porters too."

"They ought to be well paid," I said, looking at one of them who was staggering past with a tower of baskets balanced on his head.

"They are," replied my new friend. "Some of them make £11 a week. They make enough during the season to keep them for the rest of the year."

"Why the hurry?" I asked. "It's the hurry that makes the confusion."

"The stuff is perishable, that's why. If the growers lose the market they're left with it on their hands. It's useless. It's a dead loss. And that's why the prices fluctuate. If there's a shortage the prices go up by leaps and bounds and if there's a glut you can buy perfectly sound stuff for half nothing. That's why I'm waiting, you see."

"That's why you're waiting?"

"I buy for a small hotel," explained the girl. "I come here three times a week and buy all the fruit and vegetables we need—flowers too, of course. At first I used to dash in early but now I've got wise and I wait for the right moment. It's a bit tricky because if you wait too long you may find that there's a shortage of the stuff you happen to want and the price has risen. You've got to judge; you've got to get the feel of the market. There's lots of stuff to-day and if I wait for a bit I shall get things cheap. That's the idea."

It seemed a funny job for a girl and I said so.

"I love it," she said, smiling. "It's fun. I know a lot of the big growers and most of them are awfully nice. They look out for me and help me no end. Of course some of them are nasty but that doesn't worry me. I used to teach in a School of Domestic Economy but I like this job heaps better. I'll have to go now," she added. "The time has come to talk of cabbages . . . perhaps I'll see you again sometime."

She faded into the crowd and disappeared.

By this time most of the lorries had finished unloading; the traffic was beginning to move and, very slowly, to disperse. But just opposite where I was standing things seemed to have got behind-hand. A huge lorry, piled high with crates of cauliflowers had pulled up at the entrance to an arcade and was beginning to unload. It was obvious from the confusion that the lorry had been delayed en route.

I crossed the street to see what was happening and was amused by the antics of a small stout man with a very red face who was superintending the operations. He was bellowing directions to the porters, cursing and swearing and waving his arms.

"This is the second time in a week you've bin late!" cried the red-faced man with a string of lurid oaths. "Engine trouble, my, foot! It's lazy—that's wot you are! I'm short-'anded any 'ow—and you turn up at this hour. Get a move on, can't you! Wot the blazes d'you think you're doing! I could 'ave sold them caulies twice over 'alf an hour ago." In their haste to get unloaded one of the men threw a crate on to the pavement where it burst like a bomb. Cauliflowers flew in all directions—the place was strewn with cauliflowers. Some of the passers-by laughed at the accident and this annoyed the red-faced man still more. He was so furious that words failed him and he began to kick the cauliflowers into the street.

"Look here!" I cried, seizing his arm. "Don't you want them? If you don't want those cauliflowers give them to me!" He gazed at me in amazement. I suppose I looked too respectably dressed to be begging for cauliflowers which were rolling in the gutter.

"Give them to me," I repeated, shouting to make myself heard above the din. "Look here—I tell you what—I'll help you to unload if you give me some of those cauliflowers."

"What the blazes—" he began.

"You're in a hurry," I said. "Well, I'll help you. You said you were short-handed. Is it a bargain?"

"All right, get on with it," he replied.

I took off my jacket and started without more ado. As a matter of fact I had been watching the porters and it had looked easy; they swung the crates as if they were full of feathers, but I discovered that the crates were very heavy indeed, it took me all my time to lift them. I was soft, of course, for I had had very little exercise all the winter and I was unskilled into the bargain. The porters were amused at my attempts to help them but they were quite decent about it; probably they thought I was doing it for a joke.

When the job was finished I went up to the red-faced man and reminded him of his promise. He had calmed down a bit by this time.

"I've bin watchin' you," he said, smiling. "Never done this before, 'ave you? 'Ot work, ain't it?"

"Yes," I agreed wiping my face. "I'm not very good at it, I'm afraid!"

"You'll learn all right. D'you want a job, young feller?"

"No, I've got a job. I'm off to it now," I told him. "I just want some of those cauliflowers."

"Take the whole blooming lot," said the red-faced man. "You can 'ave a few tomatoes too. There's a crate of bruised tomatoes somewhere. If you like to turn up same time tomorrow morning I'll give you some more. You ain't much use, but you're better than nothing."

"All right," I said.

The cauliflowers had been thrown into a corner; most of them were too badly crushed to be eaten, but I chose three which were moderately sound and I filled my pockets with tomatoes.

"'Ere, catch!" shouted the red-faced man and he threw me a couple of oranges.

There was no time to cook the cauliflowers, but they would do for supper. My breakfast consisted of a chunk of dry bread and tomatoes. I cut another chunk of bread to eat at lunch-time and put it in my pocket.

As I walked to the office I felt well and happy. There was no hardship about it. The rough brown bread had a pleasant nutty flavour; it was filling and I had plenty to last me till Friday, so there was nothing to worry about. I thought of breakfast at Mrs. Hall's; her "guests" would be eating greasy sausages or scrambled eggs swimming about in yellow water. I did not envy them. The only thing that annoyed me was the fact that I had put up with the discomforts of Mrs. Hall's boarding-house for so long and had paid so much good money for so much bad food. It was incredibly foolish of me. As a matter of fact if I had not happened to see that notice in the window of Mr. Coe's bookshop I should be there still!

The other clerks went off at half-past twelve as usual and, when I had finished typing a letter for Mr. Penman, I got a glass of water from the tap in the washing-room and sat down to my meal. I ate the bread slowly and drank the water. This was all right; indeed it was great deal more pleasant than the restaurant where I usually had lunch. The restaurant was hot and crowded and the waitresses were so busy that it was difficult to get served. Here I had peace. There was no reason why I should not continue to have my lunch here. I could make some sandwiches and bring fruit.

"Hallo, Kirke!" exclaimed Mr. Heatley. Mr. Heatley had his lunch at one; he was on his way out but he stopped and stared at me. "What's up?" he asked.

"Nothing, sir. I'm having my lunch—"

"Bread and water! What's the matter with you? Are you doing penance or something?"

"No, I like it. I mean—"

"Well, what is it? I suppose you've been gambling, you young idiot. Lost your shirt on a horse?"

"No, sir," I said.

Mr. Heatley stood and waited and I realised I should have to tell him the whole story. In a way he had a right to know. I made the story as short as I could but he kept on interrupting and asking questions, so it took some time to tell. I told him about the dirt and discomfort of the boarding-house and how I had found the flat and used all my money to furnish it.

"You should have left yourself something to feed on," commented Mr. Heatley.

"I did," I replied. "But Mrs. Hall rooked me out of two pounds; she said it was the usual thing when you gave up your room."

"Nonsense! A week's notice is the usual thing. Why didn't you ask me? A week's rent or a week's notice is all she was entitled to."

I did not reply. Mr. Heatley would have thought me an even bigger fool if I had told him the truth; if I had told him that I had paid the money because I wanted to escape, because I wanted to avoid saying good-bye to my fellow-boarders.

"How much have you got?" asked Mr. Heatley after a moment's silence.

"Fivepence, sir," I replied, smiling. "But I've got plenty of bread—"

"Fivepence! Good Lord! Why on earth didn't you ask me to give you an advance?"

" I never thought of it."

"You never thought of it! Here you are!" said Mr. Heatley, fishing in his pocket. "Take a pound. That ought to see you through."

"No, sir. I don't want it."

"You don't want it?"

"I'd rather not," I said.

"Why?" he asked, staring at me.

This was difficult to answer because I had no idea why I did not want the money.

"Why?" repeated Mr. Heatley.

"I want to be independent," I replied, groping for words. "It's—it's a sort of game, really. I want to manage on my own."

"Oh well," he said with a chuckle. "It's a sort of game, is it? A funny sort of game if you ask me! You're a fool, Kirke, but perhaps it's a pity there aren't more fools of your kidney knocking about. I can't see Ullenwood starving on bread and water because he was too proud to accept an advance—nor Wrigson either. What are you having for supper, if it isn't a rude question?"

"Cauliflowers, sir."

"Cauliflowers!"

I told him how I had acquired the cauliflowers and he laughed. "That's a good story," he said. "I'm dining out to-night and I shall tell the story of the cauliflower bomb."

This was the first time Mr. Heatley had spoken to me about anything except my work; I had thought him a stiff old poker—when I had thought of him at all—but now I realised he was human and kindly.

We were still talking when Mr. Penman came in; Mr. Penman looked at us in surprise. I had a feeling Mr. Penman was not very pleased to see me hob-nobbing with the Boss and I wondered why—it seemed absurd to suspect him of jealousy!

CHAPTER TWENTY-THREE

THAT evening I stayed on at the office later than usual to check some figures for Mr. Heatley. There was nobody in the office except myself, everybody else had gone. I finished the work quickly and, as I took my hat from the rack, I suddenly felt happy. I was going home. I was done with Mrs. Hall and her "guests." They would all sit round the table with the stained cloth in front of them and the harsh light overhead and they would carp at one another. They would all complain and nobody would listen; Madame Futrelle would poke malicious fun at Beryl—they were always up against each other—Miss Bulwer would whine about her indigestion and Mr. Kensey about the unkindness of his relations. Ned would sit, lost in gloomy dreams, wondering how he was going to make ends meet without somebody from whom he could borrow, and Mrs. Hall would preside over the table watching to see that her "guests" did not take more than their fair share of the food she provided . . . but I had decided not to think about these people any more (it depressed me to think of them and I could do them no good) so I banished them from my mind.

I locked the door of the office and ran down the steps and, as I did so, somebody moved forward and stood in front of me. It was Beryl.

"David!" she exclaimed, seizing my arm. "Oh, David, you never said good-bye!"

"How did you know I was here?"

"Mrs. Hall told me. She knew the address of the office . . . so I came to meet you. Oh, David, it was horrid of you to slink off like that without saying good-bye. I couldn't believe it when Mrs. Hall said you'd gone. I simply—couldn't—believe it!"

"I hate saying good-bye," I told her. "There's no point in it; but we can say good-bye now if that's what you want."

"Let's go and have supper together, David."

"I'm going home to supper," I told her . . . and I thought of the cauliflowers and smiled.

"Where?" she asked, looking up at me. "Where are you staying?"

"In a flat in a friend's house. I told you that before."

"Let's go there and talk, shall we? I want to see your flat so that I can think about you. Is it near Mrs. Hall's?"

"No," I said. "It's in—it's in a friend's house. He's a bachelor and he doesn't like women. I can't take you there." I held out my hand and added, "Good-bye, Beryl."

Beryl did not take my hand. "We could go to the pictures," she wheedled. "Do let's go to the pictures. I don't want to go back to Mrs. Hall's. It's worse than ever now you've gone. Mrs. Hall hasn't been able to let your room, she's as cross as a bear about it, and Ned has got the sack—so you can imagine what he's like! Let's do something together, David."

"I'm afraid I can't," I said.

"Oh, David, you're still angry! Why won't you be friends? Please be friends with me. It's so unkind and unfair of you to be angry. I told you it wasn't my fault that we drove away and left you behind. I told you I made them stop and go back."

The party seemed so long ago that for a moment I could not think what she meant. Then I remembered. "Goodness!" I exclaimed. "I'm not angry about *that*."

"You're angry about something."

"I'm not angry at all. Listen, Beryl, why don't you make it up with Ned? You and Ned both like parties; you like the same things. Ned's very fond of you—"

"Ned's selfish," she said in a trembling voice. "He thinks of himself all the time. You know he does."

I looked at her and saw her eyes were full of tears and I felt very sorry for her.

"Beryl, it's no good," I said. "I can't take you out to supper, because I've no money."

"No money! I thought you had lots of money!"

I laughed. "Well, you were wrong," I said. "I've no money to take girls out to supper or to pictures or anything else, so it isn't the slightest use for you to bother with me any more."

"But David, we're friends, aren't we?"

"Look!" I said, taking the five pennies out of my pocket. "There, Beryl! That's all I've got to last me to the end of the week."

She looked at the coppers in amazement. "How are you going to eat?" she asked.

"I've got some bread and three cauliflowers."

Beryl hesitated. I wondered if she would offer to lend me money. I would not have taken it from her, but I rather hoped she would offer it.

"I don't believe you," she said at last, but she said it without conviction.

"It's true," I told her. "That's all I've got."

"I don't believe you!" she cried. "You're just being horrid. I thought you were nice—you seemed different from the others—but you're just horrid."

"All right, I'm horrid," I agreed and I turned and walked away. I felt "horrid" too, but it was no good. I could not be friends with her. To be friends with Beryl meant spending a lot of money; it meant taking her out and giving her meals, and, even if I had wanted to do it, I could not afford it. *Even* if I had wanted to . . . and I did not want to.

When I got to the corner I looked back and she was still standing in the same place. All the way home I thought about her and argued with myself. It was absurd to feel upset about Beryl; she was a "gold-digger." Beryl wanted somebody to take her out and give her a good time—anybody would do. All the same I felt upset about her and it was not until I had cooked the cauliflowers and had my supper that I was able to get her out of my mind.

The next morning (and all that week) I got up early and helped to unload before I went to the office. I discovered that the red-faced man was called Mr. Smith and he was a decent soul in spite of his fiery temper and foul language. He gave me all I could use in the way of slightly damaged fruit and vegetables which kept me going comfortably. I had hoped to see the girl again but I was too busy to keep a look-out for her and as a matter of fact it was extremely difficult to see anybody in the crowded streets. The unwonted exercise made me stiff at first but I got used to it and I made up my mind to carry on with the job; it saved money to get fruit and vegetables for nothing. There were still things I wanted to make the flat comfortable and the more I could save the sooner I could have them.

When Friday came I was tired of nothing but bread and vegetables and although I felt perfectly fit I had lost a good deal of weight.

Mr. Heatley smiled when he gave me my week's salary. "Well, Kirke," he said. "Your fast is over, I suppose."

"Yes, sir," I replied. "It's been all right."

"I suppose your pockets are empty?"

I laughed and showed him that I still had the five pennies left.

"How did you do it?" he asked. "Well, never mind now. Come and have supper with us on Sunday night; I'll hear about it then. I told my wife the story of the cauliflowers and she wants to meet you."

I thanked him and accepted. To tell the truth I was not particularly anxious to go to supper with the Heatleys—the prospect alarmed me— but there was no way of getting out of it. Mr. Heatley's invitation was in the nature of a Royal Command.

It was good to have money to spend and when I got out of the office I went straight to the Wooden Spoon and had a solid meal and a glass of beer. It was the best meal I had ever tasted.

On Sunday evening I spruced myself up and went to supper at the Heatleys'. Mrs. Heatley was delightful, she was much younger than Mr. Heatley and full of fun. They asked me all sorts of questions, first about my "week of starvation" and then about my home. Mrs. Heatley had been to Haines, she had stayed at Drumburly when she was a girl and knew the district quite well, so there was plenty to talk about. I discovered that my host and hostess had not been married long; it was obvious that they were very fond of each other. Mr. Heatley was quite different at home; he enjoyed being teased by his wife and played up to her in the most amusing way . . . I laughed until I cried to see him fooling about and pretending to be the butler.

"You must come again soon," said Mr. Heatley as he saw me out at the door. "It's good for Sylvia to have somebody young to talk to. I'm an old fogey, you know."

"There's not much old fogey about you," I told him. I should have liked to say more but I was afraid he might think it impertinent.

It was so long since I had spoken to cheerful pleasant people and enjoyed good talk that I felt quite elated as I walked home. The streets were quiet at this hour and my footsteps sounded loud upon the pavements.

CHAPTER TWENTY-FOUR

WHEN I had been in my new abode for a week I felt settled and comfortable. I could feed myself better and live more cheaply than at Mrs. Hall's. Mr. Coe was very good to me but I helped him in various ways, so it was not one-sided. In the morning, before I went to the office, I took down the shutters for him; sometimes if I were home in time I put them up at night. They were heavy old-fashioned shutters and it was difficult for him to climb the ladder and fix the bolts. It was no bother to me.

When his knees were painful I did his shopping for him and once or twice when he wanted to go out he left me in charge of the shop. This job amused me vastly. I had never expected to serve in a shop. It reminded me of the times when Freda and I played at shops together in the old ruined cottage on the banks of the Ling.

"Good afternoon, sir!" I would say to Mr. Coe's customers.

"What can I do for you?"

Usually they looked round vaguely and said, "Where's Mr. Coe?" but when I explained that Mr. Coe was out they would tell me what they wanted. The books were not listed nor properly arranged, which made it difficult, but if I could not find the books they asked for, I could at least be polite and pleasant and suggest that they should come back later and see the proprietor.

Quite soon I realised that Mr. Coe was lonely. He knew plenty of people in the way of business but he was an individual sort of man with odd ideas and he had no real friends who could share his interests. Sometimes Mr. Coe was irritable but I knew he suffered a good deal of pain so if I found him in a grumpy mood I left him alone and did not worry.

In the evenings, when I had had my supper and washed up, I settled down to write. It was quiet and peaceful and there were no interruptions. I began to write articles for the papers but it bothered me to think of what would please editors; the articles were dull and worthless, there was no life in them. At last I gave up trying and I began to write for my own pleasure about things that interested me. I wrote about Covent Garden, about people that I saw in the Park, about the river and the Tower. I wrote about Dickens walking at night in the streets of London, with his lame leg and his seeing eye, and making friends with all sorts and conditions of his fellow citizens. I put in some history—odd scraps of history which I picked up from old books in Mr. Coe's shop—and I illustrated it as I went along with little sketches. I wrote about Haines, too. Somehow I could see Haines very clearly—it was all inside my head—and this reminded me of Robert Louis Stevenson who wrote so feelingly about the scenes of his childhood when he was living on a South Sea island thousands of miles away. Writing all this made me think of the story about Malcolm which I had written so long ago, and oddly enough the same thing happened: at first it was difficult to get going but afterwards it came easily and my pencil flew. The work gave me a great deal of pleasure and amusement; it made the evenings pass like lightning and I was obliged to make a hard and fast rule to go to bed at eleven o'clock or I should have been writing all night. No editor would look at it of course because it was just my own ideas about things. It was not a diary, nor a guide book, it was not a series of essays. In fact I could not say what it was. At the back of my mind was the idea that mother would enjoy it. When it was finished—if ever it was finished—I thought I would send it to Mother to put in the wooden chest.

The illustrations amused me too. Some were comic and others serious but they were all extremely simple. I reduced them to a minimum of lines. There was a drawing of a tiny, bow-legged Covent Garden porter carrying an enormous crate of vegetables which consisted of eight bold lines and some shading. This was my favourite.

My letters from home were addressed to the office and I left it like that and did not tell Mother I had moved. I knew she would only worry and I decided to wait until I could tell her I was settled in my new quarters. When at last I wrote and broke the news I was able to tell her it was a great success and I was comfortable and happy; I told her I had begun to write again (which I knew would please her); last but not least I was able to tell her that Mr. Heatley had raised my salary.

Mother's reaction to my letter was surprising. She replied by return of post saying she and Father were very much distressed to hear I had moved. It seemed a pity when I had got to know the people in the boarding-house—and Mrs. Hall had seemed so kindly. It would be lonely for me living in a flat by myself Who looked after me and gave me my breakfast? What would happen if I were ill?

I could not help laughing when I read Mother's letter. It was my own fault of course. I had made a point of writing home cheerfully (sometimes it had been difficult to write cheerfully from that Slough of Despond), evidently I had managed to give an entirely false picture of the conditions and to conceal the horrors from my loving parents. The best of the joke was that Mother herself would not have stayed in that boarding-house half an hour; the dirt and discomfort would have disgusted her.

Mother's letter came when I was having breakfast and I wrote off at once assuring her that I was much happier living alone, that I cooked my own meals myself and was as fit as a fiddle. It was a short note, I had no time for more, and I posted it on my way to the office. Mother replied immediately to say she was coming to London to see me and I was to book a room for her in a hotel.

The news that Mother was coming to London was absolutely staggering, it was fantastic. Mother in London! I could not believe it was true. I thought vaguely about a hotel and then I realised I could have her in the flat. I could give her my bedroom and sleep on the divan. It would be tremendous fun to entertain Mother in my own place!

When Mr. Coe heard the news he offered to lend me some furniture and I accepted gladly for I wanted to make everything as comfortable as I could. He lent me a carpet for the bedroom and a couple of chairs and a small wardrobe and a few other odds and ends.

Mr. Coe did not visit me often, but the evening before Mother's arrival he came puffing up the stairs like a small steam-tug and had a good look round.

"It's clean," he said. "I thought it would be a mess. Who cleans it?"

"I do," I said, laughing. "I had enough dirt at the boarding-house to last me all my life."

"She'll want a bedside table and a lamp. If you come downstairs I'll give them to you . . . and an eiderdown quilt. We must make her comfortable, you know. We don't want her to say it's a pig-sty and whisk you away."

"I won't let her whisk me away."

"I'd be sorry. You and I get on pretty well together. The other tenants are not my style, I've nothing in common with them. Take the Waldrons, for instance. The other day I said to Waldron I'd give him a book to read—any book he liked—and he said he never read anything except the papers. He said he liked true stories, not made-up ones. Then I said, what about history? And he said, 'That's over and done with. All that matters to me is what happens between the time I was born and the time when I die.' What can you do with a man like that, David?"

"Not much," I said.

"Not anything," declared Mr. Coe. "A man like that is no use to me. I've no patience with him."

Mother was travelling south by the night train which arrives at Euston early in the morning and I was so excited that I could not sleep. I rose at five and got everything ready and then set out to meet her. The odd thing was I still did not really believe she was coming and it was not until the train drew in and I saw her step on to the platform that I knew it was true. She did not see me at first and she looked bewildered. She looked small and lost . . . it was incredible to see her here, in London, amongst the crowds. Mother belonged to Haines, to the hills and the river; to the manse with its quiet rooms and sedate old-fashioned air.

"Mother!" I exclaimed, rushing at her in excitement.

"Oh, Davie!" she cried. "I was wondering how I would ever find my way. It *was* good of you to come and meet me so early—"

"Good of me! Of course I came! I was so excited I never slept a wink. Where's your luggage?"

She had a big suitcase and a brown wicker hamper with a lid. I picked them up and led the way out of the station and called a taxi.

So far I had not had time to look at her properly but now I saw she was exactly the same. I laughed.

"What are you laughing at?" she asked.

"You," I told her. "You, here in London! It's the best joke in the world. I couldn't believe you'd really come. I couldn't believe Father would let you."

"Father wanted me to come."

"Wanted you to come!"

"We were a bit worried about you, Davie."

"Goodness! There's no need to worry about me. I told you in my letter I was getting on famously. Why did you worry?"

"London is a big city—and you're very young."

"I was pretty green at first," I admitted. "But not now. I've learnt to look after myself and keep my end up."

"You seem—older, Davie."

"I've had some funny experiences," I said. "I've met some funny people. That teaches you."

"You booked a room for me?"

"No," I said smiling at her. "You're coming to my flat. It's a very comfortable flat and much nicer than a room in a frowsty hotel. Of course there are a lot of stairs but you won't mind that, will you?"

We were driving through the streets and already London was beginning to wake up. The sun was shining brightly, people were taking down their shutters, washing their door-steps and polishing the shop windows.

"Such a lot of people!" Mother said. "It's bewildering. Doesn't it frighten you, Davie?"

"I'm used to it now," I told her.

"I don't think I'd ever get used to it . . . and the noise! It's a frightening kind of noise . . . like wild beasts roaring in the distance."

By this time we had arrived at Covent Garden and the market was in full swing. The narrow streets were crowded; great lorries were drawn up at the kerb and crates were being unloaded, thrown on to the pavement, carried into the shops. The stalls were piled high with fruit and vegetables and gorgeous flowers; people were bargaining, shouldering their way along and dodging one another. The noise was deafening; men were bellowing to each other to move, to look out, they were shouting ribald jokes or ferocious curses.

I was used to this bedlam of course, but that morning I seemed to see it with Mother's eyes and to hear it with her ears. I glanced at her and saw she was sitting on the edge of the seat and staring at the scene with a set face.

"It's all right," I said. "This happens every morning. Nobody gets killed. As a matter of fact, it's rather fun; I often help to unload the lorries."

Mother was not listening.

The taxi crawled between the lorries—sometimes it mounted the pavement—and the driver came in for a good deal of abuse.

"Where d'you think you're going?"

"Look out, you—. Nearly 'ad me foot off!"

"'Ere, wot's the hurry?"

These and other exclamations of an unprintable nature were hurled at us from all sides. The taxi driver leaned out and replied in kind. I wondered if Mother could understand what he said, and hoped sincerely she could not.

At last we stopped at the door of the book-shop and got out. I took up Mother's suitcase and the hamper.

"What's in this?" I asked.

Mother was gazing round. "What?" she said vaguely. "Oh, the hamper! It's—it's vegetables, Davie."

She began to laugh. We laughed together. We stood on the pavement with the little hamper between us and laughed until we could hardly move. It was some time before we recovered sufficiently to climb the stairs.

It was a proud moment when I opened the door of the flat and stood aside for Mother to enter. She went in and I followed and shut the door. The little flat seemed extraordinarily peaceful after the hurly burly of the market. It looked nice, too. I had left everything ready for breakfast; the table set with a clean cloth and white china. In the middle of the table was a little bowl of spring flowers. I opened the window to the mild morning air, and hurried to put on the kettle and water for the eggs. Mother watched me; her eyes were sparkling with amusement and her mouth curled up at the corners with a smile.

"What's funny?" I asked as I bustled about. "Did you think I couldn't boil a kettle and make tea?"

"I always knew you could do anything you set your mind to," Mother declared. She looked round and added, "Your flat is nice, Davie. You've been very clever about it, I think."

"It's a home. At least that's what I feel. You don't know what a difference it makes to have a place of one's own, to be able to lock the door and keep people out."

"Who do you want to keep out?" asked Mother.

I did not answer that. While the kettle was boiling I showed her the bedroom and the kitchen and explained all my arrangements to her. I showed her my "view" and how, by leaning out of the window, it was possible to see the street far below. There was a stall piled high with vegetables and a group of people round it, bargaining with the stall-holder for his goods. This glimpse of the market started Mother to laugh all over again.

"I shall never get over it," she declared. "To think that I should have been such a fool!"

"But they're *special*. They'll taste much better because they've been grown in the manse garden."

"There's that," she agreed. "Maybe the man who carried coals to Newcastle found they burned brighter because he had brought them from his home."

While we had breakfast I talked a lot. I told Mother about the boarding-house and the dirt and discomfort and how miserable I had been.

"But you never said!" she cried. "You never told us. We thought you were happy and comfortable with Mrs. Hall. Oh, Davie, I know you did it so that we wouldn't worry, but you shouldn't have deceived us. You must promise not to deceive us again. It must have been wretched for you—badly cooked food and cracked plates!"

"The worst part was the people. They were all so miserable."

"Poor souls!" exclaimed Mother. "Poor souls! There was a girl, wasn't there? Was she miserable too?"

"Beryl?" I said. "Well—yes. She's not very happy I'm afraid."

"Do you still see her sometimes?" asked Mother in a casual sort of voice.

I could not help smiling. Mother was no actress.

"So that was why you were worrying about me!" I exclaimed. "You don't need to worry about Beryl. She doesn't attract me at all."

Mother looked at me. I think she was waiting for me to tell her more about Beryl but I was not going to tell her another word.

CHAPTER TWENTY-FIVE

IT WAS the greatest fun having Mother to stay. She was gay and happy and enjoyed everything we did. Somehow she seemed younger in London—perhaps because, she had no responsibilities. She had cast off the responsibilities of her household and of being a minister's wife, and her natural gaiety bubbled over. It was years since she had seen a play and she enjoyed those we went to with childlike zest. We went out to dinner at little restaurants in Soho; we took a steamer from Westminster to the Pool of London; we visited the Zoo and the Tower. I had to go to the office of course but she seemed quite happy to be alone . . . and when I came back it was delightful to run upstairs and open the door and find her in the flat. She always had things to tell me—funny little incidents about people she had seen in the shops or in buses—and I had plenty to tell her about what I had done. I remember thinking that being married must be something like this; but if I looked the whole world over I should never find a girl who would be such a perfect companion or suit me half as well.

My only trouble was lack of money. I wanted to give Mother a good time and it is impossible to do anything in London without money. I had spent everything I possessed on furnishing the flat and although I had saved a little in the last few weeks it soon melted away. So I went to Mr. Heatley and told him how I was situated and asked him to advance me a few pounds and deduct it from my salary. Mr. Heatley was much more approachable since I had been to supper at his house so I did not mind asking.

"Ho, ho!" he exclaimed, smiling. "Here's a come-down. I thought you liked to do things on your own and be independent!"

"This is different, sir," I said. "It's because my mother is staying with me and I want to take her about and show her things and give her a good time. If you could advance me five pounds I would be very grateful."

Mr. Heatley laughed and gave me the money. He did not believe that I wanted it to entertain my mother and I had to put up with a good deal of chaff; but it did not worry me—in fact it amused me. People often disbelieve the simple truth whereas if you tell them a thumping lie they will swallow it whole.

Somehow or other Wrigson and Ullenwood got wind of the matter and began to take some interest in me. They hinted slyly that I was a "dark horse" and when they saw I did not mind being teased they became bolder and inquired for "Mother" tenderly. Ullenwood wanted to know where "Mother" was staying and was delighted when I said she was staying with me, in my flat. Wrigson asked what I had done to entertain her. Where had we been? I said we had been to Madame Tussaud's. It was perfectly true, of course (we had been to Madame Tussaud's and enjoyed it enormously), but I knew they would not believe it—and they did not. The information was greeted by howls of laughter from my fellow clerks.

"We did, really," I said solemnly. "We went into the Chamber of Horrors. Mother was rather upset—" This also was perfectly true. Mother was so upset when she saw the guillotine that I had to take her out.

"Where are you taking 'Mother' on Sunday?" inquired Wrigson when at last he could speak.

"Hampton Court," I replied. "I don't know what's funny about it. Mother is very keen to see Hampton Court. We shall visit the maze, of course."

This made them laugh louder (as I had known it would).

"You're priceless, Kirke!" exclaimed Ullenwood, wiping his eyes.

It was thus that I acquired a reputation for wit. I wonder if anybody ever acquired a reputation for wit so easily.

The day before Mother went home I got back early. I ran down the area steps and there was Mr. Coe sitting behind the counter, reading.

Mr. Coe looked up when the shop bell tinkled.

"Oh, it's you!" he said. "A girl came here, asking for you!"

"A girl!" I exclaimed.

"A painted hussy," said Mr. Coe, looking at me over his spectacles.

I stood quite still and gazed at him. I knew who it was.

"First she asked for Penguins," continued Mr. Coe. "Then she asked for Mr. David Kirke. Wanted to know if he lived here."

"Did you—did you tell her?"

"I pretended I was surprised. 'Mr. David Kirke?' I said as if I'd never heard the name before. 'Yes,' she said. 'I know he lives here. I saw him come into this shop.' 'Lots of people come into this shop,' I told her. 'But he didn't come out again,' she said."

"She must have followed me!" I exclaimed.

"That's right," nodded Mr. Coe. "That's what she said. 'I followed him from the office and he came in here,' she said. 'He lives here,' she said. 'It's no good saying he doesn't. I'm a friend of his and I want to see him.' So then I said, 'Does he want to see you?' She didn't answer that, just stood and looked at me. Then Mrs. Kirke came in so I said, 'Oh, Mrs. Kirke, this young woman is asking about your son.'"

"Help!" I exclaimed.

"I'm sorry, David," said Mr. Coe apologetically. "I'm afraid I managed it badly. If I'd known what to say I'd have said it, but I was struck all of a heap."

"What did Mother say?"

Mr. Coe chuckled. "It was as good as a play. She knew all about the young woman; I could see that."

"Could you?"

"Of course I could. She had that young woman taped."

"But what did Mother say?"

"I couldn't tell you exactly," replied Mr. Coe, frowning thoughtfully. "Mrs. Kirke was quite polite but as chilly as an ice-berg. She gave the young woman to understand she was living here with you—well, so she is—and that choked her off properly."

I went upstairs more slowly than usual. I saw that I had been a fool not to tell Mother about Beryl. I saw I should have to tell Mother a good deal about Beryl . . . but perhaps not everything.

"So Beryl has been here!" I said as I opened the door.

Mother nodded. She was sitting near the window in the easy-chair, darning my socks. "Yes," she said. "I thought it must be Beryl."

I drew up a chair and sat down near her. "Beryl is a menace," I said. "As a matter of fact Beryl was one of the reasons why I left the boarding-house. She was worse than the cracked plates."

"Poor soul!" said Mother. "Fancy being worse than a cracked plate!"

We smiled at one another.

"Mother," I said, "I quite liked Beryl at first. I took her out to dinner one evening and we had a friendly chat . . . but after that something happened and I didn't like her any more; She keeps on saying that she wants to be friends with me but it's no use. I'm sorry for Beryl but—but that's all, really."

"I thought that was the way of it," Mother said.

"I can't do anything, can I?"

"No, David, you can't do anything."

"I feel rather a beast."

"She'll get over it," said Mother cheerfully. "She'll find somebody else. I wouldn't worry about Beryl if I were you."

While Mother was staying with me I had not been down to the Market, but the morning after she had gone I went and saw Mr. Smith.

"Ho, it's you, is it?" he said, in a grumbling voice. "I don't know as I wants you, now, young man."

"That's all right," I replied—and I turned away.

He followed me and caught my arm.

"Look 'ere," he said. "You ain't much good at portering and the porters ain't too keen to 'ave you. That's the trouble really. You might take a 'and at the blackboard if you like."

"The blackboard!" I exclaimed.

He nodded. "Jim's gone off in a 'uff and I'm pretty well stuck."

I was not surprised to hear that his assistant had left him in the lurch. His temper was so unruly that it was a wonder he had anybody to work for him. I knew about the blackboard, of course. It stood beside his stall and on it were written the prices of the produce he had for sale. The prices fluctuated so quickly that it was a whole-time job to keep them up to date. At the moment the board said "Lets 17s, Cabs 12s," which meant that lettuces were seventeen shillings a box and cabbages twelve shillings. All the stuff was wholesale, of course.

"Get on with it," said Mr. Smith, handing me a piece of chalk and a duster. "Lets are down to sixteen and nine; cabs are eleven."

"Will you pay me?" I asked. I did not see why I should take on the job for nothing.

"If you're any good," he said testily. "Get on with it, do."

I stood on a box and got on with it, altering the prices as they were called out. There was nothing difficult about it but I had to keep my ears open and follow the bargaining. As a matter of fact it amused me and I thought of Mr. Semple, the schoolmaster at Haines, and wondered what he would say if he saw me standing on a box in Covent Garden Market writing "Caulis 20s" on a blackboard. During a lull I looked across the heads of the crowd and saw the girl I had spoken to before—her eyes met mine and she smiled. Presently I felt somebody tug my coat and she was there, beside me.

"So that's your job!" she said.

"Not really, I'm just helping out. Look here, I want to speak to you. It's hopeless here and now. Come and have supper to-night at the Wooden Spoon, will you? Please come."

She looked at me in amazement (as well she might) but I did not care.

"The Wooden Spoon," I repeated. "It's just round the corner. Eight o'clock to-night."

At that moment there was a slump in the market and Smith yelled out a whole string of new prices. When I had time to look round the girl had gone.

She would not come, of course. I knew that, but all the same I brushed my suit and changed my shirt and collar and was round at the Wooden Spoon before eight. It was ten-past eight when I saw the door open and the girl come in. She looked different in a frock, older and less approachable. If she had looked like that in the morning I should not have dared to ask her to meet me.

"Look here," she said when she had made her way across the room to the table in the corner which I had engaged for our meal. "Look here—do you always pick up your female friends like that?"

"This is the first time," I told her seriously.

"It had better be the last. To be honest I don't know why I've come. I made up my mind I wouldn't."

"I'm glad you changed it."

"Who are you, anyhow?" she inquired, sitting down and taking off her gloves.

I told her who I was and where I came from and what I was doing in London. In return she told me that her name was Teddy Freer.

"You can call me Teddy," she said. "Everyone does. But before we go any further I'm twenty-eight—old enough to be your mother—and I'm engaged to a gunner who's been fighting in Korea."

"You needn't be so fierce," I said, laughing. "I want a friend, that's all. I thought you looked nice so I asked you to supper."

"I'm paying for myself."

"But I asked you—"

"I'm paying for myself, David."

"No—please—"

"All right," she said, smiling. "You can pay for my supper and I shall thank you nicely—and never come again."

"You can pay for yourself," I told her.

"Good," she said. "We understand each other."

We understood each other remarkably well—not only that night but at all our other meetings. She was lively and intelligent and interested in all the things that interested me. It was wonderful to have a real friend in London; somebody to go about with, somebody to talk to about things. Best of all Teddy liked getting out of town and we made a habit of taking a bus on Sunday afternoons and having a walk in the country.

Teddy had dark curly hair and brown eyes; she was a little like Freda to look at and perhaps that was what had attracted me to her at first but when I got to know her I found she was entirely different and I liked her for herself. She was such a dear, easy and kind and generous, nobody could have helped liking her. Sometimes I wondered what had got into me that morning at the market and made me so bold . . . and to tell the truth I wondered what had made Teddy accept my invitation to supper.

"I was bored," said Teddy when I plucked up courage to ask her. "I was bored with everything—and I thought you looked harmless. You looked about sixteen years old, standing on that box and writing sums on the blackboard."

CHAPTER TWENTY-SIX

THERE was a much better feeling at the office after Mother's visit and, although I was aware that the friendliness of my fellow clerks was founded upon a false premise, I was quite pleased about it. It was not my fault that they had not believed the sober truth.

One evening Dick Ullenwood invited me to dinner at "Kim's"; he had won some money on a horse and wanted to celebrate the occasion. I had no idea what the entertainment would be like but I accepted the invitation. Ullenwood explained that he had asked two girls and warned me in advance that Kitty was to be my partner for most of the evening.

"Don't make it too obvious, of course," said Ullenwood anxiously. "But if you *could* manage to leave Clarice to me . . . if you see what I mean."

I saw exactly what he meant and promised to carry out his instructions to the best of my ability.

"Kim's" was a very large restaurant; it was brilliantly lighted and full of little tables with red-and-white-checked table-cloths. They gave you a good plain meal and you could sit there and watch a series of music-hall turns and dramatic sketches. The place was full (all sorts of people went to "Kim's"); there were painters and art-students with long hair and flowing ties; there were casually attired undergraduates and there were a good many foreigners as well. It was cheap but clean and well-run and there was an air of natural gaiety about it.

Ullenwood had booked a table in an alcove and we settled down and prepared to enjoy ourselves. Luckily I liked Kitty much better than Clarice; she was not exactly good-looking but she was pleasant and amusing and we got on very well together.

The only untoward incident occurred about halfway through the evening. There was an interval between two of the dramatic sketches and we were discussing the performance when I became aware that somebody was standing beside me. It was Ned Mottram.

"Hallo, David!" he said. "Fancy seeing you here!" He looked at Dick Ullenwood and the two girls as he spoke and I saw he wanted me to introduce him . . . but I was determined not to do so. I rose and shook hands with Ned and asked him how he was getting on.

"Oh, all right," he replied vaguely. "I left that job at the motor show-room—the boss was an absolute stinker—but I've got another job. I'll tell you about it later. Look here, we've got a table over near the stage and we want you and your friends to join us. The more the merrier, you know." He pointed as he spoke but the room was so crowded that I could not see his companions.

" I don't think so—" I began.

"Come on, be a sport," said Ned. "We've got a much better table. It will be fun if you join us—there's Beryl and Zilla and good old Harry; you know them all, don't you?"

I knew them only too well. "I can't, Ned," I told him. "It's not my party."

"You could suggest it to them."

"No, I don't think so, Ned."

"But Beryl sent me to ask you! Look, there she is, waving."

I saw them now. Beryl was wearing the famous red dress and a large red bow in her hair; she was waving frantically—so was Zilla. Fortunately their unconstrained behaviour did not excite any interest here; "Kim's" was an unconventional place. All the same . . .

"I'm sorry, Ned," I said firmly. "You must tell Beryl that I can't do anything about it. As a matter of fact we don't want to join up with anybody. Our party is complete."

He looked somewhat crestfallen. "Oh well—" he said doubtfully. "But perhaps we could have a talk later on—just you and I. Listen, David, you could come over and join us later on. How would that do?"

This was the last thing I wanted and I realised that I should have to be firm. It had always been difficult for me to be firm where Ned was concerned because I was sorry for him. I found I was drifting into the old habit of being sorry for Ned . . . and then I looked across the room and saw Harry and Zilla and Beryl and I hardened my heart. I explained to Ned that I was a guest and it would be impossible to desert my friends.

"I shouldn't have thought that would have bothered you," declared Ned with bitter emphasis, and he went away.

"Who was that?" asked Ullenwood when I sat down.

"A fellow called Mottram," I replied. "He's rather a bore; that's why I didn't introduce him. He wanted us to go over and join his party, but I told him we were quite happy by ourselves."

The others laughed and agreed that we were.

It was odd meeting Ned again and I wished that he and his friends had chosen some other night to come to "Kim's." Although I was sitting with my back towards their table I was conscious of their presence and I was sure they were talking about me and saying nothing to my advantage. It was silly to mind what they said or thought about me, but all the same it made me uncomfortable.

Soon after that the tables were moved to the sides of the hall and a space was cleared for dancing. It was a free and easy sort of entertainment. We danced and returned to our table and drank light ale and chatted and then danced again. Ned and his party must have gone home early—or perhaps they had gone on somewhere else—for although I looked for them I saw them no more.

We went to "Kim's" several times in the next few weeks. Sometimes Wrigson came too and brought another girl, and on one occasion Ullenwood provided his sister, instead of Kitty, for my benefit. After the first party, which was Ullenwood's affair, we all paid for ourselves and the place was so cheap that my share came to very little. I enjoyed these outings; it was good to have some fun and to see life occasionally—besides I found good copy at "Kim's." I wrote a description of the place and made some amusing sketches.

There was great excitement in the office when Mr. Penman began to arrange the holidays. Of course I had intended to go home and had been looking forward to it eagerly but when I came to make my plans I realised I had not enough money for my fare. I hated borrowing—being in debt was an absolute nightmare—the advance from Mr. Heatley had worried me considerably until I had managed to pay it off. And it was not only the fare to Haines; there would be other expenses as well. It is impossible to enjoy a holiday if one has to count every penny.

When I told Mr. Coe I had decided not to go home he immediately offered to lend me five pounds, but I thanked him and refused. I told him I had made up my mind quite definitely to stay in the flat for my fortnight's holiday. It would be quite pleasant to stay in the flat. I could write as much as I pleased and browse contentedly in Mr. Coe's bookshop and I could go out with Teddy on Saturday afternoons and Sundays.

"That girl," said Mr. Coe, looking at me doubtfully. "You're not getting yourself mixed up with that girl, are you?"

"She's good for me," I replied, smiling. "We're good for each other. We keep each other out of mischief. Teddy has taught me a lot about girls—and about other things too."

"You look out," warned Mr. Coe. "It's the quiet ones are the worst. You think you're just pally with that girl, but mark my words you'll wake up one morning and find you've promised to marry her. I know girls."

"You don't know Teddy," I told him.

"I don't want to," he said gruffly. "I've no use for girls." The conversation seemed at an end and I turned to go upstairs, but Mr. Coe called to me to come back.

"David," he said. "I was wondering . . . you wouldn't consider taking on the shop would you?"

"Taking on the shop?"

He nodded. "That's right. I want to get away to the sea for a bit of a holiday. My sister lives at Margate and I always go to Margate every year—can't do without a sight of the sea. It's in my blood, I suppose. I've been looking for a chap to run the shop but I can't find anyone suitable. Of course I could shut it up like I did last year."

"Why don't you?" I asked.

"It's not satisfactory, that's why. I lost several customers last year—lost them for good and all. They're queer, customers are. They don't think anyone should have a holiday except themselves. They come along to get a book and they're fed up when they find the place shut—and off they go somewhere else."

"But I couldn't run the shop!"

"You could. You're the very man. Six pounds a week is what I'm offering."

This seemed very generous, but Mr. Coe laughed when I said so.

"Nonsense!" he exclaimed. "You'd get twice as much for carrying crates at the market."

"That would be work," I said. "Looking after the shop is easy."

"Well, it's up to you, David. I'll be pleased if you take it on. I'll enjoy my holiday better if I know you're looking after the place."

"I'll do it," I said.

CHAPTER TWENTY-SEVEN

July is a quiet month in London and Mr. Coe's customers were few. Most of them knew the shop well and did not want much attention; they preferred to come in and poke about and find what they wanted for themselves. I had plenty of time on my hands and I amused myself by writing more articles and touching up some sketches. Teddy was getting her holiday later. Her job at the hotel was no sinecure; she did all the catering, looked after the linen and arranged the flowers. Usually she got off in the afternoons, and one afternoon she looked in to see me at the shop. I had not invited her before—partly because Mr. Coe was so peculiar about women and partly because I was not sure whether she would want to come—but now that she had come of her own accord I asked her to stay to tea.

Sometimes I wondered why I was not in love with Teddy. I liked her so much, I admired her and we got on splendidly, but quite definitely I was not in love with her. It was just as well I was not, for Teddy had given me her friendship and nothing more. She had told me at the very beginning that she was engaged to be married and she did not let me forget it. Paul Dering was a major in the Gunners; they had known each other all their lives. He was still in Korea; they wrote to each other constantly and at length and their plan was to be married as soon as he got leave. I knew all this and a good deal more about Paul; I had even been shown his photograph . . . and although I was slightly prejudiced against the man (having heard too much about him) I was obliged to admit that he had a pleasant face.

The day Teddy came to tea she was tired and dispirited—Paul's letter was overdue and all sorts of silly little things had gone wrong at the hotel—but when I took her into Mr. Coe's sitting-room and made tea she cheered up and became more like herself.

"You are a dear," she said. "I'm sorry I was so wet; but you know how it is, David. Some days everything seems to go wrong, you're scared of shadows and you daren't look at the future."

"Fears shall be in the way," I told her. "The grasshopper shall be a burden and desire shall fail."

"That describes it exactly," declared Teddy in a tone of surprise. "I suppose I ought to know the quotation?"

"You would know it if you'd been properly brought up."

"Which means it's in the Bible! Remember, David, I hadn't the advantage of being brought up in a manse. You must make allowances for me."

"I do that all the time," I said, chuckling.

"This is very good tea," said Teddy, sipping appreciatively. "I didn't know you were so domesticated." She looked round the queer crowded little room as she spoke.

"This isn't my place," I said hastily. "This is Mr. Coe's sanctum—and as a matter of fact he'd have a fit if he could see you sitting there so comfortably in his own particular chair. Mr. Coe is terrified of women; he says he's been running away from them all his life."

"Is he as attractive as all that? I *do* think you might have asked me to meet him."

"Paul wouldn't like it," I said.

"But David—seriously—is it true he dislikes women? And if so why are we having tea here?"

"It's perfectly true—and we're having tea here because I've got to listen for the shop-bell. My flat is five flights up; I told you it was in the attic, didn't I? If you can wait till closing time I'll take you up and show it to you."

"Not to-day—I've got to go back to that wretched hotel—but I'll come some other time if I'm asked."

"You'll like it, Teddy," I said. "It's so quiet and peaceful. Mother thought it was awfully nice when she stayed with me."

Teddy was looking at me thoughtfully. "You talk about your mother a lot."

"Only to you," I replied. "Mother is rather—special."

"Would I like her, David?"

I thought about that quite seriously. "Yes," I said. "You'd like her and she'd like you. I'll show you a photograph of her when you come to my flat, but it isn't very good. No photograph could give you any idea of Mother. Once, long ago, an old woman said 'It makes your heart glad to look at her' so I went home and looked at her and I saw it was true."

"That's—lovely," said Teddy, in a low voice.

We were silent for a little and then the shop-bell tinkled and I had to go. I looked about for something to amuse Teddy while I was busy and my eye fell upon a piece of manuscript; it was a short article about the Pool of London which I had just completed that afternoon.

"Here's something to look at," I said, dumping it into her lap. "I shan't be longer than I can help."

Teddy was still reading it when I returned. "David!" she exclaimed. "This is frightfully good! I've read it twice and I liked it even better the second time. I had no idea you could write like this."

"You knew I wrote things."

"But not like this!" She looked at me and added. "Isn't it funny?"

"Funny?"

"I thought you knew quite well," explained Teddy.

I saw what she meant of course.

"Have you written other things like this?" Teddy inquired.

"Dozens of them," I told her, smiling. "When I've finished one I start another. I shove them into the cupboard. There's a great untidy pile of manuscripts and sketches which nobody will ever read."

"But this is good! Why on earth don't you send them to a magazine and have them published? People would like to read them and you'd get money for them."

"It sounds easy," I admitted. "But somehow it doesn't work. I tried writing articles for the papers but they all came back like a flock of homing pigeons and I found it so depressing that I gave it up. The fact is I can only write about things that interest me; the moment I begin to write with a view to selling it to a paper it all goes flat and there's no sparkle."

"But of course!" she cried. "The answer is to write what interests you and then sell it. I like this Pool of London thing immensely."

"You like it because you like me—at least I hope you do."

"A bit," she replied teasingly. "Just a little tiny bit, David . . . but I'm beginning to see what you mean. There's a lot of *you* in it."

"There always is," I told her. "It's the only way I can write. My own personality flavours everything and who wants to read David Kirke's ideas about the Pool of London? The answer is, nobody who doesn't know David Kirke."

Teddy nodded. "Yes, but all the same it seems a pity. How would it do to make them into a book?"

"A book?"

"I believe that would be best. If the articles were collected and made into a book people would have time to get interested in the author's personality. Do you see what I mean, David?"

"Yes," I said doubtfully. "I don't know . . . perhaps some day . . ."

Teddy's words stuck in my mind and that evening when I had finished supper I decided to have a look at the manuscript which lay on the bottom shelf of the cupboard in my sitting-room. I had not looked at it for months but had kept on adding to it so there was a mass of writings and sketches mixed up in confusion. When I started the job I thought an hour would finish it but it took a great deal longer than that. I sat on the floor beside the cupboard and went on reading, turning over the untidy dog-eared sheets and coming across all sorts of things which I had forgotten. Did I write this? I asked myself in amazement (probably everybody who writes experiences the same feeling when he reads over his own work).

The manuscript was not just a mass of bits and pieces (as I had thought), it was by no means shapeless. In a way it was a history of the last year, a chronicle of all I had seen and done. The bits and pieces were like beads upon a string, and the string was myself. I saw now what Teddy had meant when she suggested that people might become interested in the author's personality.

It was very late when at last I went to bed and I was too excited to sleep. I tossed and turned. One moment I decided that the book was no good at all—who would want to read a hotch potch of my ideas and experiences? The next moment I changed my mind; Teddy had liked that thing about the Pool of London and it was by no means the best. The one about Covent Garden Market was much more amusing . . . and the one about Kim's . . . and the one about the London streets at different hours of the day and the different types of people to be seen.

The next day I had another look at the pile of manuscript and before I knew what I was doing I had begun to revise it and put it in order. I had decided to go ahead and have a try. It would have to be typed of course (I had no time to do it myself and no typewriter) and typing it would cost a good deal, but I could use the money I was getting from Mr. Coe for looking after the shop. I thought of names for my book—it was an odd sort of book, neither fact nor fiction, so it should have an odd name—but I could think of nothing that satisfied me. Various tides suggested themselves but none would do; they were too whimsy or too stodgy or too long and clumsy.

Teddy was in on all this of course. She came to supper one evening and helped me to sort out the papers . . . and suddenly after a long silence she raised her head and said, "The Inward Eye."

It was perfect; the more I thought about it the more I liked it. Wordsworth had said the inward eye was "the bliss of solitude" and the book had been exactly that to me. It had filled my solitary hours with pleasure. Undoubtedly it was "The Inward Eye."

Mr. Coe returned from Margate bronzed and cheerful and full of sea air but I did not envy him. I envied nobody who had not written a book. *The Inward Eye* looked splendid when I had revised it and had it typed. It was bound in soft cardboard folders and the sketches were inserted between the typescript. When I read it over I was very pleased with it and felt sure no publisher would be able to resist it.

Mr. Coe knew about the book and asked if he might read it. I gave it to him one afternoon and he handed it back to me the next morning.

"Here, David," he said. "You had better take this. I don't want it to lie about and get dirty."

"Have you read it?" I asked in surprise.

"It's a queer sort of book," he replied. "It's not the sort of book I like—that's the truth, David. I like a story with a good plot."

"Did you—did you read it all through?"

"Yes, every word. I finished it at two o'clock this morning. Don't know why it was—I just went on reading the damn' thing—couldn't put it down—but it's no good, David. No publisher would look at it."

"Oh!" I exclaimed, somewhat taken aback.

"I'm sure you could write a novel," said Mr. Coe encouragingly. "A novel with a plot. You should have a go, David."

"Yes," I said doubtfully.

As a matter of fact Mr. Coe's verdict did not depress me unduly. His taste was for novels—preferably the novels of Dickens—and *The Inward Eye* was a very different work. If it had kept him out of bed until two o'clock in the morning it could not have bored him. I took comfort from that.

I was full of hope when I sent off *The Inward Eye* but the publisher (whom I had chosen to have the felicity of putting it into print) returned the manuscript with regrets; he said it fell between two stools, it was neither a Guide Book nor a series of essays. I had known that before of course so it did not surprise me. Nothing daunted I packed it up and sent it to another publisher forthwith. The second publisher kept the manuscript for weeks and then returned it saying he had enjoyed the book; the articles were well-written and the drawings were amusing but it would cost a lot to produce and he was afraid there was no money in it. The third publisher said it was not the sort of book to start with. My name was unknown to the public. If I wrote a successful novel he would be very pleased to publish *The Inward Eye* afterwards. The fourth publisher advised me to break it up and send the articles separately to a magazine and he volunteered the information that certain well-known journals in America were interested in articles about London.

By this time I was sick of the whole thing and had lost all faith in it; only sheer stubborn mulishness kept me from giving up the struggle. I thought about America . . . but I was determined not to break up my book. America could have it whole or not at all. Was it worth while trying? The manuscript was dirty and crushed; it looked as if it had been read by scores of people and I realised that if I were going to send it to America it would have to be retyped. I had saved up for a new suit, which I badly needed, but I could use the money for *The Inward Eye*. For several days I swithered and then I took a half-crown out of my pocket and tossed: heads a new suit for myself, tails a new suit for *The Inward Eye*.

It was tails!

The nice crisp manuscript went off to America in February. It was a spring-like day and the shop-windows were full of spring suits, light tweeds and worsteds, I could not help looking at them as I passed. Already I regretted having spent my hard-earned savings on having the book retyped. I pushed the parcel across the post-office counter and made up my mind to think no more about it.

All this time Teddy had been helpful and encouraging and indeed if it had not been for her I should have given up the struggle long ago. Our friendship had continued on exactly the same lines, it was a most satisfactory friendship.

One evening, soon after I had sent *The Inward Eye* to America, Teddy came as usual to have supper with me at the Wooden Spoon. I was there first, sitting at our usual table, when the door opened and she came in. The moment I saw her I knew what had happened—there was no need for her to tell me.

"Paul is coming home!" I exclaimed as I rose to greet her.

"Yes," she said breathlessly. "Yes—I had a letter this morning—but how on earth did you know?"

"It's written all over you, Teddy."

She sat down. Her cheeks were pink and her eyes were shining like stars. "He's on his way," she said. "He wants me to meet him at Liverpool. I've given up my job. Oh, David, I can hardly believe it!"

"You'll be married at once?"

She nodded. "As soon as possible. Paul says we've waited long enough. Oh, David, isn't it marvellous?"

I was glad for Teddy's sake but desperately sorry for myself.

"This isn't good-bye," she continued, smiling at me. "For all we know Paul may be posted to the War Office—or somewhere near London— and—and—"

"Yes," I said. "Yes, of course, but—"

"You'll like Paul," she declared.

I felt sure I should dislike him intensely. I felt perfectly certain he was not nearly good enough for her.

"Dear David," she said. "It's been grand. I've been rather miserable sometimes and you've been perfect to me."

"So have you," I mumbled. "I'll miss you horribly."

"You'll miss me, but you'll soon find other things to do." She smiled and added, "But for heaven's sake don't pick up a girl at the Market. It's a bad thing to do."

"It's a good thing to do," I told her.

"No, no! You might not be so lucky next time. You might find you'd picked a Tartar."

"I'm good at picking girls," I said, trying to smile.

"You're nothing of the sort. I've taught you a little but you're still a babe in arms. Promise me to be careful."

I laughed—not very cheerfully I'm afraid—and refused to promise. "Why should I promise you anything, Teddy? You're deserting me basely—and you're not a bit sorry. All you think about is Paul."

She looked at me in alarm. "David, you aren't—aren't being silly?"

"No," I said, smiling at her. "At least if you mean what I think you mean. I don't want to marry you, Teddy . . . but I don't want anybody else to marry you. I'm just a dog in the manger."

"Nice dog," she said, smiling in return. "Some day you'll meet the right girl and then you'll understand. She'll be a very lucky girl and I believe I feel a tiny bit jealous of her."

"Then you know how I'm feeling, Teddy."

She nodded and her eyes met mine; they were honest eyes and full of friendship.

It was dreary when Teddy had gone. I missed her even more than I had expected.

CHAPTER TWENTY-EIGHT

THE thirteenth of May began like other days with the buzzing of the alarm clock. I opened my eyes and saw the morning sunshine streaming in through the open window and heard the noise of the market. The first thing I thought of was that I could have a boiled egg for breakfast—perhaps two boiled eggs—because yesterday a box of eggs had come from Haines. It was a pleasant thought and I rose and put on the water to boil the eggs and to make tea. I felt cheerful as I dressed. There was sunshine to brighten the present moment—sunshine and boiled eggs—and in the near future was the prospect of my holiday. This year I was having the first fortnight in June. This year I was going to Haines.

Nobody who has not worked in an office, day in and day out, can possibly imagine the delight of freedom—fourteen whole days to do exactly as he likes—and looking forward to this heavenly state of freedom is almost as good as the reality. The bad part is when the slave returns to his chains and knows that he will have to wear them for eleven and a half months. But this morning I was not worrying about the end of my holiday, I was thinking of the beginning of it. I imagined myself at Euston, walking up the long wooden platform, I saw myself getting into the train.

It was so clear in my mind that to all intents and purposes I was actually sitting in the third-class compartment and the train had begun to glide out of the station when the door-bell rang. It tinkled twice which was a signal from Mr. Coe and meant that the postman had left a letter for me and I was to come downstairs and get it. I was still half dazed, but I ran down and got the letter and ran up again.

The post-mark was New York and as I came up the stairs I looked at it vaguely and wondered who on earth could be writing to me from New York. Then I remembered *The Inward Eye.*

I was so used to having the manuscript returned to me with thanks that for a moment or two I was puzzled. This was a letter, not a bulky package of manuscript! I was furious with the American publisher—it really was the limit! I had spent pounds upon having the thing typed and the man had not even the decency to return it. I tore the letter open in a rage.

It was a long letter and was written in friendly terms. The writer began by saying he had read *The Inward Eye* with interest and enjoyment; he liked it because it was original, he had never read anything quite like it before. The drawings were fascinating, so simple and fresh and unsophisticated, they struck the correct note every time. It was not often that an author was able to illustrate his own work. The sketch of the Big Business Man on his way to the City was a little masterpiece. The writer commented on various incidents in the book: this one was full of pathos, that one had sly humour. He declared that there was "a rich pattern" in *The Inward Eye.* He complimented me upon my fresh outlook.

I read all this—and more—with a feeling of unreality; I was looking for a "but." Other publishers had said they liked my book and invariably had ended their letters with a large "but" . . . "but unfortunately your name is unknown"; "but it would be expensive to reproduce the sketches"; "but it falls between two stools." I looked for the "but" in Mr. Basil Barnes's letter and looked in vain. There was no "but." Mr. Barnes seemed anxious to publish my book. I could not believe my eyes. It was not until I unfolded the enclosure that I believed my eyes. The enclosure was a contract with a space at the bottom for the author's signature. When I saw that my eyes nearly fell out and my heart began to hammer like a pneumatic drill.

It was so unexpected. It was so amazing. I had never been so excited in my life. I capered about and laughed aloud like a madman . . . then, beset with doubts, I stopped and sat down and read the letter again.

Suddenly I remembered the office! I seized my hat and ran all the way but in spite of this I was very late indeed. Mr. Penman looked up from his desk when I came in and said Mr. Heatley had been asking for me and I was to go straight to his room when I arrived.

"You're for the high jump, my child," murmured Ullenwood. "He's in a rare old wax."

Unpunctuality was one of Mr. Heatley's bugbears. It was a major crime. I knew he would be furious with me and he was.

"Look here, Kirke!" he exclaimed when I went in. "Do you realise you're half an hour late? I suppose your alarm didn't go off or you lost your collar-stud or you were delayed on the way by a street accident? I know all those excuses and I'm sick of them. You'll have to think of something fresh."

This was not very fair because I was scarcely ever late for work; but when your boss speaks to you in this tone of voice it is better to remain silent. Mr. Heatley continued. He had a fine command of invective and he slated me uphill and down dale. He asked me what I thought I was being paid for, and how I thought an office could be run efficiently if all the clerks turned up half an hour late. Then suddenly he stopped in the middle of a sentence and looked at me.

"You're ill, Kirke!" he exclaimed. "Sit down."

I was glad to sit down for, what with one thing and another, I felt a bit giddy.

"What's the matter with you?" he asked.

"Nothing, sir."

"Look here, you haven't been starving yourself again, have you?"

"No, sir. I'm all right."

"You look uncommonly queer. What have you been doing with yourself?"

"I got a letter this morning," I said. "That's what—delayed me."

"Bad news?"

I had not intended to tell Mr. Heatley about the letter but he had been very good to me in his odd brusque fashion and I felt I wanted his advice.

"No, not bad news," I said, and I took the envelope out of my pocket and handed it to him.

"What's this!" he said irritably. "What's all this about? Am I supposed to read it?" but he unfolded the letter and read it without waiting for a reply. When he had read it once he turned to the beginning and read it again more carefully. Then he unfolded the contract.

All this time there was silence. Mr. Heatley's room seemed very quiet. His room was at the back and had double windows, so the noise of London which never ceases night or day was only a far-off murmur like the sound of the wind in the pinewoods at Haines. I sat and waited. It seemed to me that Mr. Heatley took a long time to read those pages.

Presently he looked at me over the top of his spectacles and said, "So you've written a book?"

"Yes, sir."

"H'm," he said. "Lots of people write books—fewer get them published. What's the matter with English publishers?"

"I tried four. They didn't want it."

"This chap seems keen on it."

"He doesn't seem very business-like," I said doubtfully.

"There are different ways of doing business," replied Mr. Heatley. "I expect this man sits back comfortably in his chair and chats into a dictaphone. That's the American way and as a matter of fact it works. I gather this book of yours is an unusual sort of book, with pictures."

My opinion of Mr. Heatley had been high but it went higher that morning. He asked searching questions and listened with patience to all I said in reply. I had heard of people being "turned inside out" and that expression describes what Mr. Heatley did to me. When he had finished with me he knew as much as I did and the odd thing was he had helped me to see the matter more clearly. I asked him if he would witness my signature to the contract.

"No," he replied, looking at me and smiling. "Certainly not. You're consulting me professionally, I suppose."

"Yes."

"My advice is that you go to a literary agent before you put your name to that paper."

"I thought you—"

"I know nothing whatever about it," he declared. "The only thing I know about publishing is that I know nothing."

"I suppose I could find out—"

"Wait," said Mr. Heatley. "There's Tom Randall. You'll be all right with him. I'll get him on the phone."

"Tom Randall!" I said stupidly.

"He's a literary agent," explained Mr. Heatley, taking up the receiver, and without more ado he made the appointment.

"He can see you now," said Mr. Heatley. "Off you go—here, take the letter with you!"

"What is he like?" I asked.

"Go and see."

I thanked Mr. Heatley sincerely for his help and apologised for taking up his time.

"That's all right," he said. " But you'd better be here punctually to-morrow morning."

"Do you mean I'm to have the day off?"

"I do," replied Mr. Heatley. "You would be no use to me to-day. I don't want my clients' affairs mussed up by a young man with an inward eye. Take a bus into the country and sit under a tree."

"Yes," I said vaguely. "Yes, perhaps I will."

When I got to the door he called out, "Kirke, take 'Mother' with you!"

I looked back and smiled at him. "It really was Mother," I said. "And I certainly would take her if she were here. Unfortunately she lives with Father."

I could hear Mr. Heatley laughing as I shut the door.

By this time I had quite forgotten my crime. In fact I was so dazed that I had forgotten everything except my prospective interview with Mr. Randall. I passed through the outer office like a man in a dream and was taking my hat off the peg when I found Ullenwood at my elbow.

"Kirke, have you got the sack?" he whispered.

"Got the sack? No, of course not. Mr. Heatley has given me the day off."

Ullenwood stood and gaped at me . . . and then I remembered. "Cheerio!" I said, laughing. "See you to-morrow morning!" and I ran off down the steps.

Mr. Randall was surprisingly young. He was tall and well-made with a thin face and very dark brown eyes which were magnified in a curious way by the lenses of his spectacles. When he had read the letter and the contract he sat back and looked at me. "I should like to read *The Inward Eye*," he said.

This pleased me enormously and I promised to send him the copy of the typescript which had been rejected by the other publishers. "It's dirty," I said. "It looks as if it had been kicked about the floor."

"Who misused it so grievously?" inquired Mr. Randall.

"Four publishers," I replied, and I told him their names.

"We'll try a fifth," said Mr. Randall. "Meantime there's Basil Barnes. Are you satisfied with the contract?"

"Satisfied!" I cried. "Of course I am. I mean, all I want is to have the book published, Mr. Heatley said you would know if it was all right."

"It's all right, Mr. Kirke. My advice is that you sign it here and now."

I signed. It was a solemn moment.

Presently, when I had recovered somewhat from the excitement, I said to Mr. Randall, "I suppose you have to have influence to get publishers to look at a book. That's the important thing."

He smiled. "The important thing is the book, Mr. Kirke. Publishing is a business. Publishers are on the look-out for any book which will please the public. If they think a book will sell they accept it and if not they don't. That's the real truth. Of course they make mistakes sometimes, but I can assure you they will never accept a book just because some influential person has recommended it to them. Now we'll just run over the contract, shall we?"

Mr. Randall talked on, explaining the contract to me, and I began to understand what it meant. The only thing that worried me was that the publisher wanted five more books. Five more books! It seemed an impossible task.

"You'll write them," said Mr. Randall confidently.

"How do you know? How can you possibly know?"

"Basil Barnes knows. He wouldn't offer you a contract like this unless he was sure he had plenty of books in you."

This was an eye-opener to me. I began to realise that there was a good deal more in this business than I had thought. It was not just a hit or a miss. I realised that the American publisher must have read my book very carefully indeed and weighed me in the balance. In a way he was taking a gamble.

We went on talking and I found myself telling Mr. Randall not only about *The Inward Eye* but also about myself.

"But I'm wasting your time!" I exclaimed.

He smiled. "This is my business," he said. "I like to know about people. By the way, Basil Barnes will want some autobiographical details about you and a photograph of course."

"Will he?" I asked, somewhat impressed.

I was even more impressed when Mr. Randall offered me fifty pounds on account. I had told him I was going home for my holiday and I suppose he must have realised that I was pretty hard up.

"Fifty pounds!" I exclaimed in amazement. "But supposing the book doesn't sell?"

He laughed and replied that even if it were not a howling success I should get more than fifty pounds. "Take the money," he said. "You'll enjoy your holiday much more with a full pocket and when you come back you'll be ready to start another book."

He gave me a cheque and I went back to my flat. I felt too tired to take Mr. Heatley's advice and make an expedition to the country.

CHAPTER TWENTY-NINE

To MY mind early June is the most beautiful time of the year in Haines, for spring comes late and June is the transition period from spring to summer; but September is lovely too, and I have seen still, crisp days in October which I would not have exchanged for any other day in the year. It is often beautiful in winter, when the snow lies untrodden and sparkling upon the uplands and every twig on every tree is rimed with frost, and there are days in March when the wind blows cold and clear and great clouds sail majestically across the blue sky . but I could go on for ever, finding its own peculiar beauty in every month, so perhaps the truth of the matter is that Haines is my home and in my opinion there is no place like it.

This was June, so the wild hyacinths were in their glory, the woods were carpeted with blue and the gorse swept up the side of the hills like golden flames. The hedges were a mass of white may-blossom, so thick and rich that from a distance the flowers looked like snow, so fragrant that the air one breathed was heavy with their perfume.

The train stopped at Drumburly and I got out. I had five miles to walk to Haines. My parents were expecting me tomorrow, but I had got away a day earlier and was so impatient to be home that I had flung my clothes into a suitcase and caught the night-train by a matter of seconds. There was a short-cut from Drumburly to Haines, it was a steep stony path which went snaking through the woods and over the saddle between the rounded masses of hills. I set my foot to it with a will and presently I left the land of blossom and scent behind me.

June nights are short in Haines. It is scarcely dark before the light begins to glow in the east. To-day the first presage of the rising sun was a wash of palest lavender above the rounded outlines of the hills. As the light brightened the shadows of the pine-trees deepened; each rock, each tuft of coarse grass had a shadow. My own shadow, long and thin, took shape and trailed behind me on the stony path.

Here upon the hills there was space and a wide lonely freedom, and there was such purity in the morning air that my spirit was stilled, as if I were in church, to profound solemnity. London with its noise and crowds was far away in time and space. The morning was like a gift from the past when no town sullied the surface of the earth and legendary heroes strode upon the hills.

I was happy (for this was a joyous homecoming and I was the bearer of good news) but it was a solemn happiness . . . and presently when I came to the saddle I stood still and looked around me as if I had never seen the hills before. The sun was rising like a golden flame, dazzling and warming in the cloudless sky. Behind me lay the woods and the river and the little town of Drumburly, before me in the valley was the village of Haines. How small it looked! It was no more than a cluster of little grey houses on the bank of the stream. I saw the church with its pointed spire and beside it the manse embowered in a drift of fruit blossom. Just below me lay Nethercleugh farm-house with its steading and outbuildings, its byres and barns. Nethercleugh was broad awake already for farm people begin their day early. Even as I watched a thread of smoke rose from one of the chimneys; it rose straight into the air, hung there for a few moments, and then drifted down the valley in a gauzy cloud.

I wondered if Freda were at home. It would be fun to see Freda . . . and while I was thus thinking a girl came out of the house and walked across the yard. She was wearing a blue dress and although I was too far off to recognise her I felt pretty sure it was Freda, so I picked up my suitcase which I had put down to rest my arm and went down to Nethercleugh.

I could not help smiling as I opened the gate into the yard; how surprised Freda would be!

The girl had vanished by this time. I looked into the byre, but she was not there. Then I saw a flutter of blue in the stable and as I crossed in pursuit the girl emerged from the low doorway carrying a pail. She was not Freda.

For a moment I hesitated but she came forward smiling. "David Kirke!" she exclaimed. "Your mother said you were coming to-mor-row—but here you are!"

"Yes, here I am," I agreed, taking her outstretched hand. This must be Janet, of course, or perhaps Elsie. It was amazing that this slim, grown-up young lady should be one of the twins.

"Don't look so surprised!" cried the girl, laughing gaily. "People grow up, you know. Time doesn't stand still—even in Haines."

"I know. It's just—it's just that everything else seems the same."

She nodded. "Yes, I felt that when I came home from school. Everything was exactly the same except the people; they were all older. It's sad, isn't it?"

"Some people improve with age," I said, looking at her.

She certainly had improved for she was slender and straight, her deep blue eyes were sparkling with intelligence and her silky brown hair had golden lights in it. As we were talking she tossed it back from her face and fixed a clip in it and I remembered tying the ribbon for her, that day of the picnic. This was Janet, not Elsie. I was certain it was Janet.

"Come and have breakfast," she suggested. "You can tell us all your news. Freda is here."

I explained that I was on my way home to the manse.

"Then we mustn't keep you," said Janet, nodding. "You must go home first of course. But there's time for a glass of milk before you go."

We went into the dairy together, it was cool and dim and beautifully clean. All round the walls there were slate shelves with pans of milk upon them, and an electric churn stood on a little platform beneath the window.

Janet took a dipper and filled two glasses. "Here's health and prosperity to David Kirke!" she said.

"Here's happy days to Janet Lorimer!" I replied.

We drank. I had forgotten how delicious milk can be; fresh milk, slightly warm with the cream all through it.

"Lovely!" I exclaimed. "You don't get milk like that in London."

"But you get other things, David. You get—you get freedom."

"Freedom!" I echoed in surprise.

She hesitated and then said uncertainly, "I'm going to London soon. I'm trying to get a job. The family is annoyed with me about it but I want to—to be on my own."

"Oh, Janet, you won't like it!"

"Perhaps not," she said rather shakily.

"Don't worry," I said quickly. "Perhaps you'll like it all right. Lots of people like living in town. I'm a country person so I feel a bit shut in. You must let me know when you come to London. You will, won't you, Janet?"

"Yes," said Janet, nodding.

"It makes a difference if you know somebody. When I went to London I knew nobody at all; there were hundreds of thousands of people hurrying along the streets and not one of them cared twopence about me. It seemed—it made me desperately lonely. But I expect you have lots of friends in London."

"Two," said Janet. "Two girls who were at school with me. They want me to go and share their flat."

"That makes three friends, doesn't it?"

She turned her head and looked at me. "Thank you, David," she said quite gravely; so gravely that I felt a trifle embarrassed.

"We'll have fun," I told her. "We'll go to a play together. You must come and see my flat—I'm rather proud of it."

"Tell me about it," said Janet eagerly.

"It's a funny little flat," I said. "Just two rooms and a tiny kitchen in the attic of a tall house in Covent Garden. The windows look out on to roofs and chimney-pots—it's a sort of Hans Andersen view. I'm happy there most of the time but occasionally when the sun shines and the skies are blue I get a shut-in feeling and I long to be out of town; to have a garden that I could work in and grow flowers and vegetables."

"I suppose you could, couldn't you?" asked Janet. "Lots of people who work in London live in the suburbs and travel in and out every day."

"The suburbs are not the country," I replied.

Janet nodded understandingly. "I know what you mean, David. I'm sure I should feel the same. If I couldn't live in the real country I would rather live in the town."

We went on talking while we drank our milk and then I said I must go.

"But I shall see you again," said Janet. "You're going to be here for a fortnight, aren't you? Come to tea some afternoon."

"Yes, of course I will—and you must come to the manse, or perhaps we could arrange a picnic."

Janet followed me to the door. "David," she said, "I know it seems a funny thing to ask but would you mind not telling anybody about this morning. I mean don't say you met me. It seems—it seems funny but—but it will save a lot of bother."

"I shan't say a word," I promised.

"You don't mind?"

"Of course not."

"It seems funny," she repeated with a little smile—rather a sad little smile. "But you see I'm still the naughty one of the family."

As I went down the hill I could not help wondering why our meeting should be kept a secret. There was nothing "naughty" about it unless perhaps Janet might get into trouble for giving me a glass of milk; but I soon forgot to wonder in the excitement of coming home.

The clock on the church tower began to strike eight as I reached the bridge. It was a familiar sound and I lingered listening to its cadence.

The sun was warm by this time, it sparkled on the water of the stream and filled the world with radiance. I waited for the last stroke of the clock and then jumped over the low wall into the manse garden. I ran through the orchard and up the path and paused at the dining-room window. Father and Mother had just sat down to breakfast and it was like looking at a scene in a well-known, well-loved play. Father had begun to eat his porridge; Mother was stretching out her hand to lift the big silver teapot.

Suddenly Mother saw me. "Davie!" she cried.

I leapt in through the open window and hugged her. I put my arms round Father's neck and kissed him on the cheek. It was years since I had kissed Father—not since I was a child—but somehow I could not help it.

He rubbed his cheek and said, "Och, you and your southern manners!" but he was pleased all the same.

"What's happened!" Mother cried. "There's nothing wrong, is there, Davie?"

"Something marvellous has happened," I declared.

They were both gazing at me and in both their faces there was the same look—a look of anxiety, of apprehension.

"I've told you it's marvellous!" I said, laughing at them. "It's the most wonderful thing in the world. You'll never guess what's happened."

"I believe we could guess," said Father gravely. "But it will be better if you tell us in so many words."

"Much better," agreed Mother.

"There!" I cried, taking the letter out of my pocket. "I've written a book! It's being published in America."

Whatever they had guessed, it certainly was not that, for they were astonished beyond measure at my news and as pleased and excited as I could have wished. The porridge was left to cool upon their plates while they read and re-read the publisher's letter and asked questions about it. What kind of book was it? How long had it taken to write? Were there real people in it? Why had I sent it to America?

"I'll tell you later," I said, laughing. "I've walked four miles over the hills and I want porridge—good Scots porridge—before I answer any more questions."

"Mercy!" cried Mother. "I'm an idiot! It's so exciting that I've lost my wits!"

CHAPTER THIRTY

I HAD not been many hours in the house before the telephone bell rang; it was Freda to ask me to tea at Nethercleugh.

"It will be lovely to see you, David," she declared and her voice sounded warm and excited. "We thought you were coming to-morrow but the postie said you'd arrived this morning. Come at half-past three and I'll take you round the farm."

"To-day?" I asked in surprise.

"Yes, of course," said Freda. "You've nothing else to do, have you?"

I was not particularly anxious to go to Nethercleugh on my first day at home but I had no excuse ready, so at half-past three I was walking up the hill. I had put on grey-flannel trousers and a grey tweed jacket (which I had bought with some of the money Mr. Randall had given me) and a new blue shirt and tie. It was extraordinarily pleasant to be wearing new clothes; they were loose and comfortable and gave me a feeling of well-being. I had gone about for months in an old lounge suit; I had pressed it and sponged it and done my best to make it look respectable but it was so shabby and so tight that nothing I could do was much use. I had grown to hate the sight of that suit and, as I walked up the hill in the sunshine, I decided to give it to Mother for the Jumble Sale. I would never, never wear that suit again.

Freda was waiting for me. She was sitting on the roots of a big oak-tree at the side of the road. She waved when she saw me and came to meet me.

"Hallo, David, you've grown since I saw you last!" exclaimed Freda as she took my hand.

"I'm getting quite a big boy," I agreed, laughing.

"Well, you are! I used to be taller than you!"

It was true. I could look down on Freda now; not very far down of course, for Freda was by no means small, but her eyes were on a lower level than mine.

We walked up the hill together and as we went Freda told me her news. "I'm learning about farming," she said. "There's a lot to learn—far more than I expected—but it's very interesting. At first Father was terribly difficult (you know what he's like, don't you, David?) but now he sees I'm in earnest and he's coming round and letting me help. I go with him to sales and I keep the books and fill up forms and make myself generally useful." She laughed and added, "The other day I heard him tellin Mr. Johnstone of Mureth that I was almost as good as a son."

"That's pretty good," I said, smiling at her.

We went round the farm and I saw she knew all about it and was taking it very seriously indeed. She explained the rotation of crops; she showed me the pigs and discoursed learnedly about their breeding; she showed me the calves and the byres and the barns, and eventually she took me into the dairy.

"Isn't this splendid?" she said with pride. "We've brought it up to date. We've put in all the latest gadgets. You haven't seen it since it was a dark, dank sort of shed, have you, David?"

"You've improved it tremendously," I told her. I felt rather pleased with my answer.

"What about London?" asked Freda suddenly.

"What about it?" I asked teasingly. "You don't want me to tell you it's big and crowded and noisy, do you?"

"I want to know how you can bear it," she retorted. "I want to know how you can endure sitting in a stuffy office all day adding up columns of figures."

"Some of my work is very interesting—"

"I can't understand it! Wouldn't you rather have an out-of-doors job?"

"What sort of job?"

"Wouldn't you like to be a farmer?"

"I haven't got a farm, Freda."

"But supposing you had?"

I could not help smiling. "If I had a farm I should be a farmer, but to tell you the truth I've never thought about it. What's the use of thinking about something which never could happen? It only makes you discontented with what you've got."

"A farm is endlessly interesting," declared Freda, pursuing her own line of thought. "There's so much to think of and so many different kinds of things to do, and it's all out of doors in the fresh air."

"Except filling in forms," I said, laughing at her.

Freda did not laugh and I saw she was annoyed. Freda had always wanted people to agree with her and to share her enthusiasms and she had not changed. She wanted me to say, *Oh: you are lucky! How I wish I could be a farmer instead of a clerk in a stuffy office!* but I was determined not to say it. Perhaps I felt it, for Haines was very dear to my heart and it was looking very beautiful, but I was not going to say exactly what Freda wanted. Why should I? As I looked at her standing by the window of the dairy with the fight falling on her dark curls, I realised that she was very pretty—even prettier than I had remembered. I had thought that she and Teddy were alike, but Freda was prettier than Teddy; her features were more regular and her cheeks were rosy from her out-of-door life. But prettiness is not everything.

"Why are you looking at me like that?" asked Freda suddenly.

"Oh!" I exclaimed, taken aback. "It was just—I haven't seen you for so long. I was thinking how pretty you were."

The half-truth pleased her and she smiled. "Tell me what you've been doing," she said. "You haven't told me much about yourself, David."

I hesitated. I had intended to tell her about *The Inward Eye*, but now I did not want to.

"Have you lots of friends in London?" she asked.

"Not many. It's difficult to get to know people in London."

"But you must have some?"

"Yes . . ." I said doubtfully. "There was a girl called Teddy Freer. We used to go for expeditions together on Sunday afternoons; and there are the fellows at the office."

"What is the girl like?" inquired Freda with interest. "Is she fair or dark? Is she terribly smart and attractive? Do you take her to dances and that sort of thing?"

"What a lot of questions!" I exclaimed.

"Well, you needn't answer them," said Freda crossly.

I took her at her word (which was not what she had intended) and instead of answering her questions I began to tell her about my flat. As I talked I could see her looking at me with a puzzled expression, and I knew why. In the old days I had done what Freda wanted; my constant endeavour had been to keep the weather sunny. In the old days Freda had known she had the whip-hand and that I would do anything for peace. But now my shell had hardened and her frown no longer upset me. I understood Freda now, I realised her limitations and felt sorry for her. Beryl had taught me a good deal, and Teddy—in quite a different way—had taught me more.

When Freda saw that I was armoured against her frowns she changed her tactics and was as pleasant as could be. Which just showed . . .

At tea-time we went in and found Mr. and Mrs. Lorimer sitting at the table. They always had tea in the dining-room; it was a regular meal with scones and jam and cakes of all sorts.

"David! How nice to see you!" exclaimed Mrs. Lorimer. "Come and sit beside me and tell me everything. How do you like living in London?"

It was the usual question—everybody asked me the same thing—and I gave my usual answer. "I'm getting used to it," I said.

"They say eels get used to skinning," remarked Mr. Lorimer, with a short laugh.

"Your mother enjoyed her visit to London," said Mrs. Lorimer. "It did her a lot of good. She told me about your flat and how comfortable it was. How do you manage about meals, David? I mean who cooks for you and cleans and makes your bed?"

I was hoping to see Janet, and presently when I had answered Mrs. Lorimer's questions about my domestic arrangements I asked after the twins.

"Elsie will be down in a minute," replied Mrs. Lorimer. "I don't know where Janet can be. I haven't seen her since lunch."

"She went to Drumburly by the two o'clock bus," said Freda.

"Oh!" exclaimed Mrs. Lorimer in dismay. "What a pity! She'll be so sorry to have missed seeing David. Couldn't she have waited and gone to-morrow?"

"We needed some things," said Freda briefly.

"But surely to-morrow would have done as well. Did she know David was coming to tea?"

"Have some honey, David," said Freda. "I didn't tell you we had started bees, did I? You must try some of our special Nethercleugh honey and tell us how you like it."

"Freda—" began Mrs. Lorimer; but at that moment the door opened and Elsie appeared.

I knew it must be Elsie—because I had just been told that Janet had gone to Drumburly—but they were still exactly alike. I could have sworn that this was the girl I had met in the steading and who had taken me into the dairy and given me a glass of milk. At least that was my first impression . . . after a few moments I changed my mind and realised my mistake. In face and figure and indeed to all outward appearance the Lorimer twins were still as alike as two peas, but the girl I had met in the steading this morning had an inner brightness, a glow of life and vivid intelligence, which this girl lacked. Janet was real and vital; Elsie was a good imitation. It was such a good imitation that it could deceive you for a few minutes—but not for long. They were completely different people.

"Hallo, David," said Elsie. "How do you like London?"

"He's getting used to it," said Mr. Lorimer. "He's got a flat with a view of other people's chimneys. He cooks his own meals and sews on his own buttons and mends his own socks . . . so now you know all about it, or all you need to know. Sit down and take your tea."

"Elsie was just asking," said Mrs. Lorimer mildly.

"All this talk about London!" grumbled Mr. Lorimer. "If I have to go to London I go there and do my business and come back by the first train I can get. I wouldn't live there for the world. People seem to have gone mad about London. David has gone to live there and now Janet has started to craik about it."

"Is Janet going to London soon?" I inquired, sounding the deeps.

"Going soon!" he exclaimed. "She's not going at all if I have anything to say in the matter. What on earth does she want to go to London for?"

"Perhaps she wants a job," I suggested innocently.

"There are plenty of jobs here," declared Mr. Lorimer. "She doesn't need to go to London—or anywhere else—for a job. I don't see why she can't settle down in her own home and make herself useful."

"She would if it wasn't for Barbie France!" exclaimed Elsie. "I hate Barbie!"

"She certainly has a very bad influence on Janet," agreed Freda.

"Why can't she leave Janet alone!" cried Elsie. "Why does she keep on writing to Janet and trying to persuade Janet to go to London and share her flat? She's a perfect beast, that's what she is."

"We needn't worry," declared Mrs. Lorimer, trying as usual to pour oil on the troubled waters. "Janet has written to Barbie and told her quite definitely that she can't go to London. Janet realises that we need her at home. You see, David, we really *do* need her. Freda is helping her father with the farm and Elsie has never been very strong, so—"

"Janet *doesn't* realise it!" cried Elsie hysterically. "You may think Janet has given up the idea of going to London, but she hasn't. She had another letter from that horrible girl this morning."

"From Barbie?" asked Freda. "How do you know? Did she tell you?"

"No, she never tells me anything," declared Elsie. "I saw the letter in the pocket of her overall. Barbie is looking for a job for her—so there!"

Mr. Lorimer gave a short mirthless laugh. "Do you hear that, David?" he asked. "I'm sure you must agree that this family of mine is delightful. They spend their time spying upon one another and cribbing each other's letters. It's no wonder I'm proud of them, is it?"

"Well, you asked me!" cried Elsie in trembling tones. "It isn't fair to ask me and then blame me for telling. If it wasn't for me you'd never have known anything about it. All I can say is if Janet goes to London I shall die—and then perhaps you'll be sorry."

"Janet isn't going," said Mrs. Lorimer. "You're just upsetting yourself for nothing. I'm afraid David will think you're a very silly girl."

"He wouldn't be far wrong," remarked Freda, *sotto voce*.

There are few things more uncomfortable than to sit and listen to a family row, and the Lorimers' habit of involving their guests in their disagreements was particularly embarrassing. Fortunately Mr. Lorimer was tired of the subject under discussion; he turned to me and asked how I managed to keep fit.

"I can't keep fit without exercise," declared Mr. Lorimer. "I walk round the farm every morning and I often ride in the afternoon. I don't suppose you get any exercise at all, do you?"

"Not a great deal," I replied. "I walk to and from the office and my flat is up five flights of stairs."

"Poof—that's nothing. You used to like walking on the hills."

"I still do; but I have to earn my living."

"I told David he ought to be a farmer," said Freda, smiling at me across the table.

"I don't know anything about it—" I began.

"You'd soon learn," said Mr. Lorimer. "Farming is largely a matter of common-sense. If you went as an assistant to a good farmer you'd very soon learn."

It seemed odd that Freda and Mr. Lorimer should both have the same idea as to what I should do, and especially odd because they must have known perfectly well that I had no capital to invest in a farm. I wondered if they had been discussing the matter before my arrival, but even that would not account for it.

"You should think about it seriously, David," said Mrs. Lorimer kindly. "I'm sure you'd enjoy a country life."

"Of course I should," I agreed. "But unfortunately I see no chance of being able to change my job. Beggars can't be choosers."

"You never know," said Mr. Lorimer vaguely. "Something might turn up."

We had finished tea by this time, so I rose and said good-bye.

"You're not going!" Mrs. Lorimer exclaimed in surprise. "Freda wants to show you the farm. I thought you would stay and have supper with us. Do stay, David."

"It's very kind of you, but I think I had better go home. I only arrived this morning, you know. Freda showed me round the farm before tea."

It was difficult to escape. Mr. Lorimer discovered that I had not seen the new tractor and insisted on taking me to look at it. He talked about it and extolled its performance and made Freda drive it up and down the yard to show me how easily it turned. I had never seen Mr. Lorimer in such a pleasant mood but somehow I did not like him any better for his pleasantness.

At last I managed to tear myself away and as I said good-bye to Freda I remembered that Mother had given me a message for her:

"Mother wants you to come to tea," I told her. "She wants you and Janet and Elsie. What day can you come?"

We fixed a day next week.

Mother was writing letters when I got home. She looked up and asked if I had enjoyed myself.

"It was the usual thing," I replied ruefully. "Mr. Lorimer still has his black monkey and Elsie is intolerable."

"What about Freda?" asked Mother.

I hesitated and then I said, "She hasn't changed—not really. I mean she still likes to have her own way in everything."

"You used not to mind."

This was true and (not for the first time by any means) I realised how clever Mother was. She was clever about people which is the most important kind of cleverness. "No," I said slowly. "Perhaps I didn't mind so much. When you're very young you take people as you find them. It's only when you've had experience that you begin to measure and weigh. That's natural, isn't it? You can't measure until you have some sort of standard."

Mother waited. I saw she knew exactly what I meant and was hoping to hear how I had become possessed of a standard, but it was too difficult to explain about Teddy and I was afraid she would not understand.

"And Janet?" asked Mother at last.

"Janet wasn't there. Did you know that Janet wants to get a job in London?"

"Yes, she told me. As a matter of fact I see quite a lot of Janet. She helps me in the parish, so of course I should miss her very very badly if she went away. All the same Janet ought to get away from Nethercleugh and have a chance to live her own life."

"She'll get away all right," I said confidently.

"What do you know about it?" asked Mother, raising her eyebrows.

"I know you," I told her. "If you think Janet ought to get away you'll accomplish it somehow—by fair means or foul."

"I'll try fair means first," said Mother quite seriously.

CHAPTER THIRTY-ONE

THE next day was Thursday (I spent it at home and enjoyed the peacefulness of it); on Friday I went to Edinburgh for I wanted to do some shopping and to see my friends. The chief item on my shopping list was a present for my parents for their silver wedding which they were celebrating on Sunday week. Nothing had been said about this important anniversary and I was sure they thought I had forgotten about it, but I had not forgotten and now that I had money in my pocket I intended to buy them something good.

It was difficult to find exactly what I wanted and I spent some time looking about. I tried several shops which sold second-hand jewellery and silver and at last, when I was beginning to despair, I discovered a sugar-bowl of exactly the same pattern as Mother's silver teapot. It was a beautiful thing and the moment I saw it I knew I need look no further. This would please them both.

After that I visited the Dodges' shop and saw Cliffe who had gone into partnership with his father (the board over the door bore the legend DODGE AND SON in new gold lettering). Cliffe was delighted to see me and took me into the back shop for a chat. It was fun seeing Cliffe, he was always the same, big and handsome and merry; it did not matter if you had not seen Cliffe for years, you could take up your friendship where you had left it. I noticed that he had almost overcome his stammer, but not quite. Occasionally when he became excited and talked very fast it came back in the old way and tripped his tongue. We had so much to say to each other and so little time that I asked Cliffe if he would come down to Haines and spend the day with me.

"Gosh, that would be great!" Cliffe cried delightedly. "I'll m-manage it somehow. Dad won't mind . . . it's Mum who'll kick up a fuss. She thinks Haines is d-dangerous."

"Whose fault is that?" I said, laughing.

I had arranged to have lunch with Uncle Matt at his club so I took a tram up the hill to Princes Street. Uncle Matt looked older but he was in very good form and, like Cliffe, he was pleased to see me. He wanted to know when I was coming back to Edinburgh, whether I wanted to come back or preferred to stay on with Mr. Heatley. I found this a little difficult to answer.

"Maybe you should stay on," said Uncle Matt a trifle diffidently. "It's not that I don't want you, David, but we've had to reduce our staff a wee bit. That's the truth of the matter."

I told him I could easily stay on and I told him about my book. I had decided that Uncle Matt had the right to know about it.

"A book! Goodness me!" exclaimed Uncle Matt, gazing at me in surprise. "But you're not thinking of making writing your career, are you? That's a precarious sort of business. No, no, David, you stick to your work. That's your best plan."

"Yes, of course," I said. Oddly enough Uncle Matt's warning had the opposite effect from what he intended. I had never thought of giving up my work in the office and trying to make a career by my pen—never for one moment—but now Uncle Matt had put the idea into my head and I could not help thinking of it.

"Stick to your work," repeated Uncle Matt earnestly. "Writing books is all very well for a side-line, to make a little extra pocket money, but it would be madness to depend upon it for your bread and butter."

"Of course it would," I agreed.

"Good lad," said Uncle Matt, nodding. "You're a sensible lad, David. You always were. Not like Miles."

"Miles?" I asked. "What has Miles been doing?"

"Throwing away his opportunities," declared Uncle Matt in disgust. "He's supposed to be reading Law but he's just playing himself and wasting time. Tom was telling me about him yesterday."

It would have been interesting to hear more about Miles but Uncle Matt looked at his watch and rose. "I'll need to hurry," he declared. "I've to see a client at half-past two and it's almost that now. What are you doing with yourself this afternoon, David?"

"I thought I might go and see Aunt Etta."

"Etta!" exclaimed Uncle Matt in surprise. "Have you nothing better to do than that?"

"I like her," I said defensively.

Uncle Matt looked at me.

"I believe you do," he declared. "I believe you're fond of the old mule. You'll find her as daft as ever."

"She's not as daft as you think," I said, laughing.

Uncle Matt looked older, but there was no change in Aunt Etta—or none that I could see. When I went in she was sitting beside the fire in the same big chair. Her face was plump and her cheeks were pink and her silvery hair was parted in the middle and looped back smoothly over her ears. Somehow I had expected her to look different. So much had happened since I last saw her that it was amazing she should look just the same. It was incredible that Aunt Etta should have been sitting here in the same chair all these years like a wax-work in Madame Tussaud's.

"There now!" said Aunt Etta, laying down the novel which she had been reading. "Fancy you coming to-day! I've just been reading a story about a boy called David. Isn't that funny?" She looked at me with her pale blue eyes and added, "It's nice to see you, David. You haven't been to see me for quite a long time."

"I've been away," I said, kissing her lightly on her plump cheek.

"Yes, dear. You're a soldier now, aren't you? They told me you were a soldier. Who was it told me that? Oh, yes, it was Mary. Mary came to see me a little while ago and brought me a photograph of you in your uniform. She said you were in Germany."

"But that's ages ago!" I exclaimed. "That's years ago. I came to see you after I got back from Germany."

"Yes, of course," said Aunt Etta vaguely. "But really it seems quite a short time ago that you were living with Matthew and going to school, so it's funny to think of you as a soldier. I like the photograph and I have it on the table beside my bed in a silver frame—but uniforms are not nearly so becoming nowadays as they were when I was young. Men looked so smart in those days. I think it's a pity, don't you?"

"But uniforms are for fighting—"

"Oh, I know that," nodded Aunt Etta. "Soldiers have to wear that ugly khaki, so that they can hide from the enemy. It all started in the war against Kruger. You remember that of course."

"It was long before I was born," I told her.

Aunt Etta was not listening. "Duke's son, cook's son, son of a hundred kings . . . Fifty thousand horse and foot going to Table Bay . . . Each of 'em doing his country's work (and who's to look after their things?) Pass the hat for your credit's sake, and pay—pay, pay." She looked at me for approbation. "Isn't it clever of me to remember it?" she asked.

"Yes, very clever," I replied.

"Mr. Kipling wrote the poem—it's a long poem all about the Absent-Minded Beggar and the dreadful things that happened to his wife and family while he was away. There were other songs too—there was 'Good-bye Dolly Gray' which was so dreadfully sad that it always made me cry—and there was one about Tipperary . . ." She hesitated for a moment and then added, "But that was a different war, wasn't it?"

"Yes," I said. It was difficult to know whether to help her to get things straightened out or just to leave it.

"But what were we talking about, David?" she asked.

"Uniforms," I suggested.

"Uniforms," agreed Aunt Etta. "That was it. Well, I think it would be nice for soldiers to have a smart uniform for best. They don't have to fight *all* the time, do they? If they had really smart uniforms for parties—and to be married in, of course."

"Yes, but you see—"

"You're not engaged to be married yet, are you, David?"

"No, I haven't found the right girl."

"Don't do anything in a hurry," said Aunt Etta, wagging a fat finger at me. "Marriage is important and unless you found *exactly* the right girl you would be very unhappy indeed. I never got married."

"Why didn't you, Aunt Etta?" I asked.

She sighed. "Well dear, I just . . . didn't. Several gentlemen asked me of course, and Papa thought . . . but I said no. There was one of them . . . but he never asked me properly. He had no money, you see. He went away to India and a little later I heard he had been killed fighting in a battle on the North-West Frontier. James was the only one of our family who married; he was fortunate to find Mary because very few people could understand James and manage him so well."

"Yes," I agreed. As usual, Aunt Etta's conversation was a mixture of sense and nonsense and as usual I found myself trying to make up my mind whether or not she was "daft." At one moment I would decide that she was—quite definitely—and the next moment she would say something unexpectedly shrewd.

"Now tell me what you have been doing, dear," said Aunt Etta. "Tell me all about everything."

This was a large order but I did my best to find the things that I thought would interest me. I told her about my flat and about my work at the office. She listened but it was difficult to know how much she took in.

"You're very clever," she said at last. "I always said you were a clever boy and I was quite right. I could never work in an office—I would get the papers muddled up."

The idea of Aunt Etta working in an office made me smile.

"Yes, it is funny," she agreed with one of her flashes of shrewdness. "I don't wonder you're amused. It would take a whole week to sort out the papers after I had muddled them. Matthew says I'm hopeless at business." She sighed and added, "Matthew gets impatient with me when I can't understand . . . and that makes me sillier than ever. It's a pity, isn't it?"

"Yes," I said. It was difficult to know what else to say.

"I like seeing Matthew of course," she continued in a shaky voice. "If he would just come and—talk to me quietly—like you do—but it's always business when he comes. The moment he begins about business it's hopeless—I get sillier and sillier and Matthew gets more and more angry—his visits—upset me—"

"He doesn't mean it. He can't help being impatient."

"I can't help being silly," Aunt Etta said pathetically.

It was time to change the subject so I asked her how she was.

Usually Aunt Etta enjoyed discussing her health—or ill-health—but to-day even that subject was depressing.

"There's something very funny the matter with me," said Aunt Etta, looking at me anxiously with her pale blue eyes. "I don't know what it is but every now and then I feel very queer indeed. I feel as if everything was slipping away sideways and it was getting dark. What do you think it could be?"

"It must be a horrible feeling!"

She nodded. "Horrible and frightening. They don't understand. Nobody could understand the feeling unless they had had it. Have you ever felt like that, David?"

"No, but I realise it must be dreadful."

"You're a kind boy," said Aunt Etta. "Clever and kind . . ." Her voice was getting shaky again and I was very glad when the door opened and Jean appeared with the tea.

"Oh, here's Jean with tea!" exclaimed Aunt Etta. "Isn't that nice? You've brought a cup for David, haven't you, Jean?"

"Indeed I have, Miss Kirke," replied Jean. "And I sent out to the baker's for doughnuts. You like doughnuts, don't you, Mister David?"

It was all the same as ever. I wondered how often I had had tea like this with Aunt Etta; how often Aunt Etta had said, "You've brought a cup for David, haven't you?"; how often Jean had "sent out to the baker's for doughnuts." The only difference was that Jean now called me Mister David.

"I was telling David about my horrid feeling," said Aunt Etta as she watched Jean arrange the little table for tea.

"But it's better not to think about it," replied Jean, in bracing tones. "You know what the doctor said, Miss Kirke. He said not to think about it."

Aunt Etta sighed. "It's all very well for *him*. He doesn't know what it's like to have horrid feelings. Old Doctor Brown was so sympathetic."

"The new doctor is a nice young man," declared Jean. "He's too young," objected Aunt Etta. "Much too young. He doesn't sit down and talk to me like Doctor Brown used to. He's always in a hurry and I don't think he cares very much. I'm just a silly old lady—not worth bothering about—that's what he thinks—" Her eyes filled with tears.

"Look, Aunt Etta!" I said quickly. "Look, Jean has made scones! And there's strawberry jam. It's just like old times, isn't it?"

She cheered up—as I had hoped she would. It was obvious that in spite of her "horrid feelings" she still enjoyed her food. I could not stay with her much longer for I had to catch my train back to Haines but she was quite happy again. She was munching chocolate biscuits when I kissed her and said good-bye.

On Sunday I went to church and sat beside Mother in the familiar pew . . . and I felt about nine years old. I was so filled with the atmosphere of the past that when I looked down I almost expected to see two brown, bony knees instead of a pair of grown-up knees decently clad in trousers.

I was a trifle anxious when Father began his sermon, I had always admired and enjoyed his sermons and I wanted to go on admiring and enjoying them. Supposing he was less good than I had thought? Supposing he did not come up to my expectations? But I need not have worried; Father had not been speaking for two minutes before I realised that he was grand and, banishing all unworthy thoughts, I settled down to enjoy him.

Father took as the subject for his sermon Paul's Second Letter to Timothy. He did not take a text from the letter and preach from it, but took the letter as a whole and quoted various passages from it to illustrate his points. It was a human letter, Father said. We were apt to think of Paul as superhuman when we considered his life and the frightful privations he had endured for his Faith, and when we read his closely reasoned arguments. He was superhuman, no doubt, but this letter to Timothy showed his tender human heart. It was a letter from an old man to a young man whom he dearly loved. Nobody could read it without being moved by the deep affection it showed.

This letter, continued Father, was in answer to a call for spiritual help and counsel. It was a personal letter to a friend who was finding life difficult. Father said he liked to think of Timothy receiving the precious letter, taking it away to his room and reading it over and over again—pondering upon every line. What a wise, helpful letter it was! Helpful not only for the spiritual uplift and the comfort it contained comfort for an overburdened heart—but also helpful for its sound advice upon material matters connected with the young man's work, upon his personal affairs and conduct.

Paul was anxious about Timothy, as we all are anxious about those we love who are far away; and he longed to see Timothy, as we all long to see those we love. Three times in the letter Paul voiced this longing. "Greatly desiring to see thee . . . that I may be filled with joy," wrote Paul. And in another place, "Do thy diligence to come shortly unto me," and again, "Do thy diligence to come before winter."

"Do thy diligence to come before winter," repeated Father. "Paul was old and weary and he felt the approach of winter as old people still do. He felt the approach of death. He did not dread his passing for he knew that he would obtain the salvation which is in Christ Jesus with eternal glory, but he longed to see the beloved face of Timothy before he died."

That afternoon as I sat in the garden, and read the letter with more care and greater understanding than I had given it before, I wondered how many of Father's parishioners were doing the same thing. I wondered how many of them were thinking kindly of the old man who had written the letter and the young man who had received it . . . thinking of them as real people, with hopes and fears and longings like ourselves, and not as figures in a stained glass window clad in outlandish clothes. Father had done it again; he had shed new light upon an old subject. He had breathed upon dead bones and brought them to life. I realised suddenly with a shock of surprise that my small talent for seeing things and being able to write about them was probably inherited. It was a definite gift, not just a freakish facility for putting down my thoughts on paper. The thing was in my blood. I found the idea encouraging in the extreme. It was a sound foundation.

CHAPTER THIRTY-TWO

My precious days of freedom flew past only too quickly. I worked in the garden and walked over the hills and visited various people that I knew. Freda came to tea on Tuesday as we had arranged. She was wearing a green dress and looked very nice, I thought.

"I came early," said Freda, smiling. "I thought we could walk up to 'our cottage' after tea. I haven't brought the twins. You didn't want them, did you, David?"

This was difficult to answer. I had been looking forward to seeing Janet but what could I say?

"I don't know about David," said Mother with unusual asperity. "Of course I wanted the twins or I shouldn't have asked them."

"Oh!" exclaimed Freda somewhat taken aback. "Oh, well—but you can easily have them some other time, can't you, Mrs. Kirke? David and I are going for a walk."

Mother said no more but I could see she was annoyed. She had made a lot of cakes for tea and the two empty chairs stood at the table. Mother did not move the chairs, nor ask me to move them, and somehow they made conversation difficult.

The next morning I rang up Nethercleugh and asked to speak to Janet.

There was a little pause and then a voice said, "Is that David? This is Janet speaking."

"Look here," I said. "You're very elusive. When can I see you?"

"I'm awfully busy, David. There's such a lot to do. Of course I'd like to see you sometime before you go back to London; I haven't seen you for ages."

"Haven't you?" I asked.

"It's years and years . . ."

"Elsie," I said. "You've made a mistake in the date. This isn't the first of April."

"What do you mean?"

"It's Janet I want to speak to. You beetle off and get her."

"Oh!" exclaimed the voice with a sort of gasp. "Oh, David—I was just having a joke with you."

"All right, you've had your joke; so now you can go and get Janet."

"Janet has gone out."

"When will she be back?"

There was a little click. Elsie had replaced the receiver.

I was angry. For some reason the difficulty of getting hold of Janet made me determined to see her—but how was it to be done? I looked for Mother and found her in the linen cupboard.

"Mother," I said. "How can I get hold of Janet?"

"Do you want to see her specially?" asked Mother in surprise.

"Not really," I replied. "But there seems to be some sort of conspiracy to prevent me from seeing her and I don't like conspiracies."

Mother nodded. "Elsie is jealous, that's the trouble. She's jealous of all Janet's friends. Her one idea is to keep Janet to herself; it's a sort of obsession."

"Freda seems to be in the conspiracy too. It's amazing! Why can't the Lorimers behave like sensible people?"

"Because they're not sensible, I suppose. Jealousy is a dreadful thing, David."

"Yes," I agreed thoughtfully. I knew Mother's horror of jealousy. In her opinion it was the worst of all sins.

"I'm very fond of Janet," continued Mother. "I can't bear to see her life being spoilt. If only she could get away from Nethercleugh and go to London and stay with Barbie and Nell!"

"Who is this Barbie?" I asked. "They were talking about her the other day. Elsie said she was horrible."

"She's a very clever, nice, interesting, amusing creature," declared Mother. "She has a job in London with a big firm of interior decorators and she wants Janet to go and share her flat. Barbie is just the right sort of friend for Janet."

"Why don't you speak to Mrs. Lorimer about it?"

"I have," replied Mother. "I've spoken about it several times, but it's not as easy as you might think. Barbie got a holiday at Easter and she asked Janet to go and stay at her home (it's a beautiful place near Loch Lomond) and of course Janet wanted to go. There was a lot of argument about it but eventually she was allowed to accept the invitation and off she went. Elsie was miserable; she refused to eat and mooned about the place like a lost spirit and she looked so wretched that they wired for Janet to come home."

"But that's frightful!"

"I know. It's frightful. I told Elsie how selfish it was. I told her she must brace up and not let herself be so dependent upon another person, but it was useless. She went and wailed and said I didn't understand. She said she couldn't help it."

"She must help it," I said. "Janet must get away. It's absolutely intolerable."

"You tell her, David," said Mother, looking at me and smiling. "We'll get hold of Janet and you can have a talk with her about it. I'll ask her to come and help me sort out the rubbish for the Jumble Sale. She often helps me with things like that—things that nobody else wants to do. I'll ring up and see if she can come to-morrow morning and you can have a chat with her afterwards."

The parcels of clothes for the Jumble Sale were in the spare bedroom and the next morning Mother began to undo them and sort them out. I was watching from the window and shortly after eleven I saw a girl open the gate and walk down the path. I was expecting Janet of course and for a moment I thought it was she.

"Here she is!" I exclaimed, and then I added: "No, it's not Janet."

"Not Janet?" asked Mother in surprise.

"It's Elsie."

"Are you sure?"

I was certain, but I could not explain how I knew. I could not explain without telling Mother I had seen Janet on the morning of my arrival in Haines.

"They're different," I said lamely. "I mean—well—they're just different—that's all."

Fortunately there was no time for Mother to pursue the subject before the door opened and Elsie appeared.

"Hallo!" she said. "Freda told me you wanted to see me, Mrs. Kirke." She smiled at me across the room as she spoke . . . she was very like Janet when she smiled.

"It was Janet I wanted," said Mother.

"But Freda said—"

"Freda knew quite well I wanted Janet to help me with the jumbles."

"Oh!" exclaimed Elsie. "But Freda said—"

"Well, never mind," said Mother. "Now that you're here you can help me. All these parcels have to be undone and the clothes laid out in piles."

The smile had vanished from Elsie's face. She stood and looked at the job in dismay. "Oh, but I don't think I *could* . . ." she began.

"It's not difficult. I'll show you."

"But they're dirty!" bleated Elsie. "I mean—I mean I wouldn't like to—to touch them."

Mother was really angry. I knew that by the brisk way she spoke.

"Come along, Elsie," she said. "I'll lend you an apron. We've got to get the job done before lunch."

It was time for me to go and leave them to their task and as I went out of the door I saw Elsie beginning to take off her coat. She was no match for Mother (few people were a match for Mother when she was on the war-path) and I could not help chuckling inwardly as I went down the stairs and out into the garden. Elsie was not going to enjoy her morning as much as she expected; to tell the truth I felt a little sorry for her but perhaps it would do her good.

On Saturday Cliffe came down from Edinburgh for the day. He came by bus and I met him at the bridge and took him to the manse for a cup of coffee. After that we strolled along the bank of the Ling and talked our heads off. First we talked, about *The Inward Eye*—Cliffe was tremendously interested and wanted to hear all that I could tell him—and then it was Cliffe's turn to talk and he told me he was in love.

"She's wonderful," said Cliffe. "She's a m-marvellous girl. If I talked for a week I couldn't tell you how m-marvellous she is. Of course I haven't said a word to her and she has no idea of anything—I mean I'm a bit frightened, David."

"But you're splendid," I said. "Any girl would be lucky to get you."

"Not Helen," said Cliffe rather miserably. "Helen could have half a dozen chaps. If only you could see her! She's proud and beautiful and dignified. She's like a queen. I want to m-marry her more than anything in the world, but somehow I can't imagine being m-married to her. Somehow I don't think she'd like the shop."

"But of course she would!" I told him. "If she loves you she'll take an interest in the things that interest you . . ."

"You couldn't expect her to do that," declared Cliffe.

"Why not?"

"Because—well, you couldn't. Helen is not like other girls. She's—she's remote."

"Remote?" I asked in surprise.

"That's the word," nodded Cliffe. "Sometimes when you're talking to her she doesn't hear what you're saying. There's a sort of look in her eyes as if she was thinking of something wonderful . . . and of course she is."

Cliffe went on talking about Helen in this strain and at last he took a little snapshot out of his pocket-book and showed it to me and I saw that what he said was true. Helen was a beautiful creature and she had the proud air of a queen. To my mind she did not look a very comfortable sort of girl and I said so.

"Comfortable!" exclaimed Cliffe.

"Well, you'd have to live with her all your life, wouldn't you?" I said reasonably. "If you were married to her she would be there all the time—every day. I'd rather have somebody comfortable; somebody who would listen to me when I wanted to talk to her;, somebody who would be sympathetic and kind."

"What a funny chap you are!" said Cliffe looking at me in an odd sort of way, and he put the photograph back in his pocket and said no more.

At lunch Cliffe was rather shy but Mother soon put him at his ease. She asked him about his home and she told him she used to live in Edinburgh when she was a child and often passed his father's shop and looked into the window. Father asked Cliffe about his work and whether he found it interesting.

By this time Cliffe had quite recovered and was his usual cheerful self.

"It's very interesting," he said. "It's so varied. I like serving in the shop—but that's only a part of it. The other day we went over to Glasgow for a sale. We went together, Dad and I, and stayed at a commercial hotel. It was a comfortable hotel and the food was jolly good, but what amused me was there were notices all over the place saying what you were to do and what you were not to do, and they were all signed 'Flea, Proprietor.'"

"Flea?" asked mother incredulously.

Cliffe nodded. "Flea," he said. "There was a big notice over the fireplace in the lounge and it said 'All visitors must be in bed before I am. Signed Flea, Proprietor.' I pointed it out to Dad and he said it was a very sensible precaution. Mr. Flea wanted everybody to go off to bed before himself, so that he could go round and put out the lights and see that nobody was fool enough to leave a burning cigarette end on the carpet. Dad said if he was the proprietor of a hotel he would do the same. The first night Dad and I were so tired we went to bed early, but the second night Dad had just sat down to a game of cards when Mr. Flea came in and said, 'Good night, gentlemen, I'm going to bed.' Dad put down his cards and got up. 'All right,' he said. 'You want us to be off to our beds, of course.' 'Not at all, sir,' said Mr. Flea politely. 'You go when you feel inclined.' 'But what about the notice?' said Dad, pointing to it, and he read it aloud. 'All visitors must be in bed before I am.' 'No, no,' said Mr. Flea, 'you've got it all wrong. All visitors must be in bed before one A.M.' 'But look here, Mr. Flea . . .' I began. 'What did you call me?' he cried. 'I'll have you know my name is Frederick Lea . . .'"

We were all laughing so much by this time that Cliffe had to stop. Even Father was laughing. It was not so much the story, it was the way Cliffe told it. As a matter of fact I did not believe Cliffe's story—or at least not all of it—for I knew Cliffe was capable of making a good story out of very slender material.

After lunch Cliffe went along to the blacksmith's to see his uncle and aunt and at four o'clock I saw him off in the bus.

Just as Cliffe was getting into the bus he turned to me and said, "I'll think about it, David. I believe you're right, you know."

"About what?" I asked. We had been discussing so many different subjects that I could not think what he meant.

"About Helen," said Cliffe, and with that he scrambled into the bus.

There were so many people scrambling into the bus that I could not get at him, so I ran round to the window and signed to him to open it.

The window had stuck and at first he could not move it but at last he managed to open it from the top and he put his head out.

"Cliffe!" I cried. "Don't think of what I said. I haven't seen her. I'm sure she's grand. You mustn't pay any attention to what I said."

"Listen, David," said Cliffe seriously. "If Mrs. Kirke was t-t-twenty years younger I'd m-m-marry her t-t-to-morrow and n-nothing would stop me . . ."

At that moment the bus started with a jerk and Cliffe fell backwards into his seat and vanished from view.

I stood on the pavement and laughed till I cried.

While I was at home I had a look at the wooden chest. Mother got it out one evening and put it on the table for me. It was strange to see that little chest—it was smaller than I had thought but every bit as beautiful—I ran my fingers over the polished surface and all sorts of recollections flooded into my mind. Presently I opened it and took out the stories and plays that Mother had collected and the big red book in which I had written Malcolm's Story.

"Read it, David," said Mother, nodding to me. "I read it again the other day. I often read it . . . and whenever I read it I *see* Malcolm. It may be a childish story, but you accomplished what you intended when you wrote it. To my mind that's the true test."

She was right, of course. The true test of any work is to accomplish your object and already I knew that in the realm of literature that is very difficult indeed. You see the gleam and you struggle to reach it but the mere fact of struggling dims your eyes.

I began to read Malcolm's Story in a critical spirit and I saw all the faults and failings of composition and grammar—they stuck out a mile—but after a few pages I forgot about them and I saw Malcolm; a clear vivid picture of the man formed itself in my mind. I saw Malcolm on the hills with his sheep, and in the cottage sitting on the solid wooden chair he had made himself—a chair which matched his giant frame—I saw him in his garden and in his workshop; I heard his slow deep voice: "Maybe I'll get leave and come to Haines later on. You'll not forget me, David?"

Yes, this was Malcolm himself and somehow the childish simplicity of the writing made the story more real and more moving. The picture was painted in primary colours. It was the saga of a hero.

When I had finished reading and closed the book I was left with a feeling that a small miracle had been wrought and I knew that if I lived to be a hundred I should never write anything so perfect as Malcolm's Story. It was a humbling thought.

The other stories in the box were rubbish and in spite of Mother's protests I burnt them in the kitchen fire ... but at the bottom of the box was a little package done up carefully in cotton wool and tied with string.

"What's that?" asked Mother. "I saw it but I didn't open it. I thought it might be private."

"It's Malcolm's locket," I replied. I cut the string and opened it and showed her the little gold locket with the picture inside.

"But it's lovely!" she cried. "Those are real pearls, Davie."

"I know," I said. "They're real pearls. He found them himself; he said that some day he would tell me the story of the locket—we shall never know it now. You take it and wear it, Mother. I think Malcolm would like you to wear it; in fact I know he would."

Mother hesitated. "Well," she said doubtfully. "Perhaps I should. Pearls get sick if they're shut up in the dark; it's good for them to be worn. But the locket is yours, Davie, and some day when you're married you shall have it back and give it to your wife."

I could not help smiling at the idea. "The locket is yours," I told her and I put the chain round her neck and fastened it. After that Mother wore it constantly and whenever it caught my eye I thought of Malcolm and how pleased he would be if he knew she was wearing it.

CHAPTER THIRTY-THREE

IT WAS difficult to settle down to work after my holiday (all the more so because the weather was beautiful and I longed to be out of doors) but after a few days I started another book and that helped to fill my mind. The new book was a novel; it was about a young Scot who came to work in London. There was a good deal of autobiography in the story and I found it very easy to write. My hero was called Ian; he was not much of a "hero"; for he was very human with faults and failings like the rest of us, but all the same I began to get fond of him. Ian came to London to make his fortune and he got into bad company and had an "affaire" with a girl who was not unlike Beryl. I called my novel *Golden Pavements* because of the old saying that the streets of London are paved with gold; but Ian did not make his fortune as quickly as he had expected, on the contrary he had a pretty thin time of it until he had learnt to hold his own.

Every evening I rushed home from the office, cooked my supper and ate it, and then sat down and wrote. Occasionally Mr. Coe lured me out and we went to a play together and every Sunday afternoon I took a bus into the country and walked for miles.

These jaunts into the country were not nearly so pleasant as the jaunts with Teddy and I missed her greatly, especially when I visited the places we had visited together and walked over the same ground alone. But even then the new book helped and I thought out all sorts of problems connected with *Golden Pavements* as I strode along. Teddy was married now and, judging from her letters, completely happy. She and Paul were stationed at a big camp near Chester and had found a comfortable flat. They had a spare room (said Teddy) and would be delighted to have me to stay for a few days—perhaps if I were going home I could break my journey and visit them—Paul wanted to meet me. It was nice of Paul, of course, but somehow I did not share his desire for a meeting. In any case I had had my annual holiday and could not go.

The months passed quickly. I saw nobody except Mr. Coe and the people at the office but I was not lonely. As a matter of fact I had settled comfortably into a groove and was quite contented with it. Autumn came with rain and blustering winds and, before I knew where I was, it was Christmas.

My life was so economical that I had saved up a good deal of money and I toyed with the idea of going home, but a long week-end was the extent of my Christmas holiday and it seemed scarcely worth while.

Mr. Coe and I joined forces for our Christmas dinner. We ate turkey and plum-pudding with rum-butter; we drank cherry-brandy and pulled crackers and wore paper-hats. It was ridiculous, I suppose, but we enjoyed ourselves in a quiet way. I enjoyed it a great deal more than the Christmas I had spent at Mrs. Hall's.

"We're doing the right thing," said Mr. Coe solemnly. "It's the right thing to be festive at Christmas."

He looked so funny sitting there with his solemn face and his silly paper-hat that I could not help smiling.

"You can smile, David," he said. "But Dickens was a great one for Christmas festivities and what's good enough for Dickens is good enough for me. I remember one Christmas; we were at Port Louis—that's in Mauritius in case you don't know—we were stuck there for three weeks with boiler trouble and it was as hot as Hades. Port Louis is a rum place at any time but at Christmas it's at its rummest, hot and steamy and airless. The streets were full of all sorts of people of every shade of colour from white to black—not forgetting yellow. If there's a place on earth where East and West meet and mix it's Port Louis . . ."

Mr. Coe was in a reminiscent mood so I sat back and prepared to listen. He was an excellent story-teller and could yarn away for hours about all the strange places he had been to and the strange people he had met. If he could have written his stories just as he told them he would have been a second Somerset Maugham.

Soon after Christmas a large parcel arrived from Basil Barnes; it contained six copies of *The Inward Eye*, bound in dark green 24vo cloth with gold lettering and with a jacket which depicted my sketch of the Big Business Man on his way to the city. The paper was thick and the print exceedingly clear and the whole effect was most attractive. It was thrilling to handle the books and know they were mine. It was strange to think that these books were the result of the untidy pile of papers which had lain upon the bottom shelf of the cupboard. I sent one to Mother and Father and one each to Uncle Matt and Aunt Etta and I sent one to Teddy. The fifth copy I took to the office and gave to Mr. Heatley.

"Hallo!" said Mr. Heatley. "So this is the great work! It looks pretty good to me. Have you got any money for it yet?"

"Just a small advance, sir," I replied. "But I don't mind. I mean I wouldn't mind if I didn't get a penny." I meant it, too. It was enough to see *The Inward Eye* in print and to know that it was on the bookstalls in America and that people were buying it and reading it.

Two days later I received a cheque from Mr. Randall for five hundred pounds.

To say I was astonished is an absurd understatement. There is no word big enough to describe my surprise, but I was not dazed and incredulous (as I had been when I received the letter from Basil Barnes which informed me that he would publish *The Inward Eye*); indeed I felt particularly clear-headed. I was elated of course for the sum was so vast; it was more than I had expected in my wildest dreams. It was affluence—or so it seemed to me—it put my writing on a different plane. I realised that my life had changed, it had broadened and widened, I myself was all of a sudden a different person. Ten minutes ago I had been the junior clerk in a dreary little office, now I was . . . but that needed thought.

When I had washed up the breakfast dishes I put the little slip of paper into my pocket-book and hurried off to the office. I thought about it as I went. In fact I was so busy thinking about it, and watching my horizon widen, that I nearly got run over by a bus. The screech of brakes and the torrent of abuse from the driver brought me to my senses and made me take more care. It would be a pity to get run over now, with a cheque for five hundred pounds in my pocket and the world at my feet.

Mr. Heatley was smiling when I went in to take his letters and I saw that he was in a friendly mood. "Well, Kirke," he said. "I haven't had time to read your book but my wife has read it and she's tremendously impressed. She reads a great deal and she knows what she's talking about and she says it's most unusual. She wants you to come to supper one evening and talk about *The Inward Eye*."

"It's very kind of Mrs. Heatley. I'd love to," I said.

"She thinks the book should do well," he continued. "It's interesting and amusing. She thinks there ought to be quite a lot of money in it."

I took the cheque out of my pocket and laid it on his desk. Mr. Heatley looked at the cheque and then at me. "H'm," he said. "You're giving me notice, I suppose."

There was a short silence. I could not answer because I did not know what to say. With five hundred pounds in the bank I could give up the daily toil of checking figures and typing letters and could spend all my time upon the work which I enjoyed; but five hundred pounds would not last for ever. I remembered Uncle Matt's warning about the madness of trying to earn my bread and butter by writing and I had an uncomfortable feeling that for once Father would agree with Uncle Matt.

"Mr. Heatley," I said at last "I don't know what to do. You've been very kind to me, but—but I don't know what to do."

He looked at me thoughtfully. "You think you're wasting your time here?" he inquired.

It was difficult to find a reply to that.

"Perhaps you are," he said, nodding. "If you can make five hundred pounds in your spare time you certainly are wasting your time working here."

"But can I?" I cried desperately. "I mean how do I know I can go on doing it? That's the trouble?"

"That is the trouble," he agreed. "It's a risk of course but if I were your age with nobody dependent upon me I should be inclined to take it. What do you say to six months' holiday?"

"Six months' holiday!" I echoed in amazement.

"Yes, six months should be enough."

"But Mr. Heatley—"

"Look here," he said, smiling. "Just listen to me a moment. I haven't read this great work of yours but from what Sylvia says I'm pretty sure it's good. Your work in the office is only moderate; you're a bit vague at times. My idea is that you should go away and write—if that's what you want to do. In six months you'll know whether or not you can make a success of it. If you can, well and good; if not, come back to me. You'll be more use to me because you'll have got it out of your system. How's that, Kirke?"

"Yes," I said breathlessly. "It's splendid! I don't know how to thank you, sir."

He nodded. "I'll tell Penman. You had better stay on until we find another clerk."

"Of course," I said. "Yes, of course. I can't tell you . . ."

But Mr. Heatley had finished with the subject. He took up a letter and began to dictate his reply.

Mr. Penman's reaction was very different from Mr. Heatley's. He was horrified at the idea that I was giving up "a settled job with good prospects" and he did all he could to persuade me to carry on and to "put the money in War Savings for a rainy day." Wrigson and Ullenwood were incredulous at first; they thought it was another of my jokes on a par with my "nonsense about Mother." When at last a new clerk was engaged to take my place they were forced to believe it and were frankly envious.

"Gosh!" exclaimed Wrigson. "Fancy being able to lie in bed as long as you like! Fancy having nothing to do except amuse yourself!"

"But that isn't the idea at all," I told him. "I'm exchanging one job—which I'm not particularly good at—for another job which I hope to do better."

"You'll buy a car, I suppose," said Ullenwood.

"You'll paint the town red," suggested Wrigson.

I laughed and told them I was going to do neither. I was going to work harder than ever and live as economically as possible.

"You'll be back here in six months—or less," declared Mr. Penman.

My first free day was wonderful. Instead of hastening off to the office I sat down at my table and wrote. At twelve o'clock I went round to The Wooden Spoon for lunch; I spent the afternoon prowling about the streets, getting a little exercise and using my eyes, and I wrote again in the evening. This arrangement suited me well and I stuck to it. With so much time to work I soon finished *Golden Pavements*; I bought a second-hand typewriter and typed the book myself and took it along to Mr. Randall.

Mr. Randall was pleased to see me. "This is lucky," he said. "I was just going to write and ask you to look in. Sit down and have a cigarette, Mr. Kirke. I've good news for you."

I told him I did not smoke and he took a cigarette himself and lighted it. "Well, here's the news," he said cheerfully. "We've found an English publisher for *The Inward Eye*. You had better have a look at the contract. It's not as good as the American one of course but fair enough."

"If you say so that's all right," I told him.

The parcel containing the manuscript of *Golden Pavements* was still tucked under my arm. As a matter of fact I had forgotten about it.

"Is that another book?" asked Mr. Randall.

"Yes, it's a novel this time."

"Good. I'll get it sent off straight away. Basil Barnes wants it."

"But I thought you'd read it!" I cried. "You had better read it and see if it will do. I'm not sure—I mean it may be absolute rubbish!"

"I'll read it," he said, smiling. "But you needn't worry. As long as you write about things that interest you your books will interest other people. Just keep on writing. Don't stop."

"I can't stop, Mr. Randall. For one thing I want to write—it's become a sort of craze—and for another I've given up my job. It's write or starve."

He laughed. "That's the best news I've heard for a long time—and talking of starving, we might go and have lunch together if you haven't anything better to do."

We had lunch at a small restaurant with a sanded floor but I was far too excited and interested in our conversation to notice what we ate. Books were Mr. Randall's job and also his hobby; there was not much he did not know about books. Presently he asked what I thought of doing next, and I told him I thought of starting another Inward Eye. There was plenty of material at hand and I had time to wander about London.

"Why not wander about France?" he suggested.

I gazed at him in astonishment.

"It's just an idea," he said, smiling. "Far be it from me to interfere with your plans but it's worth consideration . . . France or Holland . . . or Italy if you'd rather. I can see a whole shelf of Inward Eyes waiting to be written—clamouring to be written. If you don't want to go abroad you might go and have a look at Cornwall. Why not?"

"Yes," I said in a dazed sort of way. "Yes, why not?"

"Had you never thought of it, Mr. Kirke?"

"No, never. You'll think I'm mad. It's the obvious thing to do—but—but Eve always been tied down and I've never had any money."

"You're free now and there's more money coming along. I certainly think you should travel about a bit," said Mr. Randall. "There's no need to decide at once, of course."

As I walked home to the flat Mr. Randall's words rang in my head: *you're free now and there's more money coming along*. Astonishing words! Words which opened doors and windows to the imagination!

That evening I borrowed a big atlas from Mr. Coe and had a look at the world. Should I go to France or Holland to write the next book—or should I go farther afield? The whole wide world was open to me. I could fly to South Africa or to Florida; I could visit the Caribbean or the Sahara Desert. I felt like a man with a magic carpet spread at his feet.

After a bit I came down to earth and thought about ways and means and I realised I must wait a bit before I set off on my travels. Five hundred pounds—and more to come—sounded all right, but it would not take me to the ends of the earth. I must wait and see what happened to *Golden Pavements*.

I closed the atlas and went to bed.

CHAPTER THIRTY-FOUR

20 Surrey Mansions
Mark Street
W.C.2

DEAR DAVID,

You said I was to let you know when I came to London. Well, here I am at last! It is very thrilling. In fact I can hardly believe it. I am sharing a flat with two school-friends and we want you to come and have supper with us on Monday night—if you think you could bear to have supper with three females! Do come, David—at about half-past seven. Nell is a very good cook! I am sorry to give you such short notice but don't bother to reply. Just come if you can.

Yours,

Janet

The letter arrived on Monday morning so there was no time to reply, but there was no doubt in my mind as to whether or not I should accept the invitation. Janet in London! It was splendid news. I wondered how she had managed to escape from Nethercleugh and whether Mother had had a hand in it. I wondered . . . but there was no need to wonder; I should hear all about it to-night.

Mark Street is five minutes' walk from Covent Garden Market and it was seven-thirty precisely when I climbed the stairs of Surrey Mansions and rang the bell of Number Twenty. Janet herself opened the door. Although I had expected to see her, it seemed very strange indeed to see her here.

"David!" she exclaimed. "How lovely! Nell and Barbie said you wouldn't come. They've been teasing me about it."

"Of course I came," I said, smiling. "You said Nell was a very good cook."

A tall, slim girl with dark hair emerged from the kitchen.

"That was cheating," she declared. "If I'd known you'd said *that* in your letter I wouldn't have bet you twopence he wouldn't come."

"This is Nell," said Janet.

"I thought it must be," I said.

We went into the sitting-room. It was large and airy with white walls and coloured-cretonne covers on the furniture. There were flowers in vases on the book-case and the table. It was a charming room and there was a friendly feeling about it, a feeling of happiness. Another girl—a plump girl with red hair and a smooth pale skin—was laying the table for supper.

"Here he is, Barbie!" said Janet. "This is David."

"How do you do?" said Barbie. "Welcome to Scotch Corner!"

"That's what Barbie calls this flat," explained Nell. "She says it's a bit of Scotland in the middle of London. She wanted to have tartan covers on the chairs and a picture of 'The Stag at Bay' over the mantelpiece but I wouldn't let her. I don't belong to her barbarous country. Besides, the name is quite unsuitable because Scotch Corner isn't in Scotland at all."

"There's something burning," said Barbie.

"My *ragoût*!" cried Nell, and vanished.

"Come and sit down, David," said Janet. "They're mad but quite harmless. I want to hear your news."

"I want to hear yours," I said. "How did you get away?"

"It was difficult," said Janet, suddenly grave. "I never would have managed it if Mrs. Kirke hadn't helped me. She persuaded Mother to let me come. I don't know how she did it."

Barbie came over to where we were sitting and drew up a leather stool. "Look here, David," she said. "I'm going to tell you the whole thing. Jan wants to be herself—not just half somebody else. That's why Nell and I wanted her to come and stay with us. You know her family so perhaps you can understand what I'm driving at."

"Yes," I said.

"Jan's sisters are bloodsuckers," declared Barbie.

"Shut up, Barbie!" exclaimed Janet.

"I won't shut up! You know it's true. You know perfectly well they've sucked your blood for years. You've never been able to do anything you wanted. Freda has always bossed you and Elsie has tagged along behind, clinging to your petticoats and bleating like Mary's little lamb!"

"Don't listen to her, David!" cried Janet.

"Yes, listen, David," said Barbie. "Listen to every word. How would you like to have a twin who resembles you so closely, that very few people know which is you and which isn't?"

"Not much," I said. "As a matter of fact I know—"

"It's a grim thought," declared Barbie, interrupting me. "All the more grim when that twin, though like you in appearance, is utterly unlike you inside; when that twin is as selfish as the devil and makes use of the resemblance for her own ends."

"Barbie, don't!" cried Janet. "Please be quiet!"

"All right, that's all," said Barbie.

"Not quite all," declared Nell, appearing from the kitchen with a large brown casserole in her hands. "You haven't told David that this morning she got a letter to say that her poor little twin is pining for her and can neither sleep nor eat. And it's all because horrid selfish Jan has gone away and left her."

"Stop!" cried Janet. "All that has nothing to do with David. You're making David uncomfortable. I wouldn't have asked him if I'd known you were going to be so silly."

"We won't say another word," declared Barbie, rising as she spoke. "What's in that casserole, Nell? It smells good."

"Just rabbit," replied Nell. "Rabbit and bits of bacon and mushrooms and odds and ends—"

"It's the odds and ends that make all the difference," said Barbie, sniffing in an appreciative manner. "When I cook rabbit it comes out like pieces of white rubber, but Nell's rabbit stew is fit for the gods."

"*Ragoût*, please," said Nell solemnly.

We ate Nell's *ragoût*, which was undoubtedly Olympian, and we drank cider and we talked.

"We've got your book, Mr. David Kirke," said Nell. "We've all read it and we think it's simply marvellous. As a matter of fact I was wondering whether the author would deign to inscribe it for me."

"My book!" I exclaimed in amazement.

"Thereby hangs a tale," said Barbie, laughing. "Jan had read it of course (your mother lent it to her) and she talked about it so much that Nell and I were crazy to see it. Nell has a friend who is a pilot in a Transatlantic Air-Liner . . . you can go on, Nell."

"Thank you," said Nell solemnly. "I wondered whether this was my story or yours. Well, this friend of mine—he's rather a dear, really—asked me if I'd like him to bring me nylons from little old New York and I said, bring me *The Inward Eye* by David Kirke. You needn't be too puffed up about it," said Nell, giggling in an attractive manner. "For one thing I wanted to be different—all his girl-friends ask for nylons—and I wanted to be difficult."

"Nell wanted to give him a difficult assignment," Barbie explained. "Like the hero in a fairy story who is told to bring three hairs from the dragon's tail."

"But it wasn't difficult," continued Nell. "In fact it was the easiest task in the world. He said all the book-stalls were full of *Inward Eyes* . . . and as for nylons I can't bear them now that every common little so-and-so in town is wearing the things and they've become a Music Hall joke like mothers-in-law and Wigan."

"She's taken a scunner at them," put in Barbie.

"I don't understand your barbarous tongue," declared Nell. "But all the little wenches at Winter and Greene's wear them on their nasty little legs. They wear nylons and lip-stick and crimson nail varnish, but they're too lazy to wash their necks or brush their hair. If that isn't putting off I don't know what is. Give me real silk every time," added Nell, holding out a slim elegant leg encased in fine silk hosiery.

"It looks very nice," I said.

"Don't make her more conceited than she is already!" said Barbie, laughing. "Besides I want to talk about your book. It's a peach of a book, David. It's the sort of book to keep beside your bed and read when things look blue. I laughed like anything at the bit about that restaurant and the sketches of the people feeding."

"I loved the little boy in the park," said Janet, smiling at me across the table.

"Madame Tussaud's is the best," declared Nell. "I've read it half a dozen times and it still makes me laugh."

The author of *The Inward Eye* sat and listened; to be perfectly honest he was as pleased as Punch.

All too soon the subject was changed. Barbie asked me how and where I lived and so I told them about my flat.

"I think it would be rather dull to have nobody to talk to," said Nell.

"It's better to have nobody than the wrong sort of people," I declared. "When I first came to London I lived in a boarding-house. Everybody was so miserable that it gave me the creeps. I ran away."

"You say that as if you thought it was cowardly," said Janet.

"Sometimes I think it was."

"But why?" she asked. "If you couldn't help them or do them any good. It was no use staying and being miserable yourself."

"Why were they miserable?" Barbie wanted to know.

I tried to explain. I told them about Mr. Kensey and Miss Bulwer, I told them about Madame Futrelle and Mrs. Hall; finally I told them about Ned and Beryl and the birthday party and they listened absorbed in the recital.

"They were all mad," said Janet at last. "Stark, staring mad—no wonder you ran away!"

"They were all suffering from psycho-neurosis," said Nell.

"All of them?" asked Janet.

"All of them," replied Nell, nodding. "It's a definite disease brought on by the hurry and bustle of modern life. The struggle for existence wears out their nerves, so they worry about trifles and they can't sleep."

"But they couldn't all be suffering from that," objected Janet.

"Perhaps it's infectious," said Nell thoughtfully. "Yes, that's the answer, it's an infectious disease. I'm sure it is. This morning when I was waiting in a queue to buy the rabbit I noticed that everybody looked miserable and after a bit I began to feel miserable myself."

"Perhaps it's something to do with money," suggested Janet. "If people had more money and didn't have to worry about the future . . ."

"It isn't that," I said. "Mr. Kensey had plenty of money but he was just as miserable as the others and I'm sure Madame Futrelle didn't worry about the future—nor Beryl, either."

"Now, look here," said Barbie at last. "You've talked and talked. I've just been sitting here listening and wondering whether any of you would hit on the explanation. I can tell you why people are miserable and discontented and why they have to show off and get tight and behave like morons. It's because they aren't Christians."

"But, Barbie—" began Nell.

"They don't believe in God," declared Barbie, putting her elbows on the table and fitting her chin into her cupped hands. "They—don't—believe—in God."

"But they do!" I exclaimed. "They go to church—"

"Poof!" said Barbie. "They go to church and they say their prayers but that milk-and-watery sort of thing is no good. It wouldn't move a feather, far less a mountain. Do you realise that if we had the right sort of faith we could move mountains?"

"But wasn't that meant metaphorically?" Nell inquired.

"Metaphorically my foot!" said Barbie in her downright way. "Read it carefully and you'll see. It was a definite serious statement of fact and I believe it's absolutely true. If you and I and Jan and David had the right sort of faith we could go out and move Ben Nevis into the middle of Loch Lomond."

"You mean nobody believes?" I asked.

"Some people believe more than others, but nobody believes enough."

There was a short silence. Nell took a cigarette, fitted it into a holder and lighted it; she blew a cloud of smoke through her nose.

"You've got something there," she said. "It's frightfully exciting when you think of it. I mean, you wouldn't want to move a mountain, it would be a bit pointless, but there are other things . . ."

"How could you make yourself believe enough?" asked Janet.

"I can answer that," I told her. "You'd have to want it enough, that's all. You'd have to want it as much as the man who said, 'Lord, I believe, help Thou mine unbelief.'"

"Of course!" cried Barbie, looking at me and smiling. "That's the answer. You must want it desperately. Nothing else is any use."

"I want to want it like that," said Janet slowly. "That's all I can say truthfully."

By this time we had finished supper (a chocolate meringue had followed the *ragoût* and had been disposed of with appreciation in spite of the interesting talk). Nell rose to collect the plates and clear the table.

"Let me help," I said. "I'm an experienced washer-up."

"Nonsense," said Barbie. "Nell and I are the washers-up to-night. You're to sit down and have your coffee and talk to Jan. It's all fixed. Nell and I have talked and talked—as a matter of fact we can't help it, we're made that way—but it's about time you and Jan had a little peace. Do what you're told, David," she added, seizing a plate out of my hands. "You'll never be asked to Scotch Corner again if you don't do what you're told."

"We've got to do what Barbie says," declared Janet, smiling at me. "Barbie is terribly autocratic."

I had noticed that Nell and Barbie called her Jan and I liked the little name. It seemed to suit her. I found I had begun to call her Jan, myself.

We sat down together on the sofa. From the kitchen came the clatter of plates and the humming sound of voices in earnest discussion.

"They're still at it," said Jan with a little laugh. "They're terrific talkers—both of them. Sometimes I'm surprised they don't talk in their sleep! But they're darlings all the same."

"I like them awfully much," I told her.

"And they like you," declared Jan.

"Jan," I said. "You won't have to go home, will you?" She hesitated and then she said in a low voice, "Oh, David, I don't know. I'm terribly worried. Freda seems to think I should go home, but how can I? You see Nell got me this job at Winter and Greene's. It's a good job and I only got it because Nell has been there for two years and recommended me to the manager, so I simply can't let her down. Besides it takes three of us to run this flat and they got rid of another girl so that I could come. How can I possibly rush off home and leave them stranded?"

"You can't, Jan."

"But if Elsie is really ill?"

"Surely she can't be really ill. It's fantastic."

"We're twins," said Jan slowly. "There's something odd about being a twin. It isn't a matter of liking or disliking; it's something much queerer and more difficult to understand. Either you want to be with the other one all the time—or else you don't. Oh David, it sounds horrid, but that's how it is. That's how it has always been. I've always wanted to get away and be myself. Are you disgusted with me?"

"No, of course not, Jan. It's right that you should want to lead your own life."

"But if she's really ill?"

"I'll write to Mother," I said. "Would that be any good?"

"Oh yes!" she exclaimed. "Yes, write to Mrs. Kirke. She could go and see Elsie, couldn't she?"

"I'll write and explain everything," I said. "Mother will know. Don't worry about it any more."

"Now tell me about you," said Jan, turning her head and looking at me. Her eyes were wide and very blue, they made me think of a pool in the Ling, reflecting the summer sky.

"Tell you—about me?" I asked doubtfully.

"Do tell me, David. There's something different about you. I've been noticing it all the evening. You're—more alive. It's the book, isn't it? Oh, David, I wish I could tell you how much I like your book! All the time I was reading it I felt as if you were taking me with you and showing me what you saw—telling me about it. Of course I knew you weren't."

"What do you mean, Jan?"

"You weren't taking *me*," explained Jan. "You were taking some-body else."

"I believe I was taking Mother," I said thoughtfully.

She smiled at me. "Yes, that would explain it."

We were silent for a few moments and then I said, "You were asking why I seemed different; it isn't only because I've written a book, it's because I'm free."

"Free?"

"I've left the office. I'm going to see if I can make my living by writing."

"Tell me everything," said Jan eagerly.

I had not intended to tell Jan, but she was so sweet and friendly that I could not resist the temptation. It was such a relief to pour out my hopes and my plans and to find that she understood.

"It's a gamble," I said. "But you can't get anything worth while unless you're willing to take a risk. Don't tell Mother, will you? I haven't told them yet. I'm afraid they might worry."

"You'll do it," said Jan. "Of course you will. There's a sort of—a sort of successful feeling about you. But of course I won't say a word to anybody. It's a tremendously exciting secret."

"Our second secret, Jan. Do you remember the day we drank milk together in the dairy?"

"It's our third secret!"

I could not remember another secret and when I asked her what it was she only laughed.

Before I went home I invited the three girls to come to dinner at my flat. It was a little difficult to arrange an evening to suit them all—Nell, especially, seemed to have a great many engagements—but eventually we fixed a day the following week for the party.

I had a great deal to think about as I walked back to my flat; chiefly about Jan and her problem. I had realised before that she was unhappy at Nethercleugh but I understood it even better now. Barbie and Nell loved her and appreciated her and it was good for her, as well as pleas-ant, to be loved and appreciated. On no account must Jan go home . . . besides I did not want her to go home. It was delightful to have a real friend in London; somebody who knew Haines and could talk about it. I would see her again next week. I began to wonder if I could find some excuse to see her before then.

CHAPTER THIRTY-FIVE

MR. COE had gone to do his shopping and I was looking after the shop for him when the door opened and a young man walked in; a tall fellow with dark curly hair. I gazed at him in astonishment. It was Miles Blackworth!

The little shop was dim and shadowy. Miles came in and looked round. "Does Mr. David Kirke live here?" he asked.

"Miles!" I exclaimed. "Where on earth have you come from?"

"David!" he cried. "Great Scott, I didn't see it was you!"

"How are you, old boy!" I asked eagerly. "What have you been doing? Where are you staying?"

"I'm fine," declared Miles, smiling at me. "I'm staying with some friends in Kensington. I got your address from your uncle and I thought it would be fun to look you up."

"It's good to see you," I told him—and so it was—I had forgiven Miles long ago for his misdemeanours. "I'm terribly glad to see you, old boy. If you don't mind waiting a few minutes Mr. Coe will be back and we can go and have a spot of lunch together."

"Is this your job?" asked Miles in a doubtful voice. It was obvious that he did not approve of my employment.

I laughed. There was so much to tell Miles that I did not know where to begin.

"I was in an office," I said. "You remember Uncle Matt got me a job in a lawyer's office, but now—"

"Are you still living at the boarding-house?"

"No fears! It was a frightful place. Sit down and I'll tell you everything. I've had all sorts of adventures."

"I wish I'd come with you," declared Miles. "It was the family that prevented me; you know how interfering they are. They kept on telling me what a rattling good time I should have at the University but it didn't work out as I expected. For instance I was practically promised a place in the University Fifteen (I thought it was settled and I was as keen as mustard) but somehow I got up against the captain and there was a lot of bother . . ."

Miles went on talking. He perched himself on the counter with his long legs crossed and lighted a cigarette. It was obvious that he had come to tell me his news—not to hear mine—so I settled down to a role of listener and sympathiser. My first impression had been that Miles was exactly the same as ever but after a few minutes I changed my mind about him and decided that he had lost his sparkle; this was not the splendid dashing fellow who had charmed me in bygone days . . .

"You're not listening, David!" exclaimed Miles in annoyance.

"Yes, I am," I declared—I had been listening with half an ear—"you were telling me about the rugger match. By the way, I suppose you're a full-blown lawyer now?"

"Goodness no! I've chucked Law."

"You've chucked Law?"

"Yes, I've chucked the whole thing; it was too much grind, and so monotonous. Long dull lectures and heavy dull books! You've no idea what a frightful grind it was . . ." he told me about it at length and I listened patiently.

When he had finished I thought it was my turn. "I've got a flat, Miles," I said. "I furnished it myself; it was good fun—"

"I thought of taking a flat in Edinburgh," said Miles. "I was fed up with living at home; besides—well—there was a girl. We were engaged, you see. She's a dear little thing, but unfortunately she hasn't much backbone and her father came out all Victorian and asked me how I was going to support her. He was pretty nasty about it. I said we could easily wait a bit until I managed to get a job, but he made Iris break it off. People are extraordinary, aren't they?"

"Well, I don't know—" I began.

"Of course if I'd got a job it would have been all right, and if I'd come to London with you I'd have had a job. Gosh, David, I wish I had! If I've wished it once I've wished it a hundred times . . . but of course it's not too late."

"You mean Iris will wait?"

"Lord, no! That's all off. I mean to keep clear of girls and concentrate on getting a rattling good job and making a success of life." He laughed and added, "D'you remember how we were going to make our fortunes?"

"Yes, of course I remember. How are you going to begin?"

"Oh, I'm looking about. I'm not in any hurry. I don't want to rush into anything without considering it carefully. I mean it's so important to start on the right lines. I know what I don't want, of course. I *don't* want an office job—couldn't stick the monotony—and I don't want too long hours. As a matter of fact I was hoping you might be able to suggest something, but . . ." he hesitated.

"But you wouldn't like this job," I said, hiding a smile. Miles was amusing me vastly.

"Well—no," he agreed. "There wouldn't be much future in it, would there?"

"You want to make your fortune," I said understandingly.

"You're laughing at me," said Miles. "I know I used to talk a lot of rot but seriously I *do* want a job with lots of scope. A job that will lead somewhere."

I nodded. "Let me see. You want a well-paid job with lots of scope and good prospects and plenty of time off."

"Well, what's wrong with that?" asked Miles defensively.

Before I could tell him what was wrong with it a customer appeared. He was one of those annoying people who, unlike Miles, have no idea what they want. He began by asking for a book about birds, with coloured illustrations, and spent a long time looking at them. Then he looked at guide-books for various districts of England and finally he bought a second-hand novel and drifted away.

"How can you be bothered!" exclaimed Miles. "It would send me round the bend. What do they pay you, David?"

I laughed.

"Nothing," I said.

"Nothing?" asked Miles in amazement.

"No, nothing. I do it for love."

"All right, you needn't tell me," said Miles huffily. He got down from the counter and took up his hat. "You've changed, David," he added. "I thought you'd be pleased to see me—but you've changed."

"Wait, Miles!" I cried. "I'm sorry I ragged you. I'll tell you all about everything if you want to hear. The point is are you interested?"

He paused and looked at me. "You *have* changed," he declared. "You used to be . . . Oh, hell, here's another customer!"

But this time it was Mr. Coe with his shopping basket and when I had handed over to him I took Miles upstairs to my flat.

Now that I had more money to spend I was allowing myself a few luxuries so I was able to offer Miles a glass of sherry. He sat and smoked and sipped the wine.

"This is dashed good stuff!" he exclaimed in surprise.

"Yes," I agreed. "If I can't get good stuff I prefer water. You see Uncle Matt educated my palate. I'm not sure whether to be grateful to him or not. On the one hand—"

"What *are* you doing?" asked Miles. "You needn't tell me you're a shop assistant, David. You couldn't live in a comfortable flat and buy good wine on a shop assistant's screw."

"No," I agreed.

"Well, go on," said Miles. "What sort of job have you got? Why the heck are you so secretive?"

"I'm not secretive," I replied, smiling. "I've tried to tell you several times but you wouldn't listen. If you're ready to listen I'll tell you about my job. It's a pretty good job, really. It's well-paid and has plenty of scope and excellent prospects—and of course I'm my own master which is an advantage. I mean I can take a day off whenever I like." Miles gazed at me with astonishment. His face was so funny that I burst out laughing.

"There," I said, taking a copy of *The Inward Eye* out of the cupboard and handing it to him. "That's my job, Miles."

He looked at it. "D'you mean you wrote this?" he asked incredulously. "But how do you live, David? Do you get an allowance from your parents or what?"

I explained the whole matter and for once Miles was not only willing but eager to hear what I had to say.

"It's amazing," he said at last. "What made you think of writing a book? How did you begin? You know, David, I've often thought of writing a book but I've never had time to get down to it—and as a matter of fact I had no idea that there was so much money in it. Of course *this* sort of book isn't in my line, but I could write a thriller. You'd get even more money for a thriller because it would appeal to more people, wouldn't it? The only trouble is, how would one live until the book was finished?"

"That's the trouble," I agreed.

"But it wouldn't take long," continued Miles more hopefully. "Perhaps the family would stump up enough cash to keep me going for a month or two. How long did it take you to write this?"

"How long?" I repeated in surprise.

"Yes, how many hours of work did you put into it?"

I realised that he did not understand at all, and that I could never make him understand. *The Inward Eye* had been part of my life for nearly a year. Everything that I had done and seen and thought had gone into the book. The actual hours I had spent at my table writing had been a small part of the work.

"There must be some way of doing it," continued Miles frowning thoughtfully. "Authors can't live on air. I believe the thing to do would be to make an arrangement with a publisher to pay for your keep while you were writing the book."

"That certainly would be the thing to do—if you could persuade a publisher to do it."

"Why shouldn't he? It would be a business arrangement of course. I would sign an agreement promising to send him the book when it was finished."

"It sounds good," I agreed, trying not to laugh. "You should try it, Miles. I shall be interested to know what the publisher says when you put your plan before him."

"I wish you'd stop ragging," said Miles crossly. "I know what it is: you think I couldn't do it. I bet you I could write a jolly good thriller. I've always liked thrillers and I know the form; as a matter of fact I've got several ideas already."

I looked at Miles and considered the matter seriously. I had always believed Miles could do anything if he tried and there was nothing very difficult about writing. I remembered that Miles had always liked thrillers and was a connoisseur of that type of literature.

"I'm not taking the bet," I told him. "If you put your mind to it I see no reason why you shouldn't write a good thriller, but it doesn't matter what I think. You'd have to convince a publisher that you were a second Edgar Wallace before he would take any interest in you. That's the truth, Miles."

"H'm," said Miles putting down my book and clasping his hands behind his head. "Yes, there's something in that. One would have to wangle an introduction to the fellow. No good just blowing in."

I left it at that. He would have to learn for himself; it was useless to argue with Miles.

"Come and have lunch," I said. "There's a place called The Wooden Spoon where they give you a decent meal."

We had lunch together and talked about old times. Miles said no more about his thriller but I had a feeling he was still thinking about it. As I said good-bye to him it occurred to me to ask him to dinner on Thursday night. Miles was good value at parties and it would be more amusing for the girls if I had another man.

"Three girls!" exclaimed Miles. "Good lord, you're an absolute sultan! Yes, of course I'll come."

CHAPTER THIRTY-SIX

THURSDAY was cold and wet and windy. It was unseasonable and as I buttoned my waterproof up to my neck I suddenly thought of Malcolm's rhyme about the borrowing days.

The Austrian proprietor of The Wooden Spoon had agreed to send dinner up to my flat. I was a good customer and he had promised that everything should be done as I wished. The dinner was ordered but I was anxious to have a last word with him and tell him there would be five of us instead of four. When I had seen him I went home and arranged the flowers which I had bought at the market. This job took longer than I had expected and even when I had finished I was not pleased with the result. The flowers in Barbie's flat always looked so beautiful.

I could not write that day—I was excited about my party—as a matter of fact I was having a good deal of trouble with my new book. I realised that Mr. Randall was right and that I ought to go away to pastures new and gather fresh material but for some reason I did not want to go away. The mere thought of leaving London was distasteful which was odd to say the least of it. I had been thrilled with the idea when Mr. Randall suggested it to me.

Two letters arrived by the afternoon post. I collected them from Mr. Coe and took them upstairs to read. One was from Mother—it was her answer to the letter I had written about Jan's problem—and the other was from Uncle Matt. I opened Mother's first:

> *The Manse*
> *Haines*

DEAREST DAVIE,

I am very glad you went to see Janet and her friends. It is good news that she is happy and getting on well—and a great relief to my mind for it was I who persuaded Mrs. Lorimer to let her go! This was not easy of course and I had to tell Mrs. Lorimer what happened when you were here—you remember about the conspiracy to prevent you from meeting Janet? Mrs. Lorimer did not know about it and was somewhat upset when I told her. I struck while the iron was hot and said the twins must be separated, not only for Janet's sake but also for Elsie's. Things could not be allowed to go on like that. I just kept at it and got it fixed then and there—so you see what an interfering old busybody your mother is! But if Janet is happy it is worth all the trouble and unpleasantness. I went up to Nethercleugh yesterday after I got your letter to see how the land lay and I found them much as usual—you know what that means, Davie! Of course they all miss Janet and find there is a good deal more to do. Mr. Lorimer raised several hares while we were having tea. He asked in his usual pleasant way why this and that and the other had not been done and the reply was: "Janet always did it." Elsie is miserable, of course. She mopes about the house and looks pretty wretched. Mrs. Lorimer spoke to me about it, she seems worried. But my impression is that there is nothing wrong with Elsie (or at least nothing seriously wrong) she is just being naughty and "playing up." She will get tired of it in time. Freda ran after me when I was on my way home and said she thought Janet ought to give up her job in London and return to Nethercleugh—didn't I agree? I said no, I did not agree. Freda was annoyed with me but I did not care. The truth is they are all selfish. I am quite sure Janet ought not to come home. Elsie must learn to stand on her own feet and if she does not learn this now she will never learn it. Is Janet to spend her whole life playing nursemaid to Elsie? The thing is nonsense! That is what I think about it, Davie. Give Janet my love and tell her I will keep an eye on Elsie and if I think it necessary for her to come home I will write to her. Now Davie I must give you a piece of sad news. Poor old Aunt Etta died yesterday. I know you were fond of her and will be sorry, but her life was not much pleasure to her, poor soul. It must have been very dull and lonely for her living by herself and not being able to get out and about. She had a bad heart attack on Monday night and died early on Tuesday morning without recovering consciousness. Uncle Matthew rang up and told us and we are going to Edinburgh for the funeral and staying the night with him. I expect you will be writing to Uncle Matthew to tell him how sorry you are. Although he pretends to be hard-hearted I think he is genuinely upset.

I will write again soon, my dearie, I want to catch the post. Much love from us both.

MOTHER

This letter gave me a lot to think about. Poor old Aunt Etta! It was true that I was fond of her. She had always been very kind to me. I felt very sorry that I should never see her again. In one thing Mother was wrong (or so I thought), Aunt Etta had been quite contented with her life, had even enjoyed it in her quiet way. She had enjoyed her food and reading novels and the comforts with which she was surrounded; most of all she had enjoyed seeing people and talking to them. I was very glad I had paid her a visit when I was in Edinburgh and had spent an hour with her.

I put Mother's letter aside and took up Uncle Matt's; I knew now what it was about—or thought I knew—but I was somewhat surprised when I opened it and saw it was so long (Uncle Matt seldom wrote to me and, when he did, his letters were terse and business-like). Here were four sheets of paper closely written in his crabbed handwriting, which I always found difficult to decipher:

> *19 Ruthven Crescent*
> *Edinburgh*

DEAR DAVID,

You will have heard from your mother that Etta is dead. It was a shock to me for I thought her aches and pains were imaginary and that there was little the matter with her except nerves. I still think she would have been healthier if she had made an effort and taken a little exercise instead of sitting in a chair all day reading novels. However there it is. We all have to die some day. As you know she annoyed me a good deal one way and another but all the same I shall miss her.

It is sad to think I shall not see poor Etta again. She had no brain to speak of but she liked talking about the old days when we were all young. Now there is nobody to talk to about those times. I do not count your father for I could never talk to him for five minutes without treading on his corns. Now to business. Etta had very little money. She was life-rented in capital which provided a small yearly income but this was insufficient for her needs and I was obliged to supplement her income so that she should be comfortable and properly looked after. It was easy to do this without her knowledge because she had no head for business matters. Sometimes when she was particularly annoying I felt inclined to tell her but I never did. None of this affects you, of course. I am only telling you so that you may understand why there is so little money left. You are Etta's residuary legatee which simply means that when her estate has been wound up and the bequests paid you will get that blasted Green Beech Cottage and about two hundred pounds. The cottage is a white elephant and always has been. It belonged to a woman called Vera Marsden who diddled Etta out of two thousand pounds—a sum which she could ill afford—and left her the cottage in lieu. Needless to say this extremely shady transaction occurred before I took over the management of Etta's affairs. Etta should have sold the property of course, but she had some foolish sentimental ideas about it and would not take my advice. I daresay you will remember something of the matter. The cottage has been standing empty for years. I have had the roof seen to from time to time and the outside paint work has been kept in good order—but that is all. Apart from that the cottage has been neglected and probably is. in a dilapidated condition. Since it now belongs to you I advise you to go and see it. You can use the two hundred pounds to do it up and then put it into the hands of a reputable firm of house agents and sell it. You will get a better price if you have it put into reasonable repair.

Nobody wants to buy a ruin. Do it at once, David. The longer you leave it the worse it will get. I shall be thankful when the wretched place is off our hands; the mere thought of it makes me see red. The keys of the cottage are with a man called Grimble who is the proprietor of a garage on the main road. He is a decent chap and I made an arrangement with him to keep an eye on the place. As far as I know he has carried out his part of the bargain in a satisfactory manner. If you are short of cash I will advance you the two hundred pounds so that you can go ahead and get the cottage put in order without delay. Your parents are coming to stay with me for Etta's funeral. I shall need to watch out and be on my best behaviour.

Your affectionate uncle
MATTHEW KIRKE

This letter was extremely surprising. It had never crossed my mind for a moment that Aunt Etta would leave me anything in her will. She had left me Green Beech Cottage! I had forgotten all about the place long ago, in fact I had not given it a thought for years, but now, looking back, I remembered every detail of my first visit to Aunt Etta. I remembered her sitting in her chair and smiling mischievously, "It's mine and I can do what I like with it," she had said. "Matthew can't make me sell it. I don't want to sell it. You don't think I should sell it, do you, David?" I remembered, too, how angry Uncle Matt had been because she would not take his advice about it. Now, at last, Uncle Matt was getting his own way and Green Beech Cottage was to be sold.

Uncle Matt was an extraordinary man—a most astonishing mixture. He had been ruthless in his treatment of his sister; he had raved and stormed and railed against her, declaring she was daft and that there was nothing the matter with her except greed and laziness, yet all the time he had been paying out money to keep her in luxury and never saying a word about it. And paying out money meant a good deal to Uncle Matt, for he liked money. How queer people are, I thought. He could have made Aunt Etta so happy if he had been a little kinder and more sympathetic and had gone to see her more often . . . and yet he was quite upset at her death. He would miss her, he said.

I put the letters in my pocket and began to get ready for the party, but I could not put them out of my mind.

The three girls arrived first, which was fortunate because I wanted to talk to Jan about Nethercleugh. I managed to get a few minutes alone with her in the sitting-room while Nell and Barbie were taking off their coats.

"Jan," I said. "I've heard from Mother. She went up to Nethercleugh and it's all right. She says you shouldn't think of going home."

"She says that?" asked Jan in surprise. "I was sure she would say I ought to go home. I had a letter from Freda this morning and—and I had almost made up my mind to go. It seemed the right thing."

"It isn't," I said earnestly . . . and I took the letter and read out bits of it to Jan. Parts of the letter were unsuitable for Jan's ears so I had to be careful.

"There," I said, as I folded the letter and put it away. "You see what Mother says. Elsie must learn to stand on her own feet. She mustn't depend upon you. It isn't good for her."

"Yes," said Jan thoughtfully. "I never thought of it like that."

"Think of it now," I said. "Mother is wise—she is really—and you can trust her. If Elsie is really ill Mother will write and tell you."

"What's happening?" asked Barbie, coming out of the bedroom. "Is there a secret conclave taking place?"

"Not really," I replied. "I'm just telling Jan not to go home."

"Tell her you want her to stay in London," suggested Barbie.

"But of course I do. She knows that, don't you, Jan?"

By this time Nell was ready and we sat down to have sherry and to wait for Miles. It was just like Miles to be late but on this occasion I did not mind for I wanted to talk about Green Beech Cottage. Barbie was working in a firm of interior decorators and I thought she might give me some advice. I explained the whole matter and they all listened with interest to my tale.

"It's exciting, isn't it!" exclaimed Jan. "Fancy having a little house of your very own, David!"

"Yes," I said doubtfully. "But I shall have to sell it. Uncle Matt says I ought to do it up first."

"Of course you must," nodded Barbie. "You'll get more for it if it's in good repair."

"Barbie will help you," said Nell. "That's her fine."

I looked at Barbie hopefully.

She nodded. "Yes, David, of course I will. Now listen to me; this is what you must do," said Barbie taking charge in her usual energetic fashion. "You must go and see the place and decide about it. If you want to have it done up I'll put you onto the right people. It's no use your going to one of the big firms; they'd make you pay through the nose. Mr. Pendle is the man for you—I'll speak to him about it—but the first thing is to go and look at the house. Go to-morrow."

"Yes," I said. "I suppose I had better."

"Take Jan with you," suggested Nell with a significant nod. I realised what Nell meant. She thought the expedition would give Jan something to think of and would help to take her mind off her own affairs.

"Would you come, Jan?" I asked. "I don't know what it will be like, but . . ."

"Yes, of course, if you want me," said Jan. "I couldn't go to-morrow, it would have to be Sunday . . . but as a matter of fact I think you should take Barbie with you. She would be far more help."

"No fears!" cried Barbie. "You can count me out of your expedition to Green Beech Cottage. I have quite enough interior decorating all the week. You won't find this child looking at houses on a Sunday."

"But you said you'd help," Jan told her in surprise.

"So I will—later on. All you have to do on Sunday is to go and see what the place is like."

We had finished our sherry and still Miles had not come. I was beginning to be worried about the dinner, which I was keeping hot in the oven, and wondering whether we should start without Miles—when at last he arrived.

"Sorry I'm late old boy!" exclaimed Miles cheerfully. "I was at a cocktail party and I couldn't escape."

"It's all right," I said. "But we'll start dinner straight away if you don't mind. I'll just introduce you to the girls."

I introduced Miles and went to get the soup. Jan followed me. "I'll help you, David," she said.

"Not so," I told her, laughing. "This is my show. You're all to sit down and be waited on, hand and foot."

It was a very cheerful party. The dinner was good and everybody was in splendid form. Miles was always at his best on occasions of this sort; he showed up well and I was glad I had asked him. There was a constant flow of amusing talk and laughter and it was obvious that my guests were enjoying themselves.

As the evening wore on I noticed that Miles was particularly interested in Nell. I could see him looking at her admiringly; he listened to all she said and paid her subtle compliments. This amused me a good deal—for two reasons: firstly because Miles had said he meant to keep clear of girls and secondly because, although Nell was pretty, anybody could see she was the least attractive of the three.

CHAPTER THIRTY-SEVEN

THE girls went home soon after ten; but, contrary to my expectations, Miles did not offer to accompany them. He came with me to see them off and then followed me back to the sitting-room.

"I've started, David," he said in significant tones.

"Started what?" I asked.

"The thriller of course. I decided to write a bit of the story before I tackled a publisher so that he would see the idea. Besides, as I told you, I had thought of a first-class plot. I wrote to Mother and told her I was on to a dashed good thing but I wanted a little splosh to go on with." He laughed and added, "That did the trick all right."

I did not know what to say to this, so I said nothing.

"Writing is easy," continued Miles. "I'm getting along like a house on fire. Look, David, here's the stuff." He produced a couple of school-exercise books from the pocket of his overcoat and held them out to me.

"You mean I'm to read it?"

"Yes, of course."

"But Miles, I don't know much about thrillers."

"You read it," said Miles pressing the books into my hands. "Of course this is only the first part, but it'll give you an idea of the pace. Pace is the great thing in a thriller; you must get a move on from the word go. You'll like it, old boy—it's terrific—it really is damned good, tho' I ses it meself!" He chuckled and added, "There's a comic bit where the fellow steals a pie out of the old miser's larder; it'll make you laugh like a drain."

I took the books reluctantly. "Miles, look here," I said. "It would be much better for you to ask somebody else. Thrillers are not my fine of country. I'll give you the address of my literary agent—"

"No, no, I want you to read it. There's twenty-three hours' work in that little lot; twenty-three solid hours."

This seemed a strange way of measuring literary output and I said so.

"It's the sensible way," declared Miles as he hunched on his overcoat. "It's the only business-like way. If I'm going to make writing my career I naturally want to know how much money per hour I shall get for my work. . . . 'Bye, David, and thanks a lot for the party. I'll catch up the damsels and see them home." He clattered off down the stairs and vanished.

The exercise books were lying on the table and I looked at them doubtfully. I did not want to read Miles's thriller, but of course I should have to read it sometime and the night was still young. If I left it until to-morrow it would interfere with my own work. Better get it over, I thought. I adjusted the lamp and sat down. Fortunately it was easy to read for Miles affected a large, round schoolboy hand.

The thriller was entitled *Ralph's Progress* and it began with a detailed description of the hero; it was also a detailed description of the author; (so exact that I had a feeling he must have used a mirror for the job). The story went on to explain that "Ralph was languishing in Dartmoor prison where he had been unjustly incarcerated." He did not languish for long, of course. One dark foggy night he "socked a warder" and after changing clothes with his unconscious victim he walked out of the prison gates with a debonair swagger. As he ran lightly across the moor (he had won the three-mile when he was at Eton) Ralph laughed to himself at the ease with which he had outwitted his cruel gaolers; and there was a flash-back giving the story of his life and describing the court-scene where he had stood in the dock and listened to his harsh and unjust sentence.

When I had got thus far I put down the book and tried to make up my mind whether the story was really as bad as it seemed. To me it seemed very bad indeed—astonishingly bad. It was difficult to believe that Miles could have written anything so futile. Miles had read hundreds of thrillers, they were his favourite form of literature, and I had often heard him criticising them; praising one and pulling another to bits. ("Absolute tripe, old boy!" he would declare. "Not worth reading." And he would go on to explain why it was tripe and just where the author had blundered.) It seemed very strange that his critical faculty should fail where his own work was concerned. I turned back the pages and read bits of the story again and the thing seemed worse than before. It did not ring true. Ralph was not real and although I knew nothing about Dartmoor Prison I was pretty certain it was very different from this—and much more difficult to escape from. As for the writing, it was such an odd mixture that it made me laugh (though unfortunately the serious portions of the narrative were the funniest). Parts of it were in a high-falutin' style: "Ralph had been wrongly condemned and incarcerated, the iron of injustice had eaten into his soul and changed him from a happy care-free youth into an enemy of society." Other parts were written in a slangy staccato manner, slightly reminiscent of Peter Cheyney.

I took up the second exercise-book and toiled on. Ralph met various people in his progress; some were helpful and provided him with food and listened patiently to long speeches about the cruelty of the world; others were law-abiding and tried to entrap him. Ralph was a match for them of course, he realised in the nick of time what they were up to and socked them on the jaw or trussed them up like chickens with pieces of stout rope which happened to be lying about just when and where he needed them.

Presently I got to the incident of the pie. Ralph climbed up the ivy and stole the pie from the miser's larder. He was being pursued by bloodhounds but he found time to write a hasty note to the owner of the pie, explaining that he was not a thief by nature but Necessity knows no Law, and promising to return the loan when circumstances permitted . . . then he ran on chuckling to himself at the thought of the miser's surprise when he visited his larder in the morning.

Miles had predicted that I would laugh like a drain at the incident, but for the life of me I could see nothing particularly funny about it.

All this time I had been waiting for the Girl. I felt pretty certain there must be a Girl somewhere. . . . Yes, here she was! She had eyes like violets with the morning dew upon them and a skin like the petals of a rose (there was a very full description of her beauty and grace but I am afraid I skipped it). The Girl was the owner of an exceedingly powerful car—an eight-cylinder super-charged Bentley—and when Ralph appeared upon the scene she explained to him that it had died on her and obviously there was something the matter with the engine. Ralph knew all about cars and in spite of being almost blinded by the Girl's beauty he coped with the trouble in his own inimitable way and soon had the engine purring sweetly. Of course the Girl wanted to know where Ralph had come from and in answer to her question she was given his story in full. Her heart went out to him—her violet eyes were full of sympathetic tears—and she offered to take Ralph home with her and hide him from his pursuers. Luckily for Ralph she was the daughter of a baronet and lived in a moated-grange which boasted a secret passage and a Priest's Hole. Ralph realised that this was exactly what was needed and accepted her offer with alacrity.

They had just got into the car when a posse of warders and bloodhounds broke from a nearby thicket and surrounded them . . . but Ralph let in the clutch and the magnificent car bounded forward, and they sped off down the road pursued by shouts of rage by the baffled warders and bays of fury from the hounds.

By this time I was so tired of Ralph that I could accompany him on his progress no further. I put down the book and wondered what on earth to do.

It is true that quite a lot of rubbish finds its way into print, but it is amusing rubbish. Ralph did not amuse me at all. In fact I was so fed up with Ralph that I did not care what happened to him (the authorities of Dartmoor Prison were welcome to recapture him and incarcerate him for life.) I felt certain that nobody would care what happened to Ralph.

What was I to do about it? Should I write to Miles and say I had read his story and wished him luck? That would be much the easiest way out of the difficulty—but was it kind? I decided that it was neither kind nor honest. Miles had not asked for my opinion of his story but he had insisted that I should read it, so presumably he wanted to know what I thought of it. I considered the matter seriously and then I took a sheet of paper and wrote him a short note saying that it was very good of him to let me read *Ralph's Progress* and I had read it with interest. (This was perfectly true, for it was interesting—and puzzling—to discover that Miles could not write. Writing was easy and Miles was intelligent. He knew a good thriller when he saw it so why couldn't he write one?)

When I had got thus far I paused and chewed my pencil. Then I continued:

"Quite honestly, Miles, I don't think writing is your line and I suggest you should ask someone else before going any further. I enclose the address of Mr. Randall who is a literary agent. He will be able to advise you much better than I can."

I tried to think of some way of softening the blow but I knew that if I gave Miles the slightest encouragement he would seize upon it and magnify it and continue to waste precious hours upon Ralph. His nature was to see only what he wanted to see and to ignore what he disliked.

When I had written the note I packed it up with the manuscript and posted it the next morning. I had no housemaid who would seize upon *Ralph's Progress* and use it to light the fire (as in the case of Thomas Carlyle's masterpiece) but I felt a great deal more comfortable when it was out of my keeping.

THE FIFTH WINDOW

"The window was dirty and we could not see through it, so I opened it from the bottom and we looked out. . . . Now that the trees had been felled we could see for miles: we could see meadows and fields: we could see hedges with the green tint of spring upon them. In the distance, veiled in a tender haze, we could see the clustering roofs of London. The sun was declining in the west and its rosy beams irradiated the mist so that the big sprawling city looked like a city in a dream, a city of enchantment."

CHAPTER THIRTY-EIGHT

SUNDAY was a real April day. It rained in the morning, but cleared up beautifully in the afternoon and when Jan and I set off on our expedition to Green Beech Cottage the sky was blue and there was real warmth in the sun's golden beams. We took a Green Line Bus and got off at Grimble's Garage which stood back from the main road with a row of petrol pumps in front. Mr. Grimble was working on the engine of a car but he wiped his hands on a piece of waste and listened while I told him my business.

"You're putting the place in order at last," said Mr. Grimble, nodding. "Well, it's high time—that's all I say. If you hold on a minute I'll get you the key."

We waited and presently he returned and handed me a large iron key with a label attached to it.

"That's what you want," he said. "The cottage is about ten minutes' walk from here. You cross the road and go up that narrow lane . . . but I expect you know the way."

"I've never seen it," I told him.

"Never seen it!" he exclaimed. "You'll get a bit of a shock. I've done what Mr. Kirke said—kept the roof sound and the woodwork painted—but that's all."

"I suppose I shall want a gardener?"

"A gardener! Half a dozen men with axes is what you'll want."

I gazed at him in consternation.

"Well, you'll see," he said. "I'll do what I can to find someone to deal with the garden. As a matter of fact I'm glad the place is going to be put in order; it's a shame to keep it standing empty when so many people are screaming their heads off for a house."

The great main road which swept past Grimble's Garage was like a river of tar macadam, but much more noisy and congested than any river in the world. Cars and lorries and buses rolled past in an endless procession. Motor bicycles roared along hooting and weaving their way through the other traffic at perilous speed. Jan and I crossed the road, not without difficulty, and began to walk up the narrow lane.

It was a country lane, steep and stony, with trees and hawthorn hedges on either side. The hawthorn was budding and here and there a clump of primroses nestled in the bank. We came to a small sheltered field where there were some sheep with little white lambs. Gradually as we climbed the noise of the traffic became fainter.

"How funny to be in the country so suddenly!" I exclaimed.

"Yes," agreed Jan thoughtfully. "The country is real, David—the lambs and the primroses and the hawthorn buds—but the road is an artificial sort of thing. It goes across the land but doesn't affect it at all. I can't explain it properly but I know what I mean."

I knew what she meant for I had the same feeling myself. It was odd how well we understood one another.

"You could roll up the road like a carpet and take it away," continued Jan, smiling at me. "It would make no difference at all to the primroses. Is that a silly idea?"

"It's a grand idea. Let's do it some night," I suggested. "Mr. Grimble would be annoyed, but the lambs would never notice."

Presently we came to a beech hedge which was sprouting in all directions and obviously had not been trimmed for years. In the middle of the hedge was a wooden gate with GREEN BEECH COTTAGE painted on it. The gate fell to pieces as I pushed it open and we had to step over the ruins of it to enter my property.

Inside the gate was a narrow path which sloped downwards amongst a jungle of laurel bushes with twisted branches and spotted leaves. Briars and brambles and sodden yellow grass straggled all over the ground and there was a smell of decaying vegetation. A few paces further brought the cottage into view and we stood still and looked at it in silence. It was a small square house built of rosy pink brick. Ivy grew up the walls and hung round the windows in heavy dark, green masses. Even the chimneys were swathed in ivy. Trees and bushes had grown unchecked for years and, encroaching from all sides, seemed to be pressing upon the little house like a hostile army and smothering it to death. The place was so neglected and deserted that it looked as if nobody had been near it for a hundred years.

"It ought to be called Sleeping Beauty Cottage," said, Jan in a low voice.

Again she had put my thought into words.

"All this will have to be cleared," I said, trying to speak confidently. "All these laurels—I hate laurels anyway—and the ivy and those half-dead trees. It will have to be opened up to let in the air and the sunshine."

"Yes, of course," agreed Jan. "It's only—I mean where would one begin?"

There was no answer to that, or none that I could find.

Before going into the house we pushed our way along the choked-up path which led round to the back. There was a rainwater barrel at the corner, it was leaking and covered with green slime; beside the barrel were the remains of a small conservatory. At the back of the house was a veranda with a brick floor and a low brick wall. I remembered that Aunt Etta had spoken of the veranda and had said that she and her friend often had tea out here and admired the view, but there was no view now. Instead there was a jungle of trees and bushes struggling together in confusion, stretching up for room to breathe.

"It's—rather horrible," I said in a low voice.

Jan agreed. "But it's no use standing and looking at it. I wonder what the inside of the house is like."

"We'll soon see," I told her. "If it's anything like the outside the only thing to do is to burn it to the ground." We went back to the front door and I opened it with the huge key. The door squeaked crazily as I pushed it open, but I saw that all it needed was a little oil on the hinges. The door itself had been painted quite recently and the wood was perfectly sound. The hall was dark and dirty; the woodwork was painted in a hideous shade of brown and the dark-green wallpaper was peeling off the walls. On the right there was a steep flight of stairs which led to the floor above; on the left was a door.

Jan and I went all round the house without saying a word. We went upstairs and looked at the bedrooms—two good-sized bedrooms and a smaller one facing the road—we looked at the dingy little bathroom with its rusty iron bath; we came down and peeped into the dining-room and the kitchen with its old-fashioned stove and cracked, discoloured sink;

finally we went into a biggish room—obviously the sitting-room—which was on the ground floor and stretched from the front to the back of the house with windows at each end. This room was papered in a horrible pinkish red; there were big oblong patches on the walls where pictures had hung and there were cobwebs in every corner.

"Jan, it's ghastly!" I exclaimed, turning and looking at her. "I've never seen such a frightful place, have you?"

"I don't think it's bad," replied Jan.

"You don't think it's bad?"

Jan smiled. "Oh, I know it looks awful *now*, but it's only awful on the surface. It has good bones. As a matter of fact I think it's a dear little house."

"You're joking!"

"No, I'm not."

"Can you imagine anybody buying it?"

"Not in its present condition," she admitted. "But you're going to do it up, aren't you? That's all it wants." She hesitated and then added, "I've been wondering if you would like to live here yourself, David."

"Live here—myself!"

Jan nodded. She sat down on the wooden window-seat and looked out of the dirty window. "I can see it as it *could* be," she said slowly. "You're horrified at the awful wall-papers and the ugly paint but that could easily be altered. I've been wondering all the time whether it would do for you to live in—and I think it would."

"But, Jan—"

"Listen, David, you said you wished you could live in the country but you had to be near London; this is both, isn't it?"

"Yes, but there's an odd feeling about this place."

"It's sad, that's all. Nobody has cared for it or bothered about it for years and years. That's why it feels sad . . . but look at this room," said Jan, waving her hand. "Look what a lovely shape it is! Think of it with oatmeal-coloured walls and cream paint—and—and yes, a blue carpet and blue curtains to match. Your writing-table would stand just here, at the window, and the sofa *there* . . . and that little alcove only needs a few shelves to make a splendid bookcase."

Jan was making me see it. For a moment I saw the room just as she had described it and then the vision faded and I saw the pink wallpaper and the cobwebs and the dirty windows.

"Could it be like that?" I asked doubtfully.

"Of course—quite easily. Paper and paint is all it wants and Barbie knows a man who would do it . . . and the house is yours, isn't it? It's your very own. Doesn't it thrill you to feel that this is your very own house?"

To be honest it did not thrill me, but all the same I began to consider the matter seriously. If this little house could be made habitable it would solve a good many problems. The flat was all very well in its way, and up to now it had suited me none too badly, but it had various drawbacks—chief of which was the dirt. Up there amongst the chimney pots there was a constant rain of soot; black oily smuts drifted in at the windows and settled upon everything. There were other drawbacks as well. Now that I was collecting more goods and chattels I was beginning to feel cramped; there was no bath—when I wanted a bath I had to go down five flights of stairs to Mr. Coe's bathroom. Last but not least my tenure of the flat was uncertain for Mr. Coe was talking of selling his property and retiring to Margate to spend his old age by the sea. All these thoughts and considerations passed through my mind in a few moments—in much less time than it takes to tell.

"You must do something with this little house," continued Jan sensibly. "You must put the place in proper order if you're going to sell it and it seems a pity to make it nice for somebody else to live in."

"That's true," I admitted.

"Why not make it nice for yourself? Oh, David, I don't want to persuade you. I mean you've got to decide whether you would be happy here—but somehow I can see you here—I can see you sitting writing peacefully, with the windows open and the birds singing in the garden. You hate being cooped up in town, don't you?"

"Yes," I said.

"Well, here you are! Here's your very own house, waiting for you to come and live in it."

"There's an awful lot to do."

"That's the fun of it!" cried Jan. "That's the adventure! It would be a marvellous adventure putting the whole place in order."

I looked at her. She was excited at the idea. Her eyes were shining and her whole face was lit up.

"Jan," I said eagerly. "If you really think it would be fun perhaps you'd help me. I mean advise me about the wallpaper and that sort of thing."

She hesitated.

"Oh, I know it's a lot to ask," I said quickly. "But I thought you seemed interested—and I know so little about it. I should make all sorts of stupid mistakes."

"I'm frightfully interested, David, but what about Freda?"

"What about Freda!" I echoed in amazement.

Jan nodded. "Why don't you ask her to help you?"

"But—but she's at Haines!"

"She would come if you asked her."

"Jan," I said. "What are you talking about? How could I ask Freda to come and help me to choose wallpapers? She would think I had gone mad."

"Would she?"

"Of course she would. To begin with it isn't a bit the sort of thing that would interest Freda."

"You and Freda have always been such friends," explained Jan. "That's why I thought—I mean I think perhaps she would like to help you."

"Do you? Well I don't think so at all. Freda would help me if I wanted to buy a pig but she couldn't be bothered to choose wallpapers."

"It isn't exactly her line," admitted Jan, looking at me thoughtfully. "But sometimes people are quite pleased to do different kinds of things; I mean in special circumstances—but of course—I mean—I mean if you really think—I mean—"

"What do you mean?" I asked, laughing at her. "I can tell you here and now that nothing would induce me to ask Freda to help me; and, if I did, nothing I could say would induce her to leave her beloved Nethercleugh and come to London. If you think she would—well, all I can say is you don't know Freda as well as I do."

Jan gave a little laugh. "It was silly of me to suggest it."

"I didn't say that."

"But you thought it, didn't you, David?"

"Never mind," I said, taking her arm. "Let's go round the house again and make some notes for Barbie's friend; whether I'm going to live here or not the place will have to be done up from top to bottom. If you'll just give me a few ideas I daresay I can tackle choosing the papers myself."

"But I'd love to help you!" exclaimed Jan.

"Oh Jan—really?"

"Of course I should. I didn't mean I wouldn't help you; I just meant—"

"That's splendid. I don't know how to thank you."

"Don't thank me," said Jan, looking up and smiling. "You needn't thank me, or feel grateful, because I shall enjoy it. I've always wanted to have a hand at doing up a house."

"I can't help feeling grateful."

"Try, David," said Jan, laughing. "Try very hard. It will spoil everything if you feel grateful. We're going to have fun."

CHAPTER THIRTY-NINE

Jan was busy during the week so Barbie arranged for her friend, Mr. Pendle, to meet us at the cottage the following Sunday. Meantime I managed to get two men and we began to clear the garden. As Jan had said it was difficult to know where to begin, but we had to begin somewhere, and, after a short consultation, we decided to begin at the back so as to let air and sunshine into the main windows.

The men were strong hefty fellows and once they had got started on their work of destruction they laid into the job with a will. Finsbury was a tall thin chap with long arms; Noyes was older, thick-set and wiry, with a pleasant open face and a ready smile. The three of us worked together and in two days I had got to know them quite well. There is nothing like working beside a man for getting to know him. We worked together and we sat down and had our food together. I brought my own sandwiches and beer for the whole party.

After three days the place looked worse than before; it was a mass of fallen trees and grubbed-up bushes and tangled ivy. There had been rain and the soft ground was churned up and boggy. I had never seen such a mess in all my life. Noyes suggested we should make a bonfire in the field beyond the fence and try to clear the rubbish as we went along, so we got a bonfire going and we spent one whole morning clearing and burning.

Sunday was a showery day. I called for Jan as arranged and we set out together. Nell had made sandwiches for us so that we could spend the whole day at the cottage without bothering about lunch. As we walked up the hill together I tried to prepare Jan for the mess we had made in the garden so that it would not be such a shock.

"But of course it will look dreadful," she said. "It's bound to look dreadful. The only thing to do is to go ahead and cut and tear and burn."

"Yes," I said ruefully. "We've been cutting and tearing and burning for days. Come and see the result."

We went round to the back garden and I showed her what we had done and what I intended to do. The tall scrubby trees had been felled and we had grubbed up most of the laurel bushes.

"I wondered about those lilacs," I said doubtfully. "They're old and twisted and I'm not sure whether it wouldn't be better to take them out and plant new ones."

"I love lilac," said Jan. "You mustn't ask me to give them their death sentence. I couldn't bear it." She went forward and reached up to a branch and pulled it towards her gently. "Look, David, dear little buds! I wonder if they will be white, or purple."

The sun was shining now, it shone upon her brown silky hair, and as she turned her head and looked at me I saw that her eyes were soft and tender . . . suddenly I knew that I loved her.

It was the most astonishing discovery. I loved Jan. She was the girl I had been looking for all my life; the dearest thing on earth; the perfect companion. What a fool I had been not to have realised it before! It was as if I had been blind and now, suddenly, my eyes were opened; it was as if I had been deaf and now I could hear. I felt dazed and giddy and breathless.

"What's the matter, David?" asked Jan.

"Nothing," I said. "Nothing, really—"

"You've been doing too much," said Jan looking at me anxiously. "You've been working far too hard cutting down all those trees. You're quite pale, David. Come and sit down."

We sat down together on the steps of the veranda.

Up till now there had been an unembarrassed friendliness between Jan and me. We had laughed and talked and I had said exactly what I thought . . . but now, in a moment, all that was changed and I felt frightened and self-conscious. My thoughts were in a turmoil; all sorts of irrelevant things shot through my mind. I remembered Jan as a little girl; especially the day we had gone for a picnic on the banks of the Ling and Jan had collected wild flowers and made a posy of them. Her hands had been so tiny—they were bigger now but still white and soft and beautiful—I wanted to take her hands in mine and hold them. I remembered that we ran off to hide together and she had slipped her hand into mine and I had dragged her up the slope to the cave.

"The cave!" I exclaimed. "That was the other secret."

Jan turned her head and smiled. "Have you just remembered? I wonder what made you remember about the cave."

"We sat in the cave together and I tied your ribbon. Do you remember that?"

She did not answer directly but put her hands up to her hair.

"I suppose it's untidy," she said ruefully. "It's such stupid hair. Other people's hair seems to stay put, but mine slips and slides all over the place; I can't keep it tidy whatever I do."

I did not want her to keep it tidy. Jan would not have been Jan without that mop of pale-brown, silky hair. It had been quite straight when she was little but now it fell naturally into soft waves. It was the most beautiful hair I had ever seen and I longed to tell her so.

Jan was talking about the garden and what must be done, but I could not keep my mind upon what she was saying. I was wondering when I had begun to love Jan; for now I knew I had loved her for ages. There was nothing sudden about it except the realisation of the fact. Perhaps it was natural; perhaps that is the way love comes when you have known the loved one all your life—not in a lightning flash, like love at first sight, but in a gradual development from friendship. Love at first sight is easier to understand (This is she! This is the one I have been looking for!) but the love I felt for Jan was deeper and more tender for it had roots in the past.

"David," said Jan. "Are you feeling all right?"

"No," I said. "I mean yes, I'm perfectly all right. I was just thinking."

"About your book?"

"No," I said. "Perhaps I'm a little tired or something. I'm sorry I wasn't listening."

"We'll have lunch, shall we? You'll feel better after lunch. Don't talk, David. We don't need to talk, do we?" She looked at me with her bright, tender glance and my heart beat like a sledge-hammer. Why had I not seen before how sweet she was, how dear and beautiful and understanding? In the sunlight her soft hair sparkled and her skin was fresh and smooth; her eyebrows, slightly darker than her hair, were arched above her deep-blue eyes.

"You remind me of Haines!" I exclaimed impulsively.

"That's natural, isn't it?"

"Not only because you come from Haines," I told her. "I mean you yourself remind me of Haines. You make me think of the clear skies and the wind on the hills and the scent of thyme."

Her eyes were puzzled. She said, "You *are* funny to-day."

"Funny?"

"Not like yourself, David. I hope you're not going to be ill. Just sit here quietly while I fetch the lunch-basket."

As I sat and waited for her I wondered what to do. I wanted to say, "Jan, I love you," but I could not say it. Although she was so frank and natural and unaffected there was something mysterious about her; there was something about her I could not fathom—a sort of reticence. It was as if Jan had a secret in her heart and had set a guard upon it. I realised that I must be careful. It would be difficult to be careful with Jan because I had never had to be careful with her before. I had always said whatever came into my head . . . but I must be careful now. I must not frighten her.

I wanted her to help me with the house—not because of the house (that had become a secondary consideration) but because it would be so lovely to do it with her and because it would give me an excuse for seeing her as often as I wanted. If we were no longer easy friends together it would change everything. I should have to be very careful indeed.

When Jan returned with the basket I had taken a grip of myself and was able to smile at her. "You were right," I said. "I'm hungry, that's what's the matter with me. I've developed a terrific appetite in the last few days. It's all that hard work out of doors."

She sat down beside me and opened the basket. "Nell has given us masses of food, and there's coffee in the thermos. Nell is rather wonderful, you know. It's no bother to her to cook and cater; in fact she likes it. Nell's husband will be a lucky man."

"Is she engaged?" I asked, not because I wanted to know, but because Nell seemed a nice safe subject for conversation.

"Not on your life!?" replied Jan, smiling. "She has a host of admirers and she likes going out with them and having a good time." She paused and then added, "Your friend, Miles, has joined the queue."

"Oh—yes," I said doubtfully. "Yes, I saw he liked Nell, but you don't mean there's anything serious in that quarter."

Jan hesitated. "I don't know," she said. "He's a very attractive creature, isn't he? So tall and good-looking and full of life . . . and of course he's got heaps of money. I don't mean Nell is mercenary, lots of her friends haven't a penny, but it's nice to be taken about in taxis and fed at the Savoy."

"Look here!" I exclaimed. "Miles is all right in a way, but—but he isn't very—dependable—and—and I don't understand about the 'heaps of money.' Miles has no money; he hasn't even got a job."

"But he has!" declared Jan in surprise. "He's terribly well-off. He called for Nell this morning in a car and took her out for the day. Nell says he's got a very well-paid job; he wouldn't tell her what it was, but apparently it's going to make him rich in half no time." She hesitated and looked at me. "Isn't it true?" she asked.

"He thinks it's true," I told her. "Miles wouldn't deceive anybody on purpose, but it's his nature to be optimistic to an alarming degree. I wish I could tell you the whole story—perhaps I shall be able to tell you some day—meanwhile you had better warn Nell that Miles is a butterfly. He flits from flower to flower."

Jan bit a sandwich and looked across the garden with a thoughtful air. "I'll warn Barbie," she said. "Barbie will know what to do."

I nodded. "Barbie is very sound—and solid, isn't she?"

"Solid?" repeated Jan, smiling.

"I didn't mean physically," I said hastily. "I meant her character was solid. I think she would be a very good friend, staunch and loyal."

"Oh, she is! She's a marvellous friend. I can't tell you what a good friend she has been to me. I should never have had the courage to *think* of leaving Nethercleugh if it hadn't been for Barbie. Barbie understood that I couldn't be myself at Nethercleugh."

"I understand that too, Jan."

"Do you, David? I thought you might find it difficult to understand because your home is so different." She paused and then added in a low voice, "It's my own fault, of course. It's because I haven't enough courage. People with courage can be themselves anywhere."

I thought about this and saw that it was true. It was true of me, that was the reason I understood it so well. Jan and I were alike; we both hated rows and angry voices; we both lacked the particular brand of moral courage which would have enabled us to be ourselves in uncongenial surroundings.

Unfortunately there was no time to pursue the subject further, because at that moment Mr. Pendle arrived. He came round the corner of the house, picking his way carefully amongst the debris. Neither Jan nor I had seen him before but we both knew that this must be Mr. Pendle; not only because we were expecting him but because he looked exactly like his name. He was small and thin with a large dark moustache and bushy eyebrows, and he was dressed very neatly in a blue suit and a high stiff collar and a bowler hat. When he saw us sitting on the veranda he removed the hat with a flourish, and greeted us in a surprisingly deep voice.

"I'm Mr. Pendle," he said. "The bell is broken, so I took the liberty of coming round the 'ouse to look for you. I left the van at the gate."

We both shook hands with him solemnly.

"You 'aven't 'alf got a job 'ere," said Mr. Pendle, taking in the desolate garden, with a wave of his hand.

"The house isn't like this," said Jan hastily. "Of course it's been neglected for years, but it isn't in such a frightful state as the garden."

"I'll take you round the house," I said. "The sooner we get going the better. There's a great deal to be done."

"You finish your lunch," replied Mr. Pendle. "Just give me the key and I'll go round myself. I'd rather do it on my own, if it's all the same to you. I'll 'ave a look and see what's what. Then we can get down to brass tacks."

CHAPTER FORTY

Mr. Pendle was such a long time in the cottage that Jan and I were beginning to get impatient, but when at last he emerged from the door of the sitting-room, which opened on to the veranda, his eyes beneath his bushy eyebrows were shining with excitement.

"What a job!" he exclaimed. "It's the sort of job I like. We can make something good of this little 'ouse."

"The place is sound?" I asked.

"Sound as a bell, Mr. Kirke. I've been on the roof, and I've 'ad some of the boards up. That's why I was so long. There's no trace of dry rot in the place—nor wet rot neither. We can make a job of this if you give me the word. You want a plumber and a carpenter, you need a new bath and kitchen fittings. The rest is paint and paper."

"Do you know a plumber?" I asked.

"I do," he said. "I'll get my own people if that suits you. Miss France said you were in a 'urry. Well, if I get people I know on the job it saves a lot of delay."

"Yes," I agreed. "I realise that, Mr. Pendle."

"How much would it cost?" asked Jan.

"Now you're asking! The fact is it depends on a lot of things; it depends on the papers you choose and the time it takes."

"Some of the rooms can be distempered," Jan told him.

"That's right! But we've got to take all the old papers off first. It's that what takes the time. Just you come in 'ere a minute and I'll show you."

We went into the sitting-room and Mr. Pendle took out his knife and began to scrape the wall. "Two, three, four," he said, looking round and smiling. "Four papers to come off—all dirty and full of germs—before we can start putting on a nice clean one. It's interesting, isn't it? 'Ere's a satin-striped paper, green and white, and 'ere's one with flowers and birds. Those papers are good, but nobody would 'ave them as a gift nowadays. Shows the difference in taste, doesn't it?"

"I wonder who chose those papers," said Jan thoughtfully. "I wonder what they were like and what sort of clothes they wore and how the room was furnished. That green and white satin stripe would take a lot of living up to. You couldn't lounge about in old clothes with that on the walls."

"This would be the droring-room," Mr. Pendle said. "They'd 'ave those flimsy gilt chairs with satin covers I shouldn't wonder."

Jan nodded and then pulled herself together. "Well, what about an estimate," she said.

"That's what I can't give you," replied Mr. Pendle. "I couldn't give you an estimate for the work but I'll do it as cheap as I can."

"Isn't that rather unsatisfactory?" asked Jan.

"Not so unsatisfactory as an estimate which might work out too little or too much. You ask Miss France—she'll tell you. I shan't cheat you. I shouldn't dare. Miss France knows what's what and she'd be down on me like a ton of bricks. As a matter of fact I don't want to cheat you. Any friends of Miss France are friends of mine." He smiled as he made this statement and his smile was charming. I knew quite suddenly that I could trust Mr. Pendle.

"Right," I said. "You go straight ahead."

"Now that's what I like!" he exclaimed. "That's the way to do business. I'll get the pattern-books out of my van and we'll settle everything. The sooner you start the sooner you finish I always say."

When he had gone to get the books Jan looked at me and I nodded.

"He's all right," I said. "We're lucky to get Mr. Pendle. You choose, Jan. You tell him exactly what to do."

"But, David—"

"You saw it," I told her. "You saw it as it *could* be. I want oatmeal paper and blue curtains. That's what I want."

It took a long time to choose the papers, for Jan knew exactly what she wanted and nothing else would do. Her cheeks grew pink and her eyes shone and her hair became dishevelled and she looked more than ever like the eight-year-old Janet I remembered so well. As I watched her arguing earnestly with Mr. Pendle, crouching on the dirty floor and turning over the leaves of his pattern-book, my heart grew big with love. It was crazy of me not to have known before that I was in love with Jan. I had always loved her! I wondered if some day she would come here and would sit at her ease in this room with the oatmeal paper on the walls and the cream paint on the wainscotting and the blue curtains hanging at the windows . . . the mere idea made me feel quite dizzy. Would she? Could I ever summon up enough courage to put my fate to the test and say, "Jan, I love you. Will you marry me and come to Green Beech Cottage? Will you, Jan?" It seemed impossible. It was all the more impossible because we were friends, because we understood one another so well and laughed at the same jokes. How do you begin to get on a different footing with a girl who has been like a young sister, a girl you have known all her life?

"Look, David!" cried Jan excitedly. "That's what you want, isn't it?"

"Yes," I said. "Yes, of course. That's what I want."

"It wouldn't be too expensive, would it? I mean we could save on the bedrooms. Distemper would be quite nice for the bedrooms, wouldn't it?"

"Lots of people prefer distemper for bedrooms," Mr. Pendle said. He took the book and held it against the wall to show the effect of the paper.

"How do you like it?" asked Jan anxiously.

"Yes," I said. "Yes, that's the one. Oatmeal."

"Very tasteful," said Mr. Pendle. "Very tasteful indeed." For the hall and staircase Jan chose a light grey paper with a rough surface; and again Mr. Pendle applauded the choice.

"We'll have a blue stair-carpet," said Jan. "And a big rug of Persian design for the hall—at least if you think so, David."

"Couldn't be better," I told her. "It's exactly what I should like."

We went up to the bedrooms; Jan decided upon pastel shades of distemper for them and washable oil paint in pale peacock blue for the bathroom—and she insisted that all the woodwork in the house must be cream.

"A sort of butter-shade?" asked Mr. Pendle.

"No, cream," replied Jan. "Just a very light cream."

I had thought the cream paint would be easy—cream was cream in my eyes—but the colour of the paint was more difficult to settle than the papers and eventually the exact shade was left to be decided later. Jan said she would come and see it mixed so that there should be no mistake about the amount of pink and yellow which was to be blended with the white.

"To-morrow is Monday," said Jan thoughtfully. "Monday is no use . . . and Tuesday would be difficult. I could come on Wednesday afternoon."

"Just as you say," replied Mr. Pendle who by this time was eating out of her hand. "Wednesday afternoon it is. I'll bring the paint and mix it to suit you."

"How about you, David?" she asked.

"I'll be here," I said. "I'll be working in the garden." When Mr. Pendle had gone we went upstairs and had another look at the bedrooms. The largest bedroom was to be distempered in egg-shell blue.

"This will be yours," said Jan, looking round. "That alcove will make a lovely hanging-cupboard, so you won't need a wardrobe. It will be perfect when it's finished. You're happy about it, aren't you?"

"Yes, very happy," I said.

"Fancy waking up here and looking out of the window at the garden and the fields and the trees!"

The window was dirty and we could not see through it, so I opened it from the bottom and we looked out. The view was so surprising that it took my breath away, and Jan gave a little gasp of delight. Now that the trees had been felled we could see for miles; we could see meadows and fields; we could see hedges with the green tint of spring upon them. In the distance, veiled in a tender haze, we could see the clustering roofs of London. The sun was declining in the west and its rosy beams irradiated the mist so that the big, sprawling city looked like a city in a dream, a city of enchantment.

"Oh, David—how lovely!" whispered Jan.

"If it were only this it would be worth it," I said. "If it were only this view and nothing else at all. I had no idea it would be like this. You could see this view from the veranda if the bushes were taken away."

"They must go," declared Jan. "All the bushes must go—even the lilacs—the view must come first."

It was late when we got back to town. Darkness had fallen and the lamps were lighted. I wanted Jan to come and have supper with me at The Wooden Spoon, but she said she was too dirty and untidy. I walked as far as her door with her and waited until she had vanished up the stairs. Then I crossed the road and looked up at the windows of the flat. Presently I saw a light go on and I saw Jan come to the window and draw the curtains. The action shut me out. Jan was inside that room and I was outside in the dark. It was foolish to feel like that, of course, for she did not know I was there; she did not mean to shut me out; she had drawn the curtains without a thought. But somehow the action seemed symbolic and it frightened me. Supposing Jan shut me out of her life!

Suddenly I felt I must see Jan. I must see her now, at once. I wanted to see her face, to hear her voice, to touch her hand. The feeling was so overpowering that I started off across the street and was halfway up the stairs before I came to my senses and realised that I was behaving like a fool. How could I go blundering into the flat without any excuse? What could I say? I leant against the wall and thought about it and the more I thought about it the more miserable I became.

After a bit I went down the stairs and home to my flat.

CHAPTER FORTY-ONE

NEXT day was Monday; I got up early and went out to the cottage. Noyes had borrowed a ladder and had begun on the ivy which smothered the building; he was cutting it ruthlessly. Finsbury and I set to work on the bushes which obscured the view from the veranda. I felt so wretched that I worked like a madman and by lunch-time I was exhausted and could do no more. I went back to the flat and tried to write but it was hopeless; I tried to think of some excuse to go and see Jan.

Jan had said Monday was "no good" but she had not said why. Perhaps she was going out with somebody else, going out to dinner or to see a film. I wandered about the flat and thought about her. I felt a sense of urgency. It was no use dillying and dallying while Jan went out to dinner with somebody else; but what was I to do? How did you show a girl that you liked her—that you loved her to distraction? How did you begin? Quite suddenly I thought of flowers. You began with flowers, of course . . . and Jan loved flowers. I could buy some and take them to her.

Covent Garden Market was closed, but there was a big flower shop in the Strand. I had often passed on my way to the office and looked in at the windows. I seized my hat and rushed out and down the street. The window was full of gorgeous flowers, great sprays of lilac and mimosa, huge bunches of tulips and daffodils. I pushed open the door and went in.

"I want flowers," I said. "I want the best you've got. They're for—for a lady."

The girl was very helpful but all the same it took a long time to choose and when at last I came out I had an armful of flowers. People stared at me in the street as I walked along and I heard them making remarks. It was embarrassing so I hurried and I was thankful when I got to the house. I went in and up the stairs. Jan would be out, of course, so I would not see her but I could leave the flowers with Barbie. I would ring the bell and when Barbie—or Nell—opened the door I would give her the flowers and say, "They're for Jan with my love," and make off before she had time to answer. It would be better that way.

I rang the bell and waited. After a few moments I heard footsteps and the door was opened. It was Jan. I was so surprised to see Jan that I was speechless. I gazed at her like a fool.

"David!" she exclaimed. "I didn't know you were coming. I told you Monday was no good. The others have gone out and I've been washing my hair."

"For you—" I said, thrusting the flowers into her hands.

She took them and stood there looking at me, her eyes wide with surprise. Her hair was still wet; it looked darker than usual and it was in little flat curls all over her head with a net over it.

"For me!" she said in an amazed voice. "Oh David—what a lot—and how beautiful they are!"

"I thought you'd be out," I told her. "I meant to—to leave them for you—that's all—" and I turned to go.

"Won't you come in?" she asked.

"No, it doesn't matter. I just wanted you to have them."

She put out her hand and said, "Oh David, thank you! They're lovely."

A big spray of mimosa slipped out of her arms and fell on the floor and as she stooped to pick it up she dropped some of the others, so I went back and we picked them up together and carried them into the flat.

"You like flowers, don't you?" I babbled. "I just wanted to give you some because you like them. The lilac wasn't out at Green Beech Cottage, was it?"

"No," said Jan. "No, it was just in bud. Oh David, you shouldn't have got all these flowers for me. You shouldn't, really."

We took them into the little pantry and Jan began dividing them. I could see by her face and by the way she handled them that she really liked them a lot.

"It's nothing," I said. "I know you like flowers and there were so many different kinds in the shop; it was difficult to choose."

She said softly, "It's sweet of you, David. Nobody has ever given me such lovely, lovely flowers."

"Nobody has ever loved you so much," I said. The words burst out of me. I was amazed when I heard myself say them. I had meant to go slowly and carefully; the flowers were just to have been the beginning.

"David!" Jan exclaimed, looking up in astonishment. "What do you mean?"

"Nothing," I said quickly. "I mean of course I mean it. I love you frightfully, but it's too soon. I meant to begin with the flowers and work up."

"Oh David, you are funny!" she cried, but her eyes were soft and bright.

As I put my arms round Jan a whole lot of flowers tumbled on to the floor, but it did not matter. Nothing mattered except the light in her eyes and the softness of her lips and the clean smell of her wet hair.

"Are you sure?" she asked when she could speak.

"Sure! Of course I'm sure. You don't know how unhappy I've been!"

"Unhappy?"

"Miserable. I've been wandering about like a lost soul—trying to think how I could possibly tell you how much I loved you. Darling Jan! I've been thinking about you all the time, remembering how you looked and what you said. I've been miserable ever since I saw you ."

"But you saw me yesterday!"

"It feels like weeks."

"But yesterday," said Jan, withdrawing herself from my arms. "You never said anything—yesterday."

"I was a fool," I told her. "I've loved you for ages, but I didn't realise that I loved you—and then suddenly I knew."

"It isn't—long—" she began doubtfully.

"Darling, don't you understand? I've loved you for ages. I was blind, that's all. I thought we were friends and then suddenly I knew I loved you."

"Yes, I see," she said. "I must dry my hair. You don't mind, do you?"

Jan went into the sitting-room and sat down by the rug in front of the fire. "You don't mind if I dry my hair," she repeated.

Something had gone wrong and I did not know how to put it right.

" Jan," I said. "We're engaged, aren't we?"

"No," said Jan in a low voice. "No, I don't think so. Of course I like you very much, but—but it's too soon."

"Oh Jan!"

"We ought to wait a little . . . until we're sure."

"But we are sure!"

"It's too soon. Really it is. We must wait. I hate people who rush and get engaged—and then find—it's a mistake."

"But we're not like that. We've known each other for ages!"

"Yes," said Jan, smiling rather sadly. "Yes, I know, but there isn't any hurry. We'll wait, David. I'd rather wait for a little."

"Don't you love me? Oh Jan, you do!"

She turned her head and looked into the fire. "I'm very fond of you. We were both rather excited, David. It was so sweet of you to bring me all those lovely flowers. Let's leave it for a little."

"But why?"

"There are all sorts of reasons."

"What reasons?"

"There's my job. I can't throw it up all of a sudden."

"But you needn't, Jan. I only want you to be engaged to me, that's all. We can get married later. Please, Jan!"

"And I ought to go home," said Jan in a low voice. "I don't know what to do about that. I don't know what to do about anything. I feel—upset—unsettled. It's awfully difficult."

I went on talking and trying to persuade her but it was no use; she kept on saying we ought to wait and not decide anything in a hurry. "It's too soon," she repeated. "You said yourself it was too soon."

"I didn't mean it like that, Jan!" I cried. "I meant it was too soon for me to tell you I loved you. I ought to have waited—but now there's no reason for us to wait."

"There are all sorts of reasons," repeated Jan.

Presently I left her sitting by the fire and went home. I felt wretched and depressed. All the time I was cooking my supper and eating it I was cursing myself for being such a fool. I had managed it very badly. I had blundered and said all the wrong things. But after a bit I began to be more hopeful about it. Jan loved me. She would never have let me take her in my arms and kiss her if she had not loved me, so it was bound to come right in the end. I should have to be patient and wait until she was ready. I should have to go slowly and make her understand how much I loved her, that was the only way.

CHAPTER FORTY-TWO

THE next day was Tuesday, of course. I had some shopping to do in the morning and an appointment with Mr. Randall in the afternoon, so I could not go out to the cottage. Mr. Randall had good news for me; *The Inward Eye* was selling well in America and Basil Barnes had cabled saying he liked the novel immensely and would publish it in the fall . . . and, as if this were not enough, the British publisher who had accepted *The Inward Eye* had accepted the novel as well. He wanted to publish *Golden Pavements* first and *The Inward Eye* afterwards. At any other time these wonderful tidings would have raised me to the seventh heaven of delight, but to-day I could think of nothing but Jan.

"It's just as you like, of course," said Mr. Randall. "If you'd rather he published *The Inward Eye* first we can hold him to his contract."

"You arrange it," I told him. "Do as you think best." The fact was I did not care.

Mr. Randall looked at me in surprise. "You've been working too hard," he said.

"I haven't been working at all," I replied. "The new book has stuck. I don't feel like writing."

"Why don't you go abroad as I suggested?"

"Perhaps I will . . . later," I said doubtfully.

"Go soon, Mr. Kirke. Take a sea voyage, or fly to Spain. Do anything you like as long as it takes you away from your present surroundings. Perhaps you think it's none of my business, but we can't have you getting stale. It's like this, you see: you're just beginning your career as a writer and you ought to keep going, you can't afford to rest upon your oars. If you go away to a new place it will buck you up and you'll feel like a different man; you'll find plenty to write about." It was good of him to take an interest in me and what he said was perfectly true; I knew I ought to go away and find fresh material . . . but it all depended on Jan. How could I go away now and leave everything unsettled?

"Oh, by the way," said Mr. Randall as I rose to go. "I'm afraid I've been a little unkind to a friend of yours."

I looked at him questioningly.

"Mr. Blackworth," explained Mr. Randall. "He said you had advised him to consult me about—er—"

"*Ralph's Progress,*" I said.

"That was it—*Ralph's Progress.* Well, I'm afraid it's hopeless. There's no other word for it. Unfortunately he wouldn't take a hint and I was obliged to tell him plainly that he couldn't write. He was rather—rather upset but it was no good beating about the bush, especially as he seemed anxious to make a financial success of his writing."

I saw that Mr. Randall was trying to hide a smile and I wondered if Miles had told him that the manuscript represented twenty-three solid hours of work.

"It's very strange," I said. "I can't understand it. Miles Blackworth is intelligent—"

"He may be intelligent but he can't write for toffee," said Mr. Randall and the smile he had been trying to hide spread across his face. "To be honest, *Ralph's Progress* is the funniest thing I've read for a long time; but unfortunately no publisher would touch it with a barge pole. It's a pity, but there it is. As a matter of fact I was sorry for the young man; he was so optimistic about his writing and so—so deflated when I had finished with him. I felt a brute."

"I wonder what he'll do," I said with some anxiety.

"I don't know," replied Mr. Randall. "As a matter of fact I told him about a job. I know a man who runs a chain store and has branches in various parts of London; he wants a secretary, someone who can drive a car and type his letters and so on. Mr. Blackworth seemed to think it was not the sort of job that would suit him, but he took the address so he may change his mind about it."

"It was very good of you," I said.

"Not at all," declared Mr. Randall.

All the way home I thought about Miles and wondered whether he would take the job and if not what he would do ... and I wondered whether he would forgive me for my plain speaking about Ralph. I had a feeling that he would. Nothing bothered Miles for long; perhaps already he had chucked Ralph into the fire and set his heart on something entirely different—something much better, something that would make his fortune.

Mr. Coe was putting up his shutters when I got back to the shop. He came down the ladder to speak to me.

"Look here, David," he said. "I believe I've gone and put my foot in it, but it isn't my fault. I couldn't help it."

"What's happened?" I asked in surprise.

"It's a girl," said Mr. Coe, lowering his voice confidentially. "She came into the shop and asked for you. I tried to get rid of her but it was no use, she wouldn't go away. She said she knew you lived here and she intended to see you—very masterful, she was."

"A girl! Where is she? What did you do with her?"

"Couldn't do anything with her," he replied ruefully. "She nipped past me like a flash and up the stairs before you could say Jack Robinson. I couldn't leave the shop and go after her, could I, David? I suppose she's waiting for you on the stairs; she hasn't come down—that's all I know about it."

"What was she like?"

"Nice looking," admitted Mr. Coe. "Not like that painted hussy that came here before, when Mrs. Kirke was here."

It was Jan, of course. Who else could it be? I rushed through the shop and up the stairs like a madman. But my visitor was not Jan after all. My visitor was Barbie.

Barbie had spread a newspaper on the top step of the stairs and was sitting on it, smoking a cigarette. She looked quite peaceful; as if she had been sitting there for some time and was prepared to sit there indefinitely.

"Hallo, David!" she said, smiling cheerfully.

"Is Jan all right?" I gasped.

"Perfectly well."

"Good," I said. I leant against the wall and panted. It was no joke running up all those stairs.

"That's a funny little man," said Barbie in conversational tones. "First he said you didn't live here—but of course I knew you did—and then he said you didn't like unexpected visitors, especially girls. Don't you, David?"

"Not awfully," I said. "But of course you're different. Come in, Barbie."

She rose at once and we went in together; fortunately I had left the room quite tidy.

"Girls?" said Barbie, looking at me thoughtfully. "Do you have to pay that funny little man to keep them off?"

I laughed. "No, of course not. Sit down, Barbie. That's the most comfortable chair."

She sat down and I took out the sherry and gave her a glass. There was a little silence and then she said, "I suppose you're wondering why I've come."

"I'm glad you've come," I told her—and so I was. I liked Barbie and it was very pleasant to see her sitting there in my chair looking so comfortable and friendly.

"It's about Jan. You know, David, I'm terribly fond of Jan and I can't bear her to be unhappy."

"Is she unhappy?"

"Yes, I'm afraid she is."

"Barbie," I said. "I've been an awful fool."

She nodded.

"I'm kicking myself," I told her. "I've mismanaged everything. I've been trying to think what on earth to do."

"We might—talk about it," Barbie suggested. "As a matter of fact that's why I came. Things sometimes get straightened out if you talk about them."

I was only too willing to talk. "It's like this," I said. "I've loved Jan for ages but it was only on Sunday that I realised I loved her. Quite suddenly I knew. I tried to think what to do about it—how to begin, if you know what I mean—and I thought of flowers. I bought a lot of flowers for her."

"You did," agreed Barbie. Her lips trembled and suddenly she was chuckling. "Oh, David, you did! It was—too many—for a beginning."

"I know. I went a bit mad. When I got into the shop and saw those flowers I wanted them all for Jan. That was the trouble."

Barbie was laughing so much that she could not speak, and her laughter was the chuckling, gurgling, infectious laughter of the plump. I had to laugh too, though I was not feeling particularly cheerful.

"Jan liked the flowers," I continued. "She liked them so much, and she was so—so adorable that I lost my head. In fact we both lost our heads and everything was marvellous. It was absolutely marvellous until suddenly something went wrong and I didn't know how to put it right."

"Jan began to think," said Barbie, nodding. "It was all right until she began to think."

"She said there were all sorts of reasons."

"I can tell you one reason," Barbie said. "One reason is that Jan has loved you ever since she was a tiny child and you used to play with her. You were her hero, David."

"But Barbie—"

"Oh, I daresay you don't think that's a 'reason,' but just try to look at it from her side. Jan has always loved you, and you've only loved her since Sunday."

I was so amazed that I was speechless.

"Of course I shouldn't have told you," continued Barbie. "It's a breach of confidence . . . though as a matter of fact Jan never told me in so many words. Girls talk to one another, you know, and if you're very fond of someone you don't need to be told things in so many words. You put two and two together."

"Look here," I said, groping for words. "I don't know what to say—I mean it's wonderful to know that Jan has always—been fond of me."

"You don't deserve it," said Barbie sternly.

"Oh, I know! I've been an absolute fool—but as I told you before I've loved Jan for years. It isn't a sudden thing, Barbie."

"You discovered it suddenly?"

"Yes—and now that you've told me about Jan I understand what she feels. Naturally she wants to wait a little. I shall have to be patient and give her time; I mustn't hurry her."

"No!" cried Barbie. "No, that's all wrong! You mustn't be patient! You silly donkey, you must be impatient and masterful!"

"But Barbie—"

"You must be a cave-man. You must seize her by the hair and drag her into your den. In other words, you must marry her."

"Marry her?"

"I suppose you want to marry her?"

"Yes, of course!"

"Well, marry her, then. Marry her straight off, for pity's sake. Don't hang about any longer."

"But Barbie, I asked her—"

"You asked her!" exclaimed Barbie scornfully. "Asking her is no good."

"But Barbie—"

"Don't keep on saying 'but Barbie.' Listen to me, David, if you dilly and daily the whole thing is hopeless. Jan says she's going home."

"Going home!" I said in dismay. "But she promised to help me with the cottage."

"She's going to the cottage to-morrow to choose the paint and then she's going home. That's her plan. She says she'll go home for a week and then come back."

"Perhaps that might be quite a good idea," I said thoughtfully. "I mean if she went home she could see how Elsie is. I could write to Freda and tell her—"

"If she goes home she won't come back," declared Barbie. "They'll persuade her to stay. Nell and I are sure of it. Jan won't come back. It isn't that she's weak and changeable, it's because she's sweet and kind and far too unselfish. We had the devil of a job getting her away from Nethercleugh but we hammered at it until we succeeded. We wanted her to come—not only for our own sakes, because we love her, but for her sake. We were sure it would be better for Jan; it would give her a chance to expand and be herself."

"I'm sure you were right!" I exclaimed. "She was being absolutely smothered at Nethercleugh. Jan is a different creature since she escaped."

Barbie nodded. "We think so too. Jan needs encouragement and—and love. She needs sunshine. There was no sunshine at Nethercleugh. I stayed there once for a few days and I was never so unhappy in my life."

"I know that only too well, Barbie."

"Well then," said Barbie. "Nell and I talked about it a lot and we decided to get her out of it by hook or by crook. We thought if only we could manage to get her here, we could keep her—but we can't. You're the only person who could keep her." Barbie looked at me and I saw with dismay that her eyes were full of tears. "Oh David, *do* something," she pleaded. "Don't be a fool and let her go. Freda and Elsie will tear her to bits between them. She's sensitive and they're as tough as blazes."

"I'll try," I said. "I'll do my level best."

CHAPTER FORTY-THREE

WHEN Barbie had gone I thought about all she had said and I decided that she was absolutely right; something desperate would have to be done. I made my plans and various arrangements and the next morning I did some shopping. Then I had lunch at The Wooden Spoon and took the bus to Green Beech Cottage.

The men had got on well in my absence; they had hacked and burnt to good effect and now it was possible to see the view from the veranda. The view was beautiful. It was different this morning, clear and bright;

the golden sun shone from a cloudless sky upon the green fields and the sprawling city.

While I was admiring the view Noyes appeared. "Could I speak to you for a moment, sir?" he said.

"Yes, of course, Noyes."

"What 'appens when we've finished clearing the place?" asked Noyes. "Are you coming to live 'ere, sir?"

"That depends," I replied. "The fact is I want to get married. If I manage to—to bring it off we shall come and five here, but if not . . . well, I don't know. I may sell the place. I haven't quite decided."

"I'm sure I wish you the best," said Noyes, smiling rather shyly. He hesitated and then continued, "I was asking because I was wanting a permanent job and I was wondering if by any chance you'd want a man. There's a lot to do in the garden even when it's cleared, isn't there?"

"Yes, that's true," I said.

"I'm a 'andy sort of feller," declared Noyes. "I wouldn't mind 'elping in the 'ouse. I can do a bit of carpent'ring and I know a bit about electric gadgets. I can turn me 'and to pretty well anything. I was an officer's batman in the war and Major Smith said as 'ow 'e'd take me on after the war, but then 'e couldn't. 'E'd give me a good chit, I know that." I thought about it seriously. I had not thought about the future before—the present was so full of complications—but now I realised that I should need a reliable man if I were coming to live at Green Beech Cottage. I liked Noyes. I had worked with him and I felt I knew him. There was something solid about Noyes.

"What I'd like is to live-in," said Noyes eagerly. "I've taken a fancy to this place. It's pretty and countrified and not too far from town. I'm sick of dirty lodgings."

I could sympathise with that. Noyes was dirty on the surface because he had been working all morning. His face was smeared with soot from the bonfire, but beneath the surface he was clean—clean and wholesome.

"You might think of it, sir," added Noyes.

"Yes, I shall certainly think of it," I told him. "I shall need somebody reliable. It would be a good plan to get in touch with Major . . ."

"Major Smith," said Noyes. "'E'll speak for me. I could move in as soon as you like, sir. It might be an advantage to 'ave someone on the spot to keep an eye on things."

"But the house is empty!"

"That wouldn't worry me," said Noyes, smiling. "A bed is all I want. I can make meself snug anywhere in 'alf no time. I'm an old soldier, you see." He spat on his hands, seized his axe, and laid in to a variegated laurel with a will.

It seemed odd to think I could engage Noyes and have him to work for me. I laughed at myself as I went into the house. "David Kirke, is this really you?" I asked. "Is this really you, standing in your own house and making up your mind to engage a man?" But I was not happy all the same. The house and the man and all the other nice things that had come to me because I had written *The Inward Eye* would be nothing but dust and ashes unless I could persuade Jan to share them with me.

Jan would be here quite soon now and I was going to put my fate to the test. I was going to gamble, to stake everything on a single throw. I was going to follow Barbie's advice. I trusted Barbie but all the same I was shaking in my shoes. At one moment my spirits soared and I felt certain that the tactics would succeed and Jan's defences would crumble; and the next moment I was crushed by the fear that she would be furious with me. I walked about the house from one room to another trying to rouse my courage and rehearsing all that I meant to say to Jan when she arrived. Barbie had told me to be a "caveman," to seize my woman by the hair and drag her into my den. "Look here, Jan!" I exclaimed aloud. "There's to be no nonsense about it. Either you marry me—or you don't. Which is it to be? Either you marry me or I go out of your life for ever!"

But that sounded a bit melodramatic, besides it was not true. I had no intention of going out of Jan's life for ever. I laughed ruefully and decided it was no use. I should have to wait until I saw Jan and say whatever came into my head. Meantime I found a window from which I could see the gate and I waited. Waiting was ghastly. If Jan did not come soon I should be sick—that was how I felt. If Jan did not come soon all my courage would have leaked away.

At last she came. I saw her walking down the path from the gate and I ran and opened the door.

"Hallo, David!" she said cheerfully but her eyes did not meet mine with their usual friendly confidence.

"Hallo, Jan!" I returned.

"Is Mr. Pendle here?"

"No, he isn't. Come into the sitting-room and see the view."

She followed me and went straight over to the window. "It's lovely," she said. "It really is magnificent. How right you were to cut down the trees and bushes and open it up."

"I'm glad you like it," I told her. "It would be a pity if you didn't like it, because you'll be seeing it every day; I mean when the cottage is ready and we move in."

She turned and looked at me with startled eyes.

"We're going to be married, Jan."

"But David—"

"At once," I said confidently. "You and I are going to be married at once, immediately, straight off."

"What do you mean?" she exclaimed.

"I mean what I say. I've found out all about it and I'm going to the Faculty Office in Westminster to-morrow morning to get a Special Licence."

"But I told you—"

"You told me to wait but I'm not going to wait. There's nothing to wait for."

"David, you're crazy!"

"Not now, Jan. I was a perfect fool but I've come to my senses now and I'm going to marry you at the first possible moment."

"David, listen—"

"Jan, I'm not going to listen to a word."

"You must listen!" she cried. "I've told you over and over again that we must wait."

"We're not going to wait. We're going to get married straight off."

"No," said Jan firmly.

I looked at her. "Why not?" I asked.

"Because—" said Jan. "Oh David, I've told you. Must we go over the whole thing again?"

"Listen," I said. "If you say you don't love me it's off and I promise faithfully I won't bother you any more. That's all you've got to do to get rid of me; just say, 'I don't love you, David.'"

She was silent for a few moments and then she said in a low shaky voice, "Why are you—rushing me?"

"Oh Jan!" I cried and I took her in my arms and held her close. "Jan, darling! I'm rushing you because I love you! Because I love you, love you, love you; because I can't live without you; because you're the only thing that matters in the whole wide world. I'm rushing you because I'm so terribly afraid of losing you."

She was hiding her face against my shoulder so I kissed her silky hair. "Now you know," I said.

"David, you're frightening me," she whispered.

"There's nothing to frighten you," I told her gently. "We love each other, so we're going to get married. It's the most natural thing in the world."

"But why not wait? Don't you love me enough to wait?"

"I love you enough to wait twenty years but we're not going to wait. Come and sit down and I'll tell you why." We sat down together on the window-seat and I took her hand in mine and held it firmly. For a moment I hesitated. "Go on," said Jan. "Tell me why."

"Because you're sweet and gentle," I told her. "Because you have a tender heart. That's why, Jan. What would happen if I let you go back to Nethercleugh?"

Jan did not answer. She turned her head away.

"What would happen?" I repeated.

"You don't understand," she said in a low voice.

"But I do understand. I'll tell you what would happen; Elsie would do everything she could to prevent you from marrying me. You said yourself there was a queer sort of bond between you and Elsie; we've got to break it, darling. It will be better for you and better for Elsie to break the bond."

"Better for Elsie?"

"Much better. It will give her a chance to develop. She'll never grow up into a normal human being as long as she has you to lean upon. I told you that before, didn't I?"

Jan nodded.

"Well then!" I cried. "There you are. If that's the trouble—"

"But it isn't," said Jan, interrupting me. "That's only part of the trouble—and not the worst part."

"What's the other part?"

Jan hesitated and then she said "I didn't mean to tell you but I suppose I must. It's Freda."

"Freda! Why should Freda mind?"

There was a little silence and I had to repeat my question. "Why should Freda mind?" I asked. "What has it got to do with Freda?"

Jan raised her eyes and looked at me sorrowfully. "You belong to Freda," she said. "You've always belonged to Freda."

"Belonged to Freda!" I echoed. "What on earth do you mean?"

"They all think so," said Jan. "Father and Mother think so. Freda thinks so."

I was dumb with astonishment.

"It's true," said Jan, nodding. "That's the real reason I can't marry you, David. You understand now, don't you?"

There was quite a long silence after that. I had to think. I had to try to understand. It meant looking back a long way down the years.

At last I said, "Jan, I simply can't believe it. I can't remember anything that could have—made anybody—think that. Of course Freda and I have always been friends and we've had tremendous fun together but neither of us has ever thought for a moment of anything else. It's a most extraordinary idea to me. Freda isn't that kind of girl. She used to say she wished she were a boy. She did really."

"Yes, she used to say that, I know."

"Well then?" I said. "Freda and I are friends, that's all. There's never been anything between us but friendship. You *must* believe me, Jan."

"I do believe you," said Jan, looking at me with her wide blue honest eyes. "But you see Freda doesn't think so."

"Freda doesn't love me," I said with conviction.

"Are you sure?"

"Certain," I replied—and so I was. When people are in love they are vitally interested in one another. They want to know everything about one another's lives. Freda was not interested in me. When I saw her at Haines she had been far more eager to tell me all about her doings than to hear about mine. I explained this to Jan and she was forced to agree.

"Yes," said Jan reluctantly. "It's true, of course, but—"

"Freda is in love with Nethercleugh!" I exclaimed. "Freda would *never* leave Nethercleugh. She's crazy about the farm and everything to do with farming."

"I know," said Jan in a low voice.

"Well then, what's the use of worrying about it any more?" Jan did not reply and for a few moments there was silence. Then gradually light broke and I began to understand.

"So *that's* the idea," I said slowly. "I'm supposed to marry Freda and go and live at Nethercleugh."

Jan was silent.

"Is that the idea?" I asked. "Am I to go to Nethercleugh and learn to be a farmer?"

"Yes, I think so." Jan's voice was little more than a whisper.

"Thank you!" I exclaimed. "Thank you very much, but I would rather starve in a garret!"

"David!"

"I would—really. Good heavens, I'd rather do anything! I'd rather be a tramp and sleep under a haystack. A tramp has freedom to live his own life and think his own thoughts! Yes, I'd much rather be a tramp."

Jan had begun to shake and I realised she was laughing. It was hysterical laughter, but I was glad she saw the funny side of the matter.

"You're—very—rude!" she gasped.

"I'm sorry," I told her. "I just wanted to make it quite clear that I find the idea unattractive and that nothing you can say will persuade me to try the experiment."

"I wasn't p-persuading you—"

"Oh, I thought you were! I thought you were trying to persuade me that it would be nice for me to marry Freda and five at Nethercleugh and breed prize pigs. I won't do it, Jan. I absolutely refuse to be brother to you. I'm going to be a husband to you—see?"

"David, I can't! They would all be furious. You've no idea how dreadful it would be!"

"Darling," I said seriously. "I can imagine how dreadful it would be and that's why we're going to be married immediately. I'm not going to let you go home until we're safely married. Once we're married it will be all right—nobody can come between us—and if anybody dares to be horrid to you they'll have to reckon with me." I put my arm round her and gave her a little squeeze. "They'll have to reckon with me," I repeated firmly.

"Oh, David, I do love you," said Jan, and she leaned her head against my shoulder.

We stayed like that for a while without speaking. It was so lovely that I did not want to spoil it. Besides there was nothing to say. I knew that I had won the battle. At one moment I had thought I was beaten but I had stuck to my guns. I felt proud and humble and thankful and very, very happy . . . and I felt strong enough to fight the whole world for Jan. If anybody dared to be horrid to Jan they would get an unpleasant surprise. I almost wished somebody would dare to be horrid to Jan.

Presently I took a little white box out of my pocket and opening it I showed Jan what was inside. There were two rings in the box—I had bought them that morning—one was a plain gold band and the other was set with diamonds. It was rather an unusual setting with one large diamond in the middle and a cluster of tiny diamonds all round. Somehow it had reminded me of a flower and that was why I had chosen it for Jan. I took Jan's left hand and slipped the ring on to the proper finger. It fitted perfectly.

"Oh David!" she said with a little gasp.

"If you don't like it we can change it," I told her. "The jeweller said coloured stones were more fashionable, but somehow—"

"It's beautiful!"

"Do you really like it?"

"I love it!" she cried. "It's beautiful! It's the most beautiful thing I've ever had . . . oh, David, you shouldn't have bought me such a marvellous ring!"

"Why not, Jan?"

"It must have cost pounds and pounds!"

"It's worth it," I told her. "I mean, if you like it—"

She moved her hand about and made the diamonds sparkle. The ring had looked lovely lying on the black velvet cloth on the jeweller's counter but it looked a hundred times better on her dear little hand. I took the hand and kissed it . . . and Jan turned and put her arms round my neck.

After a minute or two she said, "You were very sure, weren't you? What would you have done if I had said no?"

"Thrown the little box into the river," I replied.

"You wouldn't!"

"Yes, I would—and myself after it. But I was nearly sure you loved me."

"Why?" she asked.

I hesitated and then I said solemnly, "I didn't think you were the sort of girl who would let any man kiss you—I mean, any man who gave you a bouquet of flowers. You aren't, are you?"

"Of course not!" cried Jan indignantly.

"Of course not," I agreed. "You wouldn't have let me kiss you unless you loved me (flowers or no flowers) so I was nearly sure it was safe to buy the rings."

Jan changed the subject. She said, "I wonder why Mr. Pendle hasn't come."

"Oh, I told him not to."

"You told him not to come!"

"Yes," I said. "I rang up this morning and asked him to come to-morrow instead of to-day."

"But David—"

"I didn't think we'd want him to-day, and we don't, do we? I mean, it would be awfully difficult to concentrate on the exact shade of cream. Just think how horrible it would have been if we had chosen the wrong shade—too much pink in the mixture or too much yellow! We should have had to live with it for years. Don't you think I was wise to put off Mr. Pendle?"

Jan was laughing too much to reply.

I was glad I had managed to make her laugh (it was good to see Jan laughing) but I realised that I must go on without hesitation and get everything arranged in a hurry. Last time I had made the mistake of being too slow and letting Jan think, and I had nearly lost her. Our future plans must be fixed up here and now.

"Jan," I said. "Once upon a time there was a little girl with silky, brown hair. She hid in a cave with a boy and he tied her ribbon for her. He made rather a good job of it if I remember rightly."

"She thought so," said Jan, smiling. "She thought the boy was wonderful. Go on with the story, David."

"This little girl wasn't very happy at home and she made up her mind that when she was grown-up she was going to travel; she wanted to go to foreign lands where there were gorgeous flowers and gaily-coloured birds and butterflies. I think she had the right idea, don't you?"

"But David—"

"They both grew up," I continued. "They grew up and decided to get married. Fortunately they had a cottage to live in, but before they settled down they thought it would be good fun to see a bit of the world. The boy suggested that they might fly to Florida for their honeymoon . . . or to South Africa, or . . ."

"Oh David—but we couldn't!"

"We could, darling," I said, giving her another little squeeze. "We will! You shall choose where we'll go and I'll write a book about it and make lots and lots of money!"

"Do you mean it—really?"

I nodded. "Yes, seriously. Mr. Randall wants me to go abroad at once and gather fresh material for another book. He says it's important for me to keep on writing—and I want you to help me, you will, won't you?"

"Yes," said Jan breathlessly. "Oh yes, David. Perhaps I could type your manuscript or something."

"That would be splendid. Well, it's settled, then."

"But what about Haines?" she asked; and her eyes, which had been so bright and eager, clouded over. "We'll be married at Haines—"

"No," I said firmly. "No, Jan, there isn't time."

"But your father? I mean—"

"No, Jan," I repeated. "It's a pity, of course, but Father will understand why we can't be married at Haines. We'll go to Haines when we come back from our travels."

"Not before? Wouldn't it be unkind?"

"Not before," I said. "It wouldn't be a bit kind to go to Haines for a few days. For one thing it would upset Elsie. And I must get the new book started. The new book is important for my career and my career is very important indeed for both of us. I'm taking on the responsibilities of a married man so I must make a success of my writing."

"Yes," said Jan, smiling at me. "It sounds awfully funny to hear you talk like that, and of course I see your career must come first, but I still think—"

"Mr. Randall suggested Spain," I told her. "But perhaps South Africa would be more fun. We could fly there, you know. Or would you rather go to Florida? There's Greece, of course. What about Greece? Look, Jan," I continued, taking a large packet of travel-brochures out of my pocket. "I got these from the travel agency this morning so that we could decide—"

I had only one hand available and the packet slipped through my fingers and fell on the floor; it was so tightly packed that it burst asunder and in a moment the floor was strewn with highly-coloured pictures. The effect was dazzling. There were pictures of blue seas with white waves and bronzed figures surf-riding; there were pictures of coral beaches and exotic flowers; there were pictures of Grecian girls in their national costume strolling amongst tall, slender columns. There were deserts and camels; there were busy towns and quiet gardens; there were jungles impenetrably green, and rivers and lakes incredibly blue; last but not least important there were pictures of the aeroplanes and ships which were waiting to take us to any of these places we might choose to go to.

"Goodness!" cried Jan in amazement and she fell on her knees and began to gather them up. "Oh goodness! How are we ever going to decide? Athens! How marvellous! I've always longed to see Athens. Look at the girls in their lovely dresses!"

"Let's go to Athens," I suggested.

"Or Egypt," said Jan, who had discovered the picture of the desert. "What about Egypt, David? We could see the Sphinx—and here's a dear little Arab boy with a camel."

"Egypt if you like," I told her. "But we had better look at some of the other pictures, hadn't we? You wanted to go somewhere and see beautiful flowers—look at these pictures of Bermuda." I read out a description of the island. *In these semi-tropical islands the nights are like fairyland and the air is heavy with the scent of flowers. Here you may see the brightly-coloured hibiscus and the night-flowering cereus. You may like to go for a sail in the silver moonlight or listen to music borne on the soft sea breeze . . .*

Jan's head was very close to mine as we looked at the pictures together; pictures of bathing parties, of yachts with white sails skimming over blue seas. "Oh David," she said in an awed voice. "I can't believe it's true. We couldn't really go there, could we?"

"We most certainly could," I declared, kissing the tip of her ear.

"You said South Africa, David."

"I suggested it. Look, Jan, here's a picture of people sun-bathing at Cape Town . . . or we could sail up the Amazon, how would you like that? There would be marvellous flowers there. You choose, Jan. I got all these pamphlets for you to choose."

"But I want to go where you want!" she cried.

I laughed. I did not care where I went as long as Jan went with me.

"We must be sensible," said Jan, pulling herself together. "We must look at them all carefully before we decide."

Together we spread them out upon the floor and tried to be sensible . . . but it was not easy. Every picture we looked at seemed more attractive than the last.

"Is that all?" asked Jan. "There isn't another in the envelope, is there?"

I looked and there was. It was a coloured brochure of Jamaica.

"Oh David!" whispered Jan. "Oh David! It's the best."

I thought so too. There were sea-beaches for bathing; there were coconut palms and banks of vivid flowers; there was a picture of some people shooting rapids on a bamboo raft. The description of the island was very attractive and it would be a better climate than the other places we had thought of. *Even in midsummer the trade winds are cool,* announced the brochure. *You will find it fascinating to stroll through jungles festooned with orchids, fern-covered valleys, forests of mahogany, cedar and sweet-wood trees till the sea is far below. You can pick oysters that are fastened to the roots of mangrove trees under water. Jamaica is incredibly old, it is all that is left of a submerged range of mountains; it is beautiful beyond praise and, somehow, majestic . . .*

"Look at this picture," Jan was saying. "Look at the sea! It's the colour of an emerald! Could it really be like that?"

"We'll go there and make sure."

"But would you like it? Perhaps you'd rather go to—"

"Jamaica," I said. "Jamaica is the place."

"Really?" asked Jan, looking at me anxiously. "I mean don't say Jamaica because you think I want to go there. I don't mind a bit . . . but it does look heavenly, doesn't it?"

"Heavenly," I agreed.

"Emerald sea, gorgeous flowers, jungles and mountains! Here's a picture of a woman with a dear little baby . . . and here's a whole grove of banana trees . . . and look at these tall purple canes with feathery pink flowers! Sugar canes!"

"Yes," I said. "Jamaica is the place to go."

Jan hesitated. "But would it be a good place to write your book? We've got to think of that."

"I'm sure it would," I said.

CHAPTER FORTY-FOUR

JAN and I went back to my flat. I meant to take her to dinner at the Savoy to celebrate our engagement, but we were so busy looking at maps (which we borrowed from Mr. Coe) and making plans for our trip that the time slipped east unnoticed. We did not think about food until nearly nine o clock and then only because I suddenly felt hungry.

It was too late to go to the Savoy so Jan made an omelet and fried some bacon while I cleared the maps off the table and laid it for our meal. When we sat down together—just the two of us—I was so outrageously happy that I could hardly bear it. I knew exactly what the psalmist meant when he sang that his cup was full. My cup was brim-full, it was running over with joy.

After supper I took Jan home to Surrey Mansions. Barbie was there, waiting for us; she took one look at us and then hugged us both, first Jan and then me, with fervour. There was no need to tell Barbie that everything was all right, but there were all sorts of other things to tell her. We settled down beside the fire in the sitting-room and talked.

Barbie was attired in a dark-blue flannel dressing-gown, for she had gone to bed before we arrived and had got up when she heard us talking. She had a white frilly thing at her neck and her red hair was in little flat curls all over her head. But somehow it suited her—at least I thought so—I thought Barbie looked almost beautiful. Her cheeks were pink and her eyes were sparkling with excitement. She was sharing our joy.

Jan had laughed when I said Barbie was "solid," but the word described her exactly. She took our vague plans into her capable hands and shaped them for us. She solved all our problems; she asked sensible questions and when we could not answer them she found the answers herself; she took a pencil and listed all the things that must be done in the next few days.

"Let me see," said Barbie, studying her list. "I can do some of this for you. For instance you needn't bother about the cottage. I'll fix it all with

Tommy Pendle, and I'll have your furniture moved from the flat. That can be done after you've gone, of course. Now, what about passports?"

"I've got one," I told her. "I got one when I thought I might be going to France."

"You can have your wife added to it," said Barbie, and she told me exactly what I was to do.

Barbie was solid. She was like a rock in a quaking bog. Her advice and help were invaluable, but even more invaluable was her management of Jan. She swept away all lingering doubts in Jan's mind and made everything we planned seem sensible and matter of fact.

Jan mentioned Haines. "I just wondered," said Jan, looking at Barbie with an appealing air. "I mean I have a sort of feeling that it isn't right to go away without going to Haines first."

"If that's how you feel, why don't you go to Haines?" asked Barbie sensibly. "David has to go abroad at once of course (he must consider his career); but you could go to Haines yourself and follow him later. There's nothing to prevent you from doing that."

There was a moment's silence (I was terrified; I thought Barbie had gone mad), and then Jan laughed.

"Oh Barbie, I thought you meant it!" she exclaimed.

"But I do mean it," declared Barbie. "David's career is important. If he can't make a living by his writing it will be a poor look-out for both of you—therefore his career must be your first consideration, Jan!"

Jan nodded thoughtfully. She trusted Barbie. "I mustn't be selfish," she said.

"Selfish!" said Barbie, chuckling. "You won't get a chance to be selfish. If you're determined to marry an author you can make up your mind to that. There are all sorts of snags lying in wait for the wife of an author. To begin with you'll have him in the house all day long. Just think of it! You'll never get rid of the creature and have a nice quiet time to yourself. I wouldn't marry an author for the world—nor a painter! If I ever marry I shall choose a husband who will go away to his office in the morning and come home at night."

"I can shut David up in his study," said Jan, giggling.

"And go about in carpet-slippers," nodded Barbie. "Oh yes, I know! He'll raise merry hell if you use the vacuum cleaner while he's writing; that's the artistic temperament, my child."

But this was just a light interlude in the serious discussion of plans.

Although it was late when I walked home to my flat—long after midnight—I knew that another task awaited me. Before, I could sleep I must write to Mother and tell her everything; all that had happened in the last week. It was a large order: *all* that had happened in the last week! More had happened to me in the last eight days than had happened in all the years of my life. The letter would take hours to write (it would take all night most likely) but I could not rest comfortably until I had got everything related and explained.

I sat down at my table and started.

Naturally I began by telling Mother about our engagement. I told her the whole story; all about the bouquet of flowers and the effect it had produced—so different from what I had intended! I told her how miserable I had been until I had managed to put things right and how happy I was now; and how amazingly lucky I was to have won the only girl in the world that I wanted as my wife—and how amazingly silly I had been not to have realised before that Jan was that girl—and how beautiful and lovely she was and how much I adored her.

All this was easy of course. The next part of the letter was difficult and I had to rewrite it several times before it satisfied me. I had to explain why Jan and I could not be married at Haines.

I knew that Father and Mother would have liked us to be married at Haines. It was the natural thing. They would hate the idea of a Special Licence and a hole-and-corner marriage in London. Unless I could make them understand the difficulty they would be grieved and hurt beyond measure. I was sad about it, myself. It would have been perfect if Jan and I could have been married by Father in the dear old church with all our friends round us . . . but this was impossible and I had to explain why.

In spite of what I had said to Jan the necessity for hurrying on with my book was not the real obstacle. As I saw it there was only one real obstacle to our being married at Haines. All the obstacles could have been overcome quite easily except the Lorimers' crazy idea that I was Freda's property. This obstacle was insuperable. It would be impossible for Jan to return to Nethercleugh, even for a single night, with my ring on her finger. Knowing her family as I knew them it could easily be seen what sort of a welcome she would receive. I could not risk it. I was determined not to risk it. I was not going to allow my Jan to enter the lions' den.

The whole thing was ridiculous of course. I had never wanted to marry Freda—the idea had never crossed my mind—and most certainly I had never wanted to live at Nethercleugh. The Lorimers' plan was utterly without foundation. Perhaps I ought to have been flattered at their good opinion of me (obviously their opinion of my character and capabilities must be high if they were willing to entrust me with their favourite daughter and their farm) but I was not flattered; I was just plain angry. What right had the Lorimers to plan my life and to try to drag me into their detestable family circle?

I explained all this to Mother. I had to explain it fully because otherwise she would not have understood why I could not bring Jan to Haines until she and I were safely married and the dust and fury raised by our marriage had subsided.

When I had finished this part of the letter I got on more quickly. I told Mother about the success of my book and my decision to leave the office and make writing my profession. I told her all Mr. Randall had said about the importance of writing another book as soon as possible and of his advice to go abroad and see new places and gather fresh material, and I said that Jan and I were going to Jamaica for our honeymoon and I would combine business with pleasure and make notes for another book while we were there. I said I wished I could come to Haines before we started (I had considered the possibility of flying north myself, and spending one day at home) but there was so much to do and so many things to arrange that there would not be time. When we returned from our travels we would come to Haines Manse for a long visit before we settled down to our new life.

That brought me to Green Beech Cottage. Mother knew already that Aunt Etta had left me the little house, but she was under the impression that it was to be sold. I told her it was a dear little house and Jan and I liked it so much that we had decided to live there. I described it in detail and added that the whole place was to be redecorated while we were away—Jan had chosen the colour scheme and Barbie France had promised to see that everything was done according to plan. Then I told Mother about Noyes. I had made up my mind to engage Noyes if his reference was satisfactory, and I felt pretty certain it would be. Noyes would move into Green Beech Cottage and the furniture from the flat would be transferred to the cottage for his benefit. All these arrangements had been undertaken by Barbie.

Finally I said that there was no need to say anything to the Nethercleugh people. I would write to Mr. Lorimer myself and tell him all that was necessary; but not until Jan and I were safely on our way.

That was about all . . . but when I had signed my name to the letter I was struck by a sudden idea. It was a very surprising idea—it was a very funny idea—and it made me smile. I took up my pen and wrote:

P.S.—Now that I think about it, I believe you always meant me to marry Jan, didn't you?

I was chuckling as I collected the sheets and clipped them together and put the bulky packet into an envelope.

The letter was finished, but I was still so excited that I did not feel tired. I went to the window and drew aside the curtains.

Dawn was not far off. The night was clear and the stars were fading rapidly; there was a greyness in the sky. The roofs and gables and chimney-pots looked eerie and unreal in the cold, wan light. I knew this view so well. I had seen it in all weathers; I had seen these roofs baking in the sunshine and gleaming silver in the rain; I had seen them covered with snow and shrouded in wreaths of yellow London fog. They were ugly in a way, but it was a pleasing sort of ugliness—or so I thought. I leaned out of the window and looked at my view for a long time . . . and as I looked the light from the east brightened and spread.

So many things had happened since I first saw this view. So many different thoughts had visited me as I looked out of this window. Sometimes I had been homesick and miserable, sometimes I had been happy and at peace with the world; I had been in the depths of despair and on the heights of joy. It was strange to think that in a few days I should be gone from here and never look out of this window again. For a few moments I felt quite sad, and then I remembered the view from Green Beech Cottage. That was a much better view; it was peaceful and beautiful and spacious—you could see for miles from the window of Green Beech Cottage—and Jan and I would look at it together, standing side by side.

THE END

AN AUTOBIOGRAPHICAL SKETCH
by D.E. Stevenson

EDINBURGH was my birthplace and I lived there until I was married in 1916. My father was the grandson of Robert Stevenson who designed the Bell Rock Lighthouse and also a great many other lighthouses and harbours and other notable engineering works. My father was a first cousin of Robert Louis Stevenson and they often played together when they were boys.

So it was that from my earliest days I heard a good deal about "Louis", and, like Oliver Twist, I was always asking for more, teasing my father and my aunts for stories about him. He must have been a strange child, a dreamy unpredictable creature with a curious fascination about him which his cousins felt but did not understand. How could ordinary healthy, noisy children understand that solitary, sensitive soul! And as they grew up they understood him even less for Louis was not of their world. He was born too late or too early. The narrow conventional ideas of mid-Victorian Edinburgh were anathema to him. Louis would have been happy in a romantic age, striding the world in cloak and doublet with a sword at his side, he would have sold his life dearly for a Lost Cause—he was ever on the side of the under-dog. He might have been happy in the world of today when every man is entitled to his own opinions and the Four Freedoms is the goal of Democracy.

My father was old-fashioned in his ideas so my sister and I were not sent to school but were brought up at home and educated by a governess. I was always very fond of reading and read everything I could get hold of including Scott, Dickens, Jane Austen and all sorts of boys' books by Jules Verne and Ballantyne and Henty.

When I was eight years old I began to write stories and poems myself. It was most exciting to discover that I could. At first my family was amused and interested in my efforts but very soon they became bored beyond measure and told me it must stop. They said it was ruining my handwriting and wasting my time. I argued with them. What was handwriting for, if not to write? "For writing letters when you're older," they said. But I could not stop. My head was full of stories and they got lost if I did not write them down, so I found a place in the box-room between two large black trunks with a skylight overhead and I made a little nest where I would not be disturbed. There I sat for hours—and wrote and wrote.

Our house was in a broad street in Edinburgh—45 Melville Street—and at the top of the street was St. Mary's Cathedral. The bells used to echo and re-echo down the man-made canyon. My sister and I used to sit on the window-seat in the nursery (which was at the top of the house) and look down at the people passing by. I told her stories about them. Some of the memories of my childhood can be found in my novel, *Listening Valley*, in which Louise and Antonia had much the same lonely childhood.

Every summer we went to North Berwick for several months and here we were more free to do as we wanted, to go out by ourselves and play on the shore and meet other children. When we were at North Berwick we sometimes drove over to a big farm, close to the sea. We enjoyed these visits tremendously for there were so many things to do and see. We rode the pony and saw the farmyard animals and walked along the lovely sands. There were rocks there too, and many ships were wrecked upon the jagged reefs until a lighthouse was erected upon the Bass Rock—designed by my father. Years afterwards I wrote a novel about this farm, about the fine old house and the beautiful garden, and I called it *The Story of Rosabelle Shaw*.

As we grew older we made more friends. We had bathing picnics and tennis parties and fancy dress dances, and of course we played golf. I was in the team of the North Berwick Ladies' Golf Club and I played in the Scottish Ladies' Championship at Muirfield and survived until the semi-finals. I was asked to play in the Scottish Team but by that time I was married and expecting my first baby so I was obliged to refuse the honour.

Every Spring my father and mother took us abroad, to France or Switzerland or Italy. We had a French maid so we spoke French easily and fluently—if not very correctly—and it was very pleasant to be able to converse with the people we met. I liked Italy best, and especially Lake Como which seemed to me so beautiful as to be almost unreal. Paris came second in my affections. There was such a gay feeling in Paris; I see it always in sunshine with the white buildings and broad streets and the crowds of brightly clad people strolling in the Boulevards or sitting in the cafés eating and drinking and chattering cheerfully. Quite often we hired a carriage and drove through the Bois de Boulogne. My sister and I were never allowed to go out alone, of course, nor would our parents take us to a play—as I have said before they were old-fashioned and strict in their ideas and considered a "French Play" an unsuitable form of entertainment for their daughters—but in spite of these annoying prejudices we managed to have quite an amusing time and we always enjoyed our visits to foreign countries.

In 1913 I "came out" and had a gay winter in Edinburgh. There were brilliant "Balls" in those far off days, the old Assembly Rooms glittered with lights and the long gilt mirrors reflected girls in beautiful frocks and men in uniform or kilts. The older women sat round the ballroom attired in velvet or satin and diamonds watching the dancers—and especially watching their own offspring—with eyes like hawks, and talking scandal to one another. We danced waltzes and Scottish country dances and Reels—the Reels were usually made up beforehand by the Scottish Regiment which was quartered at Edinburgh Castle. It was a coveted honour to be asked to dance in these Reels and one had to be on one's toes all the time. Woe betide the unfortunate girl who put a foot wrong or failed to set to her partner at exactly the right moment!

The First Great War put an end to all these gaieties—certainly nobody felt inclined to dance when every day the long lists of casualties were published and the gay young men who had been one's partners were reported dead or missing or returned wounded from the ghastly battlefields.

In 1916 I married Major James Reid Peploe. His family was an Edinburgh family, as mine was. Curiously enough I knew his mother and father and his brothers but had never met him until he returned to Edinburgh from the war, wounded in the head. When he recovered we were married and then began the busiest time of my life. We moved about from place to place (as soldiers and their wives and families must do) and, what with the struggle to get houses and the arrival—at reasonable intervals—of two sons and a daughter I had very little time for writing. I managed to write some short stories and some children's poems but it was not until we were settled for some years in Glasgow that I began my literary career in earnest.

Mrs. Tim was my first successful novel. In it I wrote an account of the life of an Officer's wife and many of the incidents in the story are true—or only very slightly touched up. Unfortunately people in Glasgow were not very pleased with their portraits and became somewhat chilly in consequence. After that I wrote *Miss Buncle's Book* which has been one of my most popular books. It sold in thousands and is still selling. It is about a woman who wrote a book about the small town in which she lived and about the reactions of the community.

All the time my children were growing up I continued to write: *Miss Buncle Married, Miss Dean's Dilemma, Smouldering Fire, The Story of Rosabelle Shaw, The Baker's Daughter, Green Money, Rochester's*

Wife, A World in Spell followed in due succession—and then came the Second Great War.

Hitherto I had written to please myself, to amuse myself and others, but now I realised that I could do good work. *The English Air* was my first novel to be written with a purpose. In this novel I tried to give an artistically true picture of how English people thought and felt about the war so that other countries might understand us better, and, judging by the hundreds of letters I received from people all over the world, I succeeded in my object—succeeded beyond my wildest hopes. My wartime books are *Mrs. Tim Carries On, Spring Magic, Celia's House, Listening Valley, The Two Mrs. Abbotts, Crooked Adam* and *The Four Graces.* In these books I have pictured every-day life in Britain during the war and have tried to show how ordinary people stood up to the frightfulness and what they thought and did during those awful years of anxiety. One of my American readers wrote to me and said, "You make us understand what it must be like to have a tiger in the backyard." I appreciated that letter.

Wartime brought terrible anxieties to me, for my elder son was in Malta during the worst of the Siege of that island and then came home and landed in France on D-Day and went through the whole campaign with the Guards Armoured Division. He was wounded in ten places and was decorated with the Military Cross for outstanding bravery. My daughter was an officer in the Women's Royal Naval Service and was commended for her valuable work.

In addition to my writing I organised the collection of Sphagnum Moss for the Red Cross and together with others went out on the moors in all weathers, wading deep in bog, to collect the moss for surgical dressings. This particular form of war-work is described in detail in *Listening Valley.*

After the long weary years of war came victory for the Allies, but my job of writing stories went on. I wrote *Mrs. Tim Gets a Job, Kate Hardy, Young Mrs. Savage* and *Vittoria Cottage.* All these books were quite as successful as their predecessors and *Young Mrs. Savage* was chosen by the American Family Reading Club as their Book of the Month. My new novel *Music in the Hills* is in the same genre and all those who have read it think it is one of my best. A businessman, who lives in London, wrote to me saying '*Music in the Hills* is as good as a holiday and, although I have read several other books since reading it, the peaceful atmosphere lingers in my mind. I hope your next book will tell us more about James and Rhoda and the other characters for they are so real to me and have become my friends." The scene of this book is laid in the hills and valleys of the Scottish Borders and the people are the rugged individualistic race who inhabit this beautiful country. For a long time it has been in my mind to write a story with this setting and to try to describe the atmosphere, to paint an artistically true picture of life in this district. Now it is finished and I hope my large and faithful public will enjoy reading it as much as I have enjoyed writing it.

Sometimes I have been accused of making my characters "too nice". I have been told that my stories are "too pleasant", but the fact is I write of people as I find them and am fond of my fellow human beings. Perhaps I have been fortunate but in all my wanderings I have met very few thoroughly unpleasant people, so I find it difficult to write about them.

We live in Moffat now. Moffat is a small but very interesting old town which lies in a valley between round rolling hills. Some of the buildings are very old indeed but outside the town there are pleasant residential houses with gardens and fine trees of oak and beech and elm. From my window as I write I can see the lovely sweep of moorland where the small, lively, black-faced sheep live and move and have their being. Every day the hills look different: sometimes grey and cold, sometimes green and smiling; in winter they are often white with snow or hidden in soft grey mist, in September they are purple with heather, like a royal robe. Although Moffat is isolated there is plenty of society and many interesting people to talk to and entertain and it is only fifty miles from Edinburgh so, if I feel dull, I can go and stay there at my comfortable club and see a good play or a film and do some shopping.

There are several questions which recur again and again in letters from friends and acquaintances. Perhaps I should try to answer them. The first is, why do you write? I write because I enjoy writing more than anything. It is fascinating to think out a story and to feel it taking shape in my mind. Of course I like making money by my books—who would not?—but the money is a secondary consideration, a by-product as it were. The story is the thing. Writing a book is the most exciting adventure under the sun.

The second question is, how do you write? I write all my books in longhand, lying on a sofa near the window in my drawing room. I begin by thinking it all out and then I take a pencil and jot it all down in a notebook. When that stage is over I begin at the beginning and go on like mad until I get to the end. After that I have a little rest and then polish it up and rewrite bits of it. When I can do no more to it I pack it up, smother the parcel with sealing wax, and despatch it to be typed. I am now free as air and somewhat dazed, so I ring up all my friends (who have been neglected for months) and say, "Come and have a party."

Another question is, do you draw your characters from real life? The answer is definitely NO. The characters in a novel are the most interesting part of it and the most mysterious. They must come from Somewhere, I suppose, but they certainly do not come from "real life". They begin by taking shape in a nebulous form and then, as I think about them and live with them, they become more solid and individualistic with definite ideas of their own. Sometimes I get rather annoyed with them; they are so unmanageable, they flatly refuse to do as I want and take their own way in an arbitrary fashion.

All the people in my books are real to me. They are more real than the people I meet every day for I know them better and understand them more deeply. It is difficult to say which is my favourite character, for I am fond of them all, but the most extraordinary character I ever had to deal with was Sophonisba Marks (in my novel *The Two Mrs. Abbotts*.) I intended her to be a subsidiary character, an unimportant person in the story, but Miss Marks had other ideas. In spite of the fact that she was plain and elderly and somewhat deaf and suffered severely from rheumatism, Miss Marks walked straight into the middle of the stage and stayed there. She just wouldn't take a back seat. She is so real to me that I simply cannot believe she does not exist. Somewhere or other she must exist—perhaps I shall meet her one day! Perhaps I shall see her in the street, coming towards me clad in her black cloth coat and the round toque with the white flowers in it and carrying her umbrella in her hand. I shall stop her and say loudly (because of course she is deaf) "Miss Marks, I presume!"

It will be seen from the foregoing sketch that my life has not been a very eventful one. I have had no hair-raising adventures nor travelled in little-known parts of the world, but wherever I have been I have made interesting friends and I still retain them. Friends are like windows in a house, and what a terribly dull house it would be that had no windows! They open vistas, they show one new and lovely views of the countryside. Friends give one new ideas, new values, new interests.

Thank God for friends!

Someday I mean to write a book of reminiscences; to delve into the cupboard of memory and sort out all the junk. There is so much to write about, so many little pictures grave and gay, so many ideas to think about and disentangle and arrange. Looking back is a fascinating pastime; looking back and wondering what one's life would have been if one had done this instead of that, if one had turned to the left at the crossroads instead of to the right, if one had stayed at home instead of going out or had gone out five minutes later. Jane Welsh Carlyle says in one of her letters, "One can never be too much alive to the consideration that one's every slightest action does not end when it has acted itself but propagates itself on and on, in one shape or another, through all time and away into eternity."

FICTION BY D.E. STEVENSON

Miss Buncle Married (1936)
The Empty World (1936, aka *A World in Spell*)
The Story of Rosabelle Shaw (1937)
The Baker's Daughter (1938, aka *Miss Bun the Baker's Daughter*)
Rochester's Wife (1940)
Crooked Adam (1942)
Celia's House (1943)
The Two Mrs Abbotts (1943)
Listening Valley (1944)
The Four Graces (1946)
Amberwell (1955)
Summerhills (1956)
Still Glides the Stream (1959)
The Musgraves (1960)
Bel Lamington (1961)
Fletcher's End (1962)
Katherine Wentworth (1964)
Katherine's Marriage (1965, aka *The Marriage of Katherine*)
The House on the Cliff (1966)
Sarah Morris Remembers (1967)
Sarah's Cottage (1968)
Gerald and Elizabeth (1969)
House of the Deer (1970)
Portrait of Saskia (collection of early writings, published 2011)
Found in the Attic (collection of early writings, published 2013)

* see Explanatory Notes

EXPLANATORY NOTES

MRS. TIM

Mrs. Tim of the Regiment, the first appearance of Mrs. Tim in the literary world, was published by Jonathan Cape in 1932. That edition, however, contained only the first half of the book currently available from Bloomsbury under the same title. The second half was originally published, as *Golden Days*, by Herbert Jenkins in 1934. Together, those two books contain Mrs. Tim's diaries for the first six months of the same year.

Subsequently, D.E. Stevenson regained the rights to the two books, and her new publisher, Collins, reissued them in the U.K. as a single volume under the title *Mrs. Tim* (1941), reprinted several times as late as 1992. In the U.S., however, the combined book appeared as *Mrs. Tim of the Regiment*, and has generally retained that title, though a 1973 reprint used the title *Mrs. Tim Christie*. Adding to the confusion, large print and audiobook editions of *Golden Days* have also appeared in recent years.

Fortunately no such title confusions exist with the subsequent Mrs. Tim titles—*Mrs. Tim Carries On* (1941), *Mrs. Tim Gets a Job* (1947), and *Mrs. Tim Flies Home* (1952)—and Dean Street Press is delighted to make these long-out-of-print volumes of the series available again, along with two more of Stevenson's most loved novels, *Smouldering Fire* (1935) and *Spring Magic* (1942).

SMOULDERING FIRE

Smouldering Fire was first published in the U.K. in 1935 and in the U.S. in 1938. Until now, those were the only complete editions of the book. All later reprints, both hardcover and paperback, have been heavily abridged, with entire chapters as well as occasional passages throughout the novel cut from the text. For our new edition, Dean Street Press has followed the text of the first U.K. edition, and we are proud to be producing the first complete, unabridged edition of *Smouldering Fire* in eighty years.

FURROWED MIDDLEBROW

*titles available in paperback only

Printed in Great Britain
by Amazon

45985333R00155